T0390580

ALSO BY CHARLES SOULE

STAR WARS
The High Republic: Light of the Jedi

The Oracle Year
Anyone
The Endless Vessel

TRIALS OF THE JEDI

TRIALS OF THE JEDI

Charles Soule

RANDOM HOUSE
WORLDS

NEW YORK

Random House Worlds
An imprint of Random House
A division of Penguin Random House LLC
1745 Broadway, New York, NY 10019
randomhousebooks.com
penguinrandomhouse.com

Copyright © 2025 by Lucasfilm Ltd. & ® or ™ where indicated. All rights reserved.

Penguin Random House values and supports copyright.
Copyright fuels creativity, encourages diverse voices, promotes
free speech, and creates a vibrant culture. Thank you for buying an
authorized edition of this book and for complying with copyright laws
by not reproducing, scanning, or distributing any part of it in any form
without permission. You are supporting writers and allowing
Penguin Random House to continue to publish books for every reader.
Please note that no part of this book may be used or
reproduced in any manner for the purpose of training artificial
intelligence technologies or systems.

RANDOM HOUSE is a registered trademark, and RANDOM HOUSE WORLDS
and colophon are trademarks of Penguin Random House LLC.

Hardback ISBN 978-0-593-72352-4
Ebook ISBN 978-0-593-72353-1

Printed in the United States of America on acid-free paper

2 4 6 8 9 7 5 3 1

First Edition

BOOK TEAM: Production editor: Abby Duval •
Managing editor: Susan Seeman • Production manager: Erich Schoeneweiss •
Copy editor: Laura Jorstad • Proofreaders: Rachael Clements,
Jacob Reynold Jones, Laura Petrella

The authorized representative in the EU for product safety and compliance
is Penguin Random House Ireland, Morrison Chambers, 32 Nassau Street,
Dublin D02 YH68, Ireland. https://eu-contact.penguin.ie

For Mike Siglain, who made it all happen

THE STAR WARS NOVELS TIMELINE

THE HIGH REPUBLIC

Convergence
The Battle of Jedha
Cataclysm

Light of the Jedi
The Rising Storm
Tempest Runner
The Fallen Star
The Eye of Darkness
Temptation of the Force
Tempest Breaker
Trials of the Jedi

Wayseeker: An Acolyte Novel

Dooku: Jedi Lost
Master and Apprentice
The Living Force

I THE PHANTOM MENACE

Mace Windu: The Glass Abyss

II ATTACK OF THE CLONES

Inquisitor: Rise of the Red Blade
Brotherhood
The Thrawn Ascendancy Trilogy
Dark Disciple: A Clone Wars Novel

III REVENGE OF THE SITH

Reign of the Empire: The Mask of Fear
Catalyst: A Rogue One Novel
Lords of the Sith
Tarkin
Jedi: Battle Scars

SOLO

Thrawn
A New Dawn: A Rebels Novel
Thrawn: Alliances
Thrawn: Treason

ROGUE ONE

IV A NEW HOPE

Battlefront II: Inferno Squad
Heir to the Jedi
Doctor Aphra
Battlefront: Twilight Company

V THE EMPIRE STRIKES BACK

VI RETURN OF THE JEDI

The Princess and the Scoundrel
The Alphabet Squadron Trilogy
The Aftermath Trilogy
Last Shot

Shadow of the Sith
Bloodline
Phasma
Canto Bight

VII THE FORCE AWAKENS

VIII THE LAST JEDI

Resistance Reborn
Galaxy's Edge: Black Spire

IX THE RISE OF SKYWALKER

A long time ago in a galaxy far, far away. . . .

TRIALS OF THE JEDI

The final confrontation between the Jedi and the Nihil looms. The valiant Jedi are spread thin as they are put to the ultimate test on four separate fronts.

Some rally against the NIHIL MARAUDERS, who plan to punish the planet ERIADU for its resistance to their rule. Others patrol the dangerous border of the OCCLUSION ZONE, protecting planets from vicious Nihil raids. A brave few struggle to stop the mysterious BLIGHT, an infection moving from planet to planet, draining worlds of life. Still others battle the sinister MARCHION RO and his monstrous NAMELESS CREATURES.

To save the Republic, the Jedi will face their fears in their most daunting challenges yet. If they fail on just one of these battlefronts, the wave of darkness will extinguish the light of the Jedi forever. . . .

Hello, searcher. I will guide you on your way.

You may have heard things about the Force. It is an energy field. It touches all things. It is a mystical source of power. It can be used to perform feats that seem impossible, magical.

If you delve deeper, you will see that people have sought to understand the Force for millennia. Belief structures have arisen around its mysteries, factions dedicated to one interpretation or another, each with its own rules for how the Force may be used. Many of these groups organize themselves around the idea that the Force is divided into a dark side and a light. The dark consumes; the light sustains.

Is this true? Think of a river. It is a great source of life in innumerable ways. It can also drown and flood and destroy. Does the river have a light side or a dark?

Endless questions arise the moment one begins to study the Force, but all have the same answer: The Force can be used, but cannot be understood—not fully.

To truly comprehend the Force, you would need to understand everything, everything that exists as well as its relationship to every other thing. The smallest pebble, the mightiest creature, the newborn infant, and the ancient forest. This is beyond us, beyond the reach of even our mightiest thinking machines.

While our limited minds cannot fully know the Force in all its connections and convolutions, we are able to consider the implications raised by its nature. For instance: Everything that happens, happens to everything.

When seen through this light, the choices of any free-willed being become vastly powerful. Our individual decisions affect everything else that exists. Not in an abstract fashion. Literally.

In theory, the decisions of a single individual could affect everything else in drastic, terrible ways. If one person chose to use their free will to bring darkness to every other being . . . it could be done. Everything can die. Everything can be destroyed.

Even, perhaps, the Force. And because the Force is everything, if the Force dies, everything dies.

Some in the galaxy understand this possibility and have chosen to stand against it. Who are these people? Who are those that choose life and light, not just with words but with actions, with sacrifice, with every bit of strength and skill they possess?

Well, many. The list of people who stand and fight when things are at their darkest is long. But one group makes this battle against the dark their sworn duty. When all else is lost, you will find them, fighting until their last breath to save even a single life.

Because a single life, any life, all life . . . is the Force. Connected to all others, connected to all things.

This is what the Jedi believe.

This is why they fight.

For everything and everyone.

For life . . . and the light.

PART ONE

THE AIR STILLS.
THE VORTEX LOOMS.
THE PEOPLE LOOK UP
IN TERROR.

Interlude

"Come on, chop chop," Ryden Colman called. "We need to get on the road."

He glanced at the timepiece strapped to his wrist. Unnecessary. He knew what time it was—about one minute since the last time he'd checked.

Ryden knew his anxiety was getting the better of him, and for what? Even if they missed the flight scheduled to leave in a few hours, another would depart a few hours after that. There was no reason to rush. Not really. He was being irrational.

He looked out the window at the clouds of white dust streaming into the air in the far distance. They looked like smoke—but that was not what they were. They were far away . . . but the wind could always shift.

Ryden checked his chrono again.

"Family!" he shouted. "It is *time to go!*"

His son, Davet, sixteen and wonderful but also ready and excited to challenge his father's hard-earned wisdom and directions at every possible opportunity, appeared from his bedroom. A gigantic trunk of all the many things a teenager found essential floated along behind him, lifted from the ground by built-in repulsorlifts and pushed forward by the household droid, a charming model that had become utterly essential to the family's operations. They all called it Sixbee, a derivation of its model and unit number.

"I'm ready, Dad," Davet said. "First one, too, looks like. Mom and Shanna don't even have their stuff out here yet."

This was only partially true. Ryden's wife's bags were already packed into the speeder waiting on the street below, though she was making the rounds of their small apartment, trying to make sure they hadn't forgotten to pack anything they might truly need while they were away. But Shanna, their eleven-year-old, was nowhere in sight, and Ryden foresaw a battle getting her out the door.

We can still make the next transport, he thought. *But we have to be out of here in ten minutes, no more.*

Davet began working with Sixbee to get his huge trunk through the apartment's front door. Assuming it actually fit, they'd take it into the lift and down to the street. Ryden left them to it, turning back to the window.

He frowned. The streets of Estarvera were nothing but traffic, as packed as he'd ever seen. Personal speeders, larger transports, and buses, some so full of people that the passengers sat on the roof or hung out the windows. All heading in the same direction . . . to the city's spaceport, out on the edge of town. Coils of dark, oily smoke rose up above the streets here and there.

Just an accident or two, Ryden told himself. *This many vehicles, bound to be a few crack-ups.*

The faint sound of sirens reached his ears, dampened by the window but clearly audible, and from multiple locations, too.

Something caught his eye on the other side of the street—a pink, small object lying on the stonework pedestrian path. People rushed past it, ignoring the thing, intent on their own destinations. Ryden recognized its outline as a character from one of the holonet kids' shows Shanna had watched obsessively when she was a little younger (as had Davet, though he'd never admit it now).

Barko the House Mouse, something like that, Ryden thought. *Shanna had one of those toys. Wouldn't go anywhere without it.*

Ryden imagined another child, another little son or daughter, who had taken their little Barko with them when their caregiver or caregivers took them from *their* home and said, *Okay, chop chop, time to get to the spaceport, no time to waste,* and then rushed them along the street toward their own speeder or bus. He envisioned that child accidentally dropping the toy in all the hubbub, as kids would do, and crying out to stop, to let them pick it up, and the caregiver tugging them along, not willing to take even the five seconds it would require to retrieve their child's toy to make them happy, to make them feel a bit less afraid.

We don't have time, the adult would have said as the child burst into tears. *We have to go.*

Ryden pulled his eyes from the toy and raised them to look across the city. Their home had a wonderful view. Now, the family wasn't wealthy— far from it. The bakery he and his wife ran together barely covered the bills. Still, they'd somehow happened upon an upper-floor residence that afforded a view of half the city and the great sea-plains beyond. The sheets of clear water teemed with the many living things that sustained the city's industry and population, including endless kelptree fields. Normally, the languid plants were blue-green, and sunlight shone through them like panes of stained transparisteel. Now huge swaths had turned gray-white. He could see great clouds of an ash-like substance blowing off them in the breeze, as if they were disintegrating before his eyes.

At first, the holonet broadcasts had called it a blight. But now that it had appeared on more and more worlds across the galaxy, it had become *the* Blight, a specific menace that everyone knew and everyone feared. Clouds of that stuff were slowly, lazily drifting toward the city from the desiccated kelptree fields. Toward his home. Toward his family.

What would happen if you breathed it in? he thought.

He turned away from the window, calling loudly back into the apartment.

"We don't have *time,*" Ryden said. "We have to *go.*"

Two hours later, the little family of four (five including Sixbee and six including Shanna's pet scalepig, Florg, whom she had categorically refused to leave behind) sat in their speeder, waiting for their opportunity to enter the spaceport and board the next ship that would take them off-world. Where they would go next almost didn't matter—anywhere that didn't have the Blight creeping across its landscape.

The strange white death moved slowly, but it was no less terrifying for its lack of speed. It advanced millimeter by millimeter in all directions, turning living things to a horrible, ashen substance, and not long after that even the stones and soil. Efforts had been made to burn it out, to build energy barriers around patches of the stuff . . . all had failed. There were even reports—unconfirmed but terrifying—that ships that flew over a Blighted zone could find their systems failing, any organic passengers becoming infected.

Now the Blight had come to Estarvera. It moved slowly but never stopped, either. New patches could appear without warning. Tiny at first, but they grew. They always grew.

Everyone who could leave the planet was leaving.

"We're almost there, Ry," his wife said, placing a reassuring hand on his arm. Ryden looked at her, looked at Calina, his partner of over twenty years. He gave her a confident nod, and she put her hand back on the speeder's control sticks, returning her focus to the road. They'd already seen a number of accidents on the road to the spaceport. The last thing they needed was another delay.

Ryden flicked his eyes toward the speeder's rear compartment. Davet was listening to music on his headphones, his eyes focused on the tense scenes outside. Shanna was busy playing with Florg, focused on trying to get the little creature to flutter into the air a centimeter or two on its stubby little wings. The family's elderly droid had folded itself up at the children's feet and gone into low-power mode to save its increasingly unreliable power cell.

"You know we probably won't be able to bring Sixbee," Ryden said to Calina, his voice quiet. "We might not even be able to bring Florg. I heard on the 'net that they're prioritizing passengers. No cargo . . . of any kind. We'll be lucky to get out with our bags."

Calina didn't answer, but he saw the little flicker at her jawline that meant she'd heard and was internalizing. The quick translation was, *Yeah, I get it, but I don't much like it.*

A quick wave of guilt washed across Ryden. The impetus to leave Estarvera—at least for the time being—had been his. Calina focused on the next day's bread; he focused on the next year's bread and their ability to keep making it. He'd been tracking reports of the Blight at the few spots in the galaxy where it had appeared, and once it showed up on their world, he put plans to be ready to leave in motion immediately.

They had enough in savings for four transport tickets offworld, with enough for living expenses in case they couldn't come back for a while. Or—and he hesitated to even consider the option—if they couldn't come back at all. They were flying to Felucia, where Calina's brother lived. It wouldn't be the most comfortable arrangement, but they'd make do, and—

A rumbling noise from ahead of them, in the direction of the spaceport. It sounded like the crashing of a wave on a beach, but deeper. And . . .

"Why are we shaking?" Shanna called from the back seat, her voice mostly just curious.

Ryden exchanged a glance with Calina.

Groundquake? was what that glance said.

He turned his head, looked back. Speeders were crammed in behind them, everyone on their way to their own trips offworld. Ahead and to either side . . . no better. The city was old, and the speeder lanes in this part of the city were narrow, not built for so much traffic.

The rumble grew louder. Now, with it, shrieks of bending metal, a great collapse, the sound becoming a roar.

"Look at that," Calina said, her voice uncharacteristically small.

The wide bowl of the spaceport dominated the view through the speeder's windshield, a beautiful silvery curve that always made Ryden think of launch trajectories and orbits and flight. He hadn't left the planet since before he and Calina got together, but he'd always admired the structure.

Now it was . . . changing. Bending, the two upturned ends of the round building curving toward each other, as if they were reaching out across the open space between, like two lovers' hands straining to touch.

It was difficult to comprehend, fast and slow all at once . . . and then it was very fast. The spaceport—what they could see of it above the intervening rows of buildings—fell. It shot downward with astonishing speed, replaced by a billowing white-gray cloudy plume that Ryden recognized. He'd seen it out the window of his home barely two hours before, wafting toward the city.

That's the blasted Blight.

"Get out," he said, his voice sharp, tighter than he wanted it to be. "Everyone. Right now. Out of the speeder."

"Ryden, how are we supposed to—"

He spun toward her, fixed her with a look that carried with it twenty years of trusted judgment that had, by and large, usually been right.

"Now, Calina. All of us. Leave everything."

At hearing the conversation, Sixbee woke up from its dormant state, the droid's sky-blue eyes lighting up.

"May I be of assistance?" the machine asked.

"Get the kids out of the speeder," Ryden said, levering his own door open.

Panic had begun to set in, not just in the family but among everyone trapped in that narrow lane approaching what had once been the Offworld Transport Terminal. Ryden could see the whole scenario in his head. He knew exactly what had happened. The Blight had appeared at the spaceport—but not at the surface. Below the enormous structure, eating away at its foundations, until it just . . . collapsed, into a yawning pit of gray-white ashen death.

Ryden took stock. His family was out of the speeder and on the street, along with many other families, people, droids, even some animals. People were beginning to understand what was happening. They were beginning to run. Someone knocked into Davet, hard, and the boy stumbled. Ryden stepped forward, grabbing his arm, steadying him.

"You okay?" he asked.

His son nodded, looking younger than he had in ages.

"You need to keep your sister safe," Ryden said. "You have to run now. Go, that way, right now. Your mother and I will be right behind you."

Davet looked for Shanna and grabbed her hand. In her other, she held the little sack containing her scalepig. And if Davet looked like a child, well, Ryden's daughter looked like a baby. Off they went, weaving between the abandoned speeders, trying to make headway within the rush of other travelers seeking safety.

Sixbee was out of the speeder, too, awaiting instructions. Ryden rapped the droid on its tarnished head and pointed in the direction his children had gone.

"With them!" he shouted over the rumbling, louder now. "Keep them safe!"

The droid beeped softly in acknowledgment, and then it, too, was gone.

Ryden turned back to the speeder, running to the driver's side, where Calina waited. She was sitting in the speeder, waiting for him, her eyes calm.

"You should go," she said.

"Forget it," he said.

Ryden bent, slung an arm around his wife's waist, and lifted her. He was practiced in the maneuver—he did it every night, moving her gently from her hoverchair to their shared bed.

He put her over his shoulder and began to run, moving as quickly as he could, immediately feeling a deep ache settle into his back, ignoring it.

Behind them, an unending dull roar, screams, bursts of noise and wind.

Is that stuff under the entire city? Ryden thought.

He couldn't run much faster. He couldn't run much farther. He did both, until he couldn't do either.

Ryden fell to the ground, Calina falling with him, her arms braced to protect her head, rolling. The roar behind them grew louder, closer, until there was nothing but the sound and the fear. Ryden crawled to his wife and held her and closed his eyes and waited for the end—they both did.

The end came.

But not the one they expected.

The roar faded away, leaving a clouded, gray silence punctuated with strange sounds—running water from ruptured pipes, sparking energy conduits, wails from the injured.

Ryden opened his eyes. He looked at his wife—she was alive, she was safe. Then he looked in the direction of what was once the Terminal District. There was nothing left. The buildings, the spaceport, any people or vehicles caught in the collapse—it was all just a deep, jumbled pit, the closest edge of which terminated not more than two meters from Ryden's left foot.

He looked into the yawning maw and saw that its edges were ashen gray. Dead, ruined, gone.

Blighted.

"Ryden," Calina said, her voice wrung out, as if the Blight itself were speaking. "Where are we going to go?"

Chapter One

THE JEDI TEMPLE

Bree went down into the dark, to a place she was not supposed to be, as she had been told to do.

She was only nine years old, a member of the Jedi Order, on the older side of the youngest group of students being trained in the Jedi's great temple on Coruscant—appropriately called younglings.

Bree descended another step, then paused to look back. Behind her, an arch of light awaited—the path back to the main levels of the Temple. She wanted to go back—to her friends, to her studies, to the sun, to the light.

But Bree had a job to do. She sighed, turned her eyes back to the stairs, and continued on her way.

The stairs were old. Everything in the Jedi Temple was old, but it didn't look like it. Maintenance droids kept everything shining and clean. These steps were different. They were crumbled at their edges, with wisps of dust and dirt, even little dead bugs. Bree didn't mind bugs. Her friend Toko was a different story, but Bree didn't care so much. Creatures were creatures, big or small.

The staircase wound down, down, down, light provided by illumination globes strung along the walls. Most of the time, Jedi didn't need lights for something like this—they carried light with them—but the globes had been installed here when it became clear that this route would need to be used more frequently.

Is it getting hotter? Bree wondered.

She put her hand against the wall. Yes. She wasn't imagining it. The wall wasn't hot, not like a flame—more like a sun-warmed patch of stone in one of the Temple's many terraces high above her. But there was no sun, not down here.

Bree pulled her hand away, frowning.

She continued down, moving faster, wanting to be done with this task.

They shouldn't have made me do this, she thought. *They're all so much stronger and older than I am. I'm just a kid. They could have found another way.*

But there was no other way. Bree was just a kid, that was true, but she had eyes, and she had ears. The grown Jedi were too busy with all the terrible crises that had landed upon their Order, one after the other. Jedi Knights were . . .

Dead, she thought. *They're dead, killed and eaten by the monsters. The Nameless.*

Not a good thought while deep beneath the Temple, descending a rapidly narrowing staircase that seemed to be closing in on her, the walls changing now from rough-cut stone blocks to a different kind of surface that looked like the rock had been melted and frozen again, like it had been *hurt.*

Bree had an important message to deliver, and she had to do it in person. This far down, the communications devices didn't work to call up to the surface. Droids were too slow, and the Order didn't have very many. The ones they did have were busy with other important tasks, too.

So who did they send? The Jedi who weren't good enough yet for anything else—the younglings.

Bree was not afraid. She was brave. The Order had taught her how to be brave. But she saw no harm in hurrying. She saw no harm, in fact, in running.

The young Jedi rushed down the stairs, leaping down two at a time,

STAR WARS: TRIALS OF THE JEDI 19

becoming increasingly certain that something was chasing her, its sharp claws clacking behind her at exactly the same moments as her own footsteps. She would reach the bottom of the stairs and there would be no one to help her—the monster would have gotten there first—nothing but chalky stone statues that used to be Jedi, and then it would get her and . . .

Bree's foot landed hard on the ground below the last step. She stumbled, fell, skidded along the ground, feeling the skin on her palms and knees scrape.

"Agh!" she cried.

She lay flat on the dirty stone, which was now most definitely not warm but hot. She breathed in and out, in and out, using the techniques she'd been taught to push back the pain, push back the shock and fear. Bree found the Force, which she thought of as a friend that could help her do amazing things if she could only find the right way to ask. Just then, she didn't think she could find the focus to ask the Force for much of anything, but even knowing it was there helped her feel better.

You are a Jedi, she thought. *Get up, girl.*

Bree pushed herself up, brushed grit from her palms and knees, and stood. She looked ahead down the dim corridor the stairs opened to and saw that the lights got brighter in the distance.

That's it. Almost there.

Bree found her way through the corridor, all but running by the time she reached its end. The corridor opened into a larger room carved out of the same raw stone as the rest of the area, now almost seeming to glisten or glow.

The Force was here, too. Bree could sense it strongly. It still felt like a friend, but the kind of friend who always had bad ideas, the kind that was always trying to get you to go along with adventures that would get you in trouble. She didn't like it.

At the far end of this new room was an open door, tall and wide, the door itself made of rusted metal, as heavy as a starship panel. That was her destination—just what she'd been told to expect.

Through the door would be, at last, other people. Bree realized how alone she had felt on that long, slow descent. She'd hated it, even though she had been taught over and over that she wasn't supposed to hate anything.

The chamber beyond the door was good-sized. Mostly empty except for Jedi, a lot of Jedi. Most were seated in a circle on the floor, eyes closed, focused-seeming. A sort of hum arose from them, although it wasn't an actual sound. It was something you could just feel. Bree thought it was her friend that was humming.

Bree couldn't see what was inside the circle, but she knew. She'd been warned about it. All the younglings were talking about it, though none had seen it. It was called the Blight, and it was a monster, too, as bad as the Nameless but scarier.

Not all the Jedi were meditating in the circle. Others were seated against the wall or stretched out on the ground, asleep, using parts of their white-and-gold temple robes as pillows. It made Bree a little sad to see how dirty the white parts of the robes had gotten down here. Up above, everything was always nice and clean.

She looked down at herself, realizing her own robes were no better. Worse, maybe, after her fall.

A few of the resting Jedi were sitting on supply crates, drinking from bulbs of water or eating nutristicks, chatting quietly to one another. Bree didn't know their names. Ever since the Council implemented the Guardian Protocols and brought everyone back to the Temple from the Jedi outposts in the Outer Rim, there were too many to keep track of.

They were a human woman with long brown hair and pale skin and a Twi'lek man, the lekku hanging from his head a beautiful blue.

The woman noticed her. "Youngling," she said, her voice weary but not unwelcoming, "you're not supposed to be here. This is a dangerous place."

"I was sent," Bree said. "They sent me. From . . . upstairs."

Bree turned and pointed back the way she had come, immediately feeling silly.

"I see," said the Twi'lek. "You come with a message from the surface world for us underground dwellers, young one?"

STAR WARS: TRIALS OF THE JEDI   21

"Please, Stalwick, can't you see the poor girl's in no mood?" said the lady Jedi.

"Apologies, Master Byre," the other Jedi said. "Was just trying to, ah, lighten things up a bit down here."

Oh, Bree told herself. *I guess he was making a joke.*

"I'm supposed to fetch Master Yoda," she said. "There's something he needs to see."

The Twi'lek's expression hardened slightly. Not a frown, more like the look her teachers would get on their faces before they demonstrated how to do something really difficult with the Force. Like a *getting ready* look.

The Jedi glanced at each other. They both stood, and each tapped another resting Jedi on the shoulder. These two nodded as well, seeming tired, so tired.

"Yoda's needed above," Master Byre said. "We need to pull him out."

Neither of the other Jedi answered, just accepted the reality of the situation, and all four moved toward the circle of meditating Jedi. They found places among them, sat down, closed their eyes, and that strange hum Bree was hearing with her sense of the Force grew louder.

But that was not all. When the Jedi had moved to make room for the new arrivals, the circle had opened up enough for Bree to see what was inside.

Despite herself, she gasped. Despite all the training, all the work her teachers had done to help her set fear aside, Bree was only nine years old, and when she saw death not five meters away, separated from her only by Jedi who seemed to be using all their strength to hold it back, yes, she was afraid.

That's the Blight, she thought. *The Blight is here. Right here, under the Temple!*

It was a patch of gray-white rot, dusty and dead. The opposite of a flower or a butterfly or any living thing or a friend.

They said nothing could stop it. That it just ate and ate and ate, killing everything it touched, turning it into more of itself. And it was here, just a staircase away from everything and everyone she knew, everything she loved. The Jedi were here holding it back, but they all looked so tired.

How long can they keep it back? Not forever.

They said nothing could stop the Blight.

Bree felt tears brimming in her eyes. This was all too much, too much.

One of the other Jedi who had been resting moved toward the circle, toward a small figure, smaller than any of the others. Pale-green skin, head bald but for a few shocks of white hair, big pointy ears. Bree knew him— every Jedi did. This was Yoda. Like every youngling in the Order, Bree had learned important lessons from the ancient Grand Master. Hundreds of years old yet he made time for every child brought into the Order's care.

Yoda was smiling. His eyes were closed, and his face radiated peace. As the other Jedi touched him lightly on the shoulder, the smile faded away like smoke from a blown-out candle. Yoda got slowly to his feet, assisted by the other Jedi, and Bree heard a groan wash across the other Knights and masters in the circle. Their bodies shifted, they sat more heavily, and Bree understood what had happened.

It took four of them to replace Yoda, she thought.

Yoda shook his head slightly, as if clearing it after waking from a dream. He looked up toward Bree and began making his slow way over to her, favoring one leg, moving with a limp. She didn't want to get any closer to the Blight, but she walked toward him, and so when he stumbled, she was there to catch him.

Yoda weighed almost nothing. He was like a baby.

She steadied the great master. He smiled at her.

"Thank you, Bree," Yoda said.

He glanced around the cavern, his gaze alighting on a short, gnarled length of wood, bent at one end to make a sort of handle. He raised one tiny green hand, and the stick whipped across the chamber to land in his outstretched palm. He set one end on the ground and leaned forward, putting his weight upon the cane.

Yoda made a slight sound of dissatisfaction, a grumbling chortle.

"An injury from times past, it is," Yoda said. "Aggravated by these exertions. Fine, I will be. Worry not."

Bree didn't know if Yoda was talking to her or to himself.

He looks old, she thought, suddenly sad. *I know he* is *old, but he's never* looked *old.*

"Sent for me, you were?" Yoda asked, his large dark eyes focused on her. "A reason, did the Council give? The climb is long, and my work here is important."

"I'm sorry, Grand Master Yoda," Bree said. "They didn't tell me much. Only that the selection of the Nine is set to begin soon. If you can be spared here, they thought—"

Yoda's eyes widened. He made a *hrrmph* sound deep in his throat, then headed for the cavern's exit, his cane clacking on the stone with every step.

"Yes, be there, I should," Yoda said. "Let us go, young Bree. This is no place for a youngling."

Bree could not agree more.

❁

The Song of the Force sang of dread, and Avar Kriss could not sleep. She sat in her chamber in the Jedi Temple, her back against the smooth stone wall, her bare legs drawn up to her chest.

Beside her, Elzar Mann lay asleep in her bed, his chest rising and falling smoothly. She listened to him breathe, and she listened to the Song.

Avar thought about what she was hearing. The Force came to her as music, and she had learned to interpret it as a source of information, but it could also be misleading. Because the Force was part of everything, its melodies chimed through the smallest insect with as much complexity as the galaxy itself. She had studied at the Jedi Temple for more than three decades. In that time, she had found ways to calibrate her perceptions, to understand what she was hearing and what it was telling her. Most of the time. Sometimes, she became wrapped up, all but lost, barely herself, and had to regain focus as best as she could.

It was this way for all Jedi who used the Force. They each experienced it their own way, but its power, its depth and breadth, its majesty . . . that was universal.

What am I hearing, then? she thought. *These notes of doom woven through the Song . . . is it the other Jedi in the Temple? We can tamp down our fears while we are awake, but when we're asleep . . . our dreams are beyond our control.*

Although Elzar might disagree, Avar considered, watching his calm, peaceful face in the dim light filtering in through her chamber's window.

Lately, they'd been spending every night together that they could. They had an unspoken acknowledgment that their obligations to the Order came before anything else. The many tasks and missions they were each assigned meant it was rare for them to be in the same place for any significant length of time. Any moments the Force gave them to be together, they tried to use well.

Dawn was coming. Avar could sense it. She sighed. No more sleep tonight.

A soft chime sounded from the datapad resting on the small, simple desk not far from her bed. Avar reached for the device. A message had come in, set at the highest priority level. She read it and froze, a chill running through her body.

"What is it?" Elzar said, his voice low, grainy with sleep.

"I'm sorry," Avar said. "I didn't mean to wake you."

"You didn't," he said, turning toward her, pushing himself up on one elbow, scratching lightly at the edge of his dark beard. "Whatever you read on that datapad did. It felt like your soul was dunked in ice water."

Avar sighed. Her link with Elzar was unique. Friendship, love, attraction, amplified and underscored through their power in the Force. They couldn't read each other's minds. It was nothing like telepathy—more that the normal Jedi sensitivity to emotional states was amplified between them. What one felt, they both felt. That bond had become stronger since they had finally allowed themselves to just . . . be what they were to each other.

Avar Kriss loved Elzar Mann, and Elzar loved her back—simple enough, and yet endlessly complicated.

"I received a message from the Jedi Council," Avar said, holding up her datapad. "They've asked me to be part of a mission designed to

STAR WARS: TRIALS OF THE JEDI

address both the Blight and the Nameless—but it's not an assignment. It's a request. If I say no, they'll move on to other Jedi."

Elzar nodded. "They're doing it this way so everyone will feel they have a true chance to refuse, if they want to," he said. "As little pressure as possible. This mission . . . it's that bad?"

Avar looked down at the datapad again, reading the words. The mission description was light on detail, but even what was there . . .

"I'm . . . not sure it's survivable," she said. "Neither are the Council. They make that clear. They know what they're asking."

Elzar reached out, taking a strand of her blond hair and tucking it behind her ear. He let his hand rest on her cheek for a moment, then lifted it and extended it toward the desk. He'd been working before they ended the previous day, researching some esoteric, near-forgotten technique of the Force. His own datapad rose into the air from the desk and moved smoothly to his outstretched hand.

Without a word, he powered it on. A moment's hesitation, then he looked at her, and she knew what he would say before he spoke.

"I don't have anything," Elzar said.

He set the datapad down on the bed, laying his hand flat on its surface. The corner of his mouth twitched upward, an acknowledgment of how little control anyone really had over their fate. Nothing was constant except that nothing was constant.

The two Jedi stared at each other. Here it was, the test they'd both known would come eventually. But so much sooner than either had expected and so much more final. A parting, one Avar knew might be the last.

"You have to go," Elzar said.

"Not yet," she replied.

Dawn broke, the sun lifting above the horizon and sending a soft glow into the chamber. She could see Elzar's face clearly now. Jedi or not, he didn't want her to leave, didn't want her to accept the mission, didn't want to lose what they had, against all odds, found together.

Neither did she. Jedi or not.

Another chime sounded, this time from Elzar's datapad. His gaze dropped to it.

"Maybe someone else declined the mission," he said. "Or maybe they're sending the requests out one at a time."

"Does it matter?" Avar said.

"Not at all," Elzar answered.

Without another word, they each tapped a button on their datapads, confirming their acceptance of the Council's request. In seconds, another message appeared, this time with details of the full briefing—its location and timing, an hour away.

"Not much time," Elzar said. "We need to get ready."

"Not yet," Avar said again, reaching for him.

Elzar Mann took a deep breath. The air smelled of growth, of rich soil and the plants and blooms that filled every centimeter of floor space, other than the walking paths laid down in meandering loops throughout the chamber. The room was built tall, and trees stretched their limbs to its roof, climbing vines dangling from them and from alcoves placed along the walls.

The ceiling was a massive artificial weather system, programmed to display a full day–night cycle for the plants. It was part of a comprehensive internal environment system that could even produce rain, in a steady, gentle bath most conducive to the needs of the vegetation.

The chamber was a great garden built within the Jedi Temple, a hidden refuge within the endless cityscape that was Coruscant, a way to encounter the natural world on a planet that so forcefully rejected it. It was called the Room of a Thousand Fountains, and yes, those too were present, fountains of every size producing a burbling music that reminded Elzar of what Avar heard when she connected with the Force. He'd heard it too, once, the first time they let themselves be together. Avar's song had never really left him.

All paths through the chamber eventually led to a large open space at its center, floored by gravel raked into intricate patterns every morning by the Temple's maintenance droids. The swirls and spirals were disrupted throughout the day by the movements of Jedi, a symbolic representation of order falling to chaos, returned again to order before the next dawn.

Elzar did not envy those droids their task that night. The patterns in the gravel had been obliterated, disturbed by the footsteps of about two dozen Jedi assembled here at the request of the High Council.

They had all received the same message. They knew why they were here. The Blight, the Nameless, or both. The end of the Jedi. The end of everything.

Eight members of the Jedi High Council were present, gathered around a short pedestal in the center of the space. This held two objects. The first was a metal rod, about half a meter long, with an ornate disk fused to one end, a single large gem at its center. The second was a large chunk of some metallic ore, crystalline in structure, reflecting the light in odd ways Elzar would have liked to examine more closely.

The eight Council members represented the entirety of that body. In better times, there would have been more. The Council had twelve seats. Four sat empty because the three Jedi Masters and one Grand Master who had held them were dead. Not for centuries had so many losses been suffered at once.

Master Adampo, Master Ada-Li Carro, and Grand Master Pra-Tre Veter were killed by the Nameless, those implacable beasts who seemed evolved precisely to counter all the Jedi's strengths.

The last empty seat on the Council belonged to Stellan Gios, and he had died a different way.

He held the seat for what . . . a few months? Elzar thought. *Until the Nihil murdered him like they murdered so many others.*

Elzar allowed himself to remember Stellan for a few moments—his goodness, his strength—then set the past aside and returned to the now. He looked toward Avar—she felt Stellan's loss as keenly as he did. Once, it had just been the three of them. The Firebrands, an unbreakable trio—until they were broken.

A strand of Avar's golden hair had escaped the diadem she wore—a gift from him to replace one lost during her time behind enemy lines in the Nihil Occlusion Zone. He wanted to adjust it but held himself back. Elzar did not particularly care what people thought about him and knew Avar did not, either—but there was a time and a place.

He took in the other Jedi gathered in the chamber, all wearing the bright white-and-gold temple robes. Elzar knew everyone present—a sampling of the very best and brightest in the entire Order. Not just the members of the High Council, extraordinary Jedi almost by definition, but many others. Elzar noted Reath Silas and his former master Cohmac Vitus, Bell Zettifar and the Wookiee Burryaga, the Kotabi bond-twins Terec and Ceret, the blademaster Zaviel Tepp. Even someone who was not a Jedi at all but once had been, the Tholothian monster-hunter Ty Yorrick. She stood alone, apart from the Jedi, giving off an impression of formidability and skill.

Elzar was glad to see her. Ty was a sort of mercenary—she hunted great beasts for a living. She carried a lightsaber, but that was far from the end of her personal armory. They had worked together more than once, and he'd found her reliable, resourceful, and good in a fight. He suspected the Council had asked her here on his own recommendation, though he wasn't quite certain why Ty had decided to accept. She'd left the Order as a teenager, for reasons that did not seem to have dimmed with time. He resolved to find a moment to ask her.

Vernestra Rwoh was here, too. The young Knight gave Elzar a cool nod, which he returned.

She doesn't like me very much, he thought.

Vernestra had been the Padawan of Stellan Gios. It saddened Elzar that he had been so close with Stellan but could not find a way to connect with his most promising student.

Ultimately, though, Vern's dislike of him didn't matter, any more than the fact that Avar Kriss *did* like him very much. All of that needed

STAR WARS: TRIALS OF THE JEDI

to fade away. They were all Jedi, nothing more, nothing less. Ties of emotion, history, and duty connected and strengthened everyone in the chamber. They had fought together, studied together, loved and lost together. Strands of obligation and memory and expectation and shared experience swirled through the room.

Grand Master Ry Ki-Sakka, known for his preternatural calm and piercing gaze, clapped his hands together twice. The chamber fell silent but for the fountains.

"We chose this place to meet," said the Grand Master, gesturing toward the room with one outstretched hand, "because it is filled with *life*. A reminder of all that will be lost if we fail."

His eyes roamed across the assembled Jedi before he continued, his voice tinged with sadness, "Every living thing in the galaxy is under threat of death. This is not hyperbole. Our studies, our observation, what we sense through the Force, and reports from across the galaxy all point to the same conclusion. The Blight, if not stopped, will consume the living Force from all life in existence. It might happen slowly, it might speed up, we are uncertain. But if nothing is done, it will happen. Everything—everything—will die."

A chill ran through the room. Elzar sensed it clearly. The Jedi learned to conquer fear early in their training, so what he sensed could not be fear . . . but it surely felt like it.

"We have prepared a plan," Master Rosason said from a few steps to the left of Grand Master Ki-Sakka.

Elzar held great admiration for Teri Rosason despite occasional friction between them in the past. Master Rosason had strong opinions and was unafraid to voice them. She was the sort of Jedi Elzar aspired to one day be, when his own hair turned gray and his face became a deeply lined record of a life deeply lived.

"There is no greater enemy for the Jedi Order than the Blight," Rosason said with great dignity. "Whatever we must do to stop it, whatever cost is paid, that is what we will do. Does everyone in this room understand?"

Again, a pause. No one spoke. Master Rosason looked toward Yarael Poof, the long-necked, slim-headed Quermian.

"With the help of the hard work performed by Jedi Knight Reath Silas and . . . others . . ." Yarael said, "we are now certain that the Blight is directly connected to the creatures we have come to call the Nameless. The Blight is spreading because the Nameless were removed from their homeworld by Marchion Ro and his Nihil."

A stir in the room. Some of the gathered Jedi were already aware of this fact, but many were not. The idea that any living beings were so connected to the Force that their physical location in the galaxy might affect literally everything else . . . it was quite a bit to take in.

"Through the efforts and sacrifice of a number of your fellow Jedi, we have captured twelve Nameless. They are secured here, within the Temple."

More than just a stir this time. The idea that those beasts, those Jedi Killers, attuned so specifically to their weaknesses, were somewhere in the same building . . .

"The younglings," said Bell Zettifar. "You can't keep them here if there are Nameless."

"The Nameless are well secured and under constant guard, Knight Zettifar," said Yarael Poof, his head weaving slowly back and forth on his long, thin neck. "There is no safer place for younglings than the Jedi Temple.

"In any case, the Nameless will not be here for long. We will return them to their homeworld. That is the mission."

"Will that be enough?" Bell asked, clearly deciding that if he'd questioned the Council once, he might as well do it twice. "We only have twelve Nameless. We know the Nihil must have stolen many more than that. Taking the creatures back to their homeworld is a good deed . . . something we should do—but will returning just a dozen create enough balance to stop the Blight?"

"We have no idea," said another member of the Council, Oppo

Rancisis, his bright eyes peering out from the mane of luxurious white hair covering his entire face and head.

The tip of the Thisspiasian Jedi Master's serpentine tail thumped against the floor—once, twice—a movement Elzar interpreted as frustration.

"We also have no choice," Rancisis continued. "Do you not understand? This is the end. This is all we have."

Master Lahru spoke next, the resonance chambers in his enormous pinnacle of a head sending bass notes through everyone in the room.

"We will send a team of Jedi with the captured Nameless. They will release the creatures, and will then determine if anything else must be done to return the galaxy to balance and end the Blight."

"Is that all?" said Vernestra Rwoh. "I mean no disrespect, but is that the entire plan, Master Lahru?"

"Patience, Vernestra," Master Lahru intoned. "We realize there are many unknowns, but time is short. Every moment we wait, the Blight spreads. The only place we have ever stopped it was Kashyyyk, but it required the Drengir. They are now gone. That solution cannot be implemented elsewhere. To echo the words of Master Rancisis . . . this is all we have."

Lahru raised his hand, extending it toward the Jedi assembled in the center of the chamber.

"The team will consist of nine people. A second, comprising an additional nine, will remain in reserve in case the first team runs into difficulties and requires assistance or extraction. These are the Jedi we can spare—our resources are spread thin between the efforts to hold back the Blight beneath the Temple and other trouble spots throughout the galaxy. But the Jedi on both teams are carefully chosen, and those who travel with the Nameless will not attempt their mission unprepared."

Master Lahru reached down and lifted the odd metal rod from the pedestal. Elzar would have given all his credits, if he had any, for a closer look. It was clearly some sort of artifact, something attuned to the Force.

Elzar had spent more time down in the Temple archives than almost any Jedi he knew, and he'd never seen anything exactly like it.

"This is the Rod of Ages," Lahru said, "obtained at great cost. An ancient and potent artifact. In its center rests an Echo Stone. In certain circumstances, these stones can resonate with the Force itself, allowing for various unusual applications. Marchion Ro has been observed to use a similar artifact to control the Nameless. While we do not yet know if the Rod of Ages offers the same capability, our hope is that the artifact could be of significant use during the mission."

He shifted his massive hand to indicate the piece of metal resting on the pedestal before him, glinting in the chamber's artificial sunlight.

"Next—this is a sample of ore retrieved from the planet Tolis, sourced by Reath Silas, Cohmac Vitus, and Padawan Amadeo Azzazzo. It is highly resistant to the Blight. We do not have a large supply of the material. However, Masters Govena and Infil'a in the armory believe they can use what we do have to create protective armor that may fend off the debilitating effects Jedi usually suffer in close proximity to the Nameless. Nine suits, no more—it will have to be enough."

Elzar considered the Jedi that Master Lahru had just named. Reath, Cohmac, the rest. And beyond them, so many others, everyone in the Order contributing to the fight against the Nihil and all their horrors. Some—far too many—had given all they had, their very lives.

Master Soleil Agra spoke for the first time, her huge, dark eyes scanning across the Council Chamber. "The primary team will take the Nameless to their homeworld using the *Ataraxia*. The cruiser and its shuttle have been outfitted with special containment chambers that will allow the creatures to be transported safely. We will also request personnel from the Republic to travel with us—non-Force-wielders immune to the Nameless effect. If the chancellor grants that request, we will have additional support in handling the creatures."

The golden-skinned Nautolan hesitated as if to heighten the suspense. But Elzar knew Soleil. She was above such a maneuver. Master Agra had paused because she felt deep anxiety, almost despair, at the thought of sending nine Jedi to what might well be their deaths.

"These are the ones we will send," she said. "These are the Nine.

"Terec, Burryaga, Arkoff, Bell Zettifar, Reath Silas, Ty Yorrick—"

Many eyes turned to look toward the outsider. Her face was set in an expression that was not exactly a frown but certainly conveyed an unspoken challenge to anyone who would question her right to be there.

"Elzar Mann, Avar Kriss, and . . ."

Soleil Agra paused again, and Elzar realized he didn't even particularly care about the final name. Whatever happened, he and Avar would be together. Then Master Agra said it, and he realized he did care, he cared quite a bit.

"Azlin Rell," she finished.

A ripple moved through the room. Elzar was not particularly thrilled about the idea of going anywhere at all with Azlin Rell, and he clearly was not alone in the sentiment.

"With respect, Master Agra," he said, "you can't mean that. Azlin Rell has embraced the dark side. For a mission like this, we need to be able to trust one another, rely on one another for our lives. We can't worry about a Sith stabbing us in the back the first chance he gets."

Soleil's mouth tightened, but before she could respond, Reath Silas spoke from where he stood beneath one of the tall trees, his arms wrapped around himself. The young Knight looked exhausted, his voice hollow.

"Azlin isn't a Sith," Reath said. "He's just afraid. We need him. He knows more about the Nameless than anyone else alive, and can see them in ways we can't. Azlin will be essential in determining the path forward once we get to their homeworld."

"If Azlin's safe, Reath," Bell said, "then why is he in a cell on the Temple's detention level?"

The attention of every Jedi focused on Reath. The young scholar knew the former Jedi better than anyone in the room, even Yoda, and his opinion here mattered.

"I can handle Azlin," Reath said. "I . . . understand him."

"If you can't," Bell said, "we will."

Reath nodded. "It won't come to that."

Bell exchanged a glance with Burryaga.

Vernestra Rwoh stepped forward, moving through the Jedi toward the Council members.

"I do not wish to question your wisdom," she said. "But I need to be on the primary team. I am the only person who knows the route to the Nameless homeworld—Mari San Tekka gave it to me. It needs one of the Nihil Path Engines to work, but the *Ataraxia* has one. I have to be on the mission."

Yoda spoke for the first time. "Part of the backup team, you are, Vernestra," he said, his voice gentle but firm.

"But . . . how will the Nine get to the Nameless homeworld?" Vernestra said. "I'm the only person with the Path. I can't write it down—something happens in my head. It's like I'm the only one who can use it."

The young Knight seemed bewildered.

Yoda spoke again. "Transcribe it you cannot, but recite it you can. Reviewed your reports, we have. You have spoken the Path aloud before . . . for a Shani woman, hmm?"

"You mean Deva Lompop," Vernestra said. "I . . . I can do that. Of course I can. That's what I'll do."

"That is not the only reason, Vernestra," Ry Ki-Sakka said. "We have allocated Jedi between the two teams to create balance. The second team will function as a direct backup if things go wrong with the primary mission. If a rescue is required, it will be crucial to have someone on the second team with direct knowledge of the route to the Nameless planet. That is you, Vernestra. The Council has carefully constructed each team to give the best chance of success to the mission as a whole."

Grand Master Ki-Sakka continued, listing the other members of the backup group—the medic Torban Buck, Ceret, Indeera Stokes, Cohmac Vitus, Lily Tora-Asi, Zaviel Tepp, Kirak Infil'a, and even a member of the Council—Yarael Poof.

Elzar considered both lists, seeing the wisdom in the Council's decisions. Everyone chosen was particularly skilled in their own way or possessed unique insight into either the Blight or the Nameless. The connections between the group were strong as well. Arkoff was an extraordinary warrior with extensive experience fighting the Nameless but was also Azlin Rell's former master. Ty Yorrick was uniquely skilled with creatures and had worked closely with Elzar more than once. Burryaga was the first Jedi to understand the Blight's nature and how to hold it back through the Force—and also Bell's closest companion in the Order. And so on. Every member of the Nine had clearly been selected for not just their abilities but their ties to the other members of the group, the shared history.

That said, Elzar wasn't entirely sure why they'd chosen him. He tried things other people didn't. That was about it. But he was sure the Council had their reasons.

Avar Kriss, though . . . her selection was easily explained. She would hold them all together. He turned to look at her. Her face was unreadable, her spirit anything but. Beautiful.

"Looks like we're off to save the galaxy," she said, her voice quiet. "Nine of us. As one."

As one, he thought.

The briefing complete, the Jedi in the room broke into small groups. Elzar saw Reath, Burryaga, and Bell chatting. Bell had his hand on Reath's shoulder. He was smiling at the withdrawn young Knight, offering some kind of reassurance. Terec and Ceret stared into each other's eyes, lost in the silent mind-to-mind communication no one outside their bond could access.

Vernestra stood alone, staring down at the chunk of ore resting on the pedestal.

"Talk to her," Avar said. "You know what it's like for the Council to hold back something you think you've earned."

He nodded and moved through the garden to approach the young woman.

"Vernestra," Elzar said. "I'm sorry they didn't choose you. I can tell it came as a surprise."

Vernestra looked at him, her green-skinned face carefully neutral.

"I just didn't think it would go this way, Elzar," she said. "I thought, after carrying that Path in my head all this time . . . I just thought it would be useful. That I'd use it."

"You are using it, Vernestra—just not the way you expected. We need that information—the galaxy needs it. You're helping everyone alive by sharing your knowledge and skill, just as we all are."

Vernestra did not seem convinced.

"A while ago, you shared one of Stellan Gios's teachings with me," Elzar said. "It's never left my mind. 'It doesn't matter how good we are or how much we want to help. The only thing that matters is that we've done everything in our power to be the best we can be.' You told me it's how you judged yourself when you began to lose faith, to doubt. Those words helped me. Perhaps they can help you now as well."

Vernestra gave Elzar a long, considering look, then nodded once.

A voice cut through the discussions in the room—a high growling warble. Burryaga.

"He's asking when we leave," Bell translated.

"Every moment we delay, more is lost," said Yoda, his voice resolute. "Certain preparations, we must undertake, and Masters Govena and Infil'a will forge the armor for the Nine. That will take a day, perhaps two, mm? But once that is done, go, you will."

The great Jedi looked up, at the life all surrounding them, all the life everywhere.

"You are our hope," Yoda said. "Luminous, you are. May the Force be with you."

Chapter Two

THE GALACTIC SENATE

"We have another one, Supreme Chancellor," said Norel Quo, touching a finger to his ear, where a tiny personal comm unit rested.

"*Blast it!*" shouted Lina Soh, slamming her palm against the top of her desk.

The sound tore through the cavernous interior of the Senate building like a rifle shot. At Lina's side, Matari and Voru stirred, low growls rumbling from their throats. The twin targons, yellow and red and huge, felt what she felt. The empathic link between the supreme chancellor of the great Galactic Republic and her feline bodyguards churned with rage, impotence, frustration.

"Where, Norel?" Lina spat.

Her aide spoke again, his voice calm.

"Should be coming up any moment . . . yes. There."

Norel pointed, and they both watched as a tiny cam droid flew through the spherical interior of the Senate building, headed for one of the disk-shaped platforms studding every meter of its curved walls in a gently spiraling pattern.

This space, the Grand Convocation Chamber, was designed to reflect the galaxy itself. Each platform represented a particular world or coalition in the great assembly of civilizations that constituted the Republic. The delegates would gather, each in their assigned space within the sphere, and then . . . democracy.

About 10 percent of the platforms were currently draped in black, representing the Occlusion Zone, the worlds stolen from the Republic by Marchion Ro and his Nihil.

Please, let it be one of those, Lina thought, watching the cam droid soar.

She immediately regretted the thought. The Occlusion Zone worlds were still part of the Republic—its people were citizens like any others. Their delegates were on Coruscant when the Nihil locked their worlds away behind their impenetrable Stormwall, and so they were still represented in the Senate. The Occlusion Zone senators still attended sessions, though their numbers were dwindling. Many didn't see the point. They still had a voice—but they all had only one thing to say, a request already voiced many times over. Help us.

The droid flew past the black-draped platforms, finally slowing to a stop before another. Lina knew the world it represented—she knew them all. The planet Tellion, a manufacturing and recycling world. Densely populated.

A symbol appeared on the edge of the platform, projected by the cam droid: a spiked circle in bright scarlet. This symbol was used across the galaxy, with a near-universal meaning. It indicated plague or pestilence. The Blight had appeared on Tellion.

Lina cast her eyes across the chamber, seeking out the other red-marked platforms. Not so many when you considered the vastness of the Republic—perhaps thirty in all—but yesterday there were only twenty-seven. The day before that, twenty-two. The Blighted planets were scattered across the galaxy with no discernible connections or patterns among them.

Lina had an extraordinary decision to make. This was the reason she had taken the opportunity offered by a brief scheduled hiatus from the

STAR WARS: TRIALS OF THE JEDI 39

Senate's regular sessions to order a repurposing of the Grand Convocation Chamber. Hence, the black drapery, the indications of the Blighted worlds, and many of her key advisers stationed around the chamber, ready to give her reports as needed. The huge space was remade, become an engine designed to help the supreme chancellor of the Republic find some way to save it.

Lina stood upon the pedestal placed at the very center of the sphere, surrounded by a symbolic representation of the Republic itself. All its cultures, all its beings with their diverse desires and troubles and unique offerings and desperate needs. Together in the same great chamber, but separate, each in their own space.

High above it all, a countdown clock hovered, projected in bright blue by another of the cam droids. It currently displayed just under ten minutes.

"Time grows short," Lina said.

"Perhaps Marchion Ro will be late, Madam Chancellor," Norel Quo said.

"No, Vice Chair, he won't," she replied. "This is the day his dream comes true."

She glanced at Norel, her primary aide for many years. Dutiful, precise, he knew her needs before she did.

"Your horn looks spectacular, by the way," she said.

"The occasion seemed to warrant the extra effort, Chancellor," Norel replied, clearly pleased.

Koorivar signified their social status through intricate ornamentation of the large central horn that spiraled from their skulls. Norel Quo's was even more splendid than usual—it looked gilded, with beautiful turquoise pictograms running along its curves. Lina had noticed the difference earlier that morning but had waited to mention it until a moment when the words would mean the most to her aide.

Choosing *this* opportunity to comment, when she had so much on her mind, when she was literally staring at a countdown clock for the fate of the galaxy . . . Norel would understand, and would not forget.

"Any word from the Jedi?" Lina asked.

"Not yet, Madam Chancellor," Norel said.

Lina watched the seconds tick by, frowning, then pulled her eyes from the timer and cast her gaze across the Grand Convocation Chamber. She looked at the black-draped disks representing the Occlusion Zone worlds, as stark a reminder as anything could be of one central fact: *Marchion Ro is your enemy.*

She brought to the very front of her mind the countless beings trapped under the Nihil's boot of oppression.

That *is the person who claims he can defeat the Blight,* Lina thought. That *is the person who has offered to be our savior. That murdering, lying monster. Marchion Ro.*

The targons at her side stirred restlessly, each blinking their four eyes rapidly. Her guardians, who had saved her life from assassins more than once: red-furred Matari and his twin, the bright-yellow Voru.

"Easy, friends," she murmured to the two beasts. "I'll be all right."

She wondered if it was true. She wasn't sure if anyone would be all right, in the end.

Lina's cancellarial pedestal contained controls that allowed her to communicate with any Senate disk she chose, even to bring them out from their respective berths to hover directly before her. She considered those controls now, deciding which report she needed to hear first, then tapped a button.

A disk soared from the wall, making its way smoothly toward her pedestal. Aboard it was the Republic's primary data analyst, a human named Keven Tarr. His work had saved as many lives as any Jedi during the Nihil conflict, probably more than most.

Surrounding Tarr on his disk were several of his custom-built computational droids—mechanical minds designed to calculate with a speed and precision beyond any accessible to organics. They clattered away, lights swirling across their surfaces, tiny pinpricks of energy surging back and forth like waves on a windswept sea.

"Supreme Chancellor," Keven said, bowing, then straightening and

STAR WARS: TRIALS OF THE JEDI

sweeping his unruly ginger-colored hair off his forehead with the back of a hand. "How may I serve the Republic?"

"You know as well as anyone the crisis we face, Master Analyst Tarr," Lina said. "Tell me you have found some pattern in the Blighted worlds? Have you been able to calculate where it will appear next, or what is causing it?"

"I don't want to offer false hope, Chancellor. As of yet, my work has produced no results worth sharing. I have a large team at my disposal, as well as the most state-of-the-art computational assets available."

Here he gestured at the swaying, sparkling droids around him.

"We do not know how the Blight travels between systems, or why it chooses one planet over another," Keven said, pursing thin, pale lips in a thin, pale face. "Originally, we assumed it was another Nihil weapon, but bits of information we've gleaned from worlds beyond the Stormwall tell us the Blight is present in the Occlusion Zone as well."

"I would not put it past Marchion Ro to test a weapon on his own systems," Lina said.

"I agree," Keven said, giving a tight nod. "But the Blight is present on worlds close to the Core, heavily defended planets with strong sensor networks. While the Nihil's Path technology lets them appear virtually anywhere, the likelihood of them slipping past the defenses employed in the Core, depositing the Blight, and getting away without being detected is very low."

Lina considered this, then swept an arm out toward the walls around them. "We've detected the Blight on thirty worlds. But that cannot be all there is, correct? Planets are huge. The Blight could be hiding in jungles, or in deserts, or beneath seas, or on sparsely populated or uninhabited planets. It could be coming for us even now, slowly chewing away at the very substance of our worlds."

Keven didn't respond. His silence was agreement enough.

"Just a few more questions before I return you to your work, Master Analyst," she said. "Is the Blight accelerating?"

"Our sample size is too small to be sure. We find more of the Blight every time we look, but is that because more of it is appearing, or because it takes time to search worlds? We just don't know. I have my people working on an orbital detector that should speed up the process for inhabited worlds. But sometimes with problems like this, you must make a conclusion based on the data you *don't* have, the information you feel rather than the facts you can see."

"You sound like a Jedi, Keven."

"The Force is in everything," Keven said without hesitation. "Especially numbers. But to finish my thought . . . if I had to place a bet, if I made a call based entirely on instinct, then yes, Chancellor Soh. The Blight is accelerating."

"Can we stop it?"

"Given time, the collective brilliance of the scientific minds of the Republic can do anything. Of course we can stop the Blight. Given time." He raised a single finger, and a little frown washed across his face. "But I know the question you are actually asking, Madam Chancellor. The information you need in light of Marchion Ro's offer is this: The Republic cannot stop the Blight today, and we will not be able to stop it tomorrow. It has, thus far, proven uniquely resistant to analysis and treatment."

Wonderful, Lina thought.

"I understand, Master Analyst," she said. "Do you have any recommendations?"

Keven seemed almost apologetic. He knew he was not giving her answers she wanted to hear—though her respect for him grew at his willingness to do exactly that. He said, "At this point, your scientific team recommends the evacuation of infected planets. We will complete the orbital scanners I mentioned soon, which will make that task easier."

"Abandon entire worlds?" Lina said, rolling the idea around in her mind, hating it.

"As far as we can tell, worlds *end* once the Blight appears. The only consolation is that it moves slowly. We have a chance to get people out of the way. It's not like the Great Disaster, where the Emergences moved at the speed of light. Here we still have a chance."

"Thank you, Master Analyst," Lina said.

Keven bowed again, then activated the control on his disk that would return it to its place in the Convocation Chamber's wall.

Lina watched it glide away, thinking about the logistical effort involved in evacuating an entire planet and relocating its population.

And it's not just one planet, she thought. *It's thirty. Today. Tomorrow it will be more.*

She took a moment to scratch Voru behind her ear, resulting in a purr from the targon that seemed to shake the entire pedestal. Then another scratch for Matari, who nuzzled up into her hand once he saw his twin was getting attention he was not. With that important work done, Lina tapped another control on her console, and a second disk moved forward to rest before her pedestal.

"Secretary Lorillia," Lina said, looking at the tall, slim being who stood on the disk, his hands folded before him. "Tell me we've had a breakthrough with the Stormwall."

Jeffo Lorillia, secretary of transportation for the entire Republic, was a Muun. To human eyes, their elongated skulls, dark, shadowed eyes, and downturned mouths suggested gloomy dispositions. Most Muuns Lina had met lived up to their reputation. They were a serious people by and large.

Now Jeffo's long, thin face stretched into an even deeper frown than genetics had provided. Lina was not surprised. The poor man hated the Stormwall to a degree that might exceed even that of people trapped within the Occlusion Zone.

He is the secretary of transportation, after all, Lina considered. *He works to make sure things can go from here to there. The Stormwall is designed to prevent exactly that. It's an affront to his entire career.*

"We have not yet defeated the Stormwall, Supreme Chancellor," the Muun intoned. "The Jedi have a limited ability to penetrate the Stormwall using small vessels, but we are not able to bring larger ships through. An occasional communications droid gets in or out, but the information they provide is limited. As you are aware . . ."

He cleared his throat, a process that seemed needlessly thorough and would have undoubtedly torn a human esophagus to shreds.

"As you are aware," Jeffo continued, "the Stormwall's border has moved more than once. Forward, back, then forward again. Intelligence gathered from various sources has confirmed that the control center for the Stormwall within the Occlusion Zone is Marchion Ro's flagship, the *Gaze Electric*. We must find that ship, destroy it, and cause the full collapse of the Stormwall."

"Does your team have suggestions on how this might be accomplished?"

"I am not a warrior," Jeffo responded, his tone dour. "Perhaps Admiral Kronara will have thoughts on the matter."

My thoughts exactly, Lina considered, as she sent the secretary's platform back to its designated berth within the Convocation Chamber wall.

Another tap on her console, and this time it was not a disk that came forward but a cam droid. It hovered before her pedestal and projected a large holoscreen upon which the grizzled face of Admiral Pevel Kronara could be seen. He was a human of middle age, gray-haired and fierce, like an outcropping of stone—though just then he resembled a block of rock that hadn't found time to shave in a few weeks.

"Supreme Chancellor," he said, bowing his head.

"The beard suits you, Admiral," Lina said. "Is it regulation?"

Kronara reached up to his face, scratched at his cheek.

"Regulations in the Republic Defense Coalition are more like suggestions, Chancellor," he said. "We're not a proper military. Member planets send their own ships and their own crews, all with their own way of doing things. Contradictions in policy crop up all over the place. But even if there were a hard-and-fast rule . . . command has its privileges."

And its horrors, she thought.

She cast a quick glance up at the timer hovering high above.

Five minutes.

"Admiral, give me the status of Nihil operations as you know them,

STAR WARS: TRIALS OF THE JEDI 45

and of our own fleets. I realize this is challenging due to the Stormwall. Tell me what you can."

"A sizable portion of the RDC fleet is with me. I'm commanding from the *Third Horizon*. We're positioned just outside the Stormwall, on the other side from Eriadu. We were using that planet as a staging area for Occlusion Zone operations before the last Stormwall expansion, which means a good number of RDC assets were present on the world when it was swallowed back up into the Zone."

Kronara frowned. "We had a contingency plan in place if something like that happened. Our people were supposed to work with local Eriaduan units to coordinate a defense. I hope that's how it went. The Nihil could bring enormous offensive resources to bear against that planet if they wanted to."

"The Eriaduans were planning to rebel against Nihil rule?"

"I don't know, Madam Chancellor. But if an uprising happens anywhere in the Occlusion Zone, Eriadu would be my bet. For one thing, more of our RDC units are congregated there than anywhere else in the O.Z., and the Eriaduans are formidable in their own right. You remember what happened at the Battle of Kur."

I do, she thought.

Kur was one of the early battles against the Nihil, where the Republic had won a resounding victory. Eriadu had sent its own ships to participate in the battle, part of an effort to avenge earlier Nihil attacks against their world. Once the battle was won, RDC commanders had ordered that Nihil leaders be captured for interrogation. Instead the Eriaduans executed every last one they found.

Eriaduans did as they pleased—but if they were on your side, they were a powerful ally.

"For all we know," Kronara continued, "a rebellion might already have kicked off on Eriadu. We don't have real-time communications through the Stormwall. But if the Eriaduans do start a fight, I would expect a significant Nihil response. The Eriaduans have a high opinion of themselves.

They might think they can win that fight and take their world back, but it's just as likely to end up a doomed last stand that ends with the Nihil killing everyone on the planet."

He frowned.

"I wouldn't care so much—it's their world, the Eriaduans can do what they like—but they've got forces under my command with them as well. My RDC fighters are brave, they'll do their part, but I don't want them dying for no purpose."

"Of course, Admiral," Lina said. "Are you aware of other RDC assets beyond the Stormwall? Could we use them to hunt the *Gaze Electric,* as Secretary Lorillia suggested, and make the whole question moot? If that ship is destroyed, then the Stormwall goes down, and we can bring as many ships into the Occlusion Zone as we need."

Kronara shook his head. "The Occlusion Zone is vast, Chancellor, and we don't even know if the *Gaze Electric* is still in it. Marchion Ro's flagship is equipped with Path Engines, which means he can come and go through the Stormwall as he pleases. We wouldn't know where to begin to look. Maybe you can ask the Eye of the Nihil when he calls."

Lina's eyes flicked up to the timer. *Four minutes.*

"Thank you, Admiral," she said. "Hold your position. If you receive further word from inside the Occlusion Zone, please pass it along immediately."

"Of course, Supreme Chancellor," he said, saluting. "We are all the Republic."

The hologram fizzled out before Lina had a chance to respond.

"Vice Chair, display the vidclip again, please," she said.

Norel Quo did not require additional instruction. He knew the clip to which she referred. She heard him tapping on his own datapad, and the droid that had projected Kronara's hologram displayed a different scene.

The Nihil had sent the recording, which made it immediately suspect, but Keven Tarr had analyzed the images with every tool at his command. As far as he could determine, the clip was genuine. If the video was faked, it was done using technology far beyond anything known in the Republic. The Nihil were more than capable of achieving unheard-of technological leaps—their Path Engines let them travel through the galaxy along routes unavailable to any other ships, and of course there was the Stormwall itself. But the Nihil's science seemed geared toward war, destruction, domination. Creating impeccable fake holovids seemed . . . not their style. Lina believed the images were real.

The opening shot of the holovid depicted Marchion Ro, standing on a world Tarr's analysts had pinpointed as Oanne based on the visible vegetation, the color of the soil, and other details. Behind him, a broad patch of Blight, the color of fossilized bone. In one hand, he held a long metal rod tipped at either end with purple crystals. The composition of both rod and crystals had eluded the science of the few technicians allowed to see these images.

Marchion was shirtless, the blue-gray skin of his chest exposed, spattered with tattoos of starfields and churning storms. He wore tight trousers made of dark-stained leather, and spiked boots. Nothing else. Not his trademark mask with its swirling red storm hiding his eyes, not even a holstered blaster. His dark hair whipped as the wind gusted past him, and his eyes were black pits in his angular face. He looked as he chose to, which was completely unafraid, unarmored, unprotected from the Blight that had the rest of the galaxy scrambling in terror. He looked, in short . . .

Like a conqueror, Lina thought.

As the holo continued, the Eye of the Nihil smiled, exposing just the sharp points of his teeth. He turned to face the Blight and lifted the metal rod in one hand. A faint glow surrounded the crystals, and the Blight *retreated.*

It chilled Lina every time she saw it. There was no mistaking what happened. The line of the Blight pulled back. While the desiccated plants did not return to life, it was clear that the soil was clean where Marchion forced the Blight to recede.

The holovid ended. The point was made. Marchion Ro could— *again*—do what the Republic could not.

The Nihil lie, Lina thought. *Of course they do. But about this . . . why would they? Why would they offer to remove the Blight if they couldn't actually do it? What would be the point?*

For the thousandth time, she considered Marchion's offer, made in person here on Coruscant several weeks earlier under a pretense of diplomatic immunity. It was very simple: Allow him into the Republic to remove the Blight from the galaxy and announce that he was the person who had done it.

Lina and her advisers had scoffed at the offer—clearly another Nihil trick. And then this footage had arrived. And then more worlds had reported the Blight. And then more.

Marchion Ro had literally torn the Republic apart. Accepting his offer to save it was unthinkable. But the increasingly clear reality was that Lina might not have a choice. The Senate had already indicated it would accept her judgment if she determined Marchion's offer should be put to a vote—her endorsement would ensure the measure would pass. Or, she could decline, turn from the Eye of the Nihil . . . the Senate would accept that as well. The decision had essentially been left to her alone.

Lina sank into the chair built into the pedestal, intended as a spot for the supreme chancellor to rest when senators were engaged in debate that did not require her immediate attention. She put her head in her hands and closed her eyes.

"Madam Chancellor?" came the concerned voice of Norel Quo.

Then, a tongue, licking across the outside of her hand. One of the targons—Matari or Voru—helping as best as the animal could.

"I'm fine," Lina said. "Just weighing things."

Where are the Jedi? she thought. *Why aren't they here? The Senate building is not a kilometer from their Temple, and still, they will not come when I call.*

The Jedi had never sworn oaths of loyalty to the Republic. Oh, they believed in the Republic's ideals, they said it all the time, but as far as Lina knew their only true loyalties were to the Force, the light, and their own Order. The relationship between the chancellor's office and the Jedi Temple was close and long standing, but technically the Jedi were not under her authority. She could not command them.

STAR WARS: TRIALS OF THE JEDI 49

Lina did not want to make this decision without the benefit of Jedi wisdom, but now, as the timer ticked down its final seconds . . . it was clear that she would.

But wasn't that always the way? The chancellor made the decision. And the chancellor, despite the majesty of the title, the office, the responsibility, the power, was just a person. Everyone was exactly who they were, no more, no less. Election to a position with power over uncountable lives across an entire galaxy did not convey any new wisdom.

We are all the Republic, Lina thought. *I try to be. I try to be all the Republic, to represent everyone, but that is the great lie of democracy. Even the greatest elected leaders are still only themselves. I can't be everyone. I can only be Lina Soh.*

The people who put me here expect me to make decisions as they would, or perhaps better than they could—but people do not become decider droids just because they win an election. I will make the choice that I, Lina Soh, feel is best. I will try to think of everyone, but in the end, some part of me will only be thinking of myself.

The galaxy faced destruction from the Blight. The Republic could not stop it. A murdering tyrant named Marchion Ro said he could, and had offered proof. All he wanted in return was a public acknowledgment of his power, of his supremacy.

Would it stop there? Of course not. Lina could see it as clearly as Marchion obviously did. If she allowed him to save the Republic, she would be handing it to him. Talk would begin, doubt in Republic governance, and in time, systems would willingly offer themselves up to Nihil rule. After all, the Nihil had saved them when the Republic could not. And then . . . war, when one side decided enough had been ceded or wanted more than they had. True, galaxy-wide war, a thousand times worse than the relatively contained conflict they had been fighting against the Nihil for the past several years. Centuries of hard-earned galactic peace—gone.

But what choice did she have? The supreme chancellor's job was to protect and serve the lives in the Republic. Not tomorrow's lives, today's. Perhaps saving those lives had to mean sacrificing the Republic.

I have lost, Lina thought.

"Madam Chancellor," said Norel Quo, a strange note in his voice, a touch of light, "the Jedi are here."

Lina Soh stood, to see another of the disks gliding toward her from the Convocation Chamber's wall. It was draped in black, and she knew the Outer Rim world it was assigned to—Hetzal. The once beautiful agricultural planet where the Great Disaster and the entire Nihil conflict had begun. Where the Jedi and the Republic had worked together to save billions of lives in a show of incredible collaboration, hope, and skill.

But now, it was a world lost to a different kind of cataclysm. In a direct rejection of everything the Republic had once achieved there, when the Nihil raised the Stormwall, they made Hetzal their seat of power.

The Nihil choosing Hetzal as their flagworld sent a very clear message: All that work, all that sacrifice, and in the end, the Jedi and the Republic had saved nothing at all.

The platform drew closer. A single Jedi stood upon it, wearing the bright white-and-gold formal robes they used for official duties. Droids hovered around the disk transmitting information to the other platforms in the chamber—and those outside it as well, Lina assumed. She was under no illusions about the security of this sacred chamber. The Nihil had infiltrated the highest levels of the Republic's government with their slicers and spies.

The Jedi aboard the platform looked at the chamber, the whole grand pageant of black drapery and holograms and busy aides. He seemed bemused. As the disk drew close to the chancellor's pedestal, he leapt, landing lightly beside Lina. Norel Quo offered an outraged murmur, but Matari and Voru did not stir. They knew this man posed no threat.

"Elzar, where have you been?" Lina said, moving to greet him. "The Republic is in crisis."

"I know, Lina," he said, a familiarity she would accept from few others. "We've been working on that. We've been trying to find a way to stop the Blight."

Elzar glanced at several cam droids hovering not far away. The recording devices were omnipresent within the space under ordinary circumstances, considered part of the transparency necessary for democracy. The Jedi frowned. He lifted his hand and flicked out his fingers, and every one of the little round droids was flung away, to carom off the walls of the Convocation Chamber and drift slowly to the floor far below.

"Better," Elzar said. "I'd like this conversation to remain between us. And the targons. And Vice Chair Quo, of course. How are things, Norel?"

Jedi Master Elzar Mann was handsome—square-jawed with a precisely trimmed beard, his hair dark with a bit of wave to it, his skin copper. Charming, too—quick to smile. He was the Jedi to whom Lina was closest in the Order and had become a sort of de facto liaison between her office and the Jedi Council. She liked the man. Usually. Today, not as much.

"The Blight, Elzar. What have you found? Can you stop it?" she said before the Jedi could enter into a chat with her aide about his day, asking after his nineteen children, asking how he'd gotten his horn so shiny.

"Yes, Lina, we can. In a sense," Elzar replied. "But there is other news. The Blight has appeared on Coruscant. It's beneath the Jedi Temple, down at the lowest possible level. In the old stones."

Lina remained standing, but only just. Matari and Voru trembled, closing their eyes. Elzar was still speaking, but she couldn't hear him.

I'll have to issue an evacuation order, she thought. *Over a trillion people. Where will we get the ships?*

Finding an evacuation fleet was one thing; getting the planet's population aboard it would be another entirely. Coruscant had no open space. Every level, every chamber was occupied. She imagined the chaos that would ensue when word spread that the great city-world was poisoned. Panicked, fleeing people, waves of beings crashing into one another, surging upward from the deep levels, converging at the surface, trying to get away, away, away.

I have to agree to Marchion's terms, Lina thought. *I have to let that monster save us. Even more than before, I have no choice.*

Thoughts sped through her mind, too many to process, like a droid trying to handle a system update too complex for its circuits.

Then a few of Elzar's words surged to the surface of her mind—something he had just said.

"Wait . . . *when* did the Jedi first become aware of the Blight beneath the Temple?"

"A short time ago," Elzar replied, his face serious. "Days, not weeks."

"*What?* You didn't tell me immediately?"

"We have it controlled. It's not going anywhere. One of our Knights, a Wookiee named Burryaga, first found the path to holding it back. We've refined his techniques. There was a substantial infestation on Kashyyyk we were able to eradicate entirely. You may have heard. Now, that one was a one-off—we won't be able to do that exact thing again. But—"

"*Days?*" Lina said, feeling an uncharacteristic fury grow in her, hearing the targons snarl. "We could be well into an evacuation effort by now!"

"An evacuation of Coruscant is impossible, Lina," the Jedi said. "We both know it. Announcing that the Blight is here would only cause panic and millions of deaths—if not billions. We have the situation under control, contained entirely within our Temple. The Jedi are not elected. We do not serve. We help. If we believed we could not hold the Blight back, we would have told you earlier. But we have, and we will continue to."

Elzar's tone was calm, but Lina felt like she had been slapped.

Who does he think he is? she thought, but the answer was obvious. *A Jedi.*

"Now, please, let me share something more positive," Elzar said. "We believe we can stop the Blight, Lina. Not just here but everywhere. We have a plan."

"Will it defeat the Nihil?" Lina asked.

"No. That is a task for the Republic, though we remain committed to helping however we can."

"Fine," Lina said. "Tell me what you've got."

"We have captured a small group of Nameless—the creatures Marchion Ro used to murder so many of us."

"I know what they are, Elzar. Why would you capture the beasts instead of killing them? To prevent him from using them against you?"

"Not exactly. We have a different approach in mind. I can tell you, but

STAR WARS: TRIALS OF THE JEDI

it must remain absolutely secret. There are clearly ears within the Republic that report to the Nihil, and our best chance of success lies in—"

A chime sounded. Every eye in the Convocation Chamber flicked upward, toward the timer, which had hit zero.

"It is time, Madam Chancellor," said Norel Quo.

The Senate chamber had a holoprojector built into its structure, able to display images much larger than any individual cam droid could. It activated, and Marchion Ro appeared within the chamber, enormous. Dominant. He sat on a sort of throne, wearing a long white coat and what appeared to be the same leather pants he'd worn in the Blight clip. His neck was bandaged, and a dark spatter stained his coat below the neck, running down his lapel. Whatever or whoever had hurt Marchion, he hadn't felt it necessary to change his clothes since the injury.

Marchion seemed at ease but focused. Not dismissive, not contemptuous—a foreign leader operating in his official capacity.

He glanced around the chamber, taking in the various elements— Blight indicators, the Occlusion Zone designation, and eventually Lina Soh herself.

"Impressive decorations, Lina," Marchion said in his quiet, penetrating voice, the sound of being stalked. "You have a Jedi with you. Elzar Mann, I believe. I wish . . . I were there in person, my friend."

"As do I, Marchion," Elzar said, all charm gone from his voice.

Marchion gestured out toward the Convocation Chamber.

"I see you've labeled the Blighted worlds. I can add another ten or so from within the Occlusion Zone, if that would be helpful. My scientists suggest more of this terrible scourge appears every day. I'm sure yours concur." His face took on an expression of noble sincerity. No one would ever be able to argue that he wasn't taking the crisis seriously. "I can begin immediately. I will remove the Blight from all afflicted worlds in the Republic."

"At what price, Marchion?" Lina said.

"None. I just want the credit."

The Supreme Chancellor took this moment to consider everything she had learned in the past hour—the state of the Republic she was pledged to preserve and protect.

What will it mean to say yes to him? Lina thought. *To make such a public acknowledgment of Republic weakness? Nothing would change—but of course everything would.*

The Republic would still hold nine times the territory of the Nihil, but the psychological power balance would shift. The Nihil would ask for more, ask to be treated as just another state, not an enemy, and many in the galaxy would see them that way.

The first concession is difficult, Lina thought. *Each after that, easier and easier.*

But what possible reason could she have for refusing Marchion's offer? A vague suggestion from the Jedi that they had some sort of plan? The same Jedi who had concealed material information from her—and had probably done so before and would again?

The responsibility of the supreme chancellor was to the Republic, to represent its interests and protect it as best as she could. To move it forward. To balance the needs of now against the needs of the future.

Matari and Voru stood, growling and gnashing their teeth in their throats, sensing her conflict and frustration.

Marchion Ro noted the targons' aggression. He smiled. Kindred spirits.

Lina could feel Elzar Mann's presence just behind her. She wanted to look at him, obtain his counsel even if just in the form of a nod or a shake of his head. But no. This decision was hers—hers alone.

This is the danger of consolidating so much power in one person, she thought. *Just because I have the ability to choose the future for a trillion trillion beings does not mean I will choose well.*

Lina took a deep breath and slowly released it.

What do I want? she asked herself. *What does Lina Soh want this Republic to be?*

Her targons went silent and still at her sides, icons of strength and power.

One more Great Work, she thought. *That's what I want.*

"We are all the Republic, Marchion," said the supreme chancellor. "We will solve this problem as we always have—together. You have chosen to exclude yourself from our great union, and stolen away and subjugated countless beings who chafe under your rule and wish to return to us. We will come for them. A price will be paid for everything you have done. The reckoning comes.

"The answer is no, Marchion Ro."

I choose the Republic, Lina thought.

Now and forever.

I choose the Jedi, she thought.

She cut the line, watching as Marchion's face twisted in fury.

Chapter Three

THE NIHIL OCCLUSION ZONE

Ghirra Starros was one of the most powerful people in the galaxy. Top ten, she'd say. And yet she knew, without a doubt, she could be dead in the next ten minutes if she chose the wrong dress.

Marchion Ro had summoned her—but she had no idea *which* Marchion.

Ghirra stood in front of the expansive closet in her huge cabin aboard the *Gaze Electric,* clothing hung in long rows, every color and texture represented; it was wardrobe enough to outfit a dozen women.

Finding storage space on the *Gaze* was never a problem. Its chambers and galleries rang with lonely silence. The ship was originally designed for a religious group to use as their mobile cathedral, but the cult had vanished in the distant past, and Marchion had inherited the ship through some chain of title he had never seen fit to share with her. Mostly crewed by droids, the gigantic vessel never seemed to have more than ten organics aboard.

The stink of unrealized dreams wafted through its echoing halls, of lost glory, of a hoped-for future that had never become real. The *Gaze Electric* didn't feel like a church. It felt like a mausoleum.

Ghirra hated being aboard the ship—but her life, for better or worse, was deeply tied to Marchion Ro. The Eye of the Nihil called the *Gaze Electric* his home, and therefore, until further notice, so did Ghirra Starros.

She ran her fingers along the various gowns and outfits hanging before her, trying to make a decision. Fabrics from some of the galaxy's best designers rustled across her fingertips. Velvet, silk, leather, soft, hard, simple, ornate, revealing, chaste. She could be many different Ghirras. The choice was part of the game. The thrilling, poisonous, deadly, addictive game that was her relationship with Marchion Ro.

Ghirra knew the Eye of the Nihil had just completed his call with Lina Soh. Marchion believed that conversation would result in Lina inviting him into the Republic to save them from the Blight afflicting their worlds. Ghirra did not know why he wanted this; after all, he'd spent the past several years doing everything he could to destroy the Republic.

But now, apparently, Marchion Ro wanted to save it. As usual, he had not bothered to explain himself to her. Marchion wanted what he wanted, and what he wanted, he took. If someone opposed him, he responded with brute force: violence, threats, fear.

This time, though, this time . . . she suspected those tried-and-true techniques wouldn't be as effective. Ghirra had dealt with Lina Soh many times in her own tenure as a Republic senator. The woman was subtle, complex, dangerous in ways Marchion couldn't easily overcome.

She was, in a word, a politician.

But so was Ghirra—an extraordinary one. She had risen to the top of not one but two galactic-level power structures, first as a member of the Senate and then, after certain . . . indiscretions in her term came to light, as minister of information for the Nihil State, its chief administrator.

She had weaned the chaos-addicted raiders away from their endless murder and squabbling, forced order upon them, showed the Nihil (including Marchion Ro himself) that true power lay not in destroying your enemies but in ruling over them.

All those achievements, all that *survival,* came down to one particular quality: Ghirra never allowed herself to believe she was on safe ground.

Lightning bolts could and did rain down from even the clearest sky. The woman who leapt first was the woman who lived.

She was *exactly* the person Marchion Ro needed at his side while dealing with a sanctimonious snake like Lina Soh. But still, infuriatingly, he hadn't asked for her counsel with respect to this bizarre offer he'd made to the Republic.

The result? Ghirra suspected that what Marchion Ro *expected* to happen on his little call with the supreme chancellor was not necessarily what *had* happened. Fine, so be it, he'd made his own bed. But Marchion's bed was also Ghirra Starros's bed—in every sense. They were linked, for better and for worse.

Ghirra selected a tight black leather number, pulling the dress from the closet and inspecting it, holding it against her body and looking at herself in the mirror.

I'm spectacular in this, she thought.

But she put it back.

Seduction could backfire. Wearing that outfit was an all-in play that wouldn't leave room to pivot if she found the wrong Marchion waiting for her. If it did turn out that Ghirra needed to be a temptress, well, she could do that in any outfit at all.

Ghirra started over, looking at the dresses each in turn. A sudden wave of frustration and irritation washed over her. She scowled.

What am I doing? Trying to suss out the mood of a maniac so I can survive our next business meeting? *This is nonsense. Foolish.*

A thought came to her, not for the first time but now stronger, more forceful than usual.

It's time to go. Get out. Run.

She'd been funneling credits to her own accounts for a long time, both as a senator and then as the de facto head of the Nihil government. By any measure, she was spectacularly rich.

Ghirra Starros no longer had to exist. She could become someone new. Live in splendor for the rest of her life.

It was tempting. But then there was Avon. Her daughter.

STAR WARS: TRIALS OF THE JEDI

They'd spoken not long before—nothing had been resolved. In truth, things had deteriorated. Ghirra's only daughter was now so repulsed by her mother and her decision to defect to the Nihil cause that Avon called herself Sunvale now, not Starros.

It was the decision of a child. Avon was only seventeen, psychologically incapable of understanding long-term goals. She just didn't have the wisdom. It was impossible for her to understand that her mother was working toward a higher purpose, and not every step along the way would be pretty.

I saw an opportunity with the Nihil, Ghirra thought. *Not just to gather power and wealth to myself, but to build an entire state from* nothing. *I created a functioning society out of a group of ravaging fools just as likely to kill one another as their enemies. The Nihil pay* taxes *now, for the light's sake. There's a freedom in the Nihil State, a power, unlike anything in the Republic. In a generation, this could really be something. A new way to live.*

Ghirra had only two real goals at this point: the full establishment of the Nihil State and, thereby, getting Avon to acknowledge that her mother wasn't a monster. Each would take decades—but both could be achieved.

So she would not run. She would stay with Marchion Ro and the Nihil.

For the love of her daughter.

"The blue," Ghirra said, deciding on a long gown of dark-blue veda cloth accented with sparkling crimson gems.

It was demure, covering her from neck to ankle, but also formfitting, showing off every part of her to great advantage.

The blue was . . . versatile. She could be any number of Ghirras in the blue.

She changed quickly and left her chambers, making her way through the vaulted passageways and cathedral-like empty spaces of the *Gaze Electric.* Her footsteps echoed, turning into whispers in the room's far corners, or perhaps causing them. She passed no one other than a pair of Marchion's She'ar, his elite bodyguards. One glared at her, and the other leered.

Look all you want, my friends, Ghirra thought. *Marchion elevated you to his right hand, made you feel special, but have you not noticed that you drop like flies every time he sends you on a mission? You die . . . he survives.*

She slipped past the two staring guards, not sparing them a glance.

Soon enough, you'll both be just another pair of ghosts haunting this cursed ship.

Ghirra reached the throne room, longer than it was wide and dominated by a huge banquet table, currently hosting only a few plates of decomposing food. She hadn't seen the space fully occupied since the end of the celebrations following the Nihil's successful destruction of Starlight Beacon. Those had lasted a month, a throbbing bacchanal presided over by a glowering, grinning Marchion Ro on his throne at the chamber's far end.

But now, the Eye's seat of power sat empty. It was a brutal, uncomfortable-looking thing, carved from a single slab of dark basalt, the cuts made by Marchion himself using one of the lightsabers he'd taken as a trophy from a Jedi he'd murdered.

The room's only occupant was a single She'ar guard, who sat on the steps leading up to the throne. He hummed an ugly little melody, weaving back and forth in time to its rhythm, a cup next to him on the steps.

The degenerate's blasted on steam juice or one of the other intoxicants Marchion leaves lying around, Ghirra thought, not letting her irritation show on her face.

"Where is he?" Ghirra said as she approached the throne and the drunk She'ar sitting at its base.

She thought his name was Faskir . . . but it didn't matter. Remembering the names of Marchion's bodyguards was wasted effort. They died like flies . . . and yet almost any Nihil would have given all they had to be elevated to serve the Eye so directly.

The She'ar blinked gummily, its multifaceted eyes extending on stalks from their sockets to focus on her.

"Oh," maybe-Faskir said. "He said to tell you to meet him in the red hold."

Ghirra clenched her fists but kept her face neutral, knowing Faskir would report anything she said or did that seemed disrespectful.

Marchion could have sent me a message, she thought. *Instead, this aggression, this petty attempt at control. He made me come up to the throne room, and now I'll have to head all the way back down to the cargo decks at the bottom of the ship. Why? Because Marchion Ro wants me to.*

Ghirra considered returning to her chambers—but she knew she wouldn't. Marchion could play her like a bone-harp. Ghirra wanted to know why the Eye had called for her, wanted to know what happened with Lina Soh, wanted to know what Marchion had been doing lately, disappearing into the galaxy and returning with his eyes aglow and secret ideas flitting behind them, wanted to know, above all, why he had offered to save the lives of his enemies.

Ghirra Starros had questions that only Marchion Ro could answer. She knew it, and he did, too. She unclenched her fists and left the throne room.

The red hold was the largest of four aboard the *Gaze.* Usually, it was kept empty like so much aboard the vast ship—but as Ghirra walked down the corridor leading to its hatchway, she knew that was no longer the case. A scent filled the air—ammonia and sweet milk gone off and sour dirt— possibly the worst she'd ever smelled, and one she recognized. She knew what was waiting for her.

Ghirra pressed the access panel on the red hold's hatchway. The great door slid open, and she saw them—Marchion's creatures. The ones he called the Nameless. Twisted, agonized bodies, great yawning mouths filled with crystalline teeth stained with fluids from the things they killed. The beasts were different now than when she had first seen them. Marchion had shown her the Nameless very shortly after he brought them to the Nihil—shown them off, really. To Ghirra's eyes, the degradation in the creatures was obvious. No one would ever call a Nameless beautiful, but at least in those early days, they still looked like animals. These were . . . demons.

The beasts' skin seemed to have shrunk. It was stretched tight over their bones and internal structures, even torn through at some spots. Their faces were nightmares—huge pale eyes over drooling, sharp-toothed mouths. The creatures hunched over themselves, limbs too long for their bodies ending in slashing claws. Drool and foam slid over their jaws. Some juddered and shook. Ghirra saw one chewing at the back of another. The assaulted Nameless didn't move. It just stood there, letting it happen, and that was even worse.

Ghirra knew Marchion had gathered these things because they could kill Jedi. The Nameless were key to Marchion's strategy since all the way back at the Republic Fair. The Nihil would not have succeeded without them.

But now, seeing the creatures milling about in the hold, their bones clacking and the soft hisses and snarls they made . . . Ghirra wanted them gone. Wanted them all dead. Never wanted to see one again in her life.

"Ghirra," Marchion said. "Welcome. Your dress is beautiful. What a lovely azure. Come to me."

He sat cross-legged in the middle of the red hold, surrounded by dozens of the creatures.

Ghirra hesitated.

"Don't be afraid," Marchion said, reaching out to nuzzle a Nameless under its slime-covered chin. "It's perfectly safe." He lifted a metal rod with a purple gem glowing at either end. Showed it to her, as if that was supposed to be an explanation.

Ghirra moved into the hold, the Nameless seeming to take only a desultory interest in her.

Show no fear, she thought.

Easier said than done. She wasn't a Jedi, didn't have the Force, so the Nameless couldn't feed on her—but they didn't only kill to eat. She'd seen them do it. They were very good at killing things.

One of the creatures swayed close to her, some sort of tail or tentacle or tendril touching the side of her neck as it passed, leaving a trail of slime. Ghirra wiped at her neck with her sleeve, trying to scrape it away—but the

STAR WARS: TRIALS OF THE JEDI

cloth came back unmarred. She touched her neck—it was dry. The only slime the Nameless had left was in her mind.

Ghirra shuddered and moved forward. The sooner this was done, the sooner she could leave. And shower.

She reached Marchion, and he gestured for her to sit. As if they were in some pastoral meadow surrounded by grazing shaaks as opposed to a stinking hold full of beasts with no obvious purpose other than death. Creatures under the control of Marchion Ro, animals he could turn on her in a moment if he wanted to. But wasn't that always the case? Nameless or Nihil—animals, all of them. Marchion Ro's weapons, ready to kill at his command. She was never safe with this man.

Ghirra sat, tucking her legs beneath her.

"The Republic refused my offer," Marchion said, scratching at the edge of the bacta patch on his neck.

The Eye had, for the past several months, taken up the habit of just . . . disappearing. He'd leave without explanation and return the same way. Ghirra had no idea what he was doing, and she simply ran the Nihil in his absence. The more she could be seen as the person in control, the better, as far as she was concerned.

Marchion had come back from his latest mysterious sojourn with a seeping wound in his neck, his own blood spattered down his coat. He hadn't explained how it happened, and Ghirra had known better than to inquire. There were moments she had seen the Eye of the Nihil angrier than he was that day . . . but not many.

Ghirra sat in silence, only tilted her head slightly to indicate that she'd heard the Eye's words. She still didn't know which Marchion was speaking to her. He seemed calm, but that meant nothing. He hid his true feelings and intentions better than anyone she'd ever met—even better than she did.

"Why do you suppose the Republic said no to me?" Marchion asked.

Ah. For now, at least, he just wants a conversation, Ghirra thought. *I can give him that.*

"They don't trust you, Marchion, which I understand. Your offer must have seemed bizarre to them. When one's enemy is suffering, you don't hold out a helping hand. Clearly, the Republic believes you had some other motive. It's not surprising they refused you."

"Whether the Republic trusts me is irrelevant. They *need* me," Marchion said. "The Blight appears on more worlds by the day. I can stop it."

Ghirra worked through the situation in her mind, trying to find an explanation for the Republic's refusal other than the obvious one: *They don't want help from a murderous, conquering monster.*

"Who said no, specifically? Lina Soh?" she asked.

Marchion nodded, a little sneer at the edge of his mouth.

"She's proud," Ghirra said, "even if she pretends she's not. Agreeing to you means sacrificing her authority. It might be as simple as that."

"Perhaps," Marchion said.

A Nameless lay down next to him, one of its limbs audibly snapping as it did. It made no sign of pain, just gently rested its head in Marchion's lap. He idly stroked its horrifying face.

"Hello, my little Leveler," he murmured, as the creature made an awful gurgling noise. "I'm so glad you're still with me."

With the tip of one claw, he began to carve something into the Nameless's head, in the broad space between its eyes. A few quick strokes to create a simple symbol Ghirra had seen thousands of times—a stylized, staring eye. The Eye of the Nihil.

"Can I ask you a question, Marchion?" Ghirra said, trying to ignore the sounds coming from the beast.

"Of course, my dear."

"Your goal as long as I've known you has been to let the Republic burn and die. Why did you make the offer to help them at all?"

Marchion lifted his bloody hand from the Nameless and reached to touch her cheek. She didn't flinch. Despite herself, she felt warmed. She always did, whenever they touched. She was his creature, too.

"You won't believe this," Marchion said, "but it's because of you, Ghirra."

Any politician at Ghirra's level was an expert at hiding their true

STAR WARS: TRIALS OF THE JEDI   65

feelings, at turning their face into a blank, pleasant mask, but her skepticism must have slipped through. The Eye of the Nihil laughed.

Blast him. The man could read a stone.

"I made the offer to the Republic because of you, Ghirra. That's the truth, whether you believe it or not," Marchion said, his smile fading, replaced with . . . sadness? Pride? "A while ago, not long after the fall of Starlight Beacon, you told me I could be more. That I was a conqueror, but not yet a legend. I never forgot it. You might think I don't pay attention, but I do."

I would never think that, Ghirra thought. *You pay attention to everything. There is no rest around you. You are always thinking of how to manipulate, to use, to turn things to your advantage.*

And in fact, that was part of her attraction to him. They weren't equals—Marchion would never allow that, it would never even occur to him—but they did share a certain unique point of view. They both saw other people as levers, buttons, gears. That perspective was rare, in Ghirra's experience.

"All my life, I've been a certain kind of person, Ghirra," Marchion said. "I don't regret it. That version of me is the reason I have achieved so much. That Marchion brought me to this place. But he will not suit for what is to come." Marchion offered up a rueful little laugh. "I won't pretend I'm reformed, Ghirra. I'm not, and I shouldn't be. No one wants a tamed, neutered Eye. But I can envision a future where my name inspires not only terror, but devotion."

His dark eyes shone.

I don't know if what he's saying is true, Ghirra thought, *but I know he believes it.*

"I have triumphed by destroying my enemies. Now I will triumph by being better than they could ever hope to be. The Nihil can be free and also exist within a society that offers peace and stability. It will not be easy, but nothing in my life ever is." Marchion stopped, tilting his head just the tiniest amount, his eyes locked on hers. "I'm grateful, Ghirra. That's why I asked for you to come be with me now. I wanted you to hear me say those words. *I am grateful to you.*"

He watched her face. His lips curved upward into something not a smile.

"You don't believe me," Marchion said, his voice going flat.

A brief spike of fear iced Ghirra's spine—she had entered dangerous territory. She ignored it, forced herself to be calm.

"I look forward to seeing you put all of this into practice, Marchion," Ghirra said, speaking with conviction. "I've been trying to get you to see all of this for a long time."

"Mm," the Eye said. "Well, it doesn't matter if you find my gratitude sincere. I know it's real. That's what matters."

Marchion took her face in his hands—she could feel his claws pressing lightly against the back of her head—leaned forward, and kissed her. As always, he tasted faintly of minerals and the sea. Ghirra leaned into the kiss. Whatever else they were, this had always been good.

Marchion released her and pulled back. It took Ghirra several moments to remember they were sitting in a filthy hold spattered with the stinking waste of the death beasts Marchion Ro had used to subdue a huge swath of the galaxy.

"I gave the Republic a chance to save itself. They rejected it. Fine. Let them suffer," Marchion said. "For now, I'll focus on Nihil space. I'll push back the Blight here and let the Republic focus on their own problems. The only thing I don't know is *why*. Why were they so confident they didn't need me?"

"Do you think they have some other plan?" Ghirra asked. "If they do, my spies close to Lina Soh's office haven't told me. From what I've heard, they're absolutely terrified."

"Even if they do, it won't matter," Marchion said. "Not in the end."

He seemed to retreat into himself, brooding. Ghirra recognized that mood, knew it could last for hours. She tried to head it off before it took root.

"Why have you brought the Nameless back to this ship?" Ghirra said, glancing at the dozens upon dozens of beasts surrounding them. "This

STAR WARS: TRIALS OF THE JEDI 67

must be almost your entire herd. Don't you want them out there killing Jedi?"

"This *is* my entire herd," Marchion said, stroking the Leveler's mutilated head. "Other than the ones I gave to Baron Boolan for his . . . experiments. I've received reports that my Nameless were being targeted by Republic hunters—captured, stolen. On Palagosal, on Angoth, elsewhere. I called these wondrous creatures back from their deployments to keep them here with me on the *Gaze* until I know they'll be safe. They're precious to me."

He looked up at her.

❧

"You're precious to me, too, Ghirra," Marchion lied.

The woman's face twitched, the slightest ripple of the muscle near the hinge of her jaw. If Ghirra Starros were a less practiced political operator, the movement would be a full-on eye roll. She thought she was being subtle, but to Marchion, she was laid bare.

"I can see how you'd think of our . . . closeness as a choice of convenience, made for mutual benefit," Marchion said. "That's true, of course. I'm a realist, and so are you. We use each other to get what we want."

He lifted the Rod of Power, and the Nameless in the room started to move. They shambled through anxious, irregular circles with Ghirra and Marchion at the center. Their protruding inner structures clacked against one another like rolling chance cubes.

"But what I'm about to say is just as true," Marchion lied. "You exist to me, Ghirra. I *see* you. Do you know what I mean?"

Ghirra froze. Marchion heard her breathing change, now coming quick and shallow. The poor woman was working so hard to betray nothing, yet her thoughts were as plain as if she had them written on her broad, unattractive forehead.

The Nameless circled, clacking, hissing and howling, snapping at one another.

"I do know what you mean, Marchion," Ghirra said, her voice very quiet. "I do."

"Very, very few people fit that category—the people I see," he said, being truthful. "Mari San Tekka and . . . almost no one else."

"It's like a game," Ghirra said. "And no one can play it but us. Everyone else . . . is just a piece on the board."

Marchion nodded.

"What do you need me to do, Marchion?" Ghirra asked. "I know that's why you're saying these things to me. You want something from me."

"I don't need you to do anything, Ghirra. I just wanted to tell someone the truth for once," he lied. "Don't get used to it."

He grinned, showing his teeth, and Ghirra tilted her head in the way she thought he liked.

"I wouldn't worry about that," she said. "I never get used to anything with you. It's always surprising, Marchion. Always."

Ghirra stood, then flinched as one of the Nameless hurtling around them in ever-tightening circles almost collided with her. She stepped forward, an involuntary movement toward him, seeking his protection. Marchion rose and gave her what she wanted, pulling her close, wrapping her in his arms.

"I need to return to Republic space," Ghirra said, speaking softly into his chest. "I'll go to our embassy on Coruscant. This situation with the Blight is chaotic. The Republic could change its mind, which would mean opportunities for us. I may need to negotiate quickly if circumstances change."

Well, that was easy, Marchion thought. *I need you far away, Ghirra Starros. You see too much.*

He lifted the Nameless control rod and the beasts stilled, every one of them completely focused on the glowing stones. He led the way out of the hold, the creatures falling away to either side as he and Ghirra walked, opening a path for them.

"If you see a chance to advance the interests of the Nihil, take it," Marchion said. "And if you can determine Lina Soh's plan to deal with the Blight, do so. Nan may be of assistance there."

He had no idea if Nan was still alive. He didn't particularly care, either. He hadn't thought about the little spy in longer than he could remember.

"What will you be doing?" Ghirra asked. "This is an important moment for us."

Marchion didn't know if she was referring to the Nihil or, repulsively, the two of them.

"The Blight," Marchion said. "The Blight is my focus now."

Ghirra nodded and left him.

Marchion turned back to look at the red hold. Ranks of Nameless stood quietly, their eyes locked on him. Or, rather, what he held. Marchion lifted the Rod of Power, giving a dial set into its length a savage twist with his thumb. The glow of the jewels intensified, and the Nameless began to shriek. They devolved into a roiling, screeching mass, lashing out without thought, tearing, hurting one another. The Eye of the Nihil watched, his face impassive.

This is what I need, Marchion thought. *Chaos.*

He'd asked Ghirra to try to discover the Republic's plans, said he didn't know why they had refused him, that he needed to understand. That was another lie. He didn't care about anything the Republic might do. Their time was done, even if they didn't know it yet.

The question, as always, was the Jedi Order. They clearly had a plan of their own. He'd suspected it as soon as he received the reports that his Nameless were being captured and taken by Republic task forces—not killed, but *captured.*

Full certainty had come during that brief meeting with Lina Soh. A Jedi had been standing on the platform behind the chancellor, close enough to touch her. Marchion wondered if the Jedi and the chancellor had their own special relationship, as he did with Ghirra. He wouldn't be surprised.

Everyone used everyone, and no one used anyone as much as the Republic and the Jedi used each other.

Elzar Mann. That was the Jedi's name. His face was on one of the bounty cards distributed to Nihil foot soldiers patrolling the Occlusion Zone. A master, high ranking, present during that little skirmish at Vixoseph I. Marchion wanted him dead, like he wanted all the Jedi dead.

Elzar Mann, standing on that platform up there with Lina Soh, both so smug, so arrogant.

They should have been cowering in terror, desperate for his help. But they weren't, which meant they thought they'd found some way to save themselves.

Fine. Marchion would adapt, as he always did.

He was very, very close now.

I need time, Marchion thought. *My offer to stop the Blight would have given me all I needed, but I will find another way. Chaos. That is the path now.*

Marchion lifted his arm and spoke into the comlink in his wristband, raising his voice to be heard over the shrieks of the Nameless.

"Faksir," he said.

"Boss," came the She'ar's response, his voice sounding a little murky.

"Reach out to General Viess," Marchion said, frowning. "Tell her to move the fleet. No reserves. Everything under her command with weapons and a functioning drive."

"Whoa," Faksir said. "We gonna kill something?"

"We are," Marchion said.

"Where do I tell her to go?"

"Eriadu."

Chapter Four

THE JEDI TEMPLE

"How does that feel, Reath?" said Kirak Infil'a, tugging the strap on his left pauldron. "It should be snug, secure, but not so tight that it cuts off circulation or restricts movement."

"To the extent possible, you don't want to be aware you're wearing it. It's there to protect, not distract," added Master Govena, chief armorer of the Jedi Temple.

Reath Silas lifted his arm. The armor was light—he could barely feel the weight at all. He stepped back from Kirak, Master Govena's second in command down in the armory. Both Jedi watched avidly as he swung his arms, bent at the knees, rotated at the waist.

They stood in an unadorned, thick-walled antechamber deep inside the Jedi Temple, with heavy, sealed doors leading off in various directions. Air vents built high in the walls did little to dispel the close, almost stagnant atmosphere. The level was full of cells built to withstand attacks by weapons both ordinary and not, designed to hold individuals deemed too dangerous to be left to Republic custody. The Jedi did not see themselves as jailers, and in normal times these cells usually stood empty. But this was not a normal time. The detention level was nearly full, holding more prisoners than it had in many generations—though most were the captured Nameless.

Reath didn't particularly want to be there. No one would want to be there. The Temple's armorers had come to this place to perform an experiment that would determine whether the mission to return the Nameless to their homeworld was just hideously dangerous instead of suicidal. They needed a test subject and had come to the primary and backup teams to ask for one.

Reath had volunteered—which was why he now found himself outfitted in a prototype version of the armor Govena and Kirak Infil'a hoped to provide to the Nine before they left Coruscant. The set was divided into eight pieces: pauldrons over his shoulders, vambraces protecting his forearms and wrists, two tassets hanging down from his waist and shielding his outer thighs, a chestpiece, and a helmet that included a full-face mask.

Reath knew the terms because he had looked them up. He looked up as many things as he could. Knowledge was a kind of lightsaber.

The moment he'd discovered that the Nine were going to wear armor, he'd pulled every file the archives had on the subject. There wasn't much. Jedi rarely used armor in the Order's current incarnation. The Temple Guards wore face masks, but that was about it.

The armor pieces Govena and Kirak had created were bright white with gold accents, polished until the metal was mildly reflective. There was tech built into it, too—Reath could see through the mask even though it appeared opaque from the outside, and it looked like it could also offer functions similar to a set of macrobinoculars.

"This doesn't seem particularly . . . protective," Reath said, igniting his lightsaber and running through a few forms, moving his arms and legs in patterns he would likely experience during a duel. "Open spots all over the place. It's more like patches of armor than a suit."

"The primary function here isn't to protect against physical attacks," Govena said.

"Oh," Reath said, thinking of the way non-Force-wielders had described the Nameless—their brutal talons, their rows of ice-pick teeth. "Great."

"Your lightsaber can handle anything you might need to fight," Kirak said, "and you've got that shield, too, right?"

Reath nodded. That particular artifact was currently stored back in his chambers, but he'd bring the ancient shield along on the mission. Reath wasn't great with it yet. No other living Jedi used one in combat, so he'd had to study the techniques for using them from holocrons—but he was better now than when he started.

Master Govena tapped one long finger against Reath's chestpiece.

"The idea here is to *let* you fight, to give you a chance against the Nameless's fear effect," she said. "Now, don't get me wrong—we've used an alloy here that can deflect some pretty serious attacks, a mix of durasteel and doonium. But what makes these armor pieces unique is the third element, that ore you and Cohmac brought back from that world, what was it?"

"Tolis," Cohmac Vitus said, watching the process unfold from where he leaned against the wall, his arms folded, his mouth tight.

Reath thought his former master looked much older than he had before they'd separated just after the fall of Starlight Beacon. They'd only been apart for about a year, but the man's dark hair had sprouted prominent streaks of gray.

Kirak snapped his fingers and pointed at Cohmac without looking at him. His focus was completely dialed-in on the armor.

"Tolis, that's right," Kirak said, making a minute adjustment to the placement of Reath's left pauldron.

"The Tolisian ore is the only substance we've found that can repel the Blight," Master Govena said. "We've used the samples you brought back to create this set, and we have enough to create eight more, one for each member of the Nine. We can do it quickly, but before we expend that effort—"

"You need to know if it works," Reath said. "I know."

"Reath, I can do this," Cohmac said. "Those pieces will fit me just as well as they do you."

Reath looked Cohmac in the eyes. The older Jedi's posture was tight, his expression dour. He didn't like this, didn't like any of it.

Cohmac was a full master to Reath's Knight. For a moment, Reath was tempted to relinquish the task to the other Jedi's greater experience.

No, he thought. *That's fear talking.*

"I know you could do it, Master Vitus," Reath said, "but I've been studying the Nameless for a long time. I know more about them than anyone beyond Azlin Rell, and I've faced them and survived. It should be me. I *want* it to be me."

Cohmac flinched on hearing Azlin's name. Reath suspected he felt responsible for his former Padawan being assigned as the fallen Jedi's primary liaison. When Azlin Rell returned to the Jedi Temple, Cohmac was gone, off on an extended self-imposed absence from the Order. And despite how deeply Cohmac might have believed in the philosophical objections that caused him to leave, it was still hard for Reath to reconcile with the fact that Cohmac Vitus, his master and protector, had *left him alone,* especially when the direct result was that the Council had stuck Reath with that old man and all his—

No, Reath thought. *That's anger talking. It's not true. I don't believe those things.*

Reath knocked once on his face mask, making a soft metallic chime.

"If this stuff works, I'll be able to observe a living Nameless up close. No other Jedi's been able to do that. I want to know. I want to see with my own eyes."

"I remember when books were good enough for you," Cohmac said.

"I remember that, too," Reath said. "It was a long time ago."

He reached over and put his hand on Cohmac's shoulder.

"This armor could be the difference between success and failure. We have to test it. You know the stakes."

Cohmac nodded. He didn't seem happy, his dark eyes hooded.

You and me both, Master, Reath thought.

He turned back to the armorers. "Can you tell me how it's *supposed* to work?" he asked. "Do I need to do anything?"

Govena and Infil'a exchanged a glance.

"The Tolisian ore resists the Blight," Govena said. "You, Cohmac, and that Padawan, Amadeo, saw that firsthand when you retrieved the samples for us. We've analyzed the ore and have determined that it puts out a sort of field—think of the way a magnet can affect iron filings from a distance. That field holds back the Blight. We've designed the armor to create overlapping sections that will allow the field to cover your entire body."

"Our theory—which you're about to test," Kirak added, "is that because of the connection between the Blight and the Nameless, this ore could also offer some protection against the Nameless effect. There's a lot we don't know. We're grateful for your help, Reath."

"This is madness," Cohmac said.

"Correct," said Govena, turning to him. "It's all madness. If you don't like it, perhaps you might consider leaving the Order again. You've only been back for what, a week or two? I'm sure you wouldn't even be missed."

The room fell silent.

Reath closed his eyes.

"Listen to me," he said. "I don't want to talk about this anymore. I just want to do it."

He opened his eyes and pointed at the heavy door sealing them away from the waiting Nameless.

"If this doesn't work, I'll need you. Can I depend on you?"

"Of course," Cohmac said. "Without hesitation."

"Good," Reath said.

He stepped up to the massive, thick door sealing off the detention wing. Beyond it, he knew, was a long corridor. At the end of that was another door, and then, secured within a heavy-duty energy cell, was a Nameless.

I wonder what the other Jedi would think if they knew the Order was holding a dozen of these things right below where they sleep and eat and study.

Reath thought maybe they already did. Ever since the missions to capture Nameless and bring them to Coruscant, Jedi were complaining about poor sleep. People were testy, anxious, quick to snap at one another in an uncharacteristically un-Jedi-like way. He thought that was part of what was happening with Cohmac, Govena, and Kirak.

These creatures need to be taken out of here as quickly as possible, Reath knew. *For so many reasons.*

"We'll send you in with a droid," Kirak said. "A servitor. If anything happens, they can get you out of there in no time."

"Sounds . . . good," Reath said.

He looked at the mask, the metal bucket he was supposed to put over his head. He wouldn't feel protected with the thing on—he'd feel imprisoned.

What am I doing? Why am I taking this risk? Any contact with the Nameless could be the end, or worse. Azlin Rell encountered the Nameless once *and turned to the dark side and put out his own eyes.*

Reath's gaze shifted to the large, heavy door separating him from the hallway that led to the detention cell containing the Nameless. Maybe twenty good steps away.

His gut churned, and suddenly he realized what he'd been feeling all this time. He'd experienced the Nameless effect before. He was probably close enough now to sense whatever field emanated from the creature. He wasn't actually afraid at all. Not really.

Not really.

Reath took a breath and set the helmet over his head. His field of vision shrank, but with it, his anxiety. His stomach calmed, he stood straighter.

I don't know if that's a psychological effect or something more, he thought. *And there's only one way to find out.*

He walked to the door, where the servitor droid waited. A tap of the access panel, and they passed through. It sealed behind them with a heavy thump.

Reath steeled his spirit and walked forward, the droid clanking along beside him. Eighteen steps to the next door at the far end of the corridor, another tap on an access panel, through the door, and there, behind an energy wall, clearly visible with no distorting effect . . . was a living Nameless.

He paused, fascinated, taking in a sight almost no other Force-wielders had ever seen. To Jedi, the Nameless appeared as indistinct outlines when they could be perceived at all, their features obscured, overshadowed by the dark hallucinations that also accompanied their presence. That was one of the reasons they were so dangerous. But with the armor, Reath could see the Nameless clearly, every detail laid bare.

They're so . . . sad, he thought. *And angry. Furious. Everything about them is wrong.*

The creature was a bit larger than a riding animal like an eopie or a kybuck, though it was difficult to determine its true dimensions because it was hunched in on itself, crabbed and twisted. Its skin was blue-white, translucent. Reath could see fluids and organs hanging and pulsing within the beast's core.

Mostly, he saw its eyes. Round, bulging, baleful, hateful, fixed on Reath. He was not afraid, but he was very glad a shimmering wall of energy stood between him and the Nameless. Its powers, or effect, or whatever you wanted to call it—that might be blunted, but its claws certainly weren't. They twitched at the ends of its long, bony arms, as if it was tearing Reath to shreds in its mind.

The anger radiating from the thing was palpable—Reath didn't need his Jedi training to see it—but that was not all. Beneath it, Reath sensed a deep, burning need. He understood that. After all, he'd spent all that time with Azlin studying these creatures. He knew what the Nameless actually wanted. The reason for the hunger, the violence, the pain, the rage.

It just wants to go home.

Reath raised his hand, focused on the Nameless, locked eyes with it.

What does it see when it looks at me? Food? An enemy? Maybe I can show it a different way to think about us.

He reached out with the Force, using skills he'd first learned as a Padawan. Jedi could commune with nonsentient beings on an emotional level, connect with them, understand them. It wasn't a *conversation,* but it was communication. Reath wanted to show the Nameless that his intentions were good—that he was there to help. And if he could connect, he might learn more about how the Nameless operated on their homeworld, find clues to how they could stop the Blight once they got them there.

Knowledge was the greatest tool, the greatest weapon, the greatest power. The Order had learned a great deal about these creatures, but there was still so much they did not understand. The Blight had to be solved, and yet when it came to the actual method to do that, the Jedi were as blind as Azlin Rell.

Reath narrowed his eyes, exploring the Nameless with the power of the Force.

I'm not very good at this, he thought. *I've read about the process—I know how it's supposed to work. Every being with a certain level of complexity has a sense of self beneath the basic needs it seeks to satisfy. You hold out an open hand through the Force, seek that deeper level, infuse it with the idea of* friend, *and once it echoes back, you—*

"Nyeeeeaaargh!" Reath screamed.

His whole body felt the agony of the Nameless's existence.

Pain pain pain pain PAIN PAIN!

Reath returned to himself. He was in darkness. He could not open his eyes, although he could sense that he no longer wore the mask. He was lying flat on his back. Everything ached.

He heard voices—voices he knew. They were agitated, upset. He was hearing an argument, despair, anger.

"The armor failed," Govena said, her voice flat. "I don't know what went wrong."

"This is why we did the test," said Kirak Infil'a. "We'll refine the design and try again."

"You'll call in some other *child* to sacrifice, you mean?" came Cohmac's voice, filled with rage.

Reath felt a hand at his neck, two fingers checking his pulse. He thought it was Cohmac but couldn't be sure.

"Where are the *medical droids*?" his former master said, pain in every syllable. "We should have had them here from the start. This was *foolish*."

The hand disappeared.

"This is your fault," Cohmac said. "You should never have let him take the risk."

"We aren't happy about it either, Cohmac," said Master Govena. "But Reath knew what he was doing, knew the choice he was making. He is not a child. He is a *Jedi Knight*."

"We have to inform the Council," said Kirak. "They need to know the armor doesn't work. This changes the mission profile. We'll have to ask for more Republic personnel to help wrangle the Nameless."

"Forget the *mission*," Cohmac spat. "We need to talk about responsibility. You two need to face consequences."

Cohmac didn't even sound like himself. Reath knew it was the Nameless all around them, their fear and aggression seeping into everything and everyone.

He knew he needed to speak to them, to explain, to open his eyes, but nothing on his body worked.

Have I been husked? he thought, shock flooding his body at the thought.

He took stock and thought . . . no. He could feel every part of himself. Nothing seemed to be missing or turned to stone.

Reath didn't know what had happened to him. He did know, however, that abandoning the armor was a mistake. The mission didn't need to change. They could use it, and they could leave as soon as the armorers created enough for all of the Nine.

Wasting time looking for other paths, waiting for more support to be authorized by the Republic . . . when every second that passed meant the Blight grew and spread and life was lost . . .

No, Reath thought.

He could not move his body, could not speak. But he had the Force.

He reached out to the great mystery and used it to open his eyes. Govena, Kirak, and Cohmac stood above him, their faces angry. Near them was the servitor droid that had accompanied Reath into the Nameless's cell.

The Force gave him life. It was the energy that propelled him every time he took a step, had a thought, took a breath. It was in all things. Whatever had happened to him was not stronger than the Force. It could not be.

That was just logic.

And with that thought, whatever had stolen his ability to move was gone. Reath was once again in control of his limbs.

"Oops," he said.

All three Jedi stepped back in shock, looking down at him.

"Reath!" Cohmac said, falling to his knees and placing his hand on Reath's shoulder. "Are you all right?"

"What happened?" said Master Govena, crouching next to him. "Did the armor fail? There's no shame in needing help. I know how intense the Nameless effect can feel."

"The armor was fine," Reath said, accepting an extended hand from Cohmac and sitting up.

My spine feels like a pile of broken bricks, he thought.

"It worked perfectly, as far as I could tell. It helped me focus, helped me use my own skill to push past the effect the Nameless generate. The armor wasn't the issue. The problem was . . . ah . . ." He hesitated, knowing the reaction he was about to get. "I tried to connect with the Nameless through the Force."

Reath expected a lecture or a look of disappointment. Govena and Kirak Infil'a turned to look at each other, but their shared glance was anything but disappointed. They seemed awed, impressed, curious.

"An interesting choice," Kirak said, "considering these things seem to eat the Force. Why did you do that?"

"He was trying to help the creature," Cohmac said, his mouth tightening, "learn about it, teach it about us."

He reached out and touched Reath's shoulder.

"Reath is a good Jedi, who understands the path of reason is better than the path of conflict."

STAR WARS: TRIALS OF THE JEDI

Cohmac looked toward the sealed door leading to the Nameless's cell.

"But if that is not to be, it is not to be," he said, his tone sad.

"This is fantastic," said Govena, and Reath and Cohmac turned toward the two armorers.

They had apparently removed Reath's helmet when the droid pulled him from the Nameless chamber, and were examining it, peering at it closely with tools and magnifiers and other instruments they had materialized from about their persons.

"What do you mean?" Reath said, getting gingerly to his feet.

"You've given us extraordinary news, Jedi Knight Silas," Master Govena said, holding out the helmet. "The armor works. You were able to resist the Nameless effect with much less effort than usual. The mission can proceed as planned."

What mission? Reath thought. *The one where we take a dozen Nameless back to their homeworld and set them free and hope it actually achieves something and the Blight stops? That mission?*

But he didn't say that.

That's despair talking, he thought. *And I reject it.*

"Of course the mission can go on, Master Govena," Reath said. "I am grateful for your work. We all are."

The chief armorer of the Jedi Order gave a tight nod, and then she and Kirak went back to examining the helmet, muttering to each other in highly technical language.

Reath rubbed at his face. His head was light, and he still felt like he'd been beaten with a hammer from the inside out, but he was coming back to himself.

What did I learn? he asked himself.

Every experience, good or bad, was a chance to learn.

"We are not ready for this mission," he said to himself quietly—but not so quiet that Cohmac did not hear.

"Perhaps not, Reath," Cohmac said. "But we are Jedi."

He began helping Reath remove the armor.

Chapter Five

ERIADU CITY

"One more, Joss?" the bartender asked, his voice gruff and deep, almost angry.

Joss Adren didn't take offense. The bartender wasn't mad at him. His name was Slendo. Tall, long, white beard, one of those lanky guys who weren't much more than muscle and bone. Joss had gotten to know him a little during his time on Eriadu. Nice fellow.

One more . . . Joss considered. *Should I have one more?*

That was the right question, the one any halfway decent bartender was supposed to ask, seeing as Joss's mug was empty. The answer was more complicated.

Joss squinted at his mug, then looked up at Slendo—then back down at his mug. He tried to figure it. It wasn't about whether he *wanted* another drink. Of course he did. He had the credits for it, too—Republic money, but that was still spent around here despite the Nihil's half-assed efforts to set up their own currency in the Occlusion Zone.

The heart of this was Pikka, really. He'd have to get back to her soon. But did she want him home *now* or a little bit down the road? Joss

STAR WARS: TRIALS OF THE JEDI

continued mulling it over. No need to rush. This was the kind of thing a fellow wanted to get right.

He wasn't particularly worried that Pikka would be mad at him if he grabbed another—a few ales wasn't exactly a bender for the ages. This decision was more about giving *her* what *she* needed. In fact, she was the reason he was at the bar in the first place. Pikka was pregnant, about eight months, and had been trying to take a nap back in the little apartment they'd rented here in Eriadu City. Joss had gotten up from the workbench, where he was messing with a navigational circuit for their Longbeam. He'd gone over to the kitchen to grab a piece of fruit, walking quiet as a mouse. Even took his boots off.

And then Pikka called out from the bedroom and said he was clomping around so loudly that it was waking the baby, which meant she couldn't sleep, either. Would he *please* consider vacating the premises for an hour or two?

Almost all of that tracked for Joss. Big guy, small apartment, pregnant wife who needed her rest. He was less sure about whether babies could actually hear much from inside their moms before they were born, but that was beside the point. Pikka needed some sleep, and Joss had never been much good at keeping quiet. He was a noisy guy. Good with his hands, good with his fists, loud laugh, loud feet, even in socks.

When you think about it, Joss thought, *Pikka pretty much insisted I have more than one round. Lady needs her rest.*

Joss pushed his empty mug across the bar toward the bartender.

"Sure, Slendo. Pour me another. But go easy on the suds this time. I like a little ale in my ale."

Slendo stared at Joss for a moment, then shook his head and grabbed the mug, lifting it to the tap mounted on the bar. He might have even rolled his eyes.

The newly filled ale slid across the bar, and Joss stopped it neatly with an outstretched open hand. Slendo went back to what he was doing, which was leaning against the back of the bar and staring moodily at a table of Nihil sitting and drinking near the far wall.

Joss had clocked them when he walked in. Six of them. They seemed like they might be military, but you couldn't always tell. The Nihil had lately taken up something like a dress code—pretending they were a government instead of a bunch of bloodthirsty raiders—but the rank and file adhered to it pretty indifferently. This little crew wore the standard Nihil getup of smelly, scuffed leather and matted furs and spikes sticking out of it all over the place, but Joss could also see a snappy little cap here, a couple of medals pinned to a chest there, a pair of shiny boots. The only consistency was that they all wore the Eye insignia somewhere: a pin, an armband. One lady had the mean-looking angular spiral symbol tattooed across her entire face, bright blue against her maroon skin.

The Nihil were chatting among themselves, laughing and drinking and polishing off a board of the weird black cheese and green bread that was the only food Slendo served. Acting like it was just another afternoon, like their side didn't murder innocents every chance they got, and robbed and killed and destroyed.

Sewage-souled monsters, Joss thought. *I should go over there and punch their lights out.*

But the Nihil weren't up to anything nefarious right at that moment, and Slendo's was supposed to be a live-and-let-live sort of place. Times were too tough to be turning away customers. Republic Defense Coalition personnel, Nihil, ordinary folks . . . everyone was welcome at Slendo's. Hell, Joss himself was RDC—nobody was giving *him* trouble.

That said, the proprietor himself looked as if he was rethinking his bar's admission policy. Slendo was still staring at the Nihil, a finger twining in his beard, pulling a hank of hair taut, a clear sign of frustration and annoyance if Joss had ever seen one.

Yeah, Slendo's no fan of those guys, Joss thought. *Me neither, pal. Me neither.*

He lifted the mug and took a long sip, really more of a gulp, then got a little mad at himself.

STAR WARS: TRIALS OF THE JEDI   85

Make this one last, buddy, he told himself. *You finish the second one too fast, and you'll find it real easy to have a third. Pace yourself.*

Right. Better to take it slow, even if this particular brand of Eriaduan ale went down real easy.

"This is nice," he said, lifting the mug in a little toast toward the bartender. "Good stuff."

Slendo grunted in reply, not taking his eyes from the table of Nihil.

"Pikka's at home napping," Joss said, figuring a little conversation would slow down the speed at which he drank his second and absolutely final drink. "We're having a baby, you know. Needs her rest."

"You've mentioned," Slendo said, his voice low.

"I ever tell you I like this place?" Joss said. "I do. Hospitable. Takes all kinds of folks. Welcoming."

A long silence from Slendo. The bartender knew Joss was RDC—part of the Republic Defense Coalition. There were a good number of them around. Almost all the RDC forces trapped in the Occlusion Zone had washed up at Eriadu after the Stormwall expanded the last time. Nobody advertised that allegiance too loudly, and most of the soldiers and pilots stayed stashed in secret bunkers up in the mountains outside the cities—but not all.

The whole planet seemed trapped in a strange sort of undeclared truce. Everyone knew there were RDC forces here. The Nihil occupying forces knew it, the Eriaduans knew it. But there was never any open fighting. The Nihil could, in theory, get organized and decide to hunt down the local RDC, but each day passed without them ever seeming to get around to it. That made sense to Joss. "Organization" and "taking the initiative" and "getting things done" were not concepts that seemed to resonate with members of the Nihil rank and file. Petty cruelties, sure. Banal evil, absolutely. Beyond that, they didn't seem like a particularly motivated bunch. It would take strong orders from the Nihil generals to get their lower-level grunts to pick a fight with a real military, and so far that hadn't happened.

The upshot: everyone on Eriadu, all three sides—Nihil, RDC, and Eriaduans—was playing it cool beyond the occasional muttered insult.

It couldn't last. Everyone knew that, too. The tension ratcheted upward day by day. But so far, it was holding.

"Everyone's welcome at Slendo's," the bartender said. "Customers are customers."

"Even Nihil?" Joss said, pitching his voice on the quiet side—as quiet as he could get.

"Even them," Slendo said.

But it didn't sound like he meant it.

The lights in the bar flickered—once, twice, went out. A weary groan came up from the assembled clientele. But then the lights came back on, if a little weaker than they'd been before, and everyone got back to the business at hand, drinking, playing games of chance, and complaining about the status of the city's infrastructure.

Slendo made a sound that couldn't be interpreted as anything but disgust.

"You know what happened during the Great Disaster?" the bartender asked, moving closer until he was directly opposite Joss and could speak quietly while still being heard.

"I do, friend," Joss said. "I was right in the thick of it at Hetzal. Did a lot of work preventing Emergences after that. Headed off impacts all across the galaxy. Me and my wife both."

Slendo shook his head.

"Well, you didn't do much good here, did you?"

Ah, damn, Joss thought, *of course. Eriadu got hit with a big one back then. Lots of people killed.*

"I'm sorry about that, Slendo," Joss said. "Wish I'd been able to stop that one, too."

The bartender waved off the apology.

"Wasn't your fault," he said. "It was them. Or their bosses, anyway."

Slendo let his gaze slide back toward the table of Nihil officers, who

STAR WARS: TRIALS OF THE JEDI   87

were at that moment laughing like crazy over something they found funny—probably some particularly awful thing they'd done. Cut somebody's nose off and fed it to them, something like that.

The lights flickered again, and Slendo's posture clenched into a full-body scowl.

"You ever get over to Bri-Phrang?" the bartender said.

Joss shook his head. Bri-Phrang was the city next door, like a rougher version of Eriadu City, which was plenty rough on its own. Heading over there was looking for trouble.

"Well, we get most of our energy here in Eriadu City from a big geothermal plant under Bri-Phrang," Slendo said. "That thing's never been the same since the Emergence hit. Something got messed up in the steam tunnels, down deep. We started trying to fix it, but once the Nihil came in they made us stop. They *want* our power to be unreliable. Never knowing if the lights will turn on when you flip the switch, or if the water purifiers will work, or anything."

"Sure," Joss said.

He took another long pull on his ale, looking ruefully at the rapidly diminishing contents of his mug as he set it down.

"You know," Joss said, lowering his voice even further, "you Eriaduans, as a rule, don't strike me as people who take well to being told what to do. Surprised you're just . . . well, letting yourselves be told what to do."

Slendo nodded. "You're not wrong. But we're on our own out here. We're on one side of the Stormwall, the Republic's on the other. The Nihil can bring their fleet to any world in the Occlusion Zone that tries to fight back. Even if an uprising succeeded, no single planet has enough military power to hold them off for long. They'd come back in force and kill who knows how many innocent people to make a point. They've done it to other worlds plenty of times."

Slendo sighed, then turned and pulled a bottle of bright-blue liquor and two shot glasses from a shelf on the bar. He set all that down and started pouring.

"Eriadu's tough—you're right about that. We start learning how to fight about three days after we're born. But the Nihil would burn this planet to nothing rather than let us take it back."

"Mm," Joss said.

The bartender lifted the two shot glasses, handed one to Joss. They toasted, and both downed the drinks.

Joss's eyes widened.

Could send a starship to lightspeed with that stuff, he thought, trying not to choke in front of the man. Meanwhile, Slendo seemed completely unbothered. He was already pouring them both another shot.

"I'll tell you one thing," Slendo said. "If a fight starts, we'd be all-in. That's how we think. Until our last blade breaks, until our last warrior falls."

Joss lifted the second shot, sipped it, shuddered.

"Right," Joss replied. "I can see that. You're a tough people on a tough world."

"You aren't wrong. But just because we're tough doesn't make us fools. Time and a place, my friend. Time and a place."

Joss thought about this for a moment.

"If I didn't know better, I'd say there's already a plan," he said. "It's gotten real quiet out in the streets the past few weeks. The Nihil probably think they've got you all good and subdued. I think it's something else. There's an energy in the air. Feels like folks might be waiting for some kind of signal."

Joss tilted his head slightly in the direction of the Nihil carousers, who had started to bother the next table over, pointing and jeering at a group of ordinary drinkers just trying to enjoy their afternoon.

"What do you think about that, Slendo?" Joss said. "You picking up the same vibes?"

Slendo was eyeing Joss very cautiously. Suspiciously, even. Joss downed his shot, then held up both hands, palms out.

"I'm asking, you know, as a fellow with a pregnant wife trying to take a nap. She doesn't sleep so great. If things are going to get loud, a guy

STAR WARS: TRIALS OF THE JEDI 89

might want a heads-up." Joss lowered his voice even more, almost whispering now. "There some sort of signal I should be watching out for?"

Slendo still seemed wary. "If there were, shouldn't you know it?" the bartender said. "You being RDC and all?"

Joss waved this off. "Pikka and I got here late, after most of the other RDC forces were already here. We were escorting some guy back to Republic space, got trapped in the O.Z. when the Stormwall expanded, and then we washed up here. It doesn't matter. We were worried about using open communications to reach out to the others, so we stashed our Longbeam in a hangar near our apartment. Whatever plan the other RDC forces here have, we don't know it."

Slendo nodded. "Sounds about right. Bosses don't tell us grunts what they're up to, even though we'll be the ones with our lives on the line when the fighting starts."

"When?" Joss said, keeping his tone light.

"Yes, *when* is the word. We're all waiting for that signal you mentioned, but it's not coming."

Slendo leaned forward, pretty much whispering now. "The Quintad families and the other high muckalucks have a whole plan set up with your RDC buddies. They're thinking they'll take the planet back in a real quick strike, all or nothing. Folks like me are supposed to create chaos on the ground when it starts, engage the Nihil wherever we can, keep them busy. We've been ready to go for *weeks.* But the word never comes. Supposedly, the Tarkins and the Harros and the other Quintad bosses are waiting for some perfect set of circumstances, the right moment . . . the *ideal tactical environment.*"

He snorted in disgust. "Like that even exists. Like they'd even recognize it if it happened. They're hiding out in bunkers they built up in the old mines. Meanwhile, these Nihil dig in more every day. Down here, where the people are. Where *we* are."

Joss digested this. His mug was empty, and the second shot was just a fond, acid-tinged memory. He wanted to give himself a minute to ponder, make sure what he was thinking about saying wasn't just a bit of booze-fueled bad judgment. He didn't think so. It took a lot more than two shots and a couple of ales to push Joss Adren into a place of ill-considered action. One of the benefits of basically being a hairless Wookiee, from a stature point of view.

He thought about the Nihil and everything they'd done, everyone they'd hurt. Everyone they'd killed in their selfish, thoughtless trampling march across this part of the galaxy.

Joss Adren didn't hate easily. It wasn't really in him.

I hate these ram-headed, burned-up, frizzling, deadblood, motherless, fatherless, life-poisoning piles of rotting digestive tracts, he thought. *The Nihil. They really think they're something. They're nothing.*

Joss took a deep breath, knowing well the chaos that a few words could unleash. The light knew he'd experienced that with Pikka from time to time. He wasn't good with words like she was.

But right now, he knew exactly what to say.

Would Pikka think this was okay?

He considered for a moment.

Hell, she'd have done it ten minutes ago.

"You know," Joss said to Slendo, who was busy mixing a round of complicated cocktails while simultaneously sending eye-daggers across the room at the Nihil contingent. "This isn't my place. But you said you're all waiting for that signal. That's what you said. You're ready . . . just waiting."

The bartender looked at him.

"A signal can come from anywhere," Joss said.

These words were received with a long, considering look and then a long, considering nod. Slendo completed the drinks—of course he did, the man was a professional—and lined them up on the bar for the server to transfer to their new owners.

Then he leaned back against the wall behind the bar and folded his arms.

"This isn't your world, Adren," Slendo said. "I know you have people here. I know your wife is here. But Eriadu is my life. My roots are here; my bones will stay here once I'm gone. I'm not sure I appreciate your little nudge there. As you said . . . not your place."

His gaze shifted toward the table of Nihil.

"On the other hand . . ." he said, "you're not wrong."

Slendo moved back to the taps and began filling a glass with the same delicious Eriaduan ale Joss had lately consumed.

"I come in here every day, take people's orders, let them talk about whatever they want, keep my opinions to myself. That was the job before the Nihil came, it'll be the job after. Same in every bar in the galaxy. When you're a bartender, opinions are bad for business."

He set the filled glass down, picked up another, and began to repeat the process.

"But just because I don't share my opinions doesn't mean I don't have them," Slendo said. "Eriadu is my planet, and I do love it, but this bar is my place. My world. What happens here matters more to me than just about anywhere else."

The second glass went next to the first, and Slendo took a third and pulled the tap to fill it.

"Seems to me that's just about exactly opposite of how the people who make the big decisions feel about it. The Tarkins up in their war bunker don't care about people down here, except in an abstract way. Same's true for how the Nihil see us. We exist, but we don't exist. The Nihil bosses just want us to stay quiet, serve their drinks, and cook their food. The Eriaduan and RDC leadership want us to stay quiet until they decide it's time for us to start risking our lives. In the meantime, down here, we all just endure."

Third glass full, fourth glass begun.

"So my bar, my *world*, becomes a place I don't want it to be. My life becomes something I don't want it to be. All around me, I see my friends, the people I've been serving for decades, my *regulars*. Their lives aren't how they want, either."

Fifth glass.

"I understand the point of being strategic, and I don't want to get in the way of anyone's plans. On the other hand, there's a moment when you realize there's not a lot of difference between giving up your free will to the Nihil and giving it up to the Tarkins. It's all people telling me what I'm allowed to do with my own world, telling me I can't make that world the way I want it to be."

Slendo topped off the sixth glass and set it next to its fellows, arranged in two neat rows. He looked up at Joss.

"This is my world," he said. "And here, I'm free."

The bartender placed the glasses on a tray and waved off the server as she approached. He lifted the tray and carried it skillfully through the bar, headed directly to the table of Nihil.

They looked up as Slendo approached, eyes narrowed but obviously at ease. Why wouldn't they be? They owned the planet. If they had any bad feelings, it was more due to the bartender daring to interrupt their conversation than any perceived threat.

Slendo set the tray down on the table.

"What's this?" one of the Nihil barked, the one in the fancy cap, his tone all superiority and contempt and boredom with a mild sheen of indignation and the threat of violence underlying it all.

"These are on the house," Slendo said.

The Nihil looked at one another, bemused.

"Why?" that same Nihil asked, evidently the highest ranking.

"Because dead folks can't pay their tabs," Slendo said.

In a move so smooth Joss barely saw it happen, a magic trick of violence, Slendo produced a blaster from beneath his apron and shot each of the Nihil dead.

The work of a moment.

Slendo turned to face his bar, a tiny wisp of steam wending upward from the barrel of his gun. Behind him, one of the newly deceased Nihil slumped, sliding slowly to the ground.

The remaining patrons were frozen, watching to see what would happen next.

What happened next was another group of Nihil entered the bar. They pushed through the door, all sharp-toothed grins and spiky armor and cocky confidence. They stopped as soon as they came in, noting the silence, realizing something was off.

Slendo lowered his blaster.

"This bar is now a Nihil-free zone," the bartender said, his tone edging on manic, knowing he'd set something in motion he didn't know how to stop. "You ain't welcome here no more. You have ten seconds to get out."

The Nihil took in the bar, scanning across it, stopping when they saw their dead colleagues.

"You think you can do this?" the leader of the new group said. "You'll pay. You'll all pay. We'll burn you. We'll wear your *skin*."

"Did I say ten seconds?" Slendo said. "My mistake. I meant five."

From across the bar, other drinkers pulled out their own concealed blasters, and one of them might have been named Joss Adren. *Zap, zap, zzzzap,* and the Nihil dropped dead.

Slendo nodded. He returned his own pistol to its holster beneath his apron. Just like that, he was once again a humble bartender. He took a long breath, then addressed the patrons of his establishment, his co-conspirators in whatever would happen next.

"It's time," Slendo said. "Let's kick them off our blasted planet. If they knew who we were, they'd never have come here in the first place. It's time they learned." He lifted a closed fist. "Let's show them who we are."

The bar emptied out quickly, people stepping over the Nihil piled near the entrance. Slendo made his way back to Joss, who remained where he'd been during the entire exchange.

"Was that the signal?" Joss asked, setting his blaster down on the bar.

"Looks like," Slendo said, surveying his establishment, the only other occupants being Nihil corpses.

He returned his gaze to Joss. He took his empty mug and refilled it from the tap, then set it down and slid it across the bar.

The two men eyed each other.

"You should head home to your wife," Slendo said. "Your tab's settled. Consider it payment for that nudge. This wasn't your decision, it was mine—let's make that clear. But I don't know if I'd have made it today if you hadn't walked in."

Joss reached out and curled his hand around the mug.

"Well, I'm not going to waste a free drink."

He lifted the mug, drained it in two gulps.

The sound of blasterfire arose from the street outside.

Pikka's not going to sleep through that, Joss thought.

"This won't be pretty," Joss said, not a question, a statement.

"Is it ever?" Slendo said.

He picked up a glass and began polishing it.

⁂

The word spread quickly. *The time has come.* This was a surprise to the Eriaduan nobles who thought the decision to begin the uprising would be theirs. But a people's desire to be free is a natural process, like a volcanic eruption or a groundquake. It has its own life, its own power. You can sense it looming, make preparations, but it cannot be held back.

Subjugate a people for too long, and eventually they will erupt, sweeping away everything in their path. If no one chooses the moment for them, they will choose for themselves.

The Eriaduan and RDC commanders realized the fight had begun, no matter how it was instigated. They could not hesitate. Orders were issued, and across the planet, concealed entrances ground open, leading to a vast system of tunnels and chambers bored into the world's mountain ranges. The tunnels were originally mining shafts dug to extract lommite ore, but the veins were depleted many years before. The shafts were still intact, however—hundreds of kilometers of high, broad tunnels and chambers perfect for concealing, say, a substantial military force.

This moment was long in the planning. Eriadu's leaders had coordinated with the RDC to convince the occupying Nihil they had completely subdued the planet, and no significant military assets remained on the world. Eriadu had sacrificed warriors and matériel as part of a false surrender, a strategic retreat that led the Nihil to believe they could move their vast fleet of attack ships to other trouble spots in the Occlusion Zone.

In the weeks and months since the Nihil's invasion fleet moved away from Eriadu, RDC vessels stealthily arrived at the planet in ones and twos. These were ships trapped behind the Stormwall after its most recent expansion, and they all had standing orders to converge on Eriadu if such a thing were to happen. Ship by ship, they slipped into the system, down to the planet, hiding away in the mountain bunkers.

The Nihil military high commanders back on Hetzal did observe among themselves that it was unusual that their patrols and autonomous scav droids had not found more RDC assets inside the Occlusion Zone. If they had more experience, drive, or imagination, they might have considered the idea that the missing RDC ships were massing in one place, waiting for the chance to strike a hammerblow against the Nihil regime from inside its own territory. But the Nihil high command did not have the necessary experience, drive, or imagination. It was easier to call themselves victorious and order yet another celebration in their own honor.

On Eriadu itself, the local Nihil commanders had always expected some level of resistance from the natives once the initial invasion was complete. Eriaduans were a warlike people, and it would undoubtedly take some time before the entire population understood it had been conquered. Nothing that couldn't be handled by a few carpet bombings and public executions.

The Nihil had assumed that if the Eriaduans ever did resist, it would be small actions run by local malcontents, perhaps a private army or two maintained by one of the many noble houses on the planet. The Nihil did not expect to face an entire fleet, which was what they got. Huge blast doors opened in the mountains of Eriadu, and vessels shot out, from single-pilot fighters all the way up to the powerful, intimidating *Pacifier*-class patrol cruisers maintained by the RDC. Longbeam multiuse attack transports, Z-28 Skywings—a full wing of aircraft spilled into the air.

The vessels headed toward predetermined targets—the spaceports co-opted by Nihil ships, the buildings they were using for their command-and-control points, and various other strategic spots across the planet.

The resistance force needed to move quickly. Surprise would only go so far. The Nihil could summon many more ships from other parts of the Occlusion Zone, while the joint RDC and Eriaduan fleet was alone. All potential aid was locked away on the other side of the Stormwall—Admiral Kronara in his magnificent *Third Horizon* and the rest of the RDC fleet.

The plan was straightforward. It would begin with a bombardment of Nihil air bases and spaceports to push the occupiers back to their own ships, to force them to take to the sky lest their vessels be destroyed on the ground. That would set up an air-to-air battle, where the skills and training of the RDC pilots and the local knowledge of the Eriaduans would give them an edge. The resistance would destroy every Nihil vessel in the system, then run sweeps to root out any remaining enemies, assisted by the local militias—which included essentially every adult on the planet. No Eriaduan would stay out of this fight. Simultaneously, ground units would retake and reactivate the planetary defense systems—long-range cannons, shielding, and the like—to protect the planet from Nihil reinforcements that might arrive from offworld.

The plan: Make Eriadu a fortress. Make it too costly a target for the rest of the Nihil fleet to engage when they inevitably arrived. Hit hard. Hit fast. Destroy the invaders. Take revenge.

Take back the planet.

That was the plan.

Chapter Six

THE JEDI TEMPLE

"Just incredible," said Torban Buck.

"Mm?" Indeera Stokes said, looking up at him from her hoverchair, floating at his side.

"The way things turn," Torban replied. "The Nameless are our greatest nightmare. They've taken so much from us. And now we're risking our lives to save theirs."

Here he glanced down at Indeera—she was in that chair because a Nameless had attacked her during the destruction of Starlight Beacon, and her legs had become calcified in the manner of Force-wielder flesh drained by the creatures. She chose to spend most of her time in a hoverchair rather than using an exoskeleton or having the dead limbs removed so she could be fitted for prosthetics.

Indeera gave him one of her unreadable little smiles.

"For light and life, Torban," she said.

They were in a viewing gallery overlooking the Jedi Temple's primary hangar, currently holding the great, elegant *Ataraxia,* a sleek vessel designed for significant missions requiring a large deployment. Its holds contained Vector fighters, shuttles, the Vanguard land vehicles, training bays, living quarters, a machine shop—everything the Jedi might need.

Now it would carry the Nine along with the dozen Nameless they were trying to return home. The chosen Jedi were all present in the hangar, plus the hunter, Ty Yorrick—everyone except Azlin Rell, who would presumably join the group shortly before the mission began. All wore the full suits of armor created for them by Masters Govena and Infil'a. Torban thought the armor was beautiful if a bit dehumanizing—the full-face masks were a little droidlike. Still, there was no mistaking Avar Kriss with her blond hair, now tied back in a ponytail, or Burryaga and Arkoff, or any of the others. Most were people he had known for decades. If the selection of the Nine had been up to him, these would probably be the ones he'd have chosen.

The armored Jedi stood in the hangar, to all outward signs untroubled, as lifter droids carefully moved repulsorlift pallets toward the *Ataraxia*'s hold. Positioned in a line near the droids, blaster rifles at the ready, stood a detachment of Republic specialists sent by the supreme chancellor. They had positioned themselves between the pallets and the Jedi, creating a formidable defensive wall. The operatives had done this because the floating platforms each held a Nameless, restrained by binder cables glowing with slowly pulsing energy.

The creatures were awake. Attempts had been made to sedate them, but this had resulted in many destroyed medical droids and not much else. The few successfully administered injections didn't work. The biochemistry of the Nameless seemed to be vastly different from anything ever before encountered.

Torban studied the creatures—as best as he could, anyway. Even though he was separated from the Nameless by a thick pane of transparisteel and many meters of open space, to his eyes they appeared as just a strange, swirling mass. He recognized that as what was known as the Nameless effect, and it didn't just affect his eyes. Torban felt fear coiling in his gut, an irrational urge to run screaming in any direction that would take him away from the creatures.

STAR WARS: TRIALS OF THE JEDI 99

He tamped it down. He was up here, in the viewing gallery, safe with Indeera and the rest of what he privately referred to as the Other Nine—Vernestra Rwoh, Ceret, Zaviel Tepp, and the rest. He had nothing to worry about. Down in the hangar were Jedi in *true* danger, yet none of them showed a drop of fear. Avar, Elzar, Bell, Terec, and the others just stood calmly, watching the Nameless being moved into the *Ataraxia.*

Reath Silas held the strange, beautiful rod the Council had shown them when the teams were selected—the Rod of Ages, Master Lahru had called it. Reath was displaying the artifact to Arkoff, indicating the gem set at the center of the ornate disk fused to one end, the Echo Stone. All of the Nine, and even the Other Nine, had been briefed in its use, though not very much was known for certain. The few records and ancient writings available implied that the thing could cancel out the similar artifact possessed by Marchion Ro, overruling his control of the creatures—but obviously that was impossible to confirm. It did seem to be able to influence the Nameless, but those tests had been extremely limited. No one wanted to risk hurting or killing one of the beasts.

The Jedi's presence in the hangar wasn't strictly necessary to load the Nameless for transport, Torban knew, but they had all chosen to take the opportunity to practice wearing the armor, to ensure they would be able to think and fight in close proximity to the creatures. It looked like they had all managed it . . . but he couldn't imagine it was easy.

The Nameless were terrifying. They ate Jedi, turning their bodies into crumbling stone corpses. Screaming corpses. Any one of those beasts could murder the Nine *and* the Other Nine, feed on their most essential selves, and there was nothing they could—

Enough, Buckets, Torban thought. *Pull yourself together. You're a Chagrian slab of muscle and bone, twice the size of most beings. Your skin's as blue as the sky and hard as stone, and your horns are white as snow and sharp as hell. You have nothing to fear.*

"You happy with how the armor turned out?" Torban asked Master Infil'a, desperately seeking a distraction.

"I like it well enough," the armorer replied. "It was a challenge to figure out how to integrate the Blight-resistant ore into the alloys we normally use. If we had more time, I think we'd have done better, but . . ."

"There is no time," Torban said. "The Council made that very clear."

Kirak nodded.

"Right. Anyway, we ended up finding a basic template we thought could work, though customized a bit for each wearer. They all had . . . *requests.*" The armorer offered up the expression of a long-suffering designer asked to make endless changes to satisfy a client. "It's my fault, really," he said. "Mine and Master Govena's. We told the Nine they could ask for adjustments to their armor for personal gear requirements and the like. And also so they could tell each other apart at a glance, know who's who. Before you know it, I'm redesigning Ty Yorrick's set to leave room for pouches and holsters for all those extra weapons she carries, and adding a crest to Avar's helmet."

He looked down through the viewing window toward Avar, whose armor did include a beautiful sweeping crest on the headpiece.

"Does look nice, though," Kirak said, not without pride, scratching at his chin through his bright-blue beard.

"More important, it seems to serve its intended purpose," Torban said.

He pointed down at another of the Nine, almost certainly Bell Zettifar. His lanky physique was one giveaway, but the larger clue was that the Jedi was down on one knee affectionately scratching a small, doglike black-and-orange creature behind one ear. Ember, the charhound Bell had adopted from her homeworld of Elphrona years back.

The young Knight was barely ten meters from a dozen Nameless, and there he was, perfectly composed, saying goodbye to his pet. Yes, clearly the armor worked. Torban's understanding from conversations with Master Infil'a was that it didn't cancel out the Nameless effect, but somehow made it easier for the Jedi to maintain their own focus and push past whatever energy the Nameless generated. Torban didn't understand it fully—but then again, he didn't need to, since he wouldn't be wearing a set himself.

"You'll take care of Ember while Bell's away?" Torban asked Indeera.

STAR WARS: TRIALS OF THE JEDI   101

"That's the plan," she answered. "I'd probably let Porter take her—he's a lonely man, even if he doesn't act like it—but he's off somewhere. So, looks like Ember will get some quality time with her auntie Indeera. Fine by me. She likes to hop on the bed to sleep at night. Keeps me nice and warm."

Bell gave Ember a final pat on her long, thin head and stood. He turned to walk back toward the rest of the Jedi. He seemed calm, completely unafraid. They all did.

Don't know if I could be so relaxed in his place, Torban thought.

"You wish you were going," he heard Lily Tora-Asi say.

"Is that a question, Lily?" Vernestra Rwoh replied.

"An observation, Vernestra," Lily said. "And I didn't need the Force to make it. Your feelings are written all over your face. I understand. Part of me wishes I were still on Banchii, to honor my obligations there."

"I just want to be useful," Vernestra said.

"You want to know how to do that, kid?" Zaviel Tepp said, as gruff as ever. "Focus on the task you've been given. Forget what isn't, think about what is."

Good advice, Torban thought, *though I would have delivered it a bit more kindly.*

Vernestra was young. That didn't mean she was foolish, or weak, or wouldn't have done her part if she had been chosen as one of the Nine. Torban knew how strong young people could be—he spent much of his time with Padawans and younglings, and he'd seen them navigate situations that would test even the most seasoned Jedi. If Vern was guilty of anything, it was youthful enthusiasm—hardly a crime.

"I wish I were going, too, Vernestra," Torban said. "I think we all do, on some level. It's difficult to watch our friends heading off to do something so dangerous while we stay here at the Temple."

Vernestra shot him a grateful look, and Torban smiled at her.

Do I mean what I just said, though? he asked himself. *Do I actually wish I were going?*

Torban Buck was a healer. He'd studied medicine since he was a Padawan—it was a mystery as great as the Force, and as beautiful. The

Jedi disciplines took too much of his time for him to become a full-fledged physician, but he knew enough to do good work as a field medic.

That devotion to healing didn't mean he couldn't fight, of course. No one would ever call him a coward. He would rush into battle whenever he needed to; that could be a way to save lives, too. But he was who he was. Causing injury was against his nature.

So, if he was completely honest with himself, no, he was not particularly bothered by the Council choosing him for the backup team. This felt like a mission for warriors. Better for people like Ty Yorrick the monster-hunter to go, or Avar Kriss the Hero of Hetzal, or Reath Silas the Nameless expert. If Torban was needed, he would go. But he was not displeased that his role in the endeavor would be focused on saving lives, not taking them.

A sound came from the hangar below, a shout of terror. All heads in the gallery whipped toward the viewing window.

"What's happening down there?" Zaviel Tepp said, sounding almost irritated.

One of the Republic operatives was backing away from a Nameless on its pallet, his rifle raised. The soldier seemed terrified—he was shaking his head, his mouth opening and closing soundlessly.

The man's comrades called out to him, moving forward to assist, unsure what was happening. The Jedi, too, were raising their hands, trying to help. Torban was sure some of them were using the Force to try to reach the man.

It was too late. The soldier began firing his rifle, and bolts of bright-red light shot out across the hangar. Most flew harmlessly into the air or bounced off the *Ataraxia*'s armored hull. Any blasts headed in dangerous directions were deflected by the armored Jedi, who had ignited their lightsabers almost as one. Torban raised his own hand and sensed his fellow Jedi doing the same all around him, reaching out toward the terrified operative's rifle, intending to pull it from his grasp.

It was too late. Several shots impacted the Nameless's pallet directly, and the glowing binders restraining the creature snapped with a shower of sparks.

STAR WARS: TRIALS OF THE JEDI 103

One of the Nameless was free.

Torban couldn't make the thing out, not clearly. It remained a swirl-ing, terrifying mass down on the hangar floor. The Nine spun to face the beast, their blades raised, a hissing, fizzing wave of light, but hesitated. Torban understood immediately. Every one of the Nameless needed to survive, needed to be returned intact to their homeworld. If this creature were killed, it would be one fewer to be reunited with whatever prevented the Blight on its world. Perhaps that would mean there would not be enough. Perhaps if they killed this Nameless, the Blight could never be stopped.

The Jedi could not attack.

Avar Kriss shouted something, and she and two other Jedi near her—Elzar Mann and Burryaga—lifted their free hands, trying to subdue the creature with the Force. Reath lifted the Rod of Ages, clearly attempting to use the artifact to help however he could. None of it worked. The Nameless leapt forward, landing on the specialist who had set it free. A long, drawn-out scream, suddenly cut off. The other Republic agents stumbled back, terror seeming to overtake them. They fired their own ri-fles in random directions, at targets only they could see.

The Nameless reared up—Torban could tell that much from its silhou-ette. It shrieked, the sound stabbing through the hangar. The thing moved quickly, shambling and squealing, toward . . .

By the light, no . . .

Toward the alcove that led to the rest of the Jedi Temple. The Temple filled with defenseless Jedi, and Padawans, and younglings. None wore the special armor. None knew what was coming. The Nameless would tear through any Jedi it encountered like cloth.

"Sound the alarm!" Torban shouted, but it was too late.

Far too late.

And then, a mighty roar, as Arkoff darted toward the fleeing Name-less, slamming into its side. The Wookiee's bulk was significant—the im-pact would be like being hit by, well, a falling tree. The Nameless seemed to sag, falling to one side, skittering.

Arkoff did not let go. He wrapped both of his mighty arms around what Torban guessed was the thing's neck and squeezed, holding it down to the ground. The Nameless writhed and screamed, thrashing its body, trying to escape.

It seized one of Arkoff's legs, and the Jedi screamed. Torban Buck had never heard a Wookiee in true pain, in agony. The sound froze every drop of blood in his body.

But somehow Torban's limbs still moved. He ignited his own lightsaber and, in a single slash, cut through the transparisteel window of the viewing gallery. Arkoff's wails and the Nameless's squeals were suddenly amplified. Torban leapt through the new opening and landed hard on the hangar floor, cushioning the impact of his large frame against the stone with the Force.

He was dimly aware of another Jedi descending from the observation gallery, a few steps behind him—Lily Tora-Asi. Torban recalled that Arkoff had been Lily's master when she was a Padawan. She was trying to help, ignoring her fear, unswayed by the danger. A good Jedi.

Torban sprinted forward toward Arkoff, who had not let go, despite the creature still fastened to his limb, thrashing and tearing. But . . . the Nameless was moving more weakly now. The creature was tiring. Fading and, with it, the effect it generated, otherwise Torban would have succumbed to terror as well.

As Buck approached, the beast drew into focus. Its jaws relaxed around Arkoff's leg, and it slumped back, its eyes closing as the huge Wookiee rendered it unconscious. Suddenly Torban could see the Nameless clearly, all its angular, bony structure, a physique that should not be, a creature that had to exist in a perpetual twilight of pain.

He took this in with a single quick glance, aware of other Jedi and Republic warriors and droids rushing up with binding cords and lightsabers drawn. Torban was not focused on the Nameless. The others would handle it.

Torban Buck cared about his patient.

Arkoff released the comatose Nameless. The Wookiee fell back and

STAR WARS: TRIALS OF THE JEDI   105

slid to the floor. He emitted a hiss of deep pain as he fell, followed by a deep, mournful, hooting howl. Suddenly, Burryaga was there, holding his fellow Wookiee's head in his lap, his hand on his chest, comforting him as best he could. Burry looked Arkoff in the eyes, with him no matter what happened next. He did not look at what had happened to Arkoff's leg. None of the Jedi working around them did. The injury was Torban's responsibility.

Clinical detachment fell over his mind as he looked at the limb. The patient's leg was deeply gashed where the Nameless had bitten into the flesh. Torban could see the deep red of muscle, the white curve of bone.

Hemorrhage. Significant blood loss from the primary arteries. He needs an immediate transfusion and surgical attention, or the wound is not survivable.

But the wound was not ordinary trauma. An attack from a Nameless had side effects. Rapid, deadly side effects. Torban could see the ash, the stone, creeping rapidly outward from the wounds on the patient's leg. This was what had taken Loden Greatstorm, Orla Jareni, Pra-Tre Veter, and so many others.

This was the creeping death the Nameless brought. They consumed users of the Force and turned them to corpses of crumbling stone.

Torban Buck, no doctor but a healer of great renown, knew that sometimes the choices available on the battlefield were stark. They were stark and needed to be made without hesitation. Life was everything. Preserve life no matter the cost.

"This will be unpleasant, my friend," he said, "but it will be quick."

Torban Buck ignited his lightsaber and severed Arkoff's leg just above the knee. The power of the blade cauterized the wound, and the lower leg dropped away. The progression of the Nameless effect ceased, but small flakes of gray dust crumbled away from the areas already damaged.

A great howl emerged from both Arkoff and Burryaga at the loss. Torban heard it, but only distantly. He was focused on the stump of Arkoff's leg, watching closely for signs of corruption, for indications that he had acted too late.

He watched, waited, watched, ready to act again if necessary.

Nothing, he thought after a moment. *I caught it in time.*

Torban allowed himself to relax, just a bit, and shifted to the other part of the healer's responsibility. He had cared for the patient's body. Now he would care for his spirit.

"You'll be all right, Arkoff," he said, his voice strong and calm. "Your life will change, but it will continue. Your path will hold joy and light. The pain will pass. Life, my friend, life—you are still here with us. The possibilities are endless."

Arkoff took in a long, shuddering breath. He nodded. Burryaga murmured to him in their language, Shyriiwook. Torban didn't speak it but didn't need to. He knew the sort of things Burry was saying.

Torban reached into a pouch on his belt and withdrew an injection device. He held it up, showing it to Arkoff.

"For your pain," he said.

Arkoff hooted in quick agreement, insistence even, and Torban administered the analgesic. It worked quickly, and the injured Wookiee sagged back, a peaceful expression coming over his face.

"Buckets," he heard someone say, "you need to see this."

Torban looked up from his patient. His gaze fell first upon the Nameless that Arkoff had subdued. The creature had already been restrained, returned to its pallet, and was being moved toward the *Ataraxia* by the lifter droids.

But just past it, lying on the ground, was the body of the Republic operative the Nameless had killed in its bid to escape. Several of the Nine stood around it. Elzar Mann had a hand up and was gesturing for Torban to come.

The healer pushed himself to his feet, went to see, and realized immediately that a terrible situation had gotten even worse. The Republic agent was dead—but not from his wounds. The man's remains were no longer flesh but grayish, crumbling stone.

"Was he . . . could he touch the Force?" Torban asked.

"We don't know, Buckets," Elzar replied, "but we tested all the soldiers the Republic sent to us, and none seemed attuned to the Force. That was a prerequisite, in fact. They wouldn't be able to help us effectively if they were susceptible to the Nameless."

"I was watching from above," Torban said, gesturing upward toward the viewing gallery where the Other Nine remained, standing at the edge of the broken window. "It looked to me as if this man was under the influence of the Nameless effect before he died. The others, too, I think."

The Jedi turned to look at the surviving Republic operatives. They stood in a little group on the far side of the hangar, obviously shaken, speaking quietly among themselves.

"That shouldn't be possible," Elzar said. "It didn't hit the RDC soldiers who participated in the missions to capture Nameless. Why would it affect them now?"

"It could be connected to the Blight," Reath Silas replied. "Perhaps as it spreads, consuming the Force from the galaxy, the Nameless grow hungrier, more manic—desperate for any source of food they can get. And the Force . . . well . . ."

He gestured down at the remains of the poor man lying before them.

"The Force is in all things," Avar Kriss finished for him.

"They can't go with us," Bell said, looking across the hangar. "The specialists. Not if this might happen again."

"No," Avar said, "they can't. I'll speak to them."

She moved away, toward the cluster of operatives on the far side of the hangar, all of them casting anxious looks toward the Jedi and their monsters.

Torban knew Avar could handle that particular situation. His focus had shifted to something else.

The Nine, after all, were now the Eight.

Would that be enough? He didn't know. Torban was sure of only one thing: Arkoff's armor was far too large to fit any member of the Other Nine. Except for one: a strongly built Chagrian healer who would never choose to fight but would do what needed to be done.

The galaxy is my patient, and every life within it, he thought. *Sometimes the choices available on the battlefield are stark.*

Torban walked across the hangar back to the peacefully sleeping Arkoff. He knelt, reached forward, and gently, carefully began to unbuckle the Wookiee's armor.

Chapter Seven

THE *GAZE ELECTRIC*

"Have a drink with me, Faksir," said Marchion Ro.

He lifted a bottle of turquoise wine from the table and filled a second goblet—pure dolovite, glinting crimson in the low light—then set the bottle down and gestured to a chair opposite him. Marchion had just finished eating, a meal consumed in silence at the enormous banquet table in the *Gaze Electric*'s cavernous throne room. The Eye of the Nihil and his bodyguard were the only two living beings on the entire ship. Ghirra was on her way to Coruscant, and Marchion had sent his other servants and bodyguards away, leaving just a droid crew to handle the ship's operations.

Faksir stood near the entrance to the gigantic, echoing arched chamber, loose-limbed but alert, protecting his lord from . . . droids bearing trays of food, perhaps.

The offer of a drink hung in the air. To Marchion's eyes, Faksir seemed perplexed. The guard captain's body language suggested deep surprise that the invitation had been extended. That made a certain degree of sense. In all the time Faksir had served as a member of the She'ar, making his slow rise to the top of the heap, Marchion had spoken to him in a way that wasn't a direct order perhaps twice.

Then again, "Have a drink with me" was an order, too. Faksir walked across the huge chamber, his bootsteps echoing, toward the seat opposite Marchion where the second goblet rested. He sat, clearly uncomfortable but ready to serve. Marchion smiled in the way he knew made other people feel safe and at ease.

"Have you ever thought about the way you think?" Marchion said.

"Not . . . regularly," Faksir replied.

Marchion lifted his goblet and held it out in a toast. Faksir lifted his own. Both men drank. One of the oldest rituals. Dependable. It put people on an equal footing. Overlords and servants. Enemies. Young and old.

"I'm the same," the Eye of the Nihil said. "Too busy thinking to consider much about how it happens. But lately, I've been pondering the question. I've concluded that my mind operates in a fashion that is all but unique. Things I find obvious are difficult for others to see. Connections, likely outcomes, patterns of behavior . . . and ways to disrupt or destroy them."

Faksir nodded slowly and took another sip of his wine. To Marchion, the motion was an obvious attempt by the other man to hide his spiking confusion and anxiety. But the crimson goblet obstructing Faksir's many-lipped mouth did not cover the slight trembles in his eyestalks or the increased pace with which his respiration holes fluttered open and closed.

"Other people can see some of these paths, too, of course," Marchion went on. "If you kick a rock off a cliff, even a very ignorant person knows it will eventually hit the ground. But I can see not just what that rock will do, but other rocks it might hit on the way down, and what *those* rocks will do, and the effects of those impacts too, and so on, to a level that I believe is beyond what most others can achieve. It seems like a fair assumption. If other people could do what I can, it wouldn't have been so easy for me to turn this galaxy inside out."

"Damn right," Faksir said, knowing that echoing his boss's claims of superiority had to be safe ground.

Marchion drank more of his own wine. He grinned—and this smile was for no one but himself.

STAR WARS: TRIALS OF THE JEDI

"I decided to take control of the Nihil and cause the Great Disaster just a few years ago, Faksir. Just a few years, and in that time I've taken a substantial portion of the galaxy for myself and repeatedly defeated the Republic *and* the Jedi in order to do it. Almost everyone alive knows my name."

Marchion leaned forward in his seat, his grin growing wider.

"They know my name," he said, "*and they fear it.*" He gestured languidly. "It was easy. In the end, people are just rocks, too."

Marchion watched Faksir mull that over. He thought he could almost recite the guard captain's thoughts. They were that plainly written on the fool's face.

Not me, though, Faksir was thinking. *I'm not a rock. Marchion doesn't think of me that way. If he did, I wouldn't be the head of his She'ar. He wouldn't have offered me a drink. I matter.*

"Because of my particular way of seeing things, I'm sure you'll agree that it's very difficult to catch me completely off guard," Marchion said.

"Right," Faksir said, not knowing what he was agreeing to.

"That is why it was *frustrating* to receive *reports* that a *rebellion* kicked off on Eriadu well ahead of when I expected it to, Faksir. I had plans based on it starting later."

The She'ar sat up a little straighter, his eyes sucking back into his skull with a little *schloop* sound—a sign of focus. Military action, battles, fighting, killing—these, Faksir knew. Here, he felt he could contribute.

"Do we have details, my Eye?" Faksir said. "The Eriaduans are known to be sneaky. How did it start?"

"The fighting began in several places at once over the past day. Localized, relatively small incidents, but it's all been amplified since then. A fairly significant RDC task force materialized from out of nowhere, and Eriadu's commanding echelons kept some of their own military assets secret from us as well. Hidden in caves, as I understand it. It all feels very coordinated. They seem to have been planning this for a while."

Faksir's fingers drummed on the tabletop, his ragged nails clacking away. Marchion read that as surprise that his leader wasn't acting with more urgency.

This is an emergency situation! Faksir was thinking. *Why is the Eye wasting time having a drink with me? Why, it doesn't make sense!*

"Do you have orders for me, my Eye?" Faksir said. "I can relay your commands to General Viess or the other fleet commanders. We can turn that planet into a cinder. Actually . . . wait. Didn't you ask me to . . ."

A stray thought had plainly occurred to the guard, something he found confusing.

"I ordered Viess to gather her fleet and take it to Eriadu several days ago," Marchion confirmed, his tone turned moody.

"Several days . . . but you said the fighting started yesterday," Faksir said. "You sent Viess before the rebellion even began."

Marchion raised his glass again, and the bewildered She'ar returned the toast, drank.

"Like I told you," Marchion said. "Rocks. Eriadu was an obvious hot spot. I knew RDC forces had to be hiding somewhere in the Occlusion Zone after the Stormwall's latest expansion. Eriadu was a likely candidate.

"That world never really understood it had been conquered. I suspected they'd rebel eventually, and the addition of RDC military assets to their strength made it likely to happen soon. I sent Viess so she'd be in position when it did."

Marchion waved a hand. Ancient history.

"It's fine, really," Marchion said. "Even if the Eriaduans claw themselves out a foothold, Viess will be there soon and will simply take the world back. An object lesson to the galaxy about the futility of resisting Nihil rule."

"Exactly," said Faksir, nodding.

"But it does call some things into question," Marchion added.

Faksir stopped nodding.

"I was wrong about the timing of Eriadu beginning its rebellion. I didn't expect Lina Soh to reject my offer to remove the Blight. And then there's the Jedi—they've been capturing Nameless across the galaxy. Not *killing*, Faksir. *Capturing.* I didn't see that coming, either."

STAR WARS: TRIALS OF THE JEDI 113

He frowned.

"Individually, these are small events. I'm not infallible. I'm not omniscient. I can miss things. But taken together, they suggest a system spiraling into a new, unanticipated configuration. To be honest, Faksir, it makes me nervous. What else might I be missing? Clouded vision. Clouded vision."

"Boss, look," Faksir said. "No one's better than you. We've all seen you do stuff that seemed impossible. Everyone gets a little low sometimes. Nothing strange about that. Maybe don't focus on the things you don't know. Focus on the things you do."

"That's very kind of you to say," Marchion said. "It's good advice. I appreciate it."

He watched Faksir relax a little. The man had taken a big swing, speaking so familiarly to his overlord. Faksir had taken a risk but also recognized a potential opportunity. The Eye had never confided in him this way before.

What if . . . Faksir was thinking, excitement rising in his belly as he considered all the new possibilities. *What if I could become a confidant, a trusted adviser, not just his bodyguard? Who knows what might happen?*

Marchion saw all of this, and it made him happy.

"My grandmother used to talk to me about this kind of stuff," Faksir said. "Back when I was small, afraid of things."

Behind Faksir, a figure stepped forward silently from the gloom—an older woman with long gray hair, slate-blue skin, and eyes like dark pools. Blood ran down the side of her skull, but she was smiling. This was Shalla Ro, Marchion's own grandmother. She had come wanting . . . well, who knew what she wanted? She wasn't real. None of the shades that visited Marchion with increasing frequency were real.

Sometimes he saw his father, Asgar. Sometimes he saw older ancestors he didn't recognize . . . but they all recognized him. Evereni had this ability, to see the spirits of their forebears. Something in their blood, maybe, or some shared delusion. Marchion hated it. He lived in the now, the moment. The past was dead, just like Shalla. He'd been there. Seen it happen, in fact.

Whatever the ghost wanted from him was irrelevant.

The Evereni were all gone, as far as Marchion knew. He was the last and no longer had to follow their rules, try to achieve their goals, listen to their ghosts.

He was alone, and that was good.

"Oh?" Marchion said, smiling at Faksir. "What did your grandmother tell you?"

"She said that when you get anxious, you should think about the things you have control over. No one's scared of things they can control. For me, it was a water faucet on the outside of our shack. I could turn it on, turn it off, anytime I wanted. It felt good to think about. You control a lot more than a faucet, Marchion."

"I do, Faksir, that's true. But I'll tell you something. The more you control, the more anxious you become. I know your grandmother's trick. I've known it for a long time. But because my anxieties are so great, my need for control is greater, too. It's a trap. The only thing I've found that helps is to create *absolute* control over other things, other beings. And the only way to do that—the one method that feels right—is to kill them. That's true control over another person. You must know what I mean. You've killed many while in my service."

"I . . . know what you mean," Faksir said.

His head made a little jerk, and fluid spilled from his mouth, presumably his blood. It was a bright-orange color.

Interesting, Marchion thought.

He watched as Faksir realized what was happening to him. The man would have time for just one last emotional reaction before his brain and body shut down. Marchion expected anger or fear—but no. Faksir was *hurt.* The man felt emotionally betrayed.

But Marchion is my friend, Faksir was thinking. *How could he do this to me?*

Fascinating, Marchion thought.

STAR WARS: TRIALS OF THE JEDI 115

Faksir shot to his feet. Somehow, long, curved blades had appeared in his hands. Marchion didn't move. He was legitimately astonished. The poison in the wine should be melting Faksir's body from the inside out. His failure to slump down into a puddle of goo was completely unexpected. Something about the poison's interaction with the body chemistry of Faksir's species, making it slower to achieve its results? Marchion didn't know.

The She'ar threw one of the two blades. Marchion dodged, almost too late, feeling the metal whick past his ear. He was off balance, not ready for that sort of attack—which was why Faksir had chosen it.

The man took the opportunity provided by Marchion's distraction and lunged forward across the table, his second blade outstretched. The moves were electric-quick, both the throw and the follow-up attack.

There's a reason he's my chief bodyguard, Marchion had time to think.

The Eye of the Nihil shoved himself backward, reaching up at the same time to grasp Faksir's wrist. The She'ar spat a mouthful of that lava-orange blood right in Marchion's face.

The stuff burned—what *were* Faksir's kind filled with?—and the edge of the blade moved closer to Marchion Ro's throat.

The fate of the entire galaxy, hinging on the fact that I got a dose of poison wrong.

Marchion and Faksir stayed like that for a bit, straining, struggling. Then the pressure on the blade became less, less.

"Thank you, Faksir," Marchion said. "You're a wonderful listener. I appreciate the advice."

A little *hkkt* noise, a judder, and Faksir's body relaxed. Marchion reached forward, supporting him as he slumped, the blade slipping from his hands to clatter on the floor. Faksir's eyes clouded, the stalks going limp, and he issued a final sighing breath.

Marchion let the She'ar's body slide to the table.

He felt nothing. No emotional spike whatsoever. Killing Faksir wasn't enough of a hit. He'd known it wouldn't be from the start—but you had to do *something.* What he actually needed was a Jedi to kill, or another

Starlight Beacon. But those were in short supply—and he'd already killed a Grand Master of the Jedi Council, Pra-Tre Veter. Was there a point where even killing Jedi would leave him cold?

Marchion took a cloth from the table and wiped Faksir's blood from his face, taking care not to taste it—though he wanted to. He had an antidote for the poison he'd used, but better not to need it.

At the edge of his vision, Shalla was staring at him, a smile on her ghastly face. A second figure emerged from the shadows, the blood on his chest from his cut throat looking black in the dim light. His father, Asgar. Marchion ignored the shades. They meant nothing.

Instead, he considered the Jedi. He'd always found them to be somewhat simple in their strategies and tactics. Their strength lay in their single-mindedness, their oaths—and of course their mastery of the Force. It was difficult to get a handle on their limits. Just when you thought you'd seen everything they could do, they pulled out some new trick.

"They captured Nameless but didn't kill them," Marchion said aloud, revisiting a line of reasoning he hadn't been able to discard. "Why? To study them, to learn more about how to defeat them, or protect themselves?"

Perhaps. But the reports his spies had sent were clear—the Jedi had captured at least a dozen, perhaps more.

"Why so many?" he said.

Asgar and Shalla moved closer, not walking but flickering through the shadows in an obscene parody of life. Marchion refused to look at them.

If the Jedi were using their newly acquired Nameless as experimental subjects, one or two would be enough. The Order didn't need to capture a dozen, especially considering the havoc even a single Nameless could wreak in their ranks. Taking that many was a dangerous, illogical choice—which was something the Jedi did not do. They were overconfident, sure of their own superiority, but there was always rationality to the things they did.

"Why so many?" Marchion said as his ancestors watched him.

He thought, listening to Faksir's strange blood drip off the table and splash against the floor. Drip. Drip. Drip.

"Because they know what the Nameless mean," Marchion realized, a coldness creeping up his spine. "They've come to the same understanding I have. The Nameless and the Blight . . . they're the same."

Drip.

"Each Nameless is important. Crucial."

Drip.

"They figured out the truth, and then they saved as many as they could."

Drip.

"I know what they're going to do with them. There's no other conclusion. They're taking them home."

He looked up. Shalla and Asgar were centimeters from him, bent at the waist, their eyes boring into his.

"Well," Marchion said to them. "If they have a dozen, I have a dozen dozen. And what do Nameless do? They *kill Jedi.*"

He lifted his goblet, drained it, poured himself another. His blood was up.

"They'll have sent their best. No one else would be trusted with a mission like this."

Marchion could see it already. How many would there be? How many Jedi could he . . . control . . . at once? That would feel good. That would give him what he needed.

And after that . . . there would be more good feelings to come.

Both ghosts smiled at precisely the same moment, in precisely the same way.

"Faksir," Marchion ordered, "set a course for—"

Drip.

Marchion Ro set the course himself, using one of the oldest Paths in the *Gaze Electric*'s database. The great ship leapt away.

Chapter Eight

THE *ATARAXIA*

"Have you ever seen hyperspace look like this?" Elzar Mann said.

"No. It's like a . . . like a waterfall of gems," Avar Kriss responded, looking out through the transparisteel cockpit at the swirling, changing, glowing medium the *Ataraxia* found itself traveling through.

Avar smiled, delighted. Elzar watched the way the colors played on her face, reflected off the diadem perched on her forehead.

"Do you think there's a problem?" Elzar asked, pulling his gaze to the instrument panel. "The readouts look good."

As far as the ship's sensors were concerned, the *Ataraxia* might as well be traveling the Corellian Run, as safe as any ship using the well-mapped superlane that connected Coruscant to Lamaredd and all points between. He had the pilot's seat, and Avar was to his left at the copilot's station, but for the moment there wasn't much to do. Until they arrived at their destination, it was peace, quiet, and the lights.

"The route we're traveling was given to Vernestra by Mari San Tekka—the same source as the Nihil's Paths," Avar said. "Those were roads inside roads. Hidden ways. Hyperspace looks different when you're using a Path,

STAR WARS: TRIALS OF THE JEDI   119

and it makes sense that this does, too. If you walk on a trail through a jungle, you see very different things than if you walk through the jungle itself."

"Mm. Like all the things that want to eat you, for instance."

"Plenty of those aboard this ship," Avar said.

"Sure are," Elzar said. "Speaking of the ravening beasts just a few decks below us, it's interesting that the only designation we have for their home-world is the name the old prospectors used for it: Planet X."

Avar didn't respond.

"Because that's not an actual name," he went on.

He glanced at her. Avar was looking right at him, her expression decid-edly neutral.

"Which is interesting because the species that comes from there is called the Nameless," he finished.

"Ah," Avar said, rolling her eyes and turning back to her monitors. "Good one."

"You know what, Avar Kriss, you actually *do* think that was a good one, and the reason I know is because I can sense your great amusement, which I am able to do, in short, because the Force is with me."

"What can you sense now, Elzar Mann?" Avar said.

Elzar reached out through the Force toward Avar Kriss, always easy, and sensed . . .

Ah, he thought.

"You too, huh?" he said.

"I've been trained my entire life to put aside attachment, to bring my focus to wherever it's needed. To let the Song guide me. I can balance on one fingertip in a hurricane. Well, probably—I've never tried—but I bet I could do it."

Avar was talking fast. She sounded exasperated, frustrated.

"The stakes could not be higher," she said. "There are only nine of us on this ship, and we all have a role to play. If we fail, there might not be a second chance. I should be putting all my concentration into the mission, not . . . daydreaming, remembering."

Elzar reached over, placed his hand over hers.

"Avar, listen to me. Yoda knows we've been, ah, together. If he thought we couldn't see this mission through, he wouldn't have sent us—or he'd have split us up and put one of us on the second team. You're brilliant, but if you're trying to tell me you're wiser than Grand Master Yoda . . . well, relax. You're not—and that's probably a good thing. It's Yoda's job to be wise. It's our job to be an inspiration to our fellow Jedi."

Avar rolled her eyes again and muttered something under her breath.

"Second," Elzar continued, "we're in hyperspace. The Nameless are secure. There is literally nothing to do until we get to their homeworld. We should be using this time to gather our energy for what's to come. To me, it's a good thing that we have these feelings and memories running through our minds. That's what we should be thinking about right now. We're like batteries, building up a charge."

"We're not batteries, Elzar."

Elzar ignored this, just kept talking. "You know things could get wild down on that planet," he said. "Deadly. Terrifying. If that's how it goes, what will keep us fighting, ready to do whatever we must to save the galaxy and everyone in it?" He leaned toward her. "Remembering the light. Which for me means Avar Kriss."

Color rose in her cheeks. "I know you're right," Avar said. "I just cannot fail. I *cannot*."

"Avar Kriss is a hero," Elzar said. "No matter what it costs her."

"She tries to be," Avar said.

"Well, here, right now, in this cockpit, you're just that same fumbling Padawan I met so long ago in the Jedi Temple."

"You were the fumbling Padawan, Elzar. Believe me."

"Actually, I think it was—"

"Stellan," Avar finished.

They both laughed, and Elzar was struck by what that meant. So much had been processed, so much had been understood. Stellan Gios was lost. The three Firebrands could never be again together the way they once

STAR WARS: TRIALS OF THE JEDI

had—but he was not gone, either. They'd just laughed at the thought of him.

Grief cannot exist without love, he thought. *We mourned Stellan because we loved him. But grief fades, while love does not.*

"You're remembering him," Avar said in that way she had of reading his mind that she swore she was never actually doing.

"Always," Elzar said. "I'm remembering him, but I'm thinking about you."

"What a coincidence," Avar said, watching him, colors shining in her eyes.

"There are no coincidences," Elzar said. "Only the will of the Force."

❁

"I'm going to the flight deck," Bell Zettifar said. "I want to see how long until we get to the Nameless homeworld, make sure we're on course."

He gestured out the nearest viewport, where brightly colored cascades shimmied past.

"It looks weird out there. Probably good to make sure everything's on track. You want to come, Burryaga?"

Burryaga and Bell were seated in one of the passenger areas aboard the *Ataraxia,* in a small lounge—four seats around a low table. Burryaga had found rations in the galley—he was very good at that—and had prepared a meal for himself of protein rods and various dried fruits and vegetables. It wasn't much more than a pile of dull-colored shapes on a plate, but Burryaga didn't seem bothered. It wasn't so much *what* the Wookiee ate as *that* he ate.

Burry shook his head, his mouth full of high-calorie, high-nutrient objects.

"Suit yourself," Bell said. "I'll be back in a few minutes."

Bell stood up, straightened the fit of his robes, taking a pleasurable moment to notice, once again, that his Padawan sash was gone.

Jedi Knight Bell Zettifar, he thought. *Never gets old.*

He could have been knighted almost two years before he actually was, but had consistently refused the Council's attempt to raise him up. The reason was no mystery to Bell or anyone who knew him. He couldn't bring himself to accept the honor after the death of his former master, the best Jedi he'd ever known, Loden Greatstorm. A Knight would have found a way to save Loden. Bell hadn't, and so he refused to become a Knight.

That's the way it had stayed, until another day when Bell had surged up from the depths of the ocean world of Eiram in a leaky submersible, Burryaga with him, rescued from a lonely death down in the crushing dark. Bell had brought his friend back when everyone else was certain he was dead. The Council offered him the chance at Knighthood again when he returned to Coruscant—him and Burry both—and this time he accepted.

Bell didn't think of it like a trade—his failure to save Loden wasn't canceled out or outweighed by the fact that he had saved Burryaga. Nothing so terrible and small. It was just . . .

Life is short, Bell thought. *Sometimes it's shorter than you think. Loden Greatstorm believed in me. He chose me as his Padawan, spent all that time training me to become a Knight. His teachings are the reason I was able to save Burryaga at all. Continuing to refuse Knighthood would have been the true failure.*

Bell patted Burryaga on the shoulder, then moved in the direction of the flight deck.

Or . . . he would have, if Burryaga hadn't stiffened suddenly and grabbed his arm, holding him in place.

Bell looked back. The huge, blond-furred Wookiee was one of the most emotionally sensitive beings in the entire Order. He'd used that ability to defeat Nameless, to intuit the path to holding back the Blight, and, more than anything else, to zero in on people who needed help but didn't know how to ask for it.

The point was, if Burryaga sensed something, you paid attention.

"What is it?" Bell said. "Something with the Nameless?"

Burry shook his head, tilting it slightly, squinting as if he was focusing, listening intently.

STAR WARS: TRIALS OF THE JEDI 123

The Wookiee's eyes widened, and he began the deep, repeated chuffing sound Bell knew was Burry's way of laughing—which turned into a choke as he promptly inhaled half a mouthful of chewed-up nutrient mush.

"Easy, pal," Bell said, slapping him on the back. "Just take it slow. You don't have to eat the whole blasted plate in two bites. That's like enough food for a week."

Burryaga made a mournful half retch, half whine, and then swallowed deeply with an audible glug.

"You all right?" Bell asked.

Burry nodded. He grinned.

"So what was that all about?"

The Wookiee gave a side-eyed glance toward the front of the ship, then looked back at Bell and growled and whooped out a sentence that . . .

That can't be right, Bell thought. *My Shyriiwook's gotten halfway decent, but there's no way he actually said what I think he did.*

"Did you just say . . ." Bell began, trying to think of how to finish. "Avar and Elzar?"

Burryaga nodded. He smiled, then turned back to his plate, apparently without a second thought.

"Huh," Bell said, his tone thoughtful. "Good for them."

He looked away from the cockpit door, scanning across the *Ataraxia's* passenger compartment. Torban Buck sat by himself, his eyes closed, either asleep or meditating. The younglings and Padawans called him Buckets of Blood, but Bell thought he seemed like the least warlike Jedi he knew.

A few rows back sat Terec, staring straight ahead, cybernetic implants blinking in their hairless, pale skull. Bell didn't know them well, certainly not as an individual. Terec and Ceret seemed like one person—he'd almost never seen either of the bond-twins apart. The tiniest touch of tension radiated from the Kotabi, though Bell didn't know its source. Not that there was any reason for any of the Nine to lack anxiety—they were transporting a ship full of Jedi-killing monsters to their home planet, where they fully intended to *release them.* Still, this felt different to Bell.

Whatever Terec was dealing with felt internal, something weighing on their spirit.

I'll ask Burryaga later, Bell thought. *Maybe there's something we can do.*

Farther back, speaking quietly to each other, were Reath Silas and Azlin Rell. Bell let himself . . . skate over that particular duo. It was still hard to process the reality that a fallen Jedi, a dark side adept, responsible for the death of thousands of people *that they knew of,* was just sitting there not ten meters away. Chatting.

I hope Reath has that guy under control, Bell thought. *I guess we need Azlin, or the Council wouldn't have sent him. But if he puts one step wrong . . .*

He noted that Azlin had not been supplied with a lightsaber. That was good, although Bell had studied dark side offensive techniques as a Padawan. He knew that other weapons were available to those who followed that path. If it came to it, Bell could handle those, too. If he had to.

Bell had been "handling" all sorts of things lately. He'd been taught as a Padawan that Jedi were not warriors and fought only as a last resort, to preserve life. Easy to say in a time of peace, easy to do. But this was not a time of peace, and Bell's views on the subject had evolved. For the last several months, he and Burryaga had been posted to the Stormwall frontier, assigned to rotations on RDC patrol vessels battling incursions by Nihil raiders into Republic space. He'd spent time with Coalition pilots and soldiers contributed to the cause by various RDC worlds—gotten to know them, their tools, psychology, the sacrifices they made. Soldiers swore an oath to protect, putting their own lives second to those without their training and dedication. Bell thought they were more like Jedi than many other people he'd met. It was an honor to work alongside them.

Not to mention, you got to kill Nihil, came the thought. *There was always a chance one of your patrols might run across Marchion Ro, and you'd get to kill him, too.*

Bell blinked. Burryaga paused with the last bite of food halfway to his mouth and slowly turned his head to look at him.

Where did that thought come from? Bell thought.

But he knew, and no amount of meditation or talks with Burryaga or counselors or his second master, Indeera Stokes, were addressing the problem. Just because you told yourself you'd released negative emotions didn't mean you actually had.

Why was Loden Greatstorm dead? The best Jedi Bell had ever known, and he wasn't dead because a Nameless killed him or because Bell had failed to save him. No, the true responsibility could be laid at the feet of one man: *Marchion Ro.*

The Eye of the Nihil had set the galaxy on a path to destruction that led in a straight line to Loden's death. The idea that Marchion Ro was still out there breathing and plotting and scheming and killing, living his life while Loden was dead . . . well, Bell Zettifar, Jedi Knight, found that rather difficult to stomach.

So, yes, Bell had allowed himself to be knighted, knowing it would let him volunteer for assignments to the frontier. Out there, every Nihil raider could be a momentary stand-in for the real quarry, a chance to temporarily satisfy Bell's desire to end Marchion Ro's reign . . . one way or the other.

It was not Jedi-like. It was the opposite. Attachment, born from anger and grief. It skirted the dark side. But Bell could not let it go.

At least I know what's going on with me, Bell thought. *It's not like I'm making these choices and I don't know why.*

Burryaga was staring at him.

I'm working on it, Burry, Bell thought. *I really am.*

Sometimes it wasn't always wonderful having a hyper-empathic Wookiee as your number one pal.

But usually it was.

"You want to check out the rest of the ship with me, Burry?" Bell asked. "I'd like to talk with everyone. Ty Yorrick in particular. I don't know her. She's not even a Jedi. Might be good to get a sense of what she's about if we'll be fighting beside her."

Burryaga growled out a response.

"Yes, I guess we don't know for sure we'll be fighting, Burry," Bell said. "But I'll bet you ten credits the sabers come out."

Burryaga sighed and pushed himself to his feet. They walked together toward the back of the compartment.

As they passed Torban Buck, Burry paused and put a hand on the Chagrian's broad blue shoulder. Buck opened his eyes, saw the Wookiee.

"Thanks, big guy," Torban said. "I'll be okay. Just processing. That business with Arkoff . . . nothing I haven't seen before, but still, a thing like that lingers. Ask any medic. You feel the same things anyone would at seeing pain and death—you just feel them later, after the job's done. I just need a little time."

Burryaga nodded, patting Buck's shoulder, and they moved on.

"Any news from Coruscant?" Bell asked as they approached Terec.

The Kotabi was still staring straight ahead, but now their yellow eyes shifted to look at Bell and Burry without their head moving at all. The effect was unsettling.

Then again, who knows how a human and a Wookiee come across to a Kotabi? Bell thought.

"My bond with Ceret is disrupted while we are in hyperspace, but nothing had changed on Coruscant up to the moment we departed," Terec said. "Another Blight spot was found on Levulia, though."

"Awful," Bell said. "I'm glad we were able to pull this mission together so quickly. We need to get this done."

"I agree with you," Terec said.

Their eyes slipped back so they were once again looking straight ahead. Bell thought about what they'd said, and wondered if it bothered Terec to be out of touch with their bond-twin while they were in hyperspace. Bell couldn't really imagine what that was like. Never being alone. Never *feeling* alone, and then suddenly, they were gone.

Bell and Burry moved on toward the row where Reath Silas and Azlin Rell had taken two seats next to each other.

"Hello," said Azlin Rell as they approached, in his surprisingly pleasant, wispy, seductive, pained voice.

The ancient man wore stained, once-white robes and strange round goggles with dark lenses that completely shrouded his eyes. He was human and inhuman, all at once.

Burryaga growled softly, deep in his throat.

Azlin smiled. Bell ignored him, focusing on Reath. The Jedi was a little younger than Bell, but they'd come up through much of their Padawan training together. Bell felt a little big-brotherly toward Reath and thought it was unfair so much weight had landed on him lately. Reath was bookish. He didn't always seem connected to the real world. Preferred the library to lightsabers.

And yet, the Council had selected him as the primary member of the Order to interact with a nearly two-hundred-year-old former Jedi who had embraced the dark side fully and completely. Bell knew the Council had its reasons, but he wished they had chosen an older, more experienced Jedi to work with Azlin Rell.

And then there was that armor test . . . Bell had heard about how that went. Sounded like Reath almost died.

It was no surprise the kid was looking a little drawn. It was too much to put on anyone, much less Reath Silas.

"You okay, Reath?" Bell said.

"I'm fine, Bell," Reath replied, and his voice did sound steady. "This mission is . . . well, it's a lot to think about. But I'm interested to see what Planet X will be like. I'm considering all this a chance to learn."

"It will certainly be that," Azlin said. "The home of the Nameless will teach us all a great many things."

"Uh-huh," Bell said.

He gestured to Reath's left.

"How are things going with the shield?" Bell asked, trying to engage him, distract him a little. "You figuring out how to use it?"

Reath turned to glance at the fascinating object propped up on the seat next to him. It was an ancient shield: round, basically a ring with a central bar running along its middle, made of some alloy Bell didn't recognize. When the shield was activated, its open spaces filled in with bright-blue plasma fields that could deflect blaster bolts, lightsaber blades, all kinds of attacks. Reath had found it somewhere—Bell didn't know the whole story—and now he trained with it all the time in the Temple. Jedi were set in their ways when it came to prioritizing the lightsaber, but a shield suited Reath, and Bell was glad he had it.

"It's coming along, I guess," Reath said. "I'm sorry, Bell—I'm just thinking about Arkoff. If I'd been able to figure out how to use the Rod of Ages, maybe he wouldn't have gotten hurt."

Burryaga growled in disagreement.

"I'm with Burry, Reath," Bell said. "That was no one's fault. You can't put that weight on yourself. Trying to use some strange artifact out of nowhere in the middle of a crisis like that—come on. No one could have done it."

"I could have," Azlin said. "What a shame I wasn't there."

All three Jedi turned to look at the old man, who was smiling serenely. He patted Reath lightly on the shoulder.

"Reath will be just fine," Azlin said. "Don't worry about Reath."

Bell ignored him and crouched to look the younger Jedi right in the eyes. "Listen, pal, this is a long flight. Try to get some time to yourself, know what I mean?"

Burryaga hooted in agreement, and after a short pause, Reath nodded.

"Okay," Bell said. "Have you seen Ty Yorrick around, by any chance?"

"I'm pretty sure she went down to the cargo deck," Reath replied.

"Great," Bell said, straightening. "Thank you. Remember, we're all in this together. You're not alone. If you need anything . . ."

His eyes flicked toward Azlin, whose smile broadened.

"Just give a shout."

"I'm fine, Bell," Reath said again. "But thank you. Very much."

Burryaga mewled quietly, clearly no happier to be near Azlin than Bell was.

STAR WARS: TRIALS OF THE JEDI 129

"Thank you, too, Burry. Thank you both," Reath said, watching the two Jedi amble away toward the *Ataraxia*'s aft, where the lift to the cargo deck was located.

Their easy camaraderie was clear, their obvious rapport. Their body language said, *I've got your back, no matter what comes.*

Bell and Burryaga get to have that, Reath thought.

He turned to look at the man sitting next to him, still smiling, staring at him through those thin-slitted goggles he wore.

I get this.

Azlin Rell had long, greasy hair that fell past his shoulders from a sharp widow's peak. Azlin was old, so old, but the hair was still dark like an oil slick. Reath assumed it had stained the seat's headrest—but he didn't want to look.

"Those two are good boys," Azlin said.

Reath had spent more time with Azlin Rell than almost anyone in the Order—only Yoda had more interactions with him. And Arkoff, Reath supposed—Azlin's former master in the long-ago, impossible-to-visualize time when the ancient man was a Padawan.

Arkoff would have been so helpful on the mission—a second person who knew what it was like to deal with Azlin's . . . peculiarities. But Arkoff was back on Coruscant, missing a leg. It all fell to Reath. Again.

Reath suspected he was one of only a few people Azlin had spoken to at any length in the past century and a half. Their conversations down in his cell in the Temple's detention level had ranged far and wide—they'd discussed the dark side, the light, the Nameless and Azlin's constant, all-consuming fear of them. The horrible things the former Jedi claimed he had done to protect the Order from the creatures.

Azlin was corrupted, his soul decayed. But was he evil? Reath was unsure of the point where delusion ended and evil began. The old man had *done* evil things in the name of his crusade to rid the galaxy of the Nameless, certainly. But Azlin didn't see them as evil, just . . . necessary.

Azlin Rell believed the dark side was an acceptable solution to a problem like the Nameless—had even tried to seduce Reath to the dark side during their interview sessions, to join him in the fight. Reath hadn't realized what was happening until it was almost too late. But he had, and had stepped back to the light.

Despite that, Reath felt no anger or fear toward Rell. No, the primary emotion he felt . . .

Was pity.

The thought of so many years just *lost,* just swept up in horror, so much that it was impossible to see the reality of your own actions . . . it was so sad. Azlin Rell was once a Jedi Knight, with all the training, all the vows, all the dedication to the light of any other. And now just this shell, withered away.

And yet, the Jedi needed Azlin Rell. He had shown them where to find the Tolisian ore that became the central component in the armor that protected them from the Nameless. His theories had helped prove the connection between the Blight and the Nameless, and they had allowed the Council to devise the plan that could, the light willing, save the galaxy from the Blight. The man was an endless wellspring of obscure knowledge, even if he was judicious about what he chose to share. Azlin would no doubt be incredibly useful on the Nameless homeworld itself, assuming he didn't just collapse in terror once they arrived.

"Do you think you will renounce the dark side once the Nameless are returned to their homeworld and balance is restored?" Reath asked. "After all, you won't need to be afraid anymore."

This was not an idle question. In some ways, Reath felt he and the old man were very similar. Azlin had spent his entire long life seeking understanding, finding hidden information, things others had forgotten. If things ever calmed down—and if the galaxy continued to exist, of course—that was the life Reath wanted for himself. He could still learn many things from Azlin, but that would only come to pass if the old man renounced the dark. If not, their time together would eventually come to an end. The Council would see to it.

STAR WARS: TRIALS OF THE JEDI   131

Azlin Rell let out a long, slow sigh. Reath could smell his breath. Not unpleasant—like the smell of winter dirt.

"The Order didn't capture all of the Nameless that were removed from their homeworld," Azlin said. "The hunts gathered only a dozen. Marchion Ro still has his. Assuming we find a solution to the Blight on the Nameless world, the Nihil's herd will still be out there. We must find them as well, and then kill the Eye so he will never steal more. If we don't, this will never be over, at least not for me."

He ran a hand down his cheek, his long, hooked nail rasping against wiry stubble.

"But let us say all those problems were solved, Reath. Would I renounce the dark side? It's impossible for me to know. My life has been defined by this fear, this problem, for a century and a half. My soul is in eclipse."

The old man reached up to his face, touching his goggles.

"The question isn't *Will I return to the light,* boy. It is *Will the darkness ever let me go?*"

Azlin's fingers curled around the stems of his goggles.

No, Reath thought, knowing what was coming. *Don't do it. Not again.*

"I'm afraid of everything," Azlin said. "I'm even afraid of the dark side itself. I only use it to help me find a way to destroy the Nameless. But I do . . . occasionally . . . consider what it could give me if I truly opened myself to its power."

Azlin pulled the goggles from his face with the awful *shplick* sound that came when the neural access spikes slid out from the ports in his temples. Where his eyes should be were just voids, empty sockets falling away into darkness, cavernous, shadowy pits.

"I suppose the dark side could return my eyes to me. My youth, my strength. I don't want power, Reath, or to control things." Azlin's head slumped back. He let the goggles drop to his lap. "I just want what the Nameless took from me."

Ty Yorrick stood in the *Ataraxia*'s cargo hold, studying the Nameless in their containment pen. She had her armor on, including the mask. She needed to see these animals up close and not through a video feed. This wasn't her first encounter with them, but the ones she'd faced before were clouded by the strange effect they generated—not to mention her own terror, as much as she'd tried to hold it back.

Now for the first time, she saw the Nameless as animals, not nightmares.

The beasts were mostly still, crouched down into ungainly piles of bony limbs and translucent flesh speckled with weeping sores. They seemed pathetic, nothing she should fear—but as was the case with many wild animals, appearances meant little. The tiniest insect could carry enough venom to kill a village. An ungainly, top-heavy herbivore could move with shocking speed, using its bulk to crush any perceived threats.

Ty knew what one of the Nameless had done to Reath Silas when he tried to use the Force to connect with it, not to mention what happened to Arkoff when he took one on, and of course the list of Jedi they had killed was horrifyingly long. The Nameless were dangerous, there was no question.

But animals were never dangerous for no reason. In Ty's experience, those reasons included hunger, fear, illness, or a desire to protect their young or their hunting grounds. That was pretty much it.

People often assigned motives to beasts beyond those simple imperatives. They decided a certain animal was evil because it was ugly, or had sharp teeth, or carried poison in its body. People labeled animals as monsters. They weren't. Sentient beings had motives, made decisions—animals did not.

Ty Yorrick had encountered monsters of every type, sentient and otherwise. Only people could be evil.

Which isn't to say these particular beasties can't get up to some nasty business, she thought, watching the twelve Nameless stare balefully at her through the energy wall of their containment chamber.

She moved closer to the glowing green wall. One of the Nameless

STAR WARS: TRIALS OF THE JEDI

wicked a long-clawed limb against it, causing sparks and sizzles. If not for the barrier, Ty's throat would now be a yawning, spurting hole.

"Easy, buddy, easy. I'm just curious. What are you when you aren't under these pressures?" she asked the animal. "When you're safe at home, raising your young, plenty of whatever food you like ... what are you then? That's who I'd like to meet."

The Nameless didn't respond. Not surprising.

Ty couldn't get inside these creatures' heads. Even with everything the Force gave her, the Nameless were a wall of need and pain she couldn't break through. She knew the Jedi expected her to help control the Nameless once they arrived at their homeworld. She had no idea if she'd be any help at all. The Nameless were a challenge like none she'd ever experienced.

"What do you want?" she asked the Nameless. "The Force? Do you really eat the Force?"

Ty had done her homework, reading through every bit of research the Jedi had compiled on the Nameless. The documentation was inconclusive on the question of whether the creatures actually consumed the Force. It wasn't useless against them—you could throw them back with it, for instance. If the Nameless ate the Force, you'd think that wouldn't work. Then again, the Order had retrieved the corpses of Jedi the Nameless had killed, and those did seem to be removed from their connection to the Force. The crumbling gray bodies were voids, their lives stolen in the most profound way.

"I don't know how I'll handle you once we get to your homeworld, my friends," Ty said. "But I can tell you this much—"

She lifted a finger to point at the closest Nameless.

"You don't want to give me any trouble."

The Nameless didn't respond.

Ty Yorrick earned her credits when people hired her to deal with creatures that posed a threat to settlements and the like. In that work, she did her best to find solutions that didn't involve killing the beasts. She saw herself almost as a detective, working to find and remove whatever pressure had caused the beasts to become dangerous. Destruction was a last resort—but it was one of the options. Sometimes it was the only option.

Killing a Nameless, though . . . was *that* on the table? The scattered mission briefing the Nine had received before they left Coruscant had made it clear that dire consequences would result if more Nameless died. Still, Ty considered her own death to be a pretty dire consequence in its own right.

She figured she'd make the right decisions in the moment. She usually did. She was a creature in her own way—instinct, reaction. She could leave the heavy thinking to the Jedi.

They'll have it locked down, she thought. *Avar Kriss seems like the locked-down type. Except with Elzar, maybe. Who do they think they're kidding?*

Ty shook her head. The Order's antipathy toward physical entanglements was another reason she'd left the Jedi. Nothing like a good tumble after dealing with a rockhorn stampede headed straight for a settlement, or hunting down an abraxas spider that had stolen away a family to fill out its larder.

She pulled her focus back to the problem in front of her. She'd come down here to learn more about these creatures before she was expected to wrangle them on an unknown planet, and there was really just one good way to do that.

Ty put her hands on the sides of her helmet and took a long breath.

Here goes nothing, she thought.

She lifted the helmet. Immediately, a concentration-blasting wave of sensation washed over her from the direction of the Nameless's enclosure. The beasts seemed to shimmer slightly, their forms becoming less distinct.

Interesting, she thought. *I wonder how long I'll be able to maintain my focus if I lose more of the armor.*

She reached to her waist and unbuckled first one tasset, then the other, letting them fall to the deck with a clang.

The Nameless effect intensified. The creatures wobbled, swelled, becoming grotesque inversions of their original forms.

STAR WARS: TRIALS OF THE JEDI

"Whoa," Ty said, her head swimming, her gorge rising. "This is . . . potent."

She'd never faced this many Nameless at once. No one had.

"Pull it together, Ty Yorrick," she chided herself, feeling fear grow inside her.

Ty focused on the animal nearest to her, the one that had slashed its claw against the cell. She reached out through the Force, knowing she was doing exactly what that kid Reath had done, knowing it was foolish, knowing her judgment was impaired, but doing it anyway.

I'm sure I'm better than Reath, she thought. *I do this for a living. I better be.*

"Who are you?" she hissed, searching for the core of this creature, the truth behind the pain and madness. "Nothing is pure savagery. There is always a reason."

She pushed, and the Nameless reared up, slashing its talons against the energy wall.

It's hurting itself, Ty thought, but she did not stop.

Something, hiding behind the rage . . . she could sense it.

Almost . . . there, she thought, sweat running down her forehead.

The Nameless surged and raged. It would smash itself to bits just for the chance to tear her apart, drink deep. Ty knew this through the Force, down to her core. She was *communicating* with the creature, and all it said was *rage,* and *pain,* and *hunger.*

But behind it, she saw . . . a place, a structure in the dark, itself made of the dark. Tall, beautiful figures stood arranged around something bright . . . something . . .

Ty felt veins pulsing in her forehead. Her eyes bulged.

Stop . . . stop! she thought, and then realized she wasn't thinking it, she was hearing it. Arms grasped her around the waist, large, hairy arms as strong as durasteel. They lifted, and she was pulled bodily from the containment cell chamber, despite her thrashing and kicking in an eerie echo of what the Nameless was doing.

Outside, she was released and fell to the ground, the fog slowly lifting.

"What were you *doing?*" a voice said.

She looked up and saw the Jedi whose name she couldn't remember, the dark-skinned human with close-cropped hair. He was standing next to the Wookiee Jedi whose name she also couldn't remember, the one who didn't get his leg eaten back in the Jedi Temple hangar. Buggyuggy or something like that.

"My job," Ty muttered, shaking her head to clear it.

"Either you were going to get killed or you were going to kill one of the Nameless," the human said, anger slipping into his voice. "Neither of those things can happen."

The Wookiee hooted, and Ty translated without thinking. *Don't be too hard on her, Bell. She's pretty shaken up.*

"Whatever, Buggy," Ty muttered. "I don't need you to fight my battles."

The Wookiee rumbled at her, sounding surprised.

"I don't just understand Shyriiwook, I speak it," she replied in the same tongue. "I'm very good at what I do."

"Let's hope so," the human said. "We'll need it."

He extended a hand to help her up.

"I'm Bell Zettifar, and this is Burryaga, not Buggy. Look, Ty, I know you walk a different path than we Jedi, but as long as you're with us, be *with us,* all right? We're not so bad, I promise."

Ty thought about it for a moment, but then she took his hand and let him pull her to her feet. As she did, the ship shuddered with the familiar feeling of a vessel dropping out of hyperspace.

A voice sounded over the *Ataraxia*'s intercom, and all three of them looked up.

"We have arrived," came Avar Kriss's voice. "We're at the disturbance surrounding the Nameless homeworld, the barrier known as the Veil. It's time to prep the landing shuttle to bring the Nameless down to the surface. Everything we're seeing suggests this will be a very bumpy ride. You all have your assigned tasks. Get ready."

STAR WARS: TRIALS OF THE JEDI

Avar Kriss thumbed off the communications system. She and Elzar Mann sat silently, looking out at the Veil.

"Bumpy ride," Elzar said. "That's an understatement."

"The records the Council shared with us really didn't do this justice, did they?"

"Nope."

The Veil was as ugly as the hyperspace route they'd traveled to get there was beautiful. It was a grinding, chewing sphere of vortexes and lightning strikes and zones of magnetic disturbance surrounding the planet. It looked like it had teeth. It looked like if you could hear it, it would be screaming with raw hunger. Screaming your name.

"We're supposed to take a shuttle through this?" Avar mused.

"We have the data," Elzar said. "Supposedly there's a way through. Others have done it."

"Well, good for them," Avar said.

They looked out at the maelstrom. Avar took a deep breath and set her hands on the ship's controls.

"You can do this," Elzar said. "Remember the light."

Avar looked at Elzar.

"I am," she said.

Outside the ship, the Veil screamed their names.

Chapter Nine

THE BATTLE OF ERIADU

A lot can happen *in a few hours,* thought Sevran Tarkin.

She stood in a hardened command bunker built into the mountains north of Eriadu City, an old place, a hidden fortress called the Raven's Peak. Her gaze flickered across tactical displays depicting the attempt to retake her planet from the Nihil.

The holos told a grim story. The Nihil did not care about the planet's people or anything upon it. They cared about control and terror, and had chosen fire as their tool. Great swaths of Eriadu City and other cities around the planet were burning. Sevran could appreciate the tactic even as she was horrified by its impact. Fire created confusion, and barriers for enemy infantry, and diversions of Eriaduan forces as they tried to extinguish the blazes to save civilian lives.

A surveillance droid stationed above Eriadu City's central hub relayed the progress of the fires in real time, sending them to the bunker's displays. Many of the planet's most venerable buildings and institutions were located in the city center, and the Nihil clearly knew it. The Grand Museum was a white-hot pillar of flame. Sevran watched it burn, thinking of everything kept inside the structure, including important artifacts

STAR WARS: TRIALS OF THE JEDI   139

from her own family's history. They and anyone caught in that building when the blaze went up—and the building itself—would soon be nothing but ash.

A timer ticked over on one of the displays, marking another hour since the battle for Eriadu had begun. More or less. The exact timing was imprecise—fighting had broken out in a number of places more or less simultaneously; Sevran didn't yet have full intelligence on how or why. In any case, it was mere hours since the hidden RDC forces poured from the mines and the remains of Eriadu's military began to execute the battle plan to retake their planet.

The Nihil had responded with utter savagery. Reports were pouring in from across the planet: attacks on infrastructure, from power plants to water purification. Chemical and biological weapons. Hostage taking. Desecration of corpses. The Nihil used tactics that Eriaduan and RDC forces would not even contemplate. Anything to kill or demoralize their enemy, they would do.

The brutality sent a clear message: Submit or watch everything you know and love be destroyed.

The Raven's Peak was full of military officers and representatives from the Quintad—the five ruling families of Eriadu, including Sevran's own. Since the start of hostilities, the bunker had become a well-organized hive designed to win an ongoing planetary battle. Each family had its own responsibility within the fight—ground battles, air attack, logistical support, evacuations, and so on.

Sevran held high command. Her job was the big picture. She was the only person in the bunker focused on what was happening in the battle as a whole—or perhaps the only one acknowledging the truth.

They were losing.

Originally, the plan was to push the Nihil off the surface, force them to take to their ships and retreat to orbit until their inevitable reinforcements arrived. In that brief interlude, the Eriaduan and RDC resistance fighters would re-commandeer and bring online the substantial planetary defense installations built since the Great Disaster. Those had been overwhelmed during the Nihil's initial invasion—a surprise attack that used long-range ion bombs to knock the defense grid offline. But the Nihil themselves had upgraded and hardened those defenses during their occupation. If Eriadu could regain control of the gigantic cannons, surface-to-orbit artillery, and shield generators, they could hold the planet indefinitely, even against a substantial Nihil fleet.

But Eriadu had *not* regained control. Every defense emplacement remained in Nihil hands—the enemy knew the importance of those locations as well as the Eriaduans did. They were dug in deep, and thus far could not be dislodged.

Sevran watched her world burn, desperate to take any action at all. Anything not to feel utterly helpless. Anything to fight back.

She pressed a control on her command console and spoke into a slim chrome microphone, sending her voice to the comms of all Eriaduan forces across the planet.

"This is Commander Sevran Tarkin. Eriadu belongs to us. This ground, the land. We have watered it with our blood for a hundred generations. It will always be ours. Nothing the Nihil do can destroy it. Do not lose heart at the dishonorable tactics these monsters use. Once they are gone—and they will be gone—we can rebuild. The land is all that matters, and that . . . is *eternal.*

"Take your revenge for all they have done to us. Show them how foolish they were to come to Eriadu. We are warriors. They are crawling insects. Burn them, kill them, bleed them.

"Eriadu is *our world.*

"Take it back."

She keyed off her communications system, not knowing who would listen or if it would do any good. But she was the leader. It was her job to lead.

"I need an assessment," she called to her aide, one of her distant cousins.

That capable young man quickly gathered the various battle commanders: an Eriaduan general and an admiral in charge of the native

STAR WARS: TRIALS OF THE JEDI 141

ground, air, and starship forces, and a colonel who commanded the RDC assets that had bunkered on the planet.

"All of this," Sevran said, gesturing at the battle displays, "tells me our masterstroke surprise attack has achieved essentially zero."

"Correct," said General Atreon Hazzo, a no-nonsense, thick-necked man with close-shaven white hair. "The Nihil's strategic approach does not rely on . . . coordinated maneuvers. We believe there is some sort of central command, but the Nihil cells are empowered to make whatever decisions they need to in the moment."

"Mostly, that seems to mean utter destruction," said the admiral— Mysteen Tena, whip-thin and withered, a stiletto of a woman. "We hold the airspace—for now. Our pilots are better trained and got into the sky while the Nihil only had a few light patrols in place. The problem is the ground battle. The Nihil are dug in, holing up in places like schools and hospitals, using local citizens as shields. To reach them, we'd have to execute a heavy bombing pattern that would destroy much of the territory we hope to regain, as well as kill our own troops and civilians."

For several long moments, no one spoke.

The RDC colonel cleared his throat. He was a handsome younger man named Frent. Sevran had initially considered him to be a bit soft by Eriaduan standards, but the officer had proven to have an astute tactical mind.

"I've been fighting the Nihil in various engagements for over a year—in space, on the ground, in atmosphere," Frent said. "This is business as usual for them. We were hoping for a rout, that they'd flee . . . they haven't. They're showing more resolve than we expected. There's only one reason for that."

"They're expecting reinforcements," Sevran said.

"Agreed," said the colonel. "They must have already received word that additional Nihil are on the way. I'm sure the call was sent as soon as we revealed our attack force."

His eyes flicked to the timer, back to Sevran.

"We're running out of time."

"Obviously," she said.

Sevran pointed at a slowly rotating holo displaying the entire planet, rendered in bright green. Five stars were visible on the globe, distributed evenly, placed at strategically advantageous spots. These were the primary planetary defense emplacements. All were displayed in red, with readouts next to them indicating they were offline, in enemy hands.

"We need those defense bunkers, and we need them now," she said. "Everything else is secondary. Even one would be significant, to buy us time to take back the others. Give me ideas."

Her three commanders stood silent, their eyes taking in the data, trying to find a workable strategy.

"A small team," Admiral Tena said. "Two, maybe three. Highly skilled, able to handle threats significantly larger than their numbers would suggest. They could navigate the obstacles the Nihil have placed in the way, access the bunker, and—"

"Jedi," Sevran said. "You're talking about Jedi."

"There are some on world. A number of Jedi arrived on Eriadu just prior to the Stormwall's last expansion for a personal matter—a wedding in Bri-Phrang."

"Jedi get married?" General Hazzo blurted out.

"Unclear, and not relevant," Frent said. "The point is, there are something between six and twelve Jedi on the planet. They reached out to us when hostilities began. They were planning to assist with local resistance efforts but said they would make themselves available to us if need be."

Sevran studied the map of defense emplacements. She stabbed a finger through the hologram at one of the locations, built in an industrial neighborhood on the outskirts of Eriadu City.

"This one," she said.

She looked at the three commanders, all waiting to see what she would tell them to do.

"These are my orders. Colonel Frent, coordinate with the Jedi. Ask them to provide two of their number for a mission at my particular request. General Hazzo, they'll need a local guide. Find me a commando, someone who knows the area, someone deadly, who can get them to the defense station. Admiral Tena, I'll rely on you to use your air assets to deliver the team to the target."

The officers nodded, acknowledging the orders. The objective was clear.

"Unless you have an objection, Madam Tarkin," said General Hazzo, "I'd like to send your brother with the Jedi."

"Navaj?" Sevran responded, considering the idea.

"Exactly. He's got the skills you described and then some. In my opinion, he's wasted on general infantry operations."

"Agreed," Sevran said.

The Tarkins should be on the front lines, she thought. *That's why we're Tarkins.*

"Colonel Frent—one final word," Sevran said, turning to the RDC officer. "Make it clear to the Jedi that this is no time for caution, recriminations, trying to reform the enemy, trying to wound instead of kill, for light and life or any of their more *peaceful* inclinations. This is war. The Nihil are murdering innocents like they are threshing grain. They have forfeited their right to consideration. *We* are all the Republic. The Nihil have made it clear that they are not."

"Acknowledged," Frent said. "For what it's worth, I agree completely. I'll make sure the Jedi understand the gravity of the situation."

"See that they do," Sevran said.

Her eyes flickered to the timer. Every second was a second lost. Every second brought doom closer.

Hurry, she thought.

※

Major Pargo Coffin of the Nihil Irregulars, part of the Occlusion Zone Occupying Force placed on Eriadu, was bored. He sat in the control room of a huge planetary defense station on the outskirts of Eriadu City, waiting for something to happen.

Something *was* happening, that was clear—explosions and blasterfire were faintly audible through the many-meters-thick walls of the defense bunker—but that was far away. Down here, it was quiet.

He was part of a three-person crew assigned to this mission, not that there was anything for any of them to do. One of them, a Weequay named Bogard, called over from his own station, where he sat wearing a headset crammed onto his bizarre gourd of a skull.

"Still no word, Major," Bogard said.

"I told you, just call me Coffin," Coffin said. "You've known me a long time. Just Coffin. None of the fancy stuff."

"Uh-huh," Bogard said.

He just does it to tick me off, Coffin thought. *The ugly little toenail.*

The other man did sort of look like a toenail. An old, yellow, snaggly one, cracked and curling over and ugly as, well, a toenail. And now the toenail was grinning.

Yeah, he calls me Major because he knows I don't like it. Keep it up, toenail. We'll see how it goes for you. Why, I could open the bunker doors right now and kick you out into that bloodgrinder outside—see if you feel like smiling then.

Coffin could almost see himself doing it. The door controls were no more than two meters away. He'd enter the access code, slam the big red button, wait for the huge magnetic locks to pull back and the blast doors to slide aside, and then he could haul Bogard out and toss the insubordinate bastard to the maniacs outside.

Eriaduans. Coffin shuddered. What were the Nihil thinking, coming to this world?

Yeah, the Nihil laid claim to everything in the Occlusion Zone, sure, and that meant this planet, too . . . but the people of Eriadu were scary. They had this whole hunter/warrior thing going on. Took themselves very seriously. Very quick to pull out a knife.

Not that Coffin wasn't. That's part of how he'd risen to the rank of Storm back when there were still Tempests. Back in the good old days. Now he was a major, the rank assigned to him when General Viess reorganized the Nihil fighters into what she considered a proper military.

STAR WARS: TRIALS OF THE JEDI   145

Coffin was good with a blade, sure. But it was one thing to stab someone and another thing entirely to *get* stabbed. Walking around Eriadu City, it felt like all any of the locals were thinking about was sticking a knife into you. It grated, after a while.

And now here he was stuck in this bunker, defending it from stab-happy fanatics, with only Bogard the Toenail and Gilch for company. Gilch was a short-statured Dug who almost never said a blasted word, just sat there in the corner. Her only contribution to the bunker's conversation was letting out a foul odor from time to time, and it was hard to tell which of the little lady's many openings it was from. Bogard, on the other hand, talked plenty but never had anything particularly interesting or pleasant to say.

Getting so damn stuffy *in here,* Coffin thought.

Coffin thought about opening the bunker door again—not necessarily because of Bogard, but because some fresh air sounded awfully nice and, more than that, because it was a choice he could make all on his own. No waiting for orders, just doing what he wanted to do when he wanted.

That's how the Nihil used to be, he reflected. *Free. Free and easy.*

Coffin sighed. He glanced over the few flickering displays running at his own terminal. Bogard had managed to slice them up some power, which was how they were staying apprised of the way the battle was going outside. So far, it seemed like it was going pretty well.

You could give the Nihil fancy titles, try to domesticate them into a proper society all you wanted, but on some level they'd always be a bunch of metal-chewing freaks. Coffin's friends and colleagues were out there burning, slashing, poisoning, toxifying, and wrecking everything and everyone they could. Teaching this planet a lesson.

Part of Coffin was sorry to be missing the fun, but on the whole, he was happy to be safe and sound, locked away in the bunker. Sure, the Nihil were out there causing chaos, but the Eriaduans had durasteel in their veins, and they didn't forget or forgive. He had a feeling plenty of Nihil were getting theirs, too.

But at the same time, it would *be fun . . .* he thought. *Maybe I'll order the team here to gear up and head out. We can cause a little ruckus and get back in here. No one the wiser.*

Then again . . . he'd heard rumors there were Jedi on the planet. That wasn't substantiated—just a few transmissions out of Bri-Phrang, that ratty little city across the bay—but enough to give him pause. He'd rather fight ten Eriaduans than a single Jedi.

Why didn't the bosses give us one of those Jedi-killer creatures? he thought. *The ones Marchion Ro uses.*

Now, *those* were something special. Whatever they were, wherever the Eye of the Nihil had found them . . . Coffin had never seen one up close, but he'd met a few folks who had. They sounded amazing. Razor-mouthed killers. The spirit of the Nihil made flesh.

But honestly, even if they did encounter a Jedi when they went outside, would they even need one of Marchion's Jedi killers? Maybe not. Coffin was a veteran. So were Bogard and Gilch. They'd fought together at Valo. Now, that was a good time. Jedi were all over the place on Valo, but the three of them had made it through all right.

"Why should *we* be afraid?" Coffin muttered. "We're the terror. We're the masked death. We're the Storm."

"Eh?" Bogard said. "What's that, Major?"

"Get your gear together," Coffin said. "Both of you."

"Feelin' pretty comfortable in here," Gilch said, or rather croaked.

"Don't care. I'm the boss. We're going outside to get some of the action. You want all the fighting to be over before we get our piece?"

"But our orders were—" Bogard began.

"You see anyone here with higher authority than me?" Coffin shouted. "I give the orders."

He pulled out his blaster. He didn't point it at anyone, but it was pretty clear that he could if he wanted to.

"Now get yourselves ready," Coffin said, lowering his voice a bit, returning to a dignified, commanding kind of tone. "I want to go out there, so that's what I'm going to do."

I want to open the bunker door, he realized.

STAR WARS: TRIALS OF THE JEDI   147

He really, truly did.

Coffin quickly tapped in the security code and, ignoring the imprecations from his subordinates, slapped the big red button that initiated the exit procedure.

A softly chiming alarm, a low groaning noise, and the huge, impenetrable blast doors began to retract.

Coffin felt a great sense of peace and relief wash over him.

Yes, he thought. *This is right. This is exactly what I want to do.*

"Oh, bother," he heard Gilch say.

Coffin glanced at her, then back toward the still-opening doors. The slabs of reinforced metal had parted to reveal . . .

Three people. Two of them wore long, dark robes and carried all-too-familiar swords made of light. One of the blades was yellow and one was blue, and that was all Coffin had time to register before the shooting started.

Kantam Sy deactivated their lightsaber. They holstered it, then hooked a length of their long, unruly hair behind their ear. Normally, Kantam kept it tied back, but some had come loose during the brief skirmish that had left three Nihil corpses lying on the floor and sprawled across consoles inside the defense bunker. Three deaths they and Emerick Caphtor had been unable to prevent.

In Kantam's view, every entity had its time, and there was little to be done to adjust it. The cosmic Force rolled and churned in its unknowable way and placed people where they were meant to be. From that perspective, this was the moment the Force had predetermined for the three Nihil to die. That was all.

Emerick Caphtor had a very different way of looking at these issues—they'd discussed it. Kantam was what you might call a philosopher when it came to the Force, open to the idea that there were things that could never be understood but only be experienced, accepted. Emerick, on the other hand, thought *everything* could be understood. Reason governed all. Cause and effect. With the application of enough time and effort, the connections among all things could be uncovered. Kantam didn't know if that perspective was somehow related to Emerick's age—he was a bit older, with touches of gray at his temples, rather fetching against his dark skin. Perhaps Emerick had learned things in his greater years that Kantam had not. He was known for his wisdom and insight, after all. Emerick's role within the Order was akin to a detective or investigator, tasked to find the truth behind all manner of mysteries. He often worked with non-Jedi liaisons from security offices across the galaxy, solving crimes that intersected with the Order in some way.

With all of that in mind, although Kantam hadn't specifically asked Emerick how he was feeling about the fact that they had just killed three Nihil warriors, the other Jedi's views were relatively easy to divine. Emerick would lay it out thusly: Neither he nor Kantam had swung their lightsaber in offense. Both had merely redirected the killing shots fired by the Nihil. The Nihil had, in essence, killed themselves. Cause and effect.

"Wasn't sure that would work," said the third member of their group, an Eriaduan commando, yet another member of the Tarkin clan, a young man named Navaj.

He was tall and olive-skinned, with straight dark hair shaved into a topknot. Navaj had been very useful in bringing them to this place. His knowledge of the local environment had allowed him to guide the Jedi through the battle outside, finding the fastest, safest route through the chaos to the entrance to the defense bunker.

"You try running the mind touch on someone you can't see, through two meters of hardened durasteel," Emerick said. "Bet it takes you a few tries, too."

Kantam made a sound that might have been a chuckle, hastily stifled. They weren't completely sure of their own emotions at that moment. They could believe the Force had chosen this time for these people to die—but that didn't take away the fact that they had been the Force's instrument. Death, proximity to it . . . no matter the situation, it was heavy.

The trio moved into the control chamber, taking in the command stations, screens, and all the other elements of a facility designed to channel massive energies against invaders appearing in orbit around the planet. It was quickly obvious that the Nihil had not just occupied the defense bunker . . . they had destroyed it. Panels were torn open, wiring ripped out, control boards and circuits smashed.

"Oof," Kantam said. "Not promising. Not surprising, really, but not promising."

Navaj made a circuit of the room, examining the systems as quickly as he could. The man did not seem as displeased as Kantam would have expected. He threw a sharp little smile back toward the Jedi.

"They didn't get all the backup components," Navaj said. "Definitely needs repair, but there's still hope. We can do this. This can actually work."

He pulled a comm from his belt, a tight-beam, military-spec device designed to overcome the signals jamming currently being layered over Eriadu City by both sides.

"Command, this is Captain Navaj Tarkin with the Jedi infiltration team. We've accessed and secured the bunker, but it looks like the Nihil did a fair amount of damage. We'll need a repair crew before we can get it up and running, but it's doable. Send us the best technicians you have, right away."

A long pause from the comm. Too long. Kantam caught Emerick's eye, and the older man nodded. They both sensed something was wrong.

"We appreciate your efforts," came Sevran Tarkin's voice, finally, "but it's too late."

Alarms blared. A few of the cracked screens lit up with threat indicators, data pouring into the system's still-functioning sensors.

Kantam, Navaj, and Emerick watched, none of them saying a word.

"Is that . . . the entire Nihil fleet?" Kantam asked, staring at the innumerable red dots slicing into the atmosphere above Eriadu's surface, each an enemy vessel, a ship of war.

"All of the fleet that matters," Emerick said, his voice like ash. "I know that flagship."

He pointed to a large, wedge-shaped icon in the center of the enemy formation.

"That's General Viess."

Chapter Ten

THE *ATARAXIA*

The modified cargo shuttle took up most of the room in the *Ataraxia*'s hangar. Aboard it: the group of brave Jedi and Jedi-adjacent who had come to think of themselves as the Nine, and a mobile containment cell holding twelve of the creatures that seemed expressly evolved to kill them.

The Nine were determined to bring the Nameless home.

"The Force is with us," Avar Kriss said to herself.

She was alone in the cockpit. The shuttle was too small for a copilot's station. Under most circumstances, it wouldn't need one; the craft's primary purpose was traveling from starships in orbit down to the surface and back again. Its maneuvering capabilities were basically limited to up or down. Maybe a bit of side-to-side. This was not a Vector, not a Skywing or a Longbeam. It was a box with a thruster at the back.

Avar looked out through the shuttle's viewport at the Veil, spinning and grinding just beyond the magnetic shield that prevented the *Ataraxia*'s life support from leaking from the hangar's access port into open space.

It's like a mouth made of saws made of flame, she thought. *How am I supposed to get through that?*

A safe path through the Veil did exist. Supposedly. The route had come to the Order through a long chain of Jedi Knights over the course of centuries. It began with a long-deceased but well-traveled Jedi named Barnabas Vim who had visited the Nameless homeworld centuries before. His reports were discovered hidden in the Occlusion Zone by Emerick Caphtor in the course of his investigations into the source of the Nameless. Emerick had managed to send the data through the Stormwall back to Republic space using an ancient EX communications droid. Finally, Elzar Mann had received the information and analyzed it as best as he could, passing along his findings to Avar.

She wondered at the series of events that had led to her having this crucial information at this crucial moment. The Order was not just its current form—the Jedi alive at that time. It was all the Jedi who had ever lived, all their work, their choices and discoveries and battles for the light. It grew, and evolved, and became something so much greater than any one Jedi could ever achieve on their own.

Barnabas Vim could not have realized his work would someday be instrumental in saving the galaxy. And yet it was.

Vim's reports were incomplete, garbled in parts, but Elzar had analyzed them thoroughly and had become certain that safely transiting the Veil required two things: First, a traveler needed to access the barrier at precisely the correct entry point. Then, somehow—Elzar was much less definitive about this second part—the Veil itself would reveal the way through. Not very much to work with, but Avar did have the starting coordinates, and she was uniquely positioned to be able to see whatever the Veil decided to show her. Or, rather, to hear it.

Avar Kriss reached out through the Force toward the Veil. The Song grew louder in her ears, and she narrowed her focus. She had learned years ago to tune her perceptions, to hear only the music generated by one person, location, threat, rather than the enthralling, gorgeous cacophony of the Force entire. Now Avar dialed herself in until she was listening to the Veil, nothing else.

It's not as chaotic as it appears, she thought, hearing something like a repeated bass figure underlying the thrashing, swirling mess of notes. *There's something holding it all together. An ostinato beneath it all. That's the path.*

Avar tapped a control and opened an intercom channel to the eight people in the shuttle's passenger compartment—she supposed the twelve Nameless could hear, too, though she did not expect the creatures to be particularly interested in her words.

"I'll take us in and through," she said, keeping it simple. "Brace yourselves. I won't lie. This will be rough."

The shuttle rose, its landing skids retracting, and Avar brought the ship around in a smooth curve, heading straight for the hangar's launch window and the glowscreaming Veil beyond.

Fine so far, she thought as she piloted the shuttle toward the coordinates Elzar had provided to her.

The Veil loomed. The shuttle began to tremble. Avar checked her instruments—the turbulence was within the craft's tolerances, though it wasn't exactly pleasant. A vision leapt into her head: She lost control, and the shuttle smashed into one of the toothed vortexes spinning out ahead. The ship was ripped apart and everyone aboard spilled out into space and certain death, all these people she cared about . . . loved.

Not to mention the rest of the galaxy in due time, turned to dust by the Blight.

Avar gritted her teeth, listened for that bass motif hidden deep within the Veil's own Force-song, and shoved the control sticks forward.

The shuttle responded immediately, diving with greater speed than she would have given the thing credit for. The Veil loomed closer, closer, closer, and this was the moment. Death, or possibly . . .

A path forward. Avar could see it. The moment she passed through what she now thought of as the Veil's entry gate, a zone of clear space could be seen, a passage descending deeper into the turmoil. A kind of alley, free of the spinning, shredding energy whorls and city-sized lightning blasts.

That's it.

Avar steered as best she could, wishing she were in a Vector. Those ships were built for things like this, little flitting insect vessels able to turn on a whim and outrun anything that might decide to chase them.

This thing's a tub, Avar thought, wrestling with the controls as the Veil worked to take the ship from her. *It's like trying to fly the Senate building.*

But still, somehow, she managed. The shuttle was not nimble, but it did what it was told . . . if slowly.

If I just . . . set up the turns well in advance . . . Avar thought, *give this clunker the time it needs . . .*

The shuttle made its way through the Veil, shuddering and clanging but intact. In time, it approached what Avar assumed to be the exit— a patch of clear space through which she could see a slice of blue-white planet. The goal was in sight.

She keyed the intercom.

"We're almost through," Avar said. "I'll take us down to the surface, and then—"

A flash of light too bright to understand. It slapped Avar's head back against her seat's headrest and was immediately followed by a sound so loud she could almost see it, a snapping bang like the sound of a planet splitting in two.

Dazed, Avar did not notice at first that her instrument panels had gone blank. She also failed to observe, due to the keening brightness of the Veil still pouring through the viewport, that the lights in the cockpit were extinguished. Her fuzzed-out perceptions did not let her recognize that the life-support systems were no longer circulating and refreshing the air or pushing back the black cold of vacuum, and that all shields were down, and the engines were out.

It took many long moments for Avar to return to herself and to understand that one of the Veil's mountainous ion blasts had skewered the shuttle, ripping through its shield as if it were a soap bubble, rendering it nothing more than a metal box weighing many tons, kilometers above a planet whose gravity was already yanking it rapidly downward, containing the only chance for the uncountable beings of the Republic to survive the Blight.

STAR WARS: TRIALS OF THE JEDI

Everyone in the galaxy, Avar thought, *killed by a single bolt of lightning.*
The shuttle fell.

Torban Buck felt his stomach climb up into his throat, and knew it meant the shuttle was descending at a rate of speed not generally conducive to a safe landing—at least not when the power was clearly out, a situation undoubtedly connected to the huge blast of light and sound that had cracked through the ship a few seconds back.

He looked around the passenger compartment, seeing the others all realizing the same thing, their eyes going wide, understanding what was happening. What was about to happen.

Except Terec, maybe, Torban thought. *They seem a little—*

The Kotabi was staring straight ahead, eyes wide, their mouth moving quickly but with no sound emerging.

Talking to Ceret while they still can, Torban realized.

Torban wondered who he would talk to right now, if he had the same ability. Lula Talisola, probably, or one of the other Padawans he'd taught, helping to shepherd them toward becoming full Jedi Knights. Teaching Padawans was one of the great tasks of the Order, ensuring that the accrued wisdom of the Jedi, the lived experience, survived from generation to generation. A direct line of legacy could be traced back to the very earliest Jedi.

I am part of that, he thought. *If this is my time, then I am at peace with it. I have done my best to live well, and I believe the galaxy was better for my presence. What more could a person ask for?*

With that settled, Torban took stock of the other passengers, seeing if anyone might need his help processing the fact that they were currently falling out of the sky.

Elzar Mann looked fine—he had gotten up from his seat and was fiddling with a control panel mounted on the wall, as if he could somehow find a way to get the ship's power back on. Torban wished him luck.

Burryaga and Bell Zettifar were sitting next to each other, as were Reath Silas and Azlin Rell. Torban wished for better company for Reath, but at least none of them were alone. The only person he saw in the passenger compartment who *was* alone was the so-called monster-hunter, Ty Yorrick. The Tholothian woman gripped the arms of her seat, her eyes tightly closed.

The Order would have helped you to handle your fear, Torban thought, and then chided himself for being uncharitable.

He unbuckled his seat harness and made his unsteady way back several rows to where Ty was sitting. The ship bucked and twisted as it fell into the planet's atmosphere, buffeted by savage winds.

"Buckets will sit with you, Ty Yorrick!" he said, forcing bravado into his voice. This was a character he played from time to time, usually when things became dangerous on one mission or another, and he saw a need to comfort, distract, or amuse. Now, usually the people he performed for were Padawans and younglings, but just because Ty was grown didn't mean she couldn't use some comfort.

"This is no time to be alone, am I right?" Torban said.

Ty gave a tight nod, keeping her eyes closed. Torban lowered himself into a seat next to the woman. He reached over and took her hand. She squeezed his in return, and not for the first time he was glad of his tough Chagrian skin and the strong bones beneath.

"Peace," Torban said.

Ty nodded again, and he thought he felt her grip relax, if only a bit.

A shearing, hissing sound came from the front of the cabin. A bright-green lightsaber blade shot out from the sealed metal door that led to the shuttle's cockpit. Three quick slashes and most of the door fell away to reveal . . . Avar Kriss.

"Avar, what are you doing?" Elzar said. "Shouldn't you be at the controls? The ship, it's—"

"There's no point, Elzar. Power is gone. The systems are fried. All of them," Avar said. "There's no fixing them—not in the time we have."

She extinguished her lightsaber and pulled herself to the first row of seats, bracing herself against the shuttle's unpredictable shakes and twists.

STAR WARS: TRIALS OF THE JEDI 157

"We're . . . crashing?" Reath shouted.

"There are worse deaths," Azlin said. "Many worse deaths."

Burryaga moaned, and while Torban didn't understand Shyriiwook, it didn't take a protocol droid to comprehend the sentiment.

"I knew this was a bad idea," Ty hissed. "I'm a fool. Jedi business. Should've *known better.*"

Her hand tightened again, though she didn't open her eyes—she didn't even really seem to be aware he was there. Torban realized she wasn't afraid but angry. Furious at herself for being in a situation she couldn't solve, couldn't hunt, couldn't subdue. He gripped her hand, offering her the serenity he could.

"We're not crashing," Avar said. "Not if we focus. All nine of us trained to use the Force in the Jedi Temple. We all know how to fall safely. It's one of the most important lessons Padawans learn."

"She's right," Bell said. "Loden Greatstorm made me go over it and over it—and I've fallen from higher than this and lived."

Elzar Mann pulled himself along to the seat next to Avar, buckled himself in.

"The shuttle is designed to work in atmosphere, at least somewhat," he said. "It's aerodynamic. It's not a glider, but if we can stabilize it, we can control the descent."

"How would we steer? How would we land?" said Terec, finally seeming to be fully in the moment.

"The shuttle's control surfaces are mechanical," Elzar said, holding out his hands with fingers outstretched and tilting them back and forth. "Flaps, rudders. We can steer it using the Force."

"This is ridiculous," Ty said, her eyes finally open, throwing an incredulous stare at Avar and Elzar. "Ridiculous! We can't see what we're doing. This ship must weigh ten thousand tons. How would we even do it? Nine people all doing different things . . . it would never work."

"We wouldn't be doing different things," Avar said, and Torban was impressed at how calm she seemed. "We'd be doing it together. I can connect us through the Force. I can coordinate the effort to steer the ship."

"Just half of us," Elzar said. "The rest should focus on slowing the shuttle's fall—lifting it, keeping it in the air. That won't take any coordination, really."

"Bell, Torban, with me," Avar said. "The rest of you, lift the ship. That will be harder than steering it."

Torban didn't know why Avar had selected him, but he was happy to help. He knew what Avar Kriss could do. He had experienced it during the *Legacy Run* disaster, when he and thousands of other Jedi across the galaxy were united within what Avar called the Song of the Force to help save a world called Hetzal.

The shuttle was shoved sideways by a particularly vicious current of air. Its nose tipped forward and the ship began to spiral, now pointed straight at the ground some unknown distance below. Beside him, Ty gasped in terror. Torban felt gravity pulling him forward and was glad for the restraint holding him to his seat.

Nausea welled up in his guts. Torban searched for the Force to settle himself—and there, waiting, was Avar Kriss. The closest metaphor he could summon was an extended hand. He grasped it and instantly found himself understanding where Avar wanted him to apply his own grasp of the Force. She'd assigned him the steering flap on the right wing. Bell had the left, and Avar had the rudder.

Together the three Jedi fought the shear, working as one. At the same time, everyone else aboard did their best to remind the shuttle through the Force that it was a flying thing, that it wanted to fly, that it was made to master the air, not be destroyed by it.

The first order of business was defeating the spin. Torban, Avar, and Bell worked in concert, pushing the flaps and rudder against the airflow, slowly, slowly pulling the shuttle back to level.

"The Nameless must be terrified," he heard Ty mutter.

"Hnh," Torban said. "Let's see how *they* like it."

Steering the shuttle felt like wrestling a tornado with his bare hands— but it was getting easier. He, Bell, and Avar were getting the hang of their makeshift control system, and the shuttle felt more nimble, more respon-

STAR WARS: TRIALS OF THE JEDI

sive by the second. Lighter, in point of fact, which had to be due to the efforts of the other Jedi applying the Force to its bulk.

Torban was starting to allow himself to feel mildly optimistic, and then, with a tearing sound like a speeder dropped from a building, a good-sized chunk of the shuttle's hull ripped away.

A shrieking wail roared into the cabin as the wind tore through the new opening. The Nine's heads all turned at once to see what had happened, assess the damage . . . and suddenly Bell Zettifar vanished from Avar's link.

"*Ember!*" he heard Bell cry.

"Bell, no!" Avar said. "I need you with me!"

But it was too late. Bell had already unbuckled his seat harness. He began climbing, leaping and springing back toward the hull breach. A storage compartment had originally taken up that space in the ship—that was gone now. The only thing that remained was a charhound named Ember, who clung for dear life by her jaws to a tight bundle of wires, her grip the only thing keeping the animal from falling out into open air beyond.

Wisps of steam poured from the charhound's nostrils. Her eyes rolled wildly in terror.

"No, Ember, don't!" Bell shouted as he moved closer to the animal. "Just stay calm, girl, relax! I'm coming for you!"

Torban was still deep in Avar's link, helping her try to maintain control of the shuttle with just two-thirds of the strength she'd had a few moments earlier. Still, he was aware of the disaster unfolding behind him. Ember was a charhound, and charhounds breathed fire when agitated or afraid. But if she did, the cables in her mouth would melt, and away she would fall, and nothing any Jedi could do would save her.

A third presence appeared in Avar's link—Elzar Mann, slipping into the opening left by Bell in what seemed like an effortless, practiced fashion.

He's done this before, Torban thought.

"Just hold on, Ember!" Bell shouted.

The charhound snorted in response, then again, which couldn't be good. One of those was bound to release some flame.

Ty Yorrick's hand squeezed his again, in gratitude, possibly, and then released. Torban let her go. He had other things to be concerned about, and if she had finally brought her emotions under control, so much the better.

The woman unbuckled her harness and sprang up, working her way back to Ember. She was close to the back of the ship and got to the rent in the hull relatively quickly. She looked back at Bell, who was still hauling himself across the passenger compartment.

"Stop yelling at the poor creature," Ty said to him, then turned and extended a hand toward the terrified charhound.

"You're a good girl, and you're safe," she said. "Nothing will happen to you. Listen to me. You are with your friends. They will protect you, as they always do."

The ship bucked and rolled, and Ember whimpered.

"It's all right, I promise," she said.

Ty dropped to her hands and knees and crawled forward toward the gap in the hull. Just a few handbreadths away was open sky, spinning clouds. Smoke poured from Ember's nostrils, whipped away by the rushing wind.

Torban watched as Ty pulled herself forward, risking her own life without hesitation. She placed a hand on Ember's heaving side. The creature's breath slowed, calmed.

"Now, Bell," she said, speaking over the wind. "Bring her in. I'd do it myself but I'm terrible with telekinesis. I don't want to risk it."

Without a word, Bell Zettifar reached out with the Force, gently taking the now calm Ember and pulling her forward into the ship. She floated through the air until she reached a seat, where she was gently deposited, a harness extending out and buckling itself around her. The charhound seemed utterly relaxed.

Bell's control is impressive, but what Ty did? Torban thought. *I couldn't have done that. No chance. She's as skilled with creatures as any Jedi I've ever seen.*

STAR WARS: TRIALS OF THE JEDI   161

"Please," Avar Kriss said, clearly speaking through teeth gritted with effort, "help me make sure that beautiful effort was not in vain. Ember is in as much danger as she ever was. *We have to land this ship.*"

The Song of the Force was loud and getting louder, its melodies clashing and clanging together into an impossible-to-interpret mess, every note in every octave in every key all at once, every frequency and the frequencies in between. The Song had become the Noise. Ordinarily, Avar could modulate its presence in her mind. The Force was always there, but if she needed to, she could turn its volume down to nothing. Now, though, it was like someone was screaming in her ear—both ears—and there was nothing she could do about it.

The reason was obvious: She and everyone else aboard the shuttle were approaching the surface of the Nameless homeworld at terminal velocity. Whatever awaited them down there—assuming they lived to see it—threw the Force into a frenzy. All she could do was try to focus.

Avar settled back into the link, feeling Bell return and take Elzar's place.

Hold, was the faint thought she directed at Elzar as he returned to the impossible task of keeping the shuttle aloft.

It wasn't the actual word, just the idea of it—the most even a strong Force connection could convey. Jedi weren't telepaths. But she knew Elzar understood. The idea she felt drift back toward her was, *Always.*

The shuttle plummeted. Down, down. Every member of the Nine had closed their eyes. They saw only what the Force allowed. Currents, energy, inertia, momentum. These were elements for which light and dark meant nothing. The wind has no intention. The wind cannot be selfish or selfless. The Nine asked the shuttle to stay in the air, and they asked the air to hold it up, and they asked the planet to not be quite so rapacious about its desire to have the shuttle crash into it at great speed.

If the craft were intact, the Nine could have set it down like a leaf falling on the surface of a pond. But with a sizable chunk of the ship's hull gone, its stability was deeply compromised. Wind shear whipped through the cabin, and deep structural groans announced the reality that the shuttle wouldn't hold together for much longer.

The ground or die, Avar thought. *Or the ground and death.*

Two blasts of wind hit the shuttle at once—one from below, one from the side—and the ship corkscrewed into an inversion. Upside down, hanging from the straps of her harness, hearing Ember howl in distress, Avar sensed the surface approaching at extreme speed. They had seconds, no more.

In perfect alignment with Torban Buck and Bell Zettifar, Avar yanked the shuttle's control surfaces into configurations that would do everything possible to slow the craft.

No, Avar! Think! she realized. *We're upside down—the flaps have to be set in the opposite direction! You're steering us right into the—*

A ripping, slashing, tearing sound from above Avar's head, which she knew had to be the sound of trees or other vegetation crashing against the ship's roof—currently the bottom of its hull.

Avar released the link with Torban and Bell, and threw everything she had into slowing the ship, lifting it, trying to keep it in one piece. The others were doing the same. Nine people, very different people, working as one, hauling backward on an invisible rope tied around a thin metal shell whipped at a planet from orbit.

A mighty, cracking thud. A roar of dirt and stone scraping against the outer hull. No one in the cabin made a sound. All was pure focus. Distraction meant death.

Finally, at last, the noises from outside eased. Ty Yorrick drew in a gigantic, sharp breath, and that was the signal the others needed. Eyes opened. The situation was assessed.

"We're down," Elzar said.

"We sure are," Bell replied, unbuckling his harness and executing a neat flip to the floor below.

He walked carefully over to a spot just below Ember and raised his arms. Using the Force, he unlocked the clasps holding her to her seat, and

STAR WARS: TRIALS OF THE JEDI   163

she fell neatly into his grasp. The charhound huffed and chuffed, nuzzling into his neck.

"Easy, girl," he said, smiling. "Aren't you the little stowaway, huh? Bet you're regretting that bright idea right about now."

Azlin Rell's harness unbuckled without his hands touching it, the straps peeling away like an obscene cocoon. He floated languidly down, rotating in midair until his bare feet with their gnarled toes and hornlike nails clattered against the hull.

"Quite a journey, but here we are," the darksider said.

He watched as the rest of the Nine found their way from the passenger seats.

"Now what?" Azlin said.

Not far from the Nine, behind a metal bulkhead and a code-locked door, was the shuttle's small cargo hold. It had survived the fall from orbit intact, as had its contents—the durasteel-framed energy cell containing the dozen Nameless the Jedi were intent on returning home.

Though built to be powered from the ship's generators, the cell had its own battery system, designed to keep it operational in the case of catastrophic power failure. Those batteries had worked well until the shuttle's impact with the planet, at which point several crucial connectors were jarred loose. This put undue stress on the capacitors inside the devices—the batteries for the batteries, in effect. One by one, they burned out. A third were already gone, scorch marks marring their surfaces.

Ordinarily, the batteries would have lasted for two days, give or take.

Under the current circumstances, they would fail in a matter of minutes.

Chapter Eleven

THE BATTLE OF ERIADU

"We have to get out of here *right now*," said Emerick Caphtor.

Kantam Sy and Navaj Tarkin looked up from the battle display in the ruined defense bunker. In a static-filled, herky-jerky way, the holos told the story of General Viess's assault fleet as it deployed above Eriadu. Entire divisions of aircraft were peeling away from the huge capital ships, headed toward significant population centers across the planet, a slow, deadly fist preparing to clench. New threat indicators appeared by the second, representing fighters and corvette-sized Nihil vessels dispersing from the larger cruisers and carriers.

General Viess's flagship was represented on the screens as a large, arrow-shaped red icon directly above Eriadu City. But Emerick had seen images of the actual ship, and he knew that Viess's *Auberge* was not designed to resemble anything so elegant as an arrowhead. It was a brutal hammer of a spacecraft. If it were ever to land on a planet, it would crush and destroy anything beneath it like a gigantic spiked boot.

"Why do you think we need to leave, Emerick?" Kantam said. "This seems like the right place to be, at least for the moment."

The delicate-featured Jedi gestured at the wrecked control panels for

STAR WARS: TRIALS OF THE JEDI

the bunker's weapons systems. "If we can get even a couple of these defenses working, it could help with the battle. We should try. Once that's done, we can go. Most of these systems are automated. We wouldn't need to stay."

Navaj nodded. "I agree. It will take time, but many of the stations have redundancies," he said. "We can rewire the—"

"*No*," said Emerick, cutting off the other man's words with a sharp chop of his hand.

They don't see it, he thought. *Cause and effect. It's right there.*

Emerick pointed at Viess's flagship on the screen.

"That ship has *orbital artillery,* and I'd guess most of the other big ships in the Nihil fleet do, too. At any moment, they'll begin a bombardment. We are standing in a planetary defense bunker, a military installation. *What do you think will be Viess's first target?*"

Kantam and Navaj looked at each other, realization dawning in their eyes.

A thundercrack shook the bunker. Dust sifted down from the ceiling above, and the heavy steel and duracrete construction groaned.

"Go!" Emerick yelled, and they did.

They moved together, in a tight group. The Jedi could have chosen differently. Their training in the Force let them move much faster than Navaj. They could have been outside in heartbeats, far from the bunker in a few more. But Navaj did not have that ability, and the Jedi would not abandon him.

The trio raced through the warren of security corridors that led back to the surface from the bunker's central control station. These were built to create choke points where enemy attackers could be forced to move in single file, to be picked off one by one by a comparatively small force of defenders. For that specific situation, the passages were well designed. But for other scenarios, such as attempting to flee the bunker before it was vaporized by laser blasts the size of buildings thrown at it from enemy starships high above, they were an utter nightmare.

Another boom and the corridor itself split, cracks spidering into the duracrete walls, small pieces of rubble falling from above. The lights flickered and went out, replaced immediately by dim amber emergency lighting. Then that, too, failed.

Two lightsaber blades snapped into life, lighting the dust-filled gloom—yellow and blue.

"Which way?" Emerick called as they approached a junction point.

"Left," said Navaj, his voice uncertain. "There are supposed to be guide paths, but with the power out—"

A *krrck* from the ceiling, and broad chunks of reinforced stone fell directly above their heads.

Emerick Caphtor slashed out with his blade, slicing one of the slabs in two. The halves crashed to the ground on either side of Navaj, leaving him unharmed. Kantam Sy did the same, and two pieces of heavy stone fell, missing Emerick.

Emerick believed Navaj would have done his part and saved Kantam if he could, but the man was not a Jedi. A jagged chunk of rock slammed into Kantam's head with a wet, ugly crunch. The blue lightsaber fell to the floor and went out, extinguished.

"Kantam!" Emerick cried out.

He fell to his knees next to the injured Jedi, gently lifting the stone off Kantam's head. It came free with a sucking sound Emerick would never forget. He held his lightsaber out to Navaj, hilt-first.

"Take it," he said. "Give me light."

He did, holding the blade at an angle to let Emerick examine the wound.

More booms and cracks from above them. The bunker was falling apart, and Kantam Sy was unconscious in the dark.

Emerick didn't know the other Jedi well. They hadn't come up as Padawans together, and now they ran in different circles. Both spent a good deal of time away from the Temple. Today was the most time Emerick had spent with Kantam that he could remember. But he knew the other Jedi's reputation—charming, cheerful, a very good master to their Padawans.

STAR WARS: TRIALS OF THE JEDI

And I am alive because they chose to save me instead of saving themselves.

Near the beginning of this whole crisis, the Council had asked him to investigate the death of Loden Greatstorm. At the time, Emerick had relished the opportunity as something new, interesting—a puzzle he couldn't immediately solve. That was naive.

That first mystery had led to the Nameless, and then to the Blight, and in the end, all he'd ever found were increasingly dire problems. Now, holding Kantam Sy's staved-in head in his hands, Emerick thought perhaps there was no solution. Only dead ends.

Blood seeped from Kantam's wound, their eyes fluttering behind half-closed lids.

Sian would know what to do, he thought, wondering where she was. He'd left her at the wedding in Bri-Phrang, where they'd danced—would that ever happen again? Was she even alive? Would any of them even survive?

"Pressure," he muttered to himself, a half-remembered lesson in field medicine from before he became a Knight. "Need to apply pressure to the wound."

"No," said Navaj. "Not for a head wound. Could damage the brain. It's the opposite. We want to relieve pressure—but we can't do that here. We need to get to a medical facility. That's it. We do that or Kantam dies."

His voice was flat and certain. Clearly, his medical training was more recent than Emerick's.

"Fine," he said.

Emerick reached out with the Force. He lifted Kantam more gently and smoothly than he ever could have with his arms. The injured Jedi offered up a faint moan.

"It's all right, my friend," Emerick said. "Just rest."

A series of crashing booms shook the corridor like a cracking whip, and both Emerick and Navaj almost fell. Kantam did not. They remained as still and safe as if they were in bed.

"Go," Emerick said. "Get us out of here. Trust yourself. You know the way."

In the end, Navaj did, leading them through the collapsing warren of tunnels. Emerick followed, his focus intense and complete. He kept Kantam steady in the air as they moved, using the Force to shield them from falling pieces of stone, flicking them to either side without conscious thought.

The trio approached the bunker's exit through bright flashes of emerald light, each burst accompanied by furnace heat and a wash of sonic devastation. They looked outside.

Jedi were taught there was no afterlife beyond a reconnecting with the cosmic Force. No reward, no punishment. Just the return.

Emerick believed that. It made sense to him.

But if there was a hell, it would look like this.

Spears of laserfire lanced down from above, landing with horrifying regularity, a rain of burning light. The bunker's entrance was located in a part of Eriadu City filled with warehouses and industrial facilities— structures three to five stories tall, containing goods and factory machines and . . . people. Many people.

Most of that was now gone, and what was left fueled a pillar of flame sending torrents of dark, toxic smoke into the air.

"We can't get through that," Navaj said, still holding the lightsaber high, as if it might somehow protect him.

He turned to look at Emerick, his gaze certain, trusting. "What do we do?" Navaj asked the Jedi, clearly expecting a miracle from the member of that great mystical Order that always had the answers, always knew the path forward.

What do we do? Emerick thought. *How the hell should I know?*

⚜

I am not the galaxy's smartest man, Joss Adren considered, crouching within an arched doorway that offered dubious protection from the all-out laser party that had erupted in Eriadu City.

To be fair, he'd had no idea that good old Slendo would end up kicking off an entire war. One minute Joss was finishing his ale, and then sounds

STAR WARS: TRIALS OF THE JEDI 169

of commotion started to filter in from outside, and laser blasts, and it was right around then he realized that this was all going south fast and he should probably get back to Pikka posthaste.

Easier said than done. The streets around the bar had erupted into firefights—did every single person on this cursed planet own seven blasters or what? Every block was a gauntlet, and several times Joss found himself roped into a bit of a back-and-forth with a dug-in group of Nihil, helping locals clear out a nest of the mask-wearing, scum-sucking, murder roaches that had taken over their planet.

That was satisfying—nothing like a little payback. The Nihil had racked up plenty of debts to one Joss Adren over the past few years, and it was nice to be able to settle some accounts. Joss didn't own seven blasters, but he owned one, a meticulously maintained WESTAR-27 that he wasn't half bad with.

I'd feel a lot better about all these little delays if I could get through to Pikka, Joss thought.

He lifted his comm and saw, yet again, the red lights indicating no available frequencies. His immediate instinct was to take the device apart and see what was wrong with it—that was the mechanic in him. He knew how to fix stuff. In this case, though, he knew better.

Jamming, Joss thought. *Could be the RDC, could be the Eriaduans, could be the Nihil . . . could be all three. Doesn't matter. This thing's useless.*

He slipped the comm back into his pocket, knowing he'd probably check it again in about thirty seconds.

If I'm still alive, he thought sourly.

Joss shifted his bulk in the little alcove where he'd taken shelter, a mostly futile attempt to get more of his body out of the line of fire.

He looked up. In the skies, RDC and Eriaduan ships were locked in what looked like an increasingly desperate battle against the huge Nihil fleet that had dropped in from hyperspace not too long ago. For a while there, things had looked pretty good. The first phase of the battle had definitely been going against the Nihil. Now, though . . .

Joss shook his head. Not so good.

Still, the streets were calming down a little. The Nihil on the surface were either dug in hard wherever they'd taken refuge, or they were dead. In Joss's opinion, it felt like everyone on the ground was waiting to see what happened with the air battle before they stuck their necks out too far.

That had a good side and a bad side. The mostly deserted streets meant he could move more quickly. But with no one else around, and no ongoing street fights to distract folks, it meant a guy that looked like three boulders stacked on top of each other was easy to spot, and easy to target.

Should have kept my damn mouth shut back at Slendo's, he thought. *Should have been quieter at home so Pikka didn't have to kick me out.*

Although . . . was it possible he'd been glomping around their little apartment because he knew that would make Pikka order him to go to the bar, and of course she knew he knew that and was happy to let him go because it would make them both happy, even if they couldn't actually just say that stuff and did the silly little masquerade instead? Yes, it was possible. Entirely possible.

Ah, marriage, Joss thought.

He slipped out of the alcove, keeping his head low, moving fast, scanning the street ahead for new spots where he could stop to make sure the next steps of his path home were clear.

His apartment with Pikka was in an industrial zone on the outskirts of the city. They'd picked it because the building had a hangarlike space next door where they could stash their starship, a *Longbeam*-class corvette on semi-permanent loan from the Republic Defense Coalition. It was designated the *Aurora III,* but they just called it the *Aurie.* The Adrens didn't stand on ceremony, generally speaking.

Technically, as RDC military personnel, they should have stashed the *Aurie* with the other RDC assets on Eriadu in one of those mines outside the city. With Pikka's pregnancy, though, it had seemed prudent to keep a ship handy if they needed it. Seemed like a smart decision now, considering. If he could get to Pikka, they had a way out of all this mess.

Joss made his way quickly along the streets, but the closer he got to his

STAR WARS: TRIALS OF THE JEDI 171

apartment, the bigger the sick, burning ball of fear deep in his chest became. For some reason, the Nihil were hitting the industrial zone hard, lashing it with blasts from high above, over and over, a typhoon of boiling green death.

The path ahead was obscured with smoke, a wall nine meters tall. Joss didn't stop. He moved faster, dived right in.

Not far now, he thought, trying to avoid breathing the acrid-smelling cloud. *Pikka's just up ahead. Just a block or two.*

And then a Nihil fighter swooped by above, chased by an RDC Skywing sending blasterfire at its tail. The turbulence in their wake cleared the smoke obscuring the street.

Oh no, Joss thought. *Oh no no no.*

The building containing his apartment was ablaze, consumed with fire. Most of it had collapsed, but a few of the lower floors were still there, and their place was on the second floor. He and Pikka had picked it because they liked to hear the street noise, the sound of people passing by.

Joss did not hesitate. He picked up the pace—he was big, but he was nimble when he wanted to be, and right now he very much wanted to be. He raced toward the building. The heat intensified as he got close—he could feel the skin on his face tightening up. He didn't stop—ran faster.

The lift will be out, but the stairs are metal, Joss thought, making his plan, thinking about how he would repair this latest malfunction. *They'll still be there. I'll run up, won't touch the railings. My boots are rated for welding, they'll hold up. I'll get to our place, kick the door down, bring 'em both out.*

And if I'm too late...

Then he'd just stay in there. Not much point being anyplace else.

Joss was about a hundred meters from the blazing building when laserfire lashed into it from above and behind him. What remained of the structure exploded, a massive blast.

He was thrown back but not too far, and was back on his feet in an instant. Joss looked toward the building and instantly knew the truth. There was no way. Just no way anyone in that building had survived.

Joss Adren closed his eyes, and then he reached into his tunic, closing his fist around his blaster, his trusty WESTAR-27. He jerked it from his holster, spinning as he did, to look up at whatever ship had just destroyed his hope, his joy, his life.

RDC, Nihil, I don't care who it is. Whoever fired those shots, they're dead.

Joss stopped, looked. He realized he was pointing his blaster at his own ship—the *Aurora III*, the *Aurie*, which was hovering above the street.

"Ah," Joss said, and somewhat lamely lowered the pistol.

The *Aurie* descended to the ground, its landing ramp extending as it came down. Joss ran to it and was in the cockpit in thirty seconds. Fifteen. Nimble when he wanted to be.

Pikka levered herself up out of the captain's chair with the little groan and attention to overall structural integrity that characterized every time she stood up these days, and Joss had her in his arms pretty much right after that.

The top of her head was just below his chin, with all its lovely dark curls, and he kissed it, breathing her in.

"Easy, big guy," Pikka said. "Nice to see you, too, but if you squeeze me too hard we'll be having this baby right here in the cockpit."

He loosened his grip and let her untangle herself from him, but he didn't let go of her hand. She looked hilarious with that huge belly alongside the rest of her, which was pretty much as it had always been, but he knew better than to say so.

"Why'd you shoot at me, Pikka?" Joss said.

"Because you weren't answering your comms and it was the only way I could think of to keep you from running into a burning, fully evacuated building to try to save me when I very obviously had already saved myself," his wife replied.

Joss was happy.

Then his senses expanded beyond the little bubble of joy in the cockpit, and he once again heard the endless, pounding hammer of the battle raging outside.

He released Pikka's hand and peered out through the cockpit's windscreen.

STAR WARS: TRIALS OF THE JEDI

"We're in trouble if we stay here," he said. "Won't be long before some Nihil gunner sees a pretty little Longbeam sitting on the ground all laid out like a snack. We need to get in the air."

"Agreed," Pikka said.

She eased herself back into the captain's chair, making her sitting-down noise in the process, significantly different from her standing-up one. Joss took the copilot's seat, buckling himself in.

"What's the decision here?" he said. "Do we try to run the Nihil blockade and head somewhere else, or get into it?"

Pikka began flipping switches, powering up engines, shields, weapons.

"We swore an oath," she said. "We're part of the RDC. We protect people who can't protect themselves."

"Yeah, but—" Joss said, gesturing to Pikka's belly.

"Our oath extends to him, too. It's unfortunate that he had the misfortune to be the kid of two of the most badass pilot types in the galaxy. Just is what it is."

"We're contractors, Pikka!" Joss said. "Fixer-uppers! Grease-grabbers! Wrench jockeys!"

"Not today, Joss. Today, we're this baby's last hope."

She pulled back on the control sticks and the Longbeam shot into the air. Through the front viewport, they had a clear view of two Nihil Strikeships riddling a Skywing with laserfire, burning the ship out of the sky.

Chapter Twelve

THE *AUBERGE*

High above the Battle of Eriadu, as the Nihil fleet used all its mighty power to transform everything on the planet below into ash and blood-scented steam, General Abediah Viess sat in a comfortable chair, sipping a nice cup of tea. She was in her tastefully appointed study aboard her flagship, thinking about the book she was intending to write. It would be filled with a (long) lifetime's worth of observations derived from her many generations of work in the military-adjacent sphere.

Her working title: *Viess: A Warrior's True Truth.*

Not too bad, not too bad.

The idea would be to ignore the obvious: Her book would only tangentially touch on the battles and strategy and tactics. Thousands of books covered those subjects more thoroughly than she had any interest in doing. No, Viess wanted to write about the *business* of war. How to make money doing it, how to build a long and fruitful career as a warrior for hire. What it was actually like to navigate the challenges of a job many people couldn't even mention without a sneer on their lips.

Like their livelihoods are any less bloody if you look beneath the surface, she thought.

A mercenary. That's what Viess was. She wasn't ashamed to say it, either. Not one bit.

Viess: Bloody Money.

Hmm, she thought. *That's not bad, either. Really comes right at it.*

She already had her opening paragraph.

> I am a mercenary, probably the most successful mercenary I can think of. I am Mirialan, which means I live a long time. As I write this, I'm older than most people ever get—let's just say I've got well over two centuries in my past and leave it there. The exact number's none of your business! But speaking of business . . . let's talk about mine. For most of my life, I've taken other people's money to fight their wars. I don't care whose money it is, and I don't care which war. You think that makes me a bad person. Well, I bet your generals in your armies get paid for their work, don't they? It's the same job. I'm just more honest about it.

From there, Viess intended to lay out her life in all its glory—starting with her young, foolish self signing up as an ordinary soldier in the army of a small-time potentate back on Mirial. It hadn't taken long for her to realize how silly it was to put your life on the line to help some powerful person make some other powerful person feel bad. You were taking the greatest possible risk for . . . what? Settling a spat between two people you'd never meet?

Forget it. Viess's life was the most precious thing she owned. Getting her to risk it needed to be *expensive.* She absorbed all the training Mirial's military had to offer—those skills clearly had value—and deserted the first minute she could, killing her stupid sergeant on the way out.

She'd leave that detail in her book. She'd leave in all the details. Viess saw no distinction between killing for yourself or killing for others or killing for money or killing because you wanted to. Killing was killing. It was all the same.

After deserting, Viess found a mercenary outfit, signed up, and got down to the business of murder for money.

Over time, she developed a ninth sense for what she called the "moment," also known as "the precise instant it was time to get the hell out of a battle before it went completely south." She saw the moment before others tended to, which meant she ran when others stood and fought, which meant she survived battles her fellow mercenaries did not. Before Viess knew it, she was a veteran. Even better, people assumed she was a better fighter than the other soldiers when in fact she was just better at running away, which meant promotions and more money. She did that for a few hundred years and eventually ended up commanding the entire Nihil military.

The end.

General Viess sipped her tea, feeling the *Auberge* shudder all around her, a smooth, sensual vibration that meant another round of bombardment munitions had just been unleashed on the hapless planet of Eriadu far below.

The best place to be in a battle, she thought, *is as far away as you can get. Ten kilometers above it, for instance.*

Viess had no idea what her gunners had just destroyed down on the planet's surface. Her orders from Marchion Ro were vague, only that she was to head to Eriadu with her fleet and "act as she felt was warranted." The Nihil armada was a moving hammer consisting of cruiser-sized Stormships, fighter-level Strikeships, and the all-purpose Cloudships. Added to that were her own personal vessels, lethal ships crewed by her own well-trained and well-paid mercenaries.

She'd brought it all to Eriadu, and when she arrived, she found a planet in revolt. Details of how it all began were sketchy, but battles between the planet's local population and their Nihil rulers were raging across the planet. The locals had even mustered up a decent little resistance fleet, including a contingent of RDC starships. If Viess hadn't shown up with her own ships, there was a decent chance the Eriaduans could have taken

STAR WARS: TRIALS OF THE JEDI   177

back their world, especially if they'd managed to access their planetary defense grid. But now . . .

Thrrrrmmm.

Something else down there doesn't exist anymore, Viess thought.

The basic strategic platform upon which Viess had built her long career was based on three simple rules.

Rule One: Win.

Rule Two: Do whatever you have to do to make sure Rule One is followed, because no one will care what you did or who you killed or how you killed them if you can provide a victory.

Rule Three: If you can't win, run.

Viess's *Auberge* and various other Nihil capital ships around the planet were busy doing their best to achieve the first rule by following the second: turning the Eriaduan defense emplacements into powder while her fighters and other attack ships engaged targets of convenience.

Viess glanced at the battle display hovering to one side of her writing desk.

Won't be needing Rule Three today, she noted, taking another sip of tea.

The fight was going their way and then some. A couple of skirmishes on the ground that could use some mopping up, especially over in Bri-Phrang, but the air battle was well in hand. Of course it was. She would have been annoyed if it wasn't.

I should go up to the bridge, Viess thought. *Victory is nigh. No better time to make an appearance.*

She sighed—her study really was very comfortable—but she did have a job to do. Viess swallowed the last of her tea and headed up toward the command bridge.

The *Auberge* was Viess's third flagship since taking command of the Nihil military. When she first signed up with Marchion Ro, she'd asked him for a vessel befitting her status. He'd delivered, giving her a pretty impressive battleship called the *Foregone Catastrophe.* That blew up when a Jedi named Porter Engle tore into it with a drill ship.

Viess hated Jedi: stuck-up hyper-virtuous freaks who thought they were above everyone else. But Porter was the worst of all of them. He actually seemed like someone she could have gotten along with in another life—rough around the edges, long-lived like her, ugly-handsome—except for the inconvenient fact that he seemed to have made it his mission in life to kill her.

Flagship number two was the *Precipitate Fire*—smaller than the *Catastrophe* but still a tough bird. That one blew up during a battle at Naboo, which, honestly, Viess should have left as soon as it started.

Cause of death for that lovely ship? Yet another Jedi—Avar Kriss.

The third ship Marchion Ro had given her, the *Auberge,* was understandably not quite as impressive as her first two command ships. It was originally the *Glitterstim Shine,* personal war cruiser of a spice dealer from Kijimi who got trapped in the Occlusion Zone when the Stormwall went up. That, of course, meant the ship immediately became a Nihil asset, the property of Marchion Ro. The spice dealer had disagreed, but the conflict had gotten worked out via the spice dealer's death.

Viess renamed the ship, had Nihil war technicians boost its armaments, and redesigned its interior to her specifications. It was all done up in sleek, shiny black paneling with purple lighting accents. Black and purple were her colors.

The general had reached the hatchway that led to the command bridge. She took a moment to smooth her clothing; presentation was important. She was dressed in her colors, too, as she almost always was—a long gown in ebony and indigo, woven from the softest wool her exorbitant compensation as Nihil minister of protection could buy.

Viess had considered wearing her armor, but she wasn't planning on giving any inspirational speeches to the troops, not in a battle this one-sided. There was no real need for showmanship, and that armor, as effective (and pricey) as it was with its beskar ornamentation to fend off attacks from Jedi lightsabers and blaster pistols alike, was uncomfortable as hell. Heavy. Like walking around inside a droid.

Life's too short, Viess thought, *when life is this long.*

STAR WARS: TRIALS OF THE JEDI 179

She paused, struck.

That's pretty good, she thought, making a mental note to drop the phrase into her book.

She tapped the control that opened the hatch. It slid aside, and she stepped onto the bridge.

"Report," said General Abediah Viess.

"We just hit the final obvious military target in or near Eriadu City, General," replied Adjunct General Pastiwell Zick.

He wasn't really a general—Zick was her second in command, a pale-skinned, potbellied Arkanian who'd been with her for over a century. He was smart, sharp as a pin, but he wasn't canny. Didn't have that ninth sense. But that's what you wanted in a second. Someone who would just focus on the goals you gave them without worrying about the big picture. Anyway, he'd always just been Zick, but ever since Viess had taken on this job running the Nihil military for Marchion Ro, it seemed like adding a little hierarchy might be the way to go. So, now he was an adjunct general—whatever the hell that was supposed to mean.

"Do you have an update to your previous orders, General?" Zick continued.

His pure-white eyes with their little dot pupils stared at her from behind a fringe of ice-colored hair that dangled limply from his mottled scalp. Pastiwell Zick, for all his virtues, looked like a marble statue left out in the weather for a few hard decades.

Viess considered her subordinate's question. This was truly an opportunity for leadership.

"Yeah, this battle's not much, is it?" she said. "I heard these Eriaduans were supposed to be tough. I'm not seeing it. Wish we could get a serious fight for a change."

Scattered agreement from the crew, a solid group of ruffians she'd collected over the years.

"I mean," Viess continued, "we've got the toughest fleet in the galaxy, but we're stuck on this side of the Stormwall. I'd love to see what you folks could do against a *real* enemy, not this wishy-washy cleanup stuff we're doing here. I'd put you up against any warship out there. RDC, Jedi, you name it."

The sounds of agreement were louder now. She saw nodding heads, little smirks of pridescorn at how tough they were compared to the pathetic Eriaduans, the Republic Defense Coalition, and especially the hidebound monks of the Jedi Order.

"Here's what we do," Viess said, reaching into one of the pockets sewn into her lovely, luxurious dress.

She produced three golden chance cubes and held them up, showing them off.

"Roll for it. Whoever wins gets to choose the next target. We'll just do that for a while. Hit whatever we feel like. Keep the cowards down there on their toes."

This got a cheer from the crew. This was interesting. This was a good time. This was fun.

Viess tossed the chance cubes to Zick, who snatched them from the air and squatted down, rattling them in his hand, waiting for the rest of the bridge crew to gather around. The tensed muscles of his thighs got her thinking.

Been a while, she thought. *Old Zick's no beauty, but he knows how to focus on the task he's been given. Goes a long way. Maybe once the battle wraps up, we'll take a tumble.*

Viess watched as the crew gambled, listened to a Lannik celebrating a winning roll, his huge, pointed ears flopping every which way. Bordak was his name, she believed.

Always learn their names, Viess thought. *Another thing to put in the book. They think you care a hundred times more than you do if you can call them by name.*

The crew moved to the weapons control console, which boasted a convenient exterior viewport set just above. Bordak lifted himself up, then gazed out through it.

"Hmm," he said, making a show of it, putting his hand on his knobbly pink chin, then pointing. "What do you think *that* is?"

"Church, maybe," said another crewmember (*Kestee:* the name appeared in Viess's mental database), "or museum. Could be a university. Something nice."

"It's big, anyway," Bordak said. "Let's shoot that. It'll be a nice explosion."

The calculations were placed into the planet-facing weapons batteries.

Thrrrrm, went the shot. Viess felt it in her soles, her calves, her thighs.

Oohs and aahs and laughter as the building turned to a mushroom of flame and smoke far below.

Goodbye, church, museum, school—whatever you were, Viess thought.

"Let me get in on this," she said, joining the crew as they circled up for the next roll.

Chapter Thirteen

THE NAMELESS HOMEWORLD

The light streaming *in from the gash in the hull has an odd quality, like nothing I have ever seen,* Terec thought, knowing Ceret heard their words as they formed them in their mind. *It looks as if it shines through a pane of faintly pink-tinted glass.*

The bond-twins each knew what the other was thinking and feeling, but sensory input was not shared the same way. Direct sights, sounds, smells—those were reserved to each bond-twin within their own experience.

I wish you could see it, Terec added, after a slight pause.

Ceret already knew that, of course. The unspoken thoughts and desires and emotions of bond-twins were relayed between them as reliably as those they specifically articulated—but the extra effort Terec made to thought-say the words underscored them, like a repetition. If Ceret were physically present, Terec would have said the words out loud, the ultimate way to demonstrate truth between them, but Ceret was half a galaxy away back on Coruscant.

Ceret did not respond to Terec's thoughts. That was not unusual, these days. Imagine the pain of a connection that persists when it is clear that one of the parties wishes to be alone. Forced, constant, unwelcome communication. Terec did not know what to do, did not want to consider that their wish for increased independence from Ceret was causing their bond-twin pain. But they did wish for these things and knew that Ceret immediately knew of these wishes at the very moment they formed in Terec's mind.

The twins' division had begun when Terec's physical appearance changed, when their body was adorned with technological augmentation to offset damage done in an attack by a Nameless. Prior to that, their physical appearance was identical to Ceret's. Now the differences were like a lens, magnifying and growing in a feedback loop that had begun to scream—to both of them simultaneously, which was part of the curse—that Terec no longer felt the same as Ceret, and no longer wanted to, and that they were not one person but two.

Terec accepted Ceret's silence as the message it was and returned to doing their assigned task on this bizarre mission: to act as a living communications relay sending the events, needs, and experiences of the Nine on Planet X back to Coruscant.

The shuttle has landed safely, Terec thought. *It is relatively intact, but its systems have suffered immense damage. It isn't likely to fly again. We have donned our armor. The Nine are safe, as is our stowaway, the charhound Ember. The poor creature is standing close to Bell Zettifar and seems more than a little alarmed.*

Ember's fear seems justified. Everything inside the shuttle is quiet, but everything outside it is not. We have gathered near the tear in the ship's hull, listening to sounds of chaos outside. Animal screams, cracks of snapped vegetation, thuds of one large thing smashing into another loud thing.

"What's going on out there?" Reath Silas says.

No one responds, but Elzar Mann moves closer to the breached hull, stepping into that oddly tinted light I mentioned earlier. It bathes him, and he seems almost to glow.

The effect is soothing—though the shrieks and battering from outside do serve to counterbalance any peaceful feelings. Odors leak in from outside as well. The scent of the world reminds me of a spice market but with more life to it. A swamp or jungle liberally dusted with soul pepper and muja sauce? A curry made from good loamy soil just after a rain? Something like that. This planet, even though I have not technically seen it yet, seems to be an extremely unique—

Elzar Mann yelps with alarm and lunges backward. Something is on his faceplate—a dark creature with five legs. It is not large, and so its aggression is unusual. I am no zoologist, but from what I have seen, animals do not attack other creatures much larger than themselves unless—

Ah. It is part of a swarm. Dozens more of the things—I'll call them pentabats, as they have small wings that help them maneuver. The wings end in savage hooks, as do the legs. Their bodies are hard-shelled with an iridescent shine. I am able to provide this level of detail because three of them have latched on to me.

The armor I wear protects me from the claws, but it does not cover every part of me. My neck, some of my joints—they are unprotected.

Around me, I hear lightsabers ignite. A lovely spray of light of many colors fills the passenger cabin. I ignite my own, adding another note of green.

It's hard to call the Nine lucky at this point in the mission. One of our original members was nearly killed before we left Coruscant, we've almost died a number of times since, our transportation is destroyed, and we are currently under attack by extremely aggressive local fauna. That said, I do think it's good that the shuttle was upside down when it crashed. It means we do not have to maneuver around the rows of seating as we fight the pentabats. The shuttle's roof—now our floor—creates an efficient zone for combat.

Focus on the work at hand, *Ceret says to me, and I agree with them.*

Terec reached out with the Force to seize all three pentabats at once, removing them from their armor and flinging them into the air. The creatures spun for a moment, disoriented, but quickly recovered and headed back for more. Terec offered up three tight, contained slashes, and the three creatures fell to the ground, each neatly bisected.

I have taken care of the three pentabats. I am checking to see if any of the other Nine require help. Unsurprisingly, they do not. They skewer and stab and slice, and the attackers fall. Azlin Rell swats the bats from the air with blasts of what I presume is the dark side of the Force.

I am extremely impressed with these people and am proud that I was chosen to be among them.

STAR WARS: TRIALS OF THE JEDI 185

*I wish you were here as well, Ceret, but I understand that because of the unique-
ness of our bond, we wouldn't be as useful to the Order if we were both here.*

We would not, *Ceret thinks.*

*I wanted this—to be more separate, to be more individual—but there is a cost to
it. The best would be to be alone but not alone, but I do not know how to achieve it.*

You wanted this, *Ceret thinks.*

A beat, and then Ceret sent an additional thought.

**Everyone here wishes to know about the status of the Nine and more about
the planet and the mission itself. They do not care about us and our . . . evolution.**

Terec frowned, then continued the narration.

*Ember is burning the last pentabat. It pops with a noise I find quite satisfying,
and an odor I find less so, like melted sulfur.*

*"That's the last of them," Torban Buck says, although none of the Nine turn off
their lightsabers.*

Nothing more emerges from the gap in the hull, and Avar Kriss takes command.

*"We need to see what's outside," she says. "Get a better sense of this place and what
we'll need to do next. See if other threats are waiting for us."*

*"I'd like to find the Rod of Ages, too," Reath says. "It was secured in a storage case
for the journey"—he glances around at the many containers of various sizes scattered
around the shuttle's interior, shaken loose in the crash—"but I lost track of it when
we fell. I want to make sure it's safe, and spend some time with it, see if it reacts to
this world, understand what it can actually do. It could be helpful when we release the
Nameless."*

"Yes," Azlin Rell says, in his strange, thin voice. "Without doubt."

*"Speaking of the Nameless," Ty Yorrick adds, "shouldn't we check on them, too?
After all, they're the entire reason we're here."*

"Ordinarily, I'd agree," Elzar Mann says.

He points at the door toward the ship's aft that leads to the cargo hold.

*"But without power, we'd have to cut through that bulkhead to get to the creatures.
Until we know what sort of situation we've, ah, landed in, I'd like to keep some good,
solid metal between us and them."*

"All right," Avar says, "I think that's it. We'll do a brief scout of the area, then set

up a perimeter around the crash site while we figure out how to safely release the Nameless. Reath and Azlin's work with the Rod of Ages could help us there. Are we agreed?"

We are.

The Nine take a moment to check one another's armor, testing straps, helping to adjust bits of equipment as needed. Every set of armor is based on the same template, but we have all taken time to customize it to our own requirements and fighting styles.

We are the same, but unique.

***The same, but unique,** Ceret says.*

Our protection in place, Burryaga and Torban Buck step up to the gap and peer out. They are taking to heart their assigned roles as our first line of defense, and will be the first outside.

"Whoa," Buck says, and Burryaga makes a low hoot of agreement.

Both Jedi leap out into this new world, and the rest of us follow.

I am now outside, and you are sensing an overwhelming feeling of . . . being overwhelmed from me. I don't know how else to describe it.

Try,** Ceret says. **That is your task.

***

The Nameless homeworld was alive. Every last part of it. The air, the plants and trees, the stones, the countless creatures visible everywhere Terec looked. It spun and churned with growth and energy and chaos. The sounds of it, as well—the *sounds*. It was wildness, power, life in all its aspects.

The shuttle had crashed in a large open field, like a meadow. At its edge, tree-like plants thrust upward from the ground in a blast of color. Everything was colors, each more intense than the last, amplified by the pink cast to the light Terec had noticed before. Most of the trees were bulbous and irregular, but some spiked straight upward, like spears. It gave the forest's edge the feeling of a palisade or walled fort.

Native species roamed everywhere. Terec could see a gigantic beast lumbering through the forest, enormous tentacle-like limbs shooting down into the trees at regular intervals, emerging with wriggling beasts stuck to their ends that disappeared into the thing's mouths. To Terec, the creature seemed larger than the *Ataraxia*. If so, that would make its snacks—the animals it was pulling from the forest—as large as a Vanguard.

We will stay out of the forest, I think, Terec sent to Ceret.

A flock of what looked like stars swooped and spun overhead, flickering between blue and red.

It is beautiful, but I fear that my words do not convey the intensity, the vividness. The trees sway and moan, their branches thrashing back and forth. Herd animals in the meadow where we landed bash themselves against one another, goading themselves into stampede and just as suddenly skidding to a stop as one, to resume crashing their bone-studded heads together.

In the far distance, great arcs of intense pink-white light shoot up into the air, as if from fountains, pushing up into the sky, then falling back to the ground below in beautiful curves. They must be each as large as a mountain. If water could be transformed into the light side of the Force, I believe it would look like this.

This is a world that commits itself to life at a level that makes all others I have seen feel pale. This place is not restrained, not ordered. It grasps and surges and swings and bites and grows and loves and births more life. I can feel it all around me. It is so beautiful and so dangerous. I wish you could see it instead of just hearing my—

"Is that a ship?" Bell said, pointing up toward the sky with his still-illuminated lightsaber.

The rest of the Nine looked in the direction Bell indicated—all but Azlin Rell, Terec noted, who was staring toward the forest's edge with a fixed gaze, as if watching for something, perhaps expecting an attack or a visitation.

High above the Jedi, barely visible at the edge of the atmosphere, was the unmistakable silhouette of a starship.

Beyond it, the swirls and electrical activity of the Veil. It occurred to Terec that the Veil could be the reason the light of this world was so strange—even the sunlight had to pass through it.

"The *Ataraxia*?" said Avar.

"No way," Elzar replied. "We left the *'Rax* on the other side of the Veil, Avar. Wouldn't be visible from here."

"We aren't the first people to come here," said Reath. "I did a lot of research on this during my work with Azlin. Barnabas Vim, of course, but also prospectors, and members of a religious organization, and who knows who else. Any of them could have left a ship in orbit."

"The ship is still up there, Reath, because everyone who comes here dies," Azlin intoned, his strange blind gaze casting around.

"I'm going to try something," Elzar said.

"Can you . . . be more specific?" Avar said, her tone wary.

Elzar raised his hands and removed his helmet before anyone could ask him why he thought that was a good idea. His eyes grew wide, and he staggered to one side.

"Whoa," he said, his voice faint.

He bent at the waist and retched into the grass, almost falling.

"Elzar!" Avar cried.

She lunged for him, snatching the helmet from his hand and unceremoniously shoving it back over his head.

"Ow," Elzar said, slowly straightening.

"What did you possibly think you were doing?" Avar asked, clearly not very happy.

"I wanted to see what the planet felt like without the armor," Elzar said, his voice getting stronger with each word.

He took a small water bottle from his belt and lifted his helmet just enough to take a sip, then spat onto the grass.

"Bad," he said. "It feels bad. Or perhaps too good. There's so much sensation here—it's overwhelming, especially through the Force. Thank the light we have the armor. I don't know how we'd operate without it."

"There were other ways we could have learned—" Avar began.

Burryaga barked out a single word.

Bell looked to him. "Where?" he said, his tone sharp.

STAR WARS: TRIALS OF THE JEDI 189

Burryaga used his own lightsaber to point, a gigantic two-handed weapon suited to his great height.

Disturbances in the grass were approaching from all directions, rippling through the grass in sinuous curves.

We set ourselves in a circle, Terec sent. *Azlin is in the center. Reath is next to him, lightsaber lit, shield raised and powered. From Reath's body language, I am not certain the young man enjoys acting as the darksider's bodyguard, but he does not complain.*

Our backs are to Azlin and Reath. We face outward, lightsabers out and buzzing, an impenetrable wall.

A wriggling, twisting thing launches out from the grass, bright red in color. It's long and relatively thin for its length, about the width around of a human torso. It has legs, many many many legs, which whip and churn in hypnotic patterns.

As it flies through the air toward me, it rears back and up, and I can see that its underside is teeth, only teeth.

Terec sliced the beast in half, then into quarters before the pieces reached the ground. The segments still moved, writhing and thrashing, leaking iridescent white liquid. Terec had no idea if it was dead. Everything on this planet was alive.

"Where are the Nameless?" Azlin shouted as lightsabers flashed and Jedi fought to keep him safe.

The ancient man seized Reath by his armor's chestpiece and pulled him close.

"You told me there would be Nameless here, Reath. I see none. Where are they?"

Reath is capable of defending himself—he has weapons and the old man does not—but he does nothing. I cannot deny that Azlin has a certain . . . strength to him. When he turns his gaze on you, it carries a deep weight. A wind of intent. Reath is well trained, impressive in many ways, but here he seems frozen against whatever influence Azlin brings to bear.

Until, that is, Burryaga closes his enormous paw around Azlin's arm and lifts, pulling the ancient man away from Reath. Whatever power Azlin possesses, it is lost on the Wookiee. Burryaga snarls.

"I would not have hurt him," Azlin stammered. "I care deeply for the boy."

A small tremor passes through Reath. I am not sure others would notice if they were not tasked to report on all details as they happen—but I see it. Is it revulsion? Pride? I do not know.

"I asked Reath about the local Nameless for a reason, Burryaga," Azlin continued, his voice gaining strength. "Finding the native versions will help us know what to do with ours. Will help us save the galaxy."

Burryaga snorted in disgust but released Azlin Rell.

"I'm fine," Reath said, to no one in particular. "It was nothing. I was just distracted for a moment."

The latest attack is over. The scarlet tooth-slugs are either dead or in retreat, or their segments are. But by now, after two unsolicited attacks by the wildlife of the Nameless homeworld, the Nine are wary. Lightsabers remain lit, and we turn our eyes toward the thrashing, churning, howling, shrieking forest.

"This place is unbelievable," Torban Buck shouted, his low, deep voice carrying over the clamor. "It's like . . . a living storm. A hurricane."

"It certainly is!" came a second voice, a new one, from behind and above the Nine.

We spin, and there, standing alone on a bluff perhaps fifteen meters away, is Marchion Ro.

The Eye of the Nihil wears a long white coat and dark pants, and lacks his trademark mask. His long, dark hair is tossed by the wind. He is a figure of menace and enormous presence. He is alone.

The Jedi move without discussion, perfectly coordinated, rushing toward the architect of so much pain and death.

Before the Jedi can reach him, Marchion Ro produces a long metal rod from within his coat, tipped at either end by a faintly glowing purple gem. He raises it, and there is movement behind him.

Shapes crest the edge of the bluff, appearing on either side of the Eye of the Nihil. Twisted, broken silhouettes, moving in shuffling, eerie silence that belies their ability to slash, cut, kill.

Nameless. There are Nameless here. Marchion's Nameless, the ones he took from the planet.

I can feel Ceret's terror for me through our bond.

Stay back, Terec, *they think, underlining the sentiment with their words.*

I do not need convincing. There are dozens of the things. Dozens, more than a hundred. The armor protects our minds—we can see them clearly—but these creatures are accomplished Jedi killers even without the fog they generate in our thoughts, and they retain the ability to consume the Force from within us, leaving our bodies empty husks.

Somewhere behind me, I hear Azlin Rell whimper in fear.

We stop our grand charge, pulling up short, unsure of Marchion's intent, reformulating our plan of attack into one of defense, moving toward each other in pairs so as to support each other when the creatures come for us.

Silence as we wait. An endless moment. Marchion is smiling, savoring his advantage.

Avar Kriss moves, shifting her feet. She is going to say something, attempt to negotiate, perhaps. But what is there to say? What leverage can she possibly attempt to employ?

From behind us, the sound of ripping, tearing metal and all-too-familiar howls. The sounds of the Nameless—though these are not Marchion's troops.

We look back, toward the crash site of the shuttle that brought us to this world, and there we see the ship's hull bending outward like petals of a flower, clawed arms reaching out from within.

"The containment cell must have failed," Elzar Mann says, his voice gone dull and dark. "The batteries should have held . . . but . . ."

He trails off.

Twelve Nameless—our Nameless, captured at great cost and with the hopes of the galaxy riding upon them—clamber up and out of the wrecked shuttle and position themselves on its hull. They peer around themselves with a sense of . . . recognition? They know this place. It is their home.

"Those do not belong to you," Marchion Ro says.

He lifts that long rod once again, and the gems at either end glow with a greater intensity, the purple light washing against Marchion's blue-gray skin, making it look bloodstained.

"They are mine," Marchion says. "They are all mine."

We watch as the Nameless—whether brought here by Marchion Ro or by the Jedi—contort themselves in obvious agony and fall to their knees. They bow in Marchion's direction, a horrible display of forced fealty. Cursed moans come from the creatures' throats, hisses of submission.

"Look at you," Marchion Ro says. "I know all of you. All of your names. Burryaga. Reath Silas. Torban Buck. Elzar Mann. Avar Kriss. I know you all. The best of the Jedi Order, plus a few scraps they dragged along."

His grin widens.

"Yes, I mean you, Azlin Rell, and Ty Yorrick, monster-hunter. Fallen Jedi. Not good enough *Jedi.*"

Terec lifted their lightsaber. Burryaga was to their right, Torban Buck to their left, and the Nameless all around them. This could well be the moment of their death. But if so, they would not go quietly.

We are trapped between two groups of Nameless under the complete control of Marchion Ro, Terec sent. *Perhaps we could fight twelve. We have no hope of defeating over a hundred.*

Terec, comes the voice of my bond-twin. They want to be here with me. They are, and they are not.

"The Gaze Electric," *I hear Bell murmur as he looks up at the ship in the sky high above us.* "I should have recognized the silhouette. Should have known Marchion was here. Should have seen this coming."

Perhaps all of us should have seen this coming. Marchion Ro has always been ahead of us, from the very start.

"None of you will ever leave this world," Marchion says.

The Nameless creak and groan to their feet. Those near Marchion start to descend the bluff. Those behind us leap down from the shuttle's hull. They draw near.

"No one will ever know what happened to you," *the Eye of the Nihil says, his voice quiet and certain.*

I will, says Ceret. I will. I am so sorry.

"No one will come to save you."

STAR WARS: TRIALS OF THE JEDI

"You are wrong, Marchion Ro!" I find myself shouting as I tighten my grip on my lightsaber and prepare for the Nameless to charge. "The Jedi will come for us! The Republic will send help!"

"Ah, but not in time, Terec, you bizarre creature," Marchion says. "You see, their attention is about to be focused elsewhere."

Marchion presses another button on his control device.

High above, the Gaze Electric *explodes.*

PART TWO

THE SKIES OPEN.
THE BRIGHT DAY BECOMES
THE THUNDER NIGHT.
THE DELUGE.

Interlude

ESTARVERA

"Where are Mom and Dad?" Shanna asked her brother, again.

"They're coming," Davet said, again.

His voice was tired. He didn't sound mad at her or anything, more like one of her toys when she hadn't charged it for a while and the battery was almost done. Like he could still do what he was supposed to but maybe not for much longer.

Shanna looked back down the street. They were sitting in a little doorway, pressed up against each other side-to-side, resting.

People moved past them, most with backpacks on or bags in their hands. No one was running, but they all looked scared, even the grownups, and that was scarier than anything else.

That's not true, Shanna thought to herself. *The scariest thing was when Mom and Dad sent us away after the spaceport fell into the ground, and Davet yanked on my arm and pulled me down the street and we just ran, running from that horrible smashing sound behind us where Mom and Dad still are.*

The scariest thing was not knowing.

The sound of the spaceport collapsing had stopped a while ago. Every so often there would be a crashing noise out in the distance, and Shanna thought that meant more parts of the city were falling down into the underground. She had a bug farm when she was in little school, some sand between two panes of glass with a lid on it, so you could see how the creatures lived their lives. They dug long, curvy tunnels all over the place in the sand, making little rooms and houses for themselves. If you looked at the farm from the top, it seemed just like a normal patch of ground. But from the side you could see how it was all hollowed out and delicate. Shanna thought that was what had happened to the city. Something underground emptied it out, and now the buildings were too heavy and everything was falling down.

She didn't think she and Davet should be just sitting here in this doorway. If the streets were hollow by the spaceport, maybe they were hollow here, too, right underneath them. It might not be safe. But Davet was older—sixteen, in his third year of second school, when she was just eleven and still in first school. She couldn't make him do anything.

Florg squirmed in his little bag, which Shanna was holding tight but not too tight in both hands. She looked down at the little creature. His cute nose poked out of the sack, snuffling around, and she gave the scale-pig a scratch under his chin. She wished she had a treat for him, but she'd left them back in the speeder when—

Nope, don't want to think about that, she thought.

"Why aren't Mom and Dad here yet?" Shanna asked, but she was thinking about her mother's hoverchair, thinking maybe that was why.

Her chair was in the speeder, so it's gone. Without it, she'd never be able to—

"They're coming," Davet said.

Her brother lifted his comm, checking its small screen as he'd done every fifteen seconds or so. It was still blank. No messages from their parents.

"Is there a signal?" she asked.

"Nope," Davet said. "Not since the spaceport fell."

"That's good," Shanna said. "It means Mom and Dad probably just can't get through on theirs, either."

"Yep," Davet said.

He looked over at Sixbee, their droid, who was standing nearby, clicking and whirring. Sixbee was part of the family, had been around since Shanna was a baby, but it wasn't too smart. It could do basic things to help out and was really important in getting her mom in and out of her chair and so on, but it could only play little-kid games and had safety locks in its programming that prevented it from doing anything too interesting. Still, Shanna was glad Sixbee was there. It wasn't a parent, but it had taken care of all of them for a long time.

"Sixbee," Davet said, his voice stronger, more confident—he'd made some kind of decision.

"Yes, Master Davet," the droid said. "How may I assist?"

"Go back to where we left our parents. See if they need our help. If they don't, either bring them to us or come back here and tell us where they want us to meet them. If they aren't there, come back and tell us that, too. Do you understand?"

"Return to Masters Ryden and Calina, assess their situation, determine a meeting point if possible. In any case, return here with relevant information."

"That's it. We'll wait right here."

The droid hesitated. Shanna could almost see it thinking.

"I was directed by your parents to remain with you and keep you safe. Your directives appear to countermand those instructions. In light of the increasingly unstable situation, I believe it might be more prudent to—"

"Override code 7G89932," Davet said, speaking quickly. "Follow my orders."

Shanna gasped.

"You're not supposed to know that!" she said. "That's for Mom and Dad!"

"Quiet," Davet hissed at her.

"Override code accepted," Sixbee said. "Following orders."

The droid spun at the waist so it was facing back the direction they'd come, toward the fallen streets and the clouds of dust billowing into the air and the people still streaming away toward . . . Shanna wasn't sure. Away from the scary stuff and hopefully toward somewhere safe, she thought.

Sixbee began clomping away, moving against the flow of people. The droid wasn't delicate, wasn't fast, but it was steady. It got out of people's way, or people got out of its.

"Pardon me," she heard Sixbee saying as it got farther away. "I apologize for the inconvenience."

Its dull silver form started to disappear into the crowd.

I'll never see Sixbee again, Shanna thought with complete certainty.

She was wrong. Someone almost bumped into the droid, a big man with a little kid on his back, and even though Sixbee moved out of the way at the last second, the man was mad. Afraid and mad, and that was a bad combination.

"Out of my way, you fool thing," the man shouted, and gave Sixbee a hard shove.

The droid had stabilizers and was good at staying on its feet—she and Davet had both had fun trying to knock it over in years past—but the street was crowded. Sixbee caromed away from the big man and toward two Nautolan women—Shanna could see their huge dark eyes and head-tentacles. The droid wasn't large, but it was made of metal and could hurt someone if it bumped into them too hard. Sixbee seemed to know this. It swerved itself away from the women, and then it was in front of a big autocart full of people and there wasn't enough time and Sixbee went down.

She and Davet both heard the crunch. The autocart didn't stop.

"Oh, damn," Davet said.

They both got up and ran forward against the crowd, pushing and weaving their way through. Shanna made sure to keep a tight hold on Florg's bag. If she dropped him, he'd be crunched, too.

Sixbee was gone. The droid's torso had a big gash in it, with wires and pieces of mechanism sticking out. The lights in its eyes were out. The droid's shell was marred by streaks and spirals of tarnish her dad always

STAR WARS: TRIALS OF THE JEDI 201

said he was going to polish but never had and never would. Shanna felt sad, sad in a way she didn't think she would have for this silly machine that had taken care of her since she was a baby, had taken care of—

"Who will help Mom now?" Shanna said. "Mom needs help, Davet."

Her skin felt hot. Tears were coming, and she started hiccupping, trying to push them back.

I can see Sixbee's insides, she thought.

Davet grabbed her arm and pulled her out of the street to another alcove, another safe spot where the flow of people fleeing the certain death that had almost certainly killed their parents, dead like Sixbee, dead like they were going to be or even worse just alone—

"Shanna," her brother said.

Davet didn't seem tired anymore. He was very focused, like Dad when he was talking about something he really cared about.

"Sixbee can't go look for Mom and Dad now, and there's still no signal on my comm. I have to go find them myself. You can come with me, or you can stay here, but if you do, you can't move. You have to stay *right here* so that when we all come back—"

"I'll come," Shanna said, the easiest decision in the world.

"Okay," Davet said, not fighting her. "Let's go."

He took her hand, and they headed back through the streets toward where they knew their parents had to be waiting. Shanna had already decided they hadn't already found them because without her hoverchair, her mom had to be moving very slowly. It made sense.

Davet was careful, making sure they didn't bump into anyone and end up like Sixbee. He kept her close, choosing their moments to dodge through the crowd, pointing at open spots for her so she knew where they were going to go.

It got easier as they went. Shanna knew why—the city was emptying out the closer they got to the bad spots the Blight had gotten underneath. She and Davet moved faster, until they came to an intersection completely empty except for two security officers. They wore their yellow uniforms and had dark masks over the bottom half of their faces. Shanna didn't like that—they looked unfriendly, like shadow monsters—but one of them spoke after holding up a hand to get them to stop, and she had a kind voice.

"You can't go this way, kids. Isn't safe."

"Our parents are over there," Davet said, pointing.

The two officers exchanged a glance, a *let's lie to these kids* maneuver that Shanna immediately understood and hated.

"Everyone this way has been evacuated," the security officer said. "The whole city's being moved. There are transports waiting on the outskirts, in the parks. That's where your parents will be, and that's where you need to go."

"Closest one is at Alowee Pond Park," the other officer said. "You know where that is, how to get there?"

He pointed up another road different from the one they'd come along.

"You take Kizgo Boulevard as far as it goes, then turn left on Nebora Street. Takes you right there."

The first officer reached into a satchel slung across her body and produced two dark shapes.

"Here," she said, handing them to Davet. "Put these on. Don't take them off until you're on the transport and out of the city."

"What are they?" asked her brother, taking both and handing one to her.

"Breathing masks," the officer replied. "High-grain filter. Won't let any toxins through."

Shanna unfolded the dark object to see that it was indeed a mask, with attachments that would let her cover the bottom half of her face, just like the officers'. She put it on, fiddled with it to get it comfortable.

"Our parents didn't have these," she said. "Is there poison?"

Another one of those glances between the officers.

You think I don't know what you're doing, she thought, suddenly angry. *You think I'm just a silly kid.*

"They were handed out to everyone," the female officer said. "Your parents do have them."

A rumbling noise sounded from deeper in the city, toward the spaceport, and both officers snapped their heads up to look up. A new cloud of bone-white dust rose slowly, leisurely, into the air.

"You need to go," said the security officer. "You can't stay. Get to your parents. They'll be waiting for you at the park."

You're just telling me that so I'll feel better and leave, Shanna thought. *Mom and Dad aren't waiting. They aren't anywhere. They're with Sixbee.*

Florg squirmed in his sack, and Shanna resigned herself. She would do what she had to do. If nothing else, she had a scalepig depending on her.

"Come on, Davet," she said and walked away up the street in the direction the officer had indicated.

After a second or two, her brother followed her.

Chapter Fourteen

THE REPUBLIC, JUST OUTSIDE THE STORMWALL

Admiral Pevel Kronara sat in his command chair on the bridge of his flagship, the *Third Horizon.*

For a galaxy-spanning power, the Republic had surprisingly few vessels operating under its own direct authority: some patrol craft, several fighter wings, *Pacifier*-class cruisers, and the *Emissary*-class megacruisers of which the *Third Horizon* was the most prominent example. The ships were designed to project power more than use it. They were, in their way, works of art—beautifully crafted by a civilization that believed its ideals would prevent its warships from ever actually needing to fight a war.

But now the *Third Horizon* was as battle-scarred as any ship Kronara had ever seen, its beautiful hull marked by near-miss explosions from Nihil missiles and barely-deflected laser blasts. Its engines and generators had been modified during the Nihil conflict to increase its maneuverability and speed, but the new systems had been installed with an eye to functionality alone. Additional power conduits lashed into place wherever they would fit. Thick sheets of armor added to the ship's weak spots. Bulky new missile batteries bolted to the exterior hull.

All those modifications could have been handled in ways that would

STAR WARS: TRIALS OF THE JEDI   205

preserve the *Third Horizon*'s vaunted aesthetics—but that would have taken time. In the years since the inciting event of the Nihil conflict—the loss of the *Legacy Run* near Hetzal—the great ship had fought battle after battle with barely enough time between to get patched up. These days, no one would mistake the *Third Horizon* for one of those *Purrgil*-class pleasure yachts.

The ship now looked like what it was: an instrument of devastating power wielded on behalf of the ideals of the great Galactic Republic.

These days, Kronara had few restrictions on how he used that power. The Nihil were a real enemy, a true enemy, and the worse they got, the fewer obstacles were put in his way to fighting them however he felt necessary.

"But how will it look if you attack with full force?" was no longer a question being asked.

Instead, another question, implied more than spoken: "What will happen to us if you don't?"

Which was why it was particularly frustrating to be stuck on the wrong side of the Stormwall. The *Third Horizon,* plus its cruiser group and all the fighters and support craft in their hangars, were just a tiny hop through hyperspace from the world of Eriadu, but they had no way to get there.

Kronara knew Eriadu was where the fighting was most likely to break out. Hell, for all he knew it already had. RDC forces under his command were bunkered on the planet. He knew some of them personally. Being unable to get to them or to know what was happening beyond the Stormwall . . . it was challenging.

Admiral Kronara was in command, was literally sitting in the command chair of the greatest warship in the Republic—and he had no commands to issue.

Hold station. That was his only order. He said those words to his XO every morning, and reaffirmed them every evening as the night watches began.

If I could just get over there, he thought, frowning, *I could clean up every bit of Nihil space. Take it all back. Remind those mask-wearing cowards we're all the blasted Republic, whether they realize it or not.*

Kronara reset his face into the mass of granite he preferred to present to his subordinates when on the bridge. The commander had to be a reflection of the indomitable spirit required to fly a starship into a threshing mill of laser blasts against impossible odds.

Stone-faced. Implacable. That was how a commander had to appear. But inside, they needed to be as sensitive as a Felucian flickerbird, attuned to changes in battle conditions, tactical scenarios, and above all the emotional temperature of the beings under their command. The true weapon of any warship was its crew, and keeping them in good order was one of a good commander's primary responsibilities.

Pevel Kronara was a *very* good commander, and so when his people started to churn with a kind of confused, excited tension—he knew it instantly.

The *Third Horizon*'s bridge was a large space, circular, with the command chair placed in the center. It offered a 360-degree view of the space around the ship via long, curved, horizontally oriented windows, which meant Kronara or his officers could see anything approaching from any direction. The ship had strong sensors, but there was no substitute for seeing the tactical environment with your own eyes.

Kronara used the controls built into his command chair to slowly rotate, surveying his domain. Almost immediately, he saw his XO, Lieutenant Commander Bekkitet, near the station of Lieutenant Meller, the comms officer. Their bodies were tense, their conversation short and clipped.

That's it, Kronara thought. *That's where this is coming from.*

"Incoming message?" he called over to them.

"Not just one, Admiral," Bekkitet said, looking up at him. "Many. We're parsing through them. Nothing we're receiving was specifically sent to us. It's more like regular communications traffic. Commercial, personal, the normal sort of chatter you'd see running through the relays out here."

"Why is that unusual?" Kronara asked.

"Two reasons come to mind, sir," Bekkitet replied. "But I would prefer to delay my report until we complete our analysis."

His executive officer was utterly reliable, a Quarren water-clock of efficiency and precision. Kronara knew she was waiting to offer up a full report until she was absolutely certain of what was going on, but he had endured too many uneventful duty shifts in this damn chair to wait for her to triple-check her conclusions.

"Continue your report, XO," he said. "Your initial impressions are fine."

"Reason one," Bekkitet said, holding up a hand with a single claw extended. "The comms traffic we're seeing was not present a few minutes ago. It popped up out of nowhere."

Odd, Kronara thought. *I wonder if Republic techs activated a new relay buoy— but ordinarily they'd notify us.*

"Reason two," his second said, producing another digit. "The origin of the signals appears to be worlds and vessels inside the Occlusion Zone."

"Inside the O.Z.? But communications signals can't penetrate the—"

The full import of her words landed, and Kronara spun his chair to look toward the *Third Horizon*'s nose. It was pointed directly toward the Occlusion Zone, straight at Eriadu and the invisible barrier that prevented him from reaching it or any of the other worlds the Nihil had stolen, worlds and populations that desperately needed the Republic's help.

"Dispatch a remote probe with hyperspace capability to confirm, Lieutenant Commander," Kronara said. "Uncrewed, just to be safe. I want confirmation ASAP. I want it yesterday."

"Acknowledged, Admiral. Right away," said Bekkitet, and the bridge sprang to life as his crew executed his orders, spinning up into readiness for whatever might come next.

The crew knows what this means as well as I do, Kronara thought. *We don't need to wait for the probe to send confirmation. It'll tell us what we already know.*

Admiral Pevel Kronara was as sure as he'd been of anything in his life. The Stormwall was down.

Viess took the chance cubes in her hand. There was, of course, a trick to them. If you tapped just the right pips, they'd push inward and shift the weighting for the next roll. That would mean she'd spin a winner, and her crew would see her as lucky, another important element for morale.

Rule One: Win, she thought. *Rule Two: Do whatever you have to do to follow Rule One.*

The chance cubes clattered across the deck, landing exactly as she expected them to, the highest possible configuration.

At the exact moment the cubes stopped rolling, an alert blared out from the threat-assessment console. Kestee shot to her feet and ran to see what was happening, but Viess could see for herself as the bridge's primary battle display updated with the data.

Ships were appearing above Eriadu. New ships, popping in from hyperspace.

They're above us, Viess thought, updating her mental model of the tactical situation like the old veteran she was. *We're still in the planet's gravity well down here. We can't get to hyperspace without getting past them.*

"Who are they?" she asked, keeping her voice calm. She asked, but she already knew. She could see the designators popping up on the holos.

A new title for her autobiography popped into her head: *Viess: The Dumbest Woman Alive, Who Will Soon Be Dead.*

"They're RDC, General," Kestee said. "A full fleet. The *Third Horizon* seems to be at the head."

"That's not possible," Viess said, knowing how pathetic she sounded, how old and confused, how weak. "The Stormwall . . ."

She trailed off. Either the Stormwall was down—wouldn't be the first time—or the RDC had figured out a way past it. It looked like she was about to engage in something she had tried to avoid for most of her career.

A fair fight.

STAR WARS: TRIALS OF THE JEDI 209

Viess took a deep breath, held it, let it out, went to her command chair, sat.

"We no longer care about holding this planet," she ordered. "We care about getting clear. Us, this ship." She paused, looking out at the faces of her silent crew. "So we can continue to command from a safe distance."

No one said anything. Who would disagree? She'd trained them all. They knew how this worked.

Rule Three.

If you can't win, run.

"Send out a request for reinforcements," Viess continued. "Every ship in the Nihil fleet. To Eriadu, now."

This was it. The battle, the war, the whole Nihil thing . . . it would be decided here, today.

Admiral Kronara watched on his own tactical displays as the Nihil fleet shifted from a surface bombardment posture to one more strategically oriented toward engaging his own ships. In other words, they turned around.

His communications team had intercepted the Nihil's call for reinforcements. Kronara had called for his own. His intelligence reports gave him a decent idea of the forces the Nihil could bring to bear, assuming all their ships actually showed up. He knew what his side could muster just as well. They were evenly matched.

Victory in battle was determined by an endless series of factors: battlefield conditions, morale, weaponry, supply chains, luck. But in the opinion of Admiral Pevel Kronara, the single most important element was this: which side had the better commander.

"Attack," he said.

Chapter Fifteen

THE NAMELESS HOMEWORLD

When Marchion Ro was a child, he discovered the meaning of life. He believed he was given this insight at such a young age as a test from the universe: *We've shown you what you're supposed to do—now show us you can do it.*

It came to him while sitting through a meal aboard the *Gaze Electric.* His father, Asgar, and grandmother Shalla were bickering about their vague plan to conquer, destroy, or kill the Jedi, or end the Republic, or just show everyone—*everyone*—that they were to be reckoned with. Marchion Ro wanted to leave the table, to go spend time with Mari San Tekka. The ancient human woman was as close to a friend as he had, even though she was stuck in a weird tank with wires running in and out of her and machines keeping her alive.

But Marchion was not allowed to do that. He was required to remain at the table until the meal was concluded, until the wine was drunk, until arguments were settled, until plans were made, remade, discarded, picked back up, and made anew.

From this small moment, staring at his empty plate, wishing to leave but not being able to, came Marchion Ro's understanding of the purpose of being alive.

"The point of life," that boy had murmured to himself, "is to make your decisions matter more than anyone else's."

So Marchion did. Over years, many years, he found ways to elevate himself, creating paths for his choices to carry more weight than those of others around him. He did this first with his family, although the method was somewhat drastic—he became the most important Ro by becoming the only Ro left. Then he took control of the Tempest Runners. Then the Nihil as a whole. The entire Occlusion Zone. Over and over, Marchion conquered problems and destroyed obstacles. He found paths to continue moving forward. The universe rose to meet him, and in greater and greater spheres, the will of Marchion Ro became the only will.

Now the ultimate confirmation of the rightness of all those many choices lay spread before him. Marchion stood atop a slight rise in the landscape of this wild, thrashing planet, looking down at the nine warriors the Jedi Order had sent to thwart him, as the remains of the *Gaze Electric* burned in the atmosphere high above. The Jedi were bunched together, back-to-back in a loose circle, helpless. Dozens of Nameless crept close to them, their eyes hungry, their mouths open and spilling slime on the strange ground of this strange world, bones clacking, tendons audibly stretching like old bands of rubber.

It was a tableau. A dream made real, an unforgettable image, and even better was the fact that in all the ways that mattered, Marchion Ro had created it.

The Jedi wore suits of armor, white and gold, and masks over their faces.

How funny, Marchion thought. *They're masked, and I'm not.*

Marchion thought the Jedi's armor must protect them from the disorienting effect generated by the Nameless—otherwise they'd all be screaming in terror, rolling around on the ground, fighting phantoms.

But no—the Jedi were focused, their lightsabers lit and humming.

Only Azlin Rell was unarmed. The old man huddled in the middle of the Jedi's protective circle, his arms wrapped tight around himself, his body like a twisted wire. Marchion wondered why the Jedi had brought a traitorous old man along on what was clearly a crucially important mission to them. No matter.

The Nameless drew closer to the Jedi, driven by their hunger, driven by the Rod of Power, currently dangling loosely from Marchion's left hand. He tapped his dark claws against its surface. He could give the final command: *Charge, kill, feast* . . . but he didn't want to. Not yet.

"You can't kill these things, you know," Marchion Ro called out to the Jedi.

Not one of the self-righteous fools shifted their gaze from the Nameless. They knew the danger they were in. Only Azlin Rell looked up, his expression unreadable through the mask but his body language radiating utter terror.

"You know how it works," Marchion said. "Every Nameless that dies means the Blight gets worse. If you kill one here, how many souls will you doom to death elsewhere in the galaxy?"

Marchion shook his head in sympathy, to show the Jedi that he, too, understood how difficult it had to be for them.

"But the Nameless can kill *you,* of course," he called. "All of *you* dying wouldn't change things at all."

He gestured down toward the circle of lost, doomed fools. The Jedi were in constant, subtle motion—shifting their feet, adjusting their stances and the angles at which they held their lightsabers, trying to prepare for the attack they knew would come. They seemed to be ignoring him, not acknowledging his presence at all—but Marchion knew they heard every word he said.

"So many of you have died horribly. Have any of those deaths actually meant anything? The Jedi couldn't stop the Nameless. You didn't save Starlight Beacon. You can't stop the Blight. I could go on, but let's just collect all your failures into one: You haven't stopped *me.*"

"We'll see," one of the Jedi said—Marchion thought it was Torban

STAR WARS: TRIALS OF THE JEDI 213

Buck. It was tricky to be certain with the masks, but the Chagrian's horns were a solid clue.

I knew you were listening, he thought.

"I could have had it all, given time," Marchion said, raising his voice. "I think we all know that. But I realized something not long after Starlight went down and the Stormwall came up. There's a . . . flaw built into the system. Something staring me in the face the whole time."

He placed a hand flat on his chest.

"Even if I ruled the entire galaxy, it wouldn't actually give me what I wanted. Coming to understand this left me very low. Very low indeed."

One of the Jedi called out, without turning from the circling Nameless—Avar Kriss, based on the blond hair and the lovely music in her voice.

"You realized power is a trap, Marchion. That's why you changed direction and offered to save the galaxy from the Blight. You can still do that. You can still be that person. It's never too late."

Energy filled Marchion. He began pacing back and forth on the bluff, just to put it somewhere.

"No, Master Kriss," he said. "That offer was never real. I was just buying time, misdirecting. You still don't understand. Saving the galaxy was never the answer for me. If I did that, even if everyone knew I'd done it, even if I was even more of a hero than *the Jedi* . . . someday I would still die. I don't want to be remembered. Eventually, everything that is remembered is forgotten. I want more."

Marchion spread his arms wide. Now the Jedi looked at him, all of them. Of course they did. He was Marchion Ro.

"I realized that what I wanted—what I needed—was to make a choice for everyone in the galaxy that could not be reversed or contradicted. This has always been about proving *the supremacy of my will.* The last decision made by anyone, anywhere, ever . . . it had to be mine."

The Jedi stiffened, their postures shifting. They understood. Marchion's predator eyes read their new attitudes as *We have to kill him, we have to stop him, we have to we have to we have to*—but we can't.

For fun, Marchion used the Rod of Power to force several of the Nameless to lunge forward toward the Jedi, claws outstretched. The Jedi reacted instantly, lifting their lightsabers, ready to . . . what? What did they think they were going to do?

Marchion considered using a Nameless to kill one of the Jedi right then, to answer a question he was curious about. Would the Jedi strike back, or would they actually let a Nameless kill them rather than possibly allow sentients to die in some other place they'd probably never see?

Marchion tapped his finger against the Rod of Power, considering . . . but no. Not yet. This was all the audience he'd ever have.

"It was difficult for me when I realized that even ruling the galaxy would not bring me peace," Marchion Ro said. "This is why I fell into despair after the Stormwall went up. I knew what I needed but could not see any way to achieve it. How does one person kill an entire galaxy? Even if I ended a million lives per day for the rest of my life, I wouldn't come close to destroying even a single world in the Core. Why had the universe been so cruel to me? It had given me the capacity to have the great insight, to see the final goal but have no way to achieve it.

"It was awful."

He watched as the Jedi tried to find a way to defend themselves from the circling, snapping, lunging Nameless without actually hurting them. The poor fools had to be terrified. It was beautiful.

"Finding a way to end everyone at once was a puzzle I could not solve," Marchion said. "I let Ghirra run her schemes, let Viess and Boolan and the others scrabble and scratch in the playground I built for them while I thought, and thought, and tried to find a way."

Marchion remembered those days so clearly—an unending span of gray, like a cloudy sky that threatened a storm but never made good on its promise.

"I persisted, pushed against the despair, and in time the universe rewarded my focus, my diligence. It handed me the Blight," Marchion said.

He stopped pacing, now talking to himself as much as to the Jedi below.

"I had no idea removing Nameless from this world would cause the Blight to happen elsewhere. In the beginning, I just wanted a weapon that would kill Jedi. But somehow, my decision to delve into my family's history, to find this place and come here . . . that simple choice ended up giving me exactly what I've desired since I was a child. Do you see how unlikely that is? That not only would I be a person who wanted the galaxy to die, but that my lineage would also be deeply connected to a way to achieve it? That connection . . . that *link* . . . the odds against it are astronomical. It could only happen if the key thing I've always believed to be true about myself is in fact true."

Marchion Ro looked up at the strange sky of the Nameless world, watching the Veil spin above.

"No one else matters," Marchion said. "Only me. Now and forever."

"Why are you telling us this?" shouted Elzar Mann—no mistaking that self-satisfied voice.

"Because if I don't tell you, you won't know," Marchion said, turning back to the Jedi. "It feels better if you know. If someone knows. This was my last chance to tell anyone. These things are important to me. I'm glad I shared them with you."

He lifted the Rod of Power, the purple stones at its ends glowing, intensifying. Below, the Nameless froze.

"Don't, Marchion!" one of the Jedi shouted. "You can't!"

"Watch me," he said.

No one could tell Marchion Ro what to do. That was the point.

The Nameless attacked. They leapt forward, their claws extended, their jaws open wide, all their savage power ready to rend, to destroy, to tear flesh from bone and swallow organs and bathe in blood.

But they did not attack the Jedi.

They attacked one another.

They did not want to do this. They had not chosen to do this. But in this, as in so many other things, Marchion's will would be done.

Every Nameless launched its body at the nearest creature like itself. They slashed, tore, slaughtered, their claws and teeth rending apart the bodies of their fellows. Skin ripped, bones snapped, internal structures burst, fluids poured and ran across the ground.

With every wound, the planet responded. From all directions, screams rose up from the creatures in the forests surrounding the killing field. The plants and trees shuddered as if they, too, were being consumed, hammered, ripped apart. The very air vibrated. Chaos.

Marchion looked up, envisioning the vast galaxy beyond.

All the bad things happening here are happening out there, too.

The Eye of the Nihil smiled like a boy surprised with a gift, the thing he's always wanted.

He looked back down the bluff. The Jedi had drawn into a tighter circle and had their hands out. They were using the Force. Marchion couldn't sense it himself, but he knew what it looked like when the Jedi worked their magic.

He watched for a little while. The Jedi called to one another, offering words of support, of advice.

Here and there, he saw evidence of their efforts—a Nameless lifted into the air or resting back on its haunches, momentarily calmed. But for every creature the Jedi tried to save, many more were destroyed. Wails of agony rose into the air.

It was a beautiful thing.

The Jedi were failing, as they always did—but their efforts would keep them busy for a while. Marchion would kill the Jedi eventually, but he wanted the Nameless dead first. There was time. There was time for everything now.

Marchion strode away into the jungle. These were not the only Nameless on the planet. He would find the rest and kill them all.

And then it would be over.

Chapter Sixteen

THE BATTLE OF ERIADU

There was no safe place in Eriadu City. Not on the ground, and not in the sky. Not for Pikka and Joss Adren.

Deadly bolts of energy slashed through the air from all directions, all around the *Aurora III;* red, green, and blue spears burning with the intent to kill. Some could be deflected by the *Aurie*'s shields, which Pikka had upgraded well beyond the Longbeam standard issue. The ship barely noticed even direct hits from fighters or handheld weaponry. Other shots, though—fired by the gigantic starships hovering above or launched from artillery emplacements on the ground—were powerful enough to turn entire neighborhoods into smoking pits. If the *Aurie* took a hit from one of those, it would vanish as if it had never been.

Other starships careened through the air, chasing, being chased, firing, fleeing. Some were damaged, leaking smoke or sparks or flame. Some weren't ships at all, but chunks of wreckage flung from exploding vessels. A collision with any of those—friend or foe—would destroy the *Aurora III* on impact.

The ground was no better. At first glance, it seemed like it should be— the bombardment of Eriadu City had largely ceased once ship-to-ship combat commenced between the big capital ships of the Nihil and the newly arrived RDC fleet. But when the salvos stopped falling from above, ground forces emerged from where they'd taken shelter and resumed fighting it out in the streets and alleys. If Pikka tried to set the *Aurie* down, the ship would be swarmed.

There was no safe place—not outside the *Aurie.* The only safety was inside it, in its cockpit, where Pikka flew with everything she had. And what did she have? Her eyes and her ears and the ship's sensors and her pilot's instincts and the will to make sure her husband, their child, and she would all survive.

Joss was across the cockpit in the navigator's seat. Well, some of the time. He was constantly leaping up to patch power between shields, engines, weapons, making repairs on the fly, taking the gunner controls when he could and firing at Nihil raider ships to supplement Pikka's own work on that front.

If they spoke, it was only to convey the barest bit of information the other needed to do their part—a word here, a grunt of acknowledgment there. Joss and Pikka Adren were united, operating like a machine designed to preserve a tiny safe place within an ocean of death, and that even smaller place inside Pikka where their child was waiting to be born. The baby didn't know what was happening, didn't know that its parents' choices had made it all too likely that it might never leave the place where it had grown. It rested, warm, waiting, just a few weeks from coming into the world.

THIS IS A SAFE PLACE! Pikka screamed in her mind, tweaking the control sticks left, then right, then up and forward to send the Longbeam into a dive, feeling the ship's engines surge and weapons fire, and then she was flying through a flower of fire that a moment earlier had been an ugly, cruel block of metal with a Nihil pilot at the helm.

"Three up," Joss said. "Shaken, no chasers."

Pikka's mouth tightened.

In their marital shorthand, Joss's words meant three enemy ships were converging on their position from different directions, with no friendly vessels close enough to help.

STAR WARS: TRIALS OF THE JEDI 219

"Need a road, Joss," she said.

"Working on it, love."

Pikka kept the Longbeam in the dive, feeling g-forces push her back in her seat, wondering how the baby interpreted these sensations, feeling it kick. It did that a lot, and its feet always felt huge—this was Joss's kid, no doubt about it.

Baby Adren probably doesn't realize anything is unusual at all. It's probably just safe and happy in its little floaty cocoon in there. It's just kicking me because it's fun to kick.

That's what Pikka Adren chose to believe.

"Upscrew, forty left," Joss said.

Corkscrew up and to the left at forty degrees. Okay. If the baby wasn't having fun before, it's sure as hell about to.

"I know it's a tricky maneuver, but it'll draw them closer together, unify their firing vector so they can't hit us from all sides," Joss went on, as if he was trying to convince himself.

"We'll need to—"

"Already on it," Joss said, levering himself up and out of his seat.

No easy feat against the g-forces from the dive. Pikka couldn't have done it. But Joss was strong.

Arms like a lifter droid, face like a lifter droid, too, he liked to say.

The rest is heart, she always thought, when he did.

"Need to pull us out of this dive," Pikka said, flicking switches that would activate specially installed maneuvering thrusters that would kick in once she pulled back on the control sticks, letting them change direction faster than their pursuers would believe possible. "You braced? Gonna be sharp."

"I'm good," Joss said from back at the shield control console, where she knew he was diverting power toward the rear shields, where, if all went as planned, they'd presently be taking quite a bit of fire. "Go."

Pikka yanked back on the control sticks. The ship's main thrusters roared in protest. The *Aurie* apparently found it frustrating that its idiot pilot was requesting a change of direction when it was already pleasantly engaged in a steep, gravity-assisted dive. Secondary thrusters on the top rear of the hull fired half a moment later, essentially *shoving* the Longbeam's tail forward and down, swinging the entire ship around in a controlled spin around its central axis.

The ship didn't much like this. Its frame groaned and shuddered around them, but Pikka knew it wouldn't fall apart. She and Joss had spent plenty of time reinforcing it with light, strong alloys that meant their *Aurie* could do things other vessels could not. It was a safe place.

Out the front viewport, all around the *Aurora III,* flashes of color as laser bolts zipped past. It was still pure death out there. Pikka put it out of her mind. You could only control what you could control.

She put the ship into a spiral, heading up at forty degrees. She didn't know what the enemy Nihil ships were doing—couldn't take focus from flying the ship to look at her scopes—but she trusted Joss. She had to. If he said this was the maneuver that gave them the best chance of surviving, then it was.

More kicks from the baby—*not a fan of all this shaking and spinning,* she thought.

Then another kick, hard, but not from inside her. This came from Pikka's right, from outside the ship, from one of the many deaths awaiting them in the not-safe spaces of the raging battle.

"Nnf!" came Joss's voice, and she heard muffled thuds and bangs that her mind immediately assembled into a picture of her husband falling backward, deeper into the ship, having lost his grip on whatever he was braced against when the laser blast hit. (She assumed it was a laser blast, anyway—a low-energy shot from a relatively distant fighter, probably not aimed at them at all, just coincidentally occupying the same space as the *Aurie* at the worst possible second.)

Are the shields up? Pikka thought, prioritizing.

That was the central question. She was worried about Joss, of course she was, but she'd seen him trip and fall off the roof of a three-story building and sit up laughing. He could get banged up and be just fine. But if he hadn't finished boosting the rear shields, then the concentrated

STAR WARS: TRIALS OF THE JEDI 221

fire of three Nihil raider ships firing on their tail at once would be enough to knock them out of the sky.

She risked a quick glance down at her indicators, focusing on the one displaying a simple outline of the *Aurora III,* with its shields represented by a glowing silhouette. Fully operational shield zones would be green. After a few direct hits, they'd turn yellow. As power levels dropped, they could be red or absent entirely. If Joss had completed his task, the rear shields would be three levels deep in green, while other areas of the ship wouldn't be shielded at all.

Blast it, Pikka thought, looking at the display. *He didn't get it done.*

That was her last thought before one, two, three more kicks hit the *Aurora III,* all right in the stern. The first knocked the shields down to red, the second to nothing, and the third . . . well, the third knocked them down.

"No!" Pikka cried as all the indicators on her control console flipped over to the red.

Main engines out, rear shields gone but other shields are holding, she thought, running the systems checklist. *Weapons up, mostly. Power dropping fast— maybe the reactor took a hit.*

The priority now was avoiding another hit at the stern. Another blast and they were done for. Pikka could still fly, could still stay in the air— those bonus maneuvering thrusters could work as primary propulsion in a pinch. They didn't have much fuel, though, and using them took a lot of focus, a lot of micromanaging.

Pikka whipped the *Aurie* into a roll, spinning it up and over and back down like a breaching aiwha splashing back down into the sea. She knew the maneuver would toss Joss around like a pebble in the back, but there was nothing to be done.

Thank the light he's built like a lifter droid, she thought.

The idea—the only one she had—was to fly the *Aurie* toward one of the other engagements between RDC and Nihil ships, to see if an allied fighter might be able to take out the pursuers on her tail. She toggled her communications, sending out a broadcast on all frequencies.

"This is the Republic Defense Coalition Longbeam designation *Aurora III.* I've taken damage and have three Nihil Strikeships on my tail. Requesting any available assistance from RDC or Eriaduan ships. Please . . . I have a child aboard."

Silence and then a response.

"Don't worry, Mommy," came a hiss from her speakers. "We're here to help."

Not an ally. The opposite, in fact.

"Joss!" she yelled, her eyes on the threat displays, seeing the Nihil lining up behind her, all in a row.

No answer.

Pikka pushed the maneuvering thrusters beyond what they were designed to do, slewing the ship to the left and right, sliding it through the air, trying to delay the inevitable. Blasterfire whipped past the ship, barely missing them.

Any one of those hits us and we're done, she thought. *That's the whole game.*

Pikka glanced back down at the threat display, then flicked her eyes back up.

Wait.

She looked again, making sure. Yes. The display now only showed two Nihil raiders on their tail, not three.

Maybe one of them got hit by a stray shot? Pikka thought.

Then a new ship appeared on the scope, closing fast, from behind the two remaining Nihil fighters. They saw it, too, and broke left and right, away from the *Aurie's* tail.

Pikka gasped in relief. Whoever was flying the mystery ship, they'd saved her life—all three of their lives. It wasn't over, but it wasn't *over,* either.

She curved the ship around in a wide arc, a far cry from the tight turns her ship could normally pull off, and looked for her as-yet-unknown savior. She wanted to help, if she could. The *Aurie's* weapons still worked.

In the end, she didn't need to do anything.

The new ship was a small fighter Pikka didn't recognize. She guessed it

STAR WARS: TRIALS OF THE JEDI 223

was some local planetary design not used outside its native system. It could move, though. The fighter went into a barrel roll, then juked to the left and down in pursuit of one of the Nihil raider ships. Pikka focused her attention on the other Nihil fighter, the last one. She was trying to line up a shot, do her part, when the new ship's canopy slid back.

Then two things happened, one of which Pikka believed and the other she did not. The thing she believed: The new ship fired its blasters, and the first of the two remaining Nihil ships flipped over and collapsed into itself, its hull disintegrating into burning fragments.

The thing she did not: A spinning arc of blue light shot out from the open cockpit of the new ship, forming into a disk about a meter in radius. It whipped out toward the last Nihil raider, *sliced it in half,* then *curved in midair,* returning in a precise arc to where it began—at which point it disappeared once again into the cockpit.

The new ship whipped past the *Aurie,* waggling its wings in acknowledgment. Its cockpit was still open, and Pikka got a glimpse of the pilot as it zipped away: a gray-bearded, long-haired, pale-skinned being with a patch over one eye, holding a short metal cylinder to his forehead in salute.

"What the *hell?*" Pikka said.

⚜

Jedi Master Emerick Caphtor meditated, connecting deep with the Force, seeking calm and peace from within. He was crouched just inside the bunker where he had taken shelter with Navaj Tarkin and his fellow Jedi Kantam Sy. The sounds and smells and sensations of war were everywhere. The thin acid scent of burning wires and electronics. The sharp snapbooms of exploding vehicles and fuel tanks. The feel of air compressed and heated by massive column-thick laser bolts sizzling through the air.

War was chaos, raw and untempered. It solved nothing, answered no questions. There was no logic to it, only horror and pain. Emerick pulled his focus inward, seeking the Force. There were no questions the Force could not answer, and it would always answer true. Emerick took refuge in it, forming a barrier of interior peace between himself and the madness just meters away.

Then, he did his best to channel that calm light toward Kantam Sy, and more specifically toward the horrible wound on the other Jedi's head. Emerick had read of healing with the Force, transferring energy from one living being to another. It was a lost technique that few living Jedi understood, but even if his attempts to send the Force toward his injured friend were unlikely to help, Emerick felt they could not hurt. Kantam's head wound had stopped bleeding. That might have nothing to do with the Force and everything to do with their body's natural processes, but it was something.

"What do we do?" Navaj had asked when they first realized they were trapped inside the nearly destroyed defense bunker, unable to leave while slowed by Kantam's injury.

Emerick still had no concrete answer. The battle raged; people died. A second fleet had appeared in the sky, recognizable as forces of the Republic Defense Coalition. Now the Nihil and the RDC slugged it out above the planet, using weapons of a scale that boggled the mind. Emerick desperately wanted to do something more—to fight, to give aid to the injured, to find help for Kantam, anything—but knew that rushing out into the burning maelstrom beyond the bunker's exit was certain death.

The chances are slim anyone's even still alive out there for me to help, Emerick thought, deep inside the Force, seeking answers he could not yet find.

"What the—?" he heard Navaj say, his voice dim and distant.

Emerick brought his senses back to the moment, hoping his meditation had done something for Kantam. The other Jedi still slept, a blood-stained strip of robe wrapped around their head.

"What is it?" Emerick said, opening his eyes and getting to his feet.

The commando pointed, up.

"That ship. I don't know who's flying it, but it's doing incredible things. It's slicing through the Nihil like they're nothing."

"The pilot's a good shot?"

"No, I mean literally *slicing.* Watch."

Emerick followed the ship Navaj had indicated as it whipped through the air, rolling and twisting through the Nihil attack fighters swarming it. More than once, the small vessel slipped out of the way of enemy fire at precisely the right moment to let the shots zip past and take out a different Nihil ship. It felt almost as if the pilot had engineered the result on purpose, letting the Nihil destroy each other rather than firing their own blasters.

Not to say this mysterious ship wasn't willing to use its weapons— lines of energy lanced regularly from the fighter's cannons, each finding a target. But still, none of that explained what Navaj had said. *Slicing.* Emerick was about to ask him to explain when he saw it.

A disk of blue light, whipping out from the open cockpit of the new ship, cutting off the wing of one of the Nihil attackers before curving back to its source.

"Lightsaber," Emerick said, flat and certain. "That pilot's a Jedi."

"Whoa," Navaj said. "Do you know who it is?"

"Yoda could do it, but he probably wouldn't. And his blade is green."

Emerick ran down the list of Jedi he knew were on Eriadu, the people who had attended Lula Talisola's wedding in Bri-Phrang. Yaddle could have pulled off the throw—maybe—but like Yoda, her lightsaber blade was green, and this didn't seem like something she would do, either. Really, there was only one likely candidate. But that wasn't possible.

But maybe it is, he thought, feeling a surge of hope.

"Do you have macrobinoculars?" Emerick asked.

Navaj pulled a set from his pack and handed them over without a word. Emerick held the device to his eyes, taking a moment to zero in on the ship at such high magnification. The macrobinoculars' stabilizers kicked in once its circuits realized what he was trying to see, and the image cleared, following the ship as it swung and curved through the air. At one point, it rolled so its cockpit was facing almost directly toward the bunker exit, and Emerick tapped the button that captured a still image.

He froze the shot, then zoomed in.

He took a breath.

By the light, he thought.

"It's . . . it's Porter Engle," Emerick said, lowering the macrobinoculars, still almost not daring to believe what he'd seen.

"Okay, fine. Who's Porter Engle?" Navaj responded.

"A very old, very experienced Jedi," Emerick said, watching the ship wheel and turn high above. "He retired from the Order but reactivated himself once the Nihil conflict began. I had no idea he was anywhere near this world. The lightsaber's been his focus for his entire career. He can do things the rest of us barely understand."

They both watched as the blue lightsaber sliced through another enemy ship. Porter's course was clear—he was headed for the Nihil flagship.

Emerick allowed the touch of a smile to cross his lips. He spoke again.

"We call him the Blade."

Chapter Seventeen

THE NAMELESS HOMEWORLD

Every hair on Burryaga's body felt like it had been dipped in electric acid. The emotional wasp's nest pouring off the Nameless as they methodically, savagely ripped each other to pieces was worse than anything he'd ever felt.

They don't want to kill, he knew. *Marchion Ro gave them no choice.*

All around him were his fellow Jedi, some of the most skilled he'd ever known. They had their lightsabers lit and ready, they had skills in the Force he couldn't imagine, and yet they were all but paralyzed.

A Nameless closed its jaws around the neck of one of its fellows, crunched, wrenched. A gout of foul, pale fluid and a headless corpse fell to the ground even as the murderer turned, swaying, snarling, looking for another victim.

The horror of what Marchion Ro had done shrieked through Burry's mind. As each Nameless fell, it was another strike at the foundations of everything. Every dead Nameless meant it was that much harder to stop the Blight—if it could be stopped at all. Burryaga was one of the first Jedi to encounter the Blight out in the wild, back on Oanne. He knew firsthand what it did to living things.

How could anyone—*anyone*—want that to happen to the galaxy? It was the opposite of anything Burryaga understood. Like holding a lightsaber hilt to the head of every living thing in the universe and activating the blade.

Marchion Ro had done it so casually. He had known exactly what would happen, and he'd done it anyway. He just lifted that rod and started the avalanche. Burryaga understood emotions, could read them from every sort of creature in the galaxy, so he knew what Marchion was feeling at that moment of death and doom.

Marchion Ro was at peace.

Burryaga roared and reached out with the Force.

With all the strength he had, he seized the two Nameless closest to him, yanking them apart, feeling them writhe and strain toward each other, trying to escape his grip so they could continue tearing each other into shreds of meat.

"Easy now, easy," he heard a voice saying—Ty Yorrick, using her particular skill with beasts on the other Nameless, trying to overpower Marchion Ro's command.

The rest of the Nine, all around him, were doing what they could. Using their own abilities, risking their lives, putting their bodies between death-maddened Nameless, trying to hold them back with the Force. Reath, the youngest among them, had pushed a Nameless back against the bluff with the Force and was now bent down, holding his shield against it, holding it back even as the creature snarled and snapped at him. Reath was shouting something, but it was difficult to understand him above the sounds of the Nameless.

So brave, Burryaga thought. *They're all so brave.*

But there were only Nine of them. Eight, really—he didn't think Azlin Rell would be of much help.

Maybe they could save a few Nameless. Maybe they couldn't save any at all. Burryaga could feel his grip on the Force weakening as the two Nameless he was holding worked to fight their way free.

Burryaga roared.

STAR WARS: TRIALS OF THE JEDI 229

He planted his feet, clenched his fists, and the two Nameless rose into the air, pulled farther apart. He anchored himself to the ground, made of himself a mighty, deep-rooted tree, as tall and strong as any wroshyr on Kashyyyk.

These two, at least, will live, he thought.

Another Nameless, a third, leapt into the air, snatching at one of Burry's two charges, its claws puncturing the beast's chest. It hung there, clawing and tearing, and the sound its victim made as it was ripped to pieces would echo in Burryaga's heart until the day he died.

Burryaga staggered back, his focus gone, and all three Nameless fell, the two survivors leaping at each other as soon as their claws touched the ground.

"Burry!" he heard Bell shout. "You okay?"

Burryaga turned, lifting a hand toward his friend. Bell was down on one knee in front of Ember, a hand on the charhound's trembling body. She could feel the turmoil churning the air as well as any of them.

He scanned across the other Jedi, each doing their part to protect life as best as they could, even if only their own. They were still trapped inside the buzz-saw circle of Nameless. Dozens still lived, though how long that would last, Burryaga couldn't say.

What are we going to do? the Wookiee thought. *Have we already failed?*

The Nameless that Reath was trying to protect slashed at his face, and the young Jedi moved his shield instinctively to protect himself—just enough to allow the creature to slip away from him and lunge toward one of the other poor beasts. But now Reath could turn and shout toward the rest of the Nine, doing everything he could to make himself heard above the sounds of the Nameless murdering each other.

"The Rod of Ages," he cried. "We have to get it—it's all we have!"

"Yes," Azlin Rell said, from the spot near the center of the meadow where he crouched, cowering in fear. "Reath is correct. The artifact can negate the influence of the other control rods. It is the only way!"

"Blast it," Elzar Mann yelled, standing back-to-back with Avar Kriss, both with their sabers out. "It's in the ship."

Burryaga looked back toward the crash site. It wasn't too far—a Force-enhanced run could bring any of them to it in perhaps ten seconds. But that was too far to leap, and snarls of enraged Nameless covered the ground between the Nine and the ship. They could cut their way through, but none of them were willing to do that.

"I'll get it," Torban Buck said.

The huge, blue-skinned Chagrian was down on one knee next to a gravely wounded Nameless. He had his hands held tight over the creature's neck, applying pressure, but it was too late. The strange gray light shining in the thing's eyes faded and went out.

Torban stood, wiping the pale blood from his hands. He turned toward the shuttle. He was closer than anyone else, by a fair stretch.

"Wait!" Avar Kriss called. "There may be another way!"

"If we wait, more die," Torban said. "I'm here to save lives."

He set himself, preparing to run.

"Clear a path for me," he said.

Burryaga shot his arm forward, sending a soft, blunt hammer of the Force out toward the shuttle wreck just as Torban Buck began his run. To either side of him, he was aware of Avar, Elzar, and Reath doing the same thing, while Bell, Terec, and Ty ignited their lightsabers and stood guard against any Nameless that might head their way. Azlin Rell shook and moaned, lost in the grip of deep, soul-churning terror.

A lane opened before Torban Buck as the Nameless were shoved back. Their claws dug furrows in the ground, and their screams turned indignant at being held back from the slaughter. Torban's boots pounded the meat-soaked dirt. He moved like a blur, leaping as soon as he was close enough to the wreck. He landed heavily on the hull, falling to one knee but quickly recovering.

Torban disappeared into the ship through the gash in its side. The Jedi released their hold on the Force, conserving their strength but freeing the Nameless.

Hurry, Burryaga thought, watching the creatures leap at one another again.

STAR WARS: TRIALS OF THE JEDI 231

Long moments later, Torban reappeared, flipping himself up out of the shuttle. Now he held a long metal rod in one hand, half the size of the one Marchion Ro used, with an ornate disk at one end—the Rod of Ages. He held it aloft.

"That's it!" Reath called. "Throw it to me! I can try to use it to—"

Torban didn't even wait for Reath to finish his sentence. He pulled his arm back, preparing to send the Nameless's salvation sailing above their kill-maddened heads directly to the young Knight's hand.

Torban Buck's arm came off at the elbow, sliced clean through by the claws of the Nameless that had crawled up the far side of the shuttle's hull. It happened fast, so fast. The limb fell, the Rod of Ages still clasped in the powerful blue hand.

Before the arm hit the hull, the Nameless had its jaws clamped at the juncture of Torban's shoulder and neck, where there was no protective armor. It bit down, hard, puncturing the Jedi's body. Torban screamed.

Burryaga ignited his lightsaber and threw it. It would take off the top of the Nameless's head, and then they could get to Torban, do what they could for him.

Burry's lightsaber froze in midair, halfway to the shuttle. He growled in surprise and frustration, and looked. Torban Buck's arm, his remaining arm, was outstretched. He had stopped the lightsaber.

He was here to save lives.

The Nameless bore Torban down to the shuttle hull and began to feed. Burryaga's lightsaber fell to the ground. Blood, buckets of it, spilled down across the hull.

Azlin Rell screamed, a sound of elemental horror.

"No!" he said. "No!"

He lifted his arms, his fingers curled into claws, and threw his head back. Burryaga sensed what he knew had to be the dark side of the Force, a cold, awful sensation. Three Nameless exploded, becoming clouds of gray-blue mist.

Brrrk! Brrk! Krrck!

"No!" cried Terec, lunging for the possessed, terrified, horrifying Azlin Rell.

Azlin's head whipped toward Terec, and the Kotabi's feet left the ground. Terec's hands went to their neck, and a strangled choking sound came from their throat.

Force energy impacted Azlin from several directions at once. He staggered as Terec fell to the ground, unconscious.

"You are fools," Azlin spat. "We're all going to die."

The Rod of Ages tore from where it lay near Torban Buck's severed arm. It whipped across the clearing, coming to meet Azlin as he moved with shocking speed, running, sprinting toward the edge of the swirling, screaming forest. It slapped into the old man's outstretched hand, and he vanished into the trees.

"Azlin! Stop!" Reath cried, running after him, followed shortly by Ty.

Burryaga fell to his knees. The Nine were now the Four. He, Bell, Elzar, and Avar. The rest of them were dead or lost or hurt. Around him, he heard the sounds of the last few Nameless finishing their slaughter.

All the creatures were dead or would be in moments—their corpses were all around the Jedi. They hadn't managed to save a single one. That fight was over. That fight was lost.

Ember came to Burryaga, nuzzling the Wookiee's neck.

The air burned with the stink of death, and the planet's surface raged.

Chapter Eighteen

EVERYWHERE

On Coruscant, far below the Jedi Temple, in the ancient dark shrine built into its foundation, an ever-growing group of Knights and masters were using all of their skill in the Force to hold back the infestation of Blight. All at once, they felt the gray-white patch of nothingness *flex*, like something had infused the infection with new power. It wanted to be free, to eat and eat and eat, everything in its path, whether living or dead.

The Jedi groaned, as if a weight they already carried had doubled. One, an older master named Astor Grane, started back to awareness from the calm halls of his meditation. His focus had been so complete—ignoring everything else in the universe beyond his task—that he had been taken off guard when the Blight surged. Master Grane felt wetness on the sides of his neck, running down from his ears. He reached up, touched it with two fingers, then brought them around to see redness on his fingertips.

Only Yoda did not react, beyond the corners of his mouth turning down into a frown.

"More difficult, our task has become," the Grand Master said. "And now all the more urgent."

His voice was quiet, but every Jedi present heard it. Those in the circle returned to their task. Master Grane closed his bloodstained fingers into a fist and sought his focus. In a way, the old Jedi considered himself lucky. What is a vow to defend the light if it is never truly tested?

Now he was setting his full strength, his very life against the darkness. This was the choice of a Jedi. He knew it, in a way the decades of peace he had enjoyed since his time as a youngling had never truly given him a chance to prove.

Yoda lifted a hand and gestured toward the Jedi outside the circle, those who had completed recent shifts holding back the Blight and were now slumped against the walls, not speaking, conserving their energy.

"Sorry I am that your rest will be cut short, my friends," the Grand Master murmured. "Need your strength, we do."

Without a word of protest, the reserve Jedi rejoined their fellows, forming a second ring around the patch of Blight, which now seemed to pulsate and thrum with malign energy.

"A runner, I require," Yoda said.

A youngling approached him, and at last Yoda opened his eyes, sparing a smile for the terrified child, a young Togruta with beautiful pink and white montrals surrounding her head.

"Hello, Toko," Yoda said. "Up, you must go, quick as you can. Tell them to send more, all who can come. Assistance, we will need, for the Blight has found new strength."

"I will, Master Yoda," the girl said. "I will be brave."

Away she went. Yoda closed his eyes.

He thought of the Nine and wondered if this change in the Blight was connected to their mission. If so, it did not bode well. But their task was theirs, and his was here. His leg hurt. His bones ached. He wished to sleep.

You are your will, Yoda thought. *You are the decisions you make. All else matters not.*

Yoda decided his body still possessed the strength he required, that it could continue this task as long as he needed it to.

And so, for the moment, it did.

***

Oanne. Ronaphaven. Norisyn. Felne 6. Vixoseph I. Cethis. Tolis. Arli. Outer Kavorn, and dozens more.

The Blight had been discovered on these worlds, wending its way through channels in the Force to places its hunger could be satiated. It carved out slices of withered death, growing with every passing moment wherever it appeared. Only Coruscant's Blight was held in check—though the guardians holding it back grew weary and would not stand forever.

But on the other worlds, including the many worlds where its presence was not yet discovered by sentients, the Blight had moved without restraint from the start.

And now, because Marchion Ro had caused the death of so many Nameless on their homeworld, itself a nexus of the Force, essential balances fell into greater imbalance. The Blight's strength grew. Its *need* grew. It began to move faster, consuming more than it had before, taking matter in every form and turning it into itself, draining the Force from everything it touched.

And still, the Blight sought more. It found worlds it had not yet touched, and there, new Blights grew. Creeping, moving, eating, hollowing out, leaving nothing in its wake, not even death.

What the Blight did was worse than death, for death is a returning, part of a cycle. All dead things become other living things in time. But what was left after the Blight was simply . . . empty. No living thing taken by the Blight would ever feed a scavenger, or have its molecules or energy recycled to become part of the next generation. It would be removed, gone forever. Torn from the endless lattice of the Force.

As the Blight grew, the Force shrank. This should have been impossible. The Force was infinite. And yet . . . it was happening.

In the Senate building, Supreme Chancellor Lina Soh watched as reports poured in from many corners of her great Republic attesting to the acceleration of the Blight. She thought of the desperation behind those reports. "Where will we go if this keeps spreading?" "Will anywhere be safe?" "Why will no one save us?"

Lina thought of the Nine. The last report she had received from the Jedi Temple confirmed that the team had landed on the Nameless's home planet with the creatures still intact and alive—but she knew nothing further.

She looked out at the Grand Convocation Chamber, where holodisplays glowed increasingly red as the reach of the Blight grew.

The Jedi have failed, Lina Soh thought.

Lina thought of her son, just returned to her after a period trapped in the Occlusion Zone via a desperate but ultimately successful rescue attempt. Would it have been better if Kitrep had been lost there? Died cleanly rather than living in terror of an unavoidable creeping death for however many months, weeks, days they all had left?

She did not know.

In the Jedi Temple, the youngling named Toko reported that the Blight had strengthened and Yoda was requesting immediate aid—but this was not the only terrible news to be passed along at that time. A small, select group of Jedi already knew that the mission of the Nine had met with disaster.

STAR WARS: TRIALS OF THE JEDI   237

The Nine's backup team had gathered in the Temple's hangar after the *Ataraxia* launched, prepared for whatever might be required. From that moment, Ceret had maintained constant contact with their bond-twin Terec, relaying to the other members of the second team all that transpired. Ceret conveyed that the Nine had encountered Marchion Ro, that the Eye of the Nihil had set the Nameless against one another, and that the Jedi's attempts to save the creatures had failed.

In unaccented, emotionless syllables, Ceret described Torban Buck's doomed charge, Azlin Rell succumbing to the dark side, and finally Terec going silent.

Indeera Stokes, Yarael Poof, and the others listened to all of this, their faces grim.

"Do you have any idea what happened to Terec?" Indeera asked Ceret. "Did you see anything through your bond? Did Terec tell you anything?"

"Either there is some kind of interference, or Terec is hurt," Ceret said and then paused, their large yellow eyes staring at a spot in the far distance. "Or Terec is dead. I do not know which. I only know that I am no longer receiving information."

The link was gone.

The Nine . . . or whatever might be left of them . . . were in the dark.

Chapter Nineteen

THE BATTLE OF ERIADU

Your ship's on fire, Porter Engle thought. *What now, old man?*

He was a few miles off the ground in a little single-seater he'd grabbed back on Naboo after that battle a few weeks back. His cockpit was open, wind whipping through his long hair. He squinted his single eye against it, gathering information from his sensors and from the Force.

Porter thought he knew which ship had tagged him: one of those ugly Nihil fighters that looked like a flying meat tenderizer. He'd been dodging fire from a few others, and that one had gotten in a lucky shot. His shields were pretty run down after fighting it out for a while, so that was that. Engines on fire.

He never should have let himself get distracted. He wasn't here to pick off Nihil fighters one-on-one or even save the good guys' ships. Nothing wrong with that, but there were literally hundreds of other ships flying around this wasp's nest of a sky that could do that job. The *actual* job, the reason he'd come to Eriadu, was to do something only he seemed to be able to do.

Completing that task was the reason Porter Engle existed, he'd come to believe.

No. It was more than belief.

I'm certain, he thought.

Porter decided to stop ruminating about the fact that his ship was ablaze, probably about to blow up. It was, and that was that. It was time to stop thinking and do something.

What now, old man? THIS.

The little fighter jerked to the left, skidding away from the next round of laserfire headed toward it. The controls were a little sticky—melted wires, maybe, or burned-out gears—so Porter gave the ship a Force-assisted push, nudging it back to the trajectory he wanted.

He took a good, long look at the sky ahead of him. Targets, threats, allies—he took it all in. Ships of all sizes, explosions, laser blasts, missiles, people living and dying. Quite a bit happening up above Eriadu that day.

Then he closed his eyes and did it all again through the Force, which pared things down significantly. To Porter Engle, the Force was a blade—double-edged, light and dark. It let you see what was what, and everything after that was just the choices you made.

The ship changed direction, curving sharply until it was headed directly at a huge, dark ship dominating that part of the sky. Obsidian-colored with purple accents, engaged in ship-to-ship broadsides with an equally gigantic but much more elegant RDC megacruiser Porter recognized as the *Third Horizon.* He didn't know the name of the dark ship, but he knew who owned it. That was why he was headed straight for it.

A last tweak of vector for Porter's ship—and he couldn't have told you if he did it with the ship's controls or the Force, so dialed-in was he at that moment. He drew very near to the gigantic dark ship, so close that it blocked out everything else in front of him. Then two things happened.

The first thing that happened: Porter Engle slapped the release catch on his harness and shoved himself out of his burning ship, pushing hard with both feet and the Force. He and the little vessel diverged, because when you push something, it moves. Porter left the dubious safety of his disintegrating starship and whipped across open air, his body still traveling at the speed his ship had been.

The second thing that happened: Porter's now-abandoned little fighter kept moving, too, even though it was now just a ball of fire with super-heated metal and polymers for a core. It had enough momentum to stay in the air for a good bit yet, though it had already started to curve down toward the planet below, gravity being what it was.

The shuttle's arc took it to the precise spot Porter had selected via the little shove when he leapt from its cockpit plus a tiny adjustment with the Force—directly into the path of the Nihil fighter that had so rudely attacked Porter Engle's ship in the first place. A flash of light, a rattling boom, and both vessels were gone.

Porter took no satisfaction from killing the Nihil pilot—it was just something that needed to happen. They had shot at him, which meant that eventually they'd shoot at someone else. Now they couldn't. He spared them not another thought.

Porter Engle had a deeper stewpot to stir—he was whipping through the air at uncounted kilometers per hour toward the hull of a gigantic starship, like a piece of fruit thrown at a stone wall.

Get this right, he thought. *No second chances with this little maneuver.*

Porter got it right—at least the first part of what he was thinking he'd try. When he jumped from his starship, he'd tried to aim himself at the entrance to the Nihil flagship's hangar bay. It was a good-sized opening, big enough for fighters and transports to move in and out. The only barrier to his passage was the magnetic energy shield that sealed off the hangar's atmosphere from open vacuum while it was in space.

Porter shot through the shield, dead on target. His skin tingled for half an instant, but that was it. No harm done.

Not yet, anyway. Technically, Porter was still in as much danger as he was before, maybe more now that he was in an enclosed space. Starships had ways to slow themselves down—thrusters, brakes. He didn't.

So now he'd attempt the second part of this little plan he'd made up on the fly. This step was, he'd freely admit, a bit of a gamble.

The hangar flashed by, and Porter took a look around. The huge space was mostly empty, which was fortunate—no ships for him to smash into.

That made sense. The Nihil ships were all outside, their pilots busy murdering people. Still, the hangar's far wall was approaching with alarming rapidity. At the speed he was traveling, he had seconds, no more.

Porter lit his lightsaber. The blue blade flashed out into existence from the emitter in the beautiful golden hilt, embellished by a smoothly curving knuckle guard that he could use as a skull rapper if the necessity arose. Porter flipped himself over so he was facing the hangar deck, then used the Force to give himself one hell of a shove in the back.

"Nnf!" he said, feeling his spine creak—but the maneuver worked. Somewhat.

Porter Engle hit the deck, literally. His body slammed into the hangar's floor, still moving at a rate of speed that was, frankly, ridiculous. He stabbed his lightsaber straight down into the deck plating, hoping he was right about an assumption he'd made back in the murky past of three seconds ago when he decided to try this move.

The lightsaber sliced through the deck, like it sliced through everything. Porter didn't feel any resistance—he almost never did. That was part of what made lightsabers so useful. They could cut through anything like it was nothing.

But nothing wasn't what he needed just then. Nothing wouldn't slow him down. Sparks shot up to either side of Porter's careening body, his blade digging a meter-deep furrow of molten metal in the deck.

Come on, you rickety piece of— he thought.

Porter had gambled on the fact that sometimes, starships were built out of alloys stronger than your average durasteel composites. Sometimes, whoever built them splurged on the good stuff. The rare stuff. The tough stuff. That happened more frequently in warships—for example, this Nihil heavy cruiser. If heavy-duty materials were used at all, they were often placed near vulnerable spots that could do with some armoring up—such as hangar bays.

Alloys used in starship armor were a bit harder to cut through than the usual varieties; they provided some resistance for a lightsaber blade. That meant—in theory—they could gradually slow a full-bodied, somewhat elderly Jedi moving at hundreds of kilometers per hour before that same Jedi was smashed into tomato paste against the far wall.

Porter Engle was not exactly a stranger to improvised maneuvers like this. He wasn't deeply analytical. He believed in figuring things out as he went. Life was too short, especially when life was this long.

Now, slashing his way across the hangar of a huge enemy starship with sparks setting fire to his beard, it was all pretty simple. Either he was right, or he was wrong. If he was wrong, well, he wouldn't have much time to regret it.

Porter was not wrong. He slowed, more quickly than he expected. His immediate concern shifted from avoiding the wall to keeping his hand on his hilt, which kept trying to yank itself from his grip as it encountered resistance in the deck armor.

He came to a stop, feeling a bit scorched but otherwise as fine as a three-hundred-some-year-old semi-retired Jedi Master could be. He eased the grip on his hilt, stretched his sore fingers.

Porter got to his feet, patting out the bits of his beard that had caught fire, taking stock, looking out across the hangar.

He saw only one ship, an ugly little Nihil whipsaw thing hooked up to a refueling tube extending from the wall. An astromech droid was supervising that process, and five Nihil stood near it—hangar techs and the pilot, presumably. Only one wore one of those ugly masks they liked, but they all had tattoos and skin painted in swirls and that crude Eye symbol on their clothing. They looked mean. They looked like they lived lives full of pain—theirs and the pain they caused others.

All of them were staring at Porter Engle in stunned silence.

He lifted his lightsaber, showing them the blade.

"Yep," he said. "It's me."

The Nihil started shooting. Of course they did. A Jedi was in their hangar, and they knew their side had killed a lot of Jedi. They probably assumed he'd come for revenge, and now they were terrified. Or maybe it was just that every Nihil Porter had ever met had a worm pit for a soul.

Porter sent the blaster bolts back toward the shooters. He didn't put

STAR WARS: TRIALS OF THE JEDI 243

them through their eyes, though he could have. He didn't send the shots right back at the blasters, though he could have done that, too. The Nihil would lose their hands, and he didn't want to take things to that level yet. The blaster bolts sizzled off his blade, whipping back at the Nihil, flashing just over their shoulders or between their legs. They just kept shooting.

Porter sighed.

He gestured with his free hand, and the fueling tube yanked free of the Nihil fighter with a metallic, fibrous tearing sound. Murky, dark-blue liquid sprayed from the torn end under pressure, and Porter twisted the tube with the Force so its open end was pointed directly at the Nihil. They realized what was about to happen an instant before it did, and good for them. They finally stopped with all the blasting just as gouts of extremely flammable fuel cascaded over them, soaking them to the skin.

The tube's self-sealing mechanisms kicked in, and the fuel slowed to a trickle, but the message was sent.

"Okay?" Porter shouted over to them, turning off his lightsaber and returning it to its holster. "We good?"

The Nihil seethed, pointing weapons they couldn't fire without blowing themselves up.

"We've got knives, too, Jedi!" the pilot yelled. "Come on over here and we'll show you, coward!"

Porter frowned. He crooked a finger, and the pilot was yanked forward as if a rope were tied around his chest, his toes dragging on the shiny metal of the deck, a wave of fuel fumes preceding his arrival.

"What are you—?" the Nihil said, scrabbling for purchase, finding none. "Stop!"

Porter deposited the man on his feet right in front of a computer console. He pointed at the screen and keypad beneath it.

"Access code," Porter said. "Intercom. Shipwide."

The Nihil, without hesitation, reached up and tapped in a code. A little green light appeared on the console below a speaker with a switch next to it. The man turned to look at Porter. Behind the mask, his eyes looked wide and terrified.

"I didn't have a choice," the Nihil pilot said. "They were going to kill me if I didn't sign up. I didn't have anything to do with Starlight Beacon or those Jedi that got killed. I'm just trying to get along."

Porter looked at the man's eyes. Not those of a young man. He wasn't as old as Porter, but few were. This Nihil was old enough to know who he was. To know better.

"Hey, friend," said Porter Engle. "You shot a blaster at me the second you realized I was a Jedi. You didn't have to do that. You decided to. If I'd died, you'd never have thought about it again, except maybe to cash in whatever reward Marchion Ro is offering. Let's not pretend you're anything other than you are."

"What are you going to do to me?" the man said.

"Wrong question," Porter answered. "You should be thinking about what *you're* going to do. Today, and for all the days you have left."

He pushed the Nihil out of the way, no longer concerned with him— either he'd learn the lesson or he wouldn't. He triggered the intercom and spoke into it, hearing his voice echo throughout the hangar and, presumably, all over the huge ship.

"My name is Porter Engle," he said. "I am a Jedi—but I am not like other Jedi. If you attack me, with blaster or blade or fist, I will send it back at you. Attack me, and I will know you are an enemy of life. If you are an enemy of life, I am your enemy." He paused. "I will do things other Jedi will not. I am the destroyer."

This was not true—not entirely true, though it had been true at other times in Porter's very long life. But this was the sort of language the Nihil understood. Saying these things would save more of their lives than asking them to surrender.

"I am here for your leader, no one else. General Viess is my target."

Long ago, she took my sister from me, and I have not stopped thinking about her ever since, Porter thought, but did not say.

Do you mean Viess or Barash? he asked himself, and did not answer.

"The general is an enemy of life, and so she is my enemy. All who ally with her are my enemy. I am certain. Choose well, my friends. Choose well."

STAR WARS: TRIALS OF THE JEDI

Porter lit his lightsaber, holding it near the intercom so its telltale *snap-hiss-hum* could be heard by everyone listening.

"If you don't believe I will do these things, that I am bluffing, that I am anything other than what I claim to be—those of you who are near General Viess, watch what she does next."

He shut off his lightsaber, the scents of spilled fuel and molten metal filling his nose, listening to the sound of the Nihil hangar crew fleeing, seeking places to hide deeper in the ship. To hide from him. Porter Engle. The destroyer.

"See you soon, Viess," Porter said.

And then he went to work.

On the bridge of the *Auberge,* General Abediah Viess flicked her eyes between her various subordinates. All of them were staring at her, unblinking, doing exactly what Porter Engle had told them to: watching to see what she would do next. She felt like a large, heavy shackle had just closed around her neck.

First the RDC fleet had appeared, trapping her between Eriadu and the relative safety of open space, and now *Porter Blasted Engle,* a nemesis of hers for a century and a half, had appeared like something from a nightmare.

Why didn't Marchion leave me one of his Force Eaters? she thought, despairing. *I'm left here, with a murderous Jedi on my ship, without the weapon I need.*

The urge to sprint for the nearest shuttle and take her chances with the battle outside was nearly overwhelming—but Viess knew the color of Nihil loyalty. If she ran, she wouldn't get two steps before she got a blaster bolt to the back. Hell, one of her own people might be the one pulling the trigger.

"General," said her second, Pastiwell Zick, who stood near one of the navigation consoles, staring intently at its screen. "We've managed to push back the RDC forces a bit. I think I could get us through. Shove past them and above the gravity well to a spot where we could get into hyperspace."

Viess almost couldn't believe it. This whole operation had turned into a monsoon of feces—the idea that some *good* news might appear seemed too audacious to believe.

"Go, Adjunct General," she said. "We'll cut our way through, leap to hyperspace, deal with this overambitious Jedi, then return to claim victory."

But not before our reinforcements arrive, Viess thought. *Actually, where are the reinforcements? I called for the rest of the Nihil fleet. They should be here by now. Cowards. They'll probably pretend they never got the transmission.*

"Setting coordinates to get us out of here, Abediah," Zick said, overly familiar but she didn't much care.

Not with Porter Engle on the way.

Win when you could. Run when you couldn't. And if you couldn't do either . . .

Kill.

"Bring me my armor," Viess said. "Bring me my sword."

Chapter Twenty

THE NAMELESS HOMEWORLD

There is no emotion, there is peace, Azlin Rell thought, or said, he didn't know which.

There is no ignorance, there is knowledge.
There is no passion, there is serenity.
There is no chaos, there is harmony.
There is no death, there is the Force.

He said the words, or thought them, as he stumbled through the jungle away from the horror, away from the creatures that had haunted his waking and sleeping moments for a hundred and fifty years. For Azlin, there was little difference. Awake, asleep, it was all a nightmare. A constant, unending nightmare.

The Jedi Code helped. It reminded him of who he was, where he'd started, what had been taken from him. He couldn't let that be taken from the rest of the Order.

"I am a good Jedi," he said, and this time he heard the words out loud.

I am a good Jedi, Azlin told himself.

A root caught his foot and he fell, dropping the Rod of Ages. He landed awkwardly, sprawled out against the sickly, soft ground of this planet. He thought he could feel it squirming against his face as he lay there, panting. Or maybe it was worms under his cheek, or insects, or any one of the other horrible ways this planet was *alive, alive to feed the Nameless, alive to breed them, to—*

He lashed out with the Force, and the root that had tripped him shattered into mossy splinters. Azlin sat up, his mouth a tight, pale line below the edge of the mask covering the upper half of his face.

He tasted blood and spat. As he did, the entire tree that had sent out the root that had dared to trip him cracked down its center.

Azlin reached for the Rod of Ages and used it to lever himself to his feet. None of the others knew what the artifact was truly capable of, not even young Reath, and Azlin had not seen fit to explain it to them. The knowledge he had was hard-won, the only treasure he owned. He had never offered it up lightly.

Insects whined and swirled around his head, a tiny fractal piece of the hissing, swirling agitation that was all around him, creatures and plants and the whole writhing, churning planet.

The bugs exploded in little pops. Azlin continued on his way, calmer but still moving as fast as he could. The Jedi would be after him, because he'd—

You did it again, Azlin, he thought. *You lost control. You were trying to show them you could help them. Prove to them that all the sacrifices you've made were for them, for the Order, and even if you were different now, you could still be with them. One of them.*

In the jungle, not far from Azlin's foot, a small amphibian exploded into a paste of flesh.

But instead you killed those Nameless, and that means the Blight will take over everything, and there will be nowhere safe to hide, and people will die and the Jedi will know it is your fault.

So? said another voice in his head.

Azlin knew it well.

My armor must be failing, he thought. *That's why I'm hearing voices. It's the Nameless effect.*

Your armor is fine. You didn't need it in any case, Azlin. I'll protect you. What is fear to one who draws power from fear?

Above Azlin's head, a strange turquoise creature with sleek fur and sharp suckered mouths all down its long, thick tube of a body coiled itself to strike at the old man.

Its spiny teeth shattered, its body curled in on itself like a knot, pulling so tight that the creature's insides spurted out through all those conveniently placed mouths.

Azlin didn't notice. He kept moving.

Don't we all have a little voice in our heads? he said to himself, as he had all the other times he'd heard this particular one.

Where are you going, Azlin?

The old man stopped, uncertain.

Take off that mask. It's clouding your vision.

Azlin considered this suggestion, and decided . . . that he agreed. He reached up and removed the headpiece, the fetid air of the planet's jungle somehow feeling cool against his nearly bald scalp.

The goggles, too.

Azlin reached to his temples and pulled out the neurospikes that connected the sensors in his goggles directly to his optical cortex. They came free with a wet squelch and that strange tug he always felt when he removed them. Like he was pulling out his own brain.

Darkness descended.

Are you afraid?

Yes.

Of what?

That the Nameless will find me, eat my power. That the Jedi will find me and execute me for betraying them.

You are afraid that others will be more powerful than you. That you will be weak. You are a foolish old man.

Don't speak to me that way. I have done my best. For all these years, I have done my best.

You haven't even come close to your best, Azlin Rell. Do you know how I know that?

Azlin didn't want to hear the answer. He sensed that beyond it was a choice, a path that led in only one direction. If he walked it, he'd no longer be able to tell himself everything he did was to protect the Jedi Order in ways they were unwilling to do themselves. No more telling himself he was still, somehow, one of them.

He did not want to hear the words, but he knew he needed to.

He knew he wanted to.

It was time.

Tell me, he thought. *Tell me how you can be so certain there is more for me beyond this constant, unending, crippling fear?*

I am certain, Azlin Rell . . . because weakness is a choice.

Light bloomed in Azlin's vision. He could . . . see, though not in the way of true sight. Many years ago, in a fit of terror from the visions that constantly haunted him, he had hooked his fingers into his eyes and plumbed the sockets clean. It had accomplished nothing but pain, regret, and darkness—but he could still remember what the world had looked like.

Whatever he was seeing now, it was not the form of sight his eyes had once given him, or the constructed simulacrum of vision his goggles fed directly to his brain.

This new sight felt natural—pure. It showed him a great web of taking, hunting, devouring, death, decay. Creatures appeared to him as ravenous bursts of orange and red—and the plants were just as hungry, consuming in their own way. Everything that lived had wants and needs, and satisfied them however it could. That . . . satisfaction was what Azlin now saw, all around him.

You see the truth, he told himself. **What will you do with it?**

Insights rolled across Azlin's mind, the first clear thoughts he'd had in two lifetimes.

I have allowed my life to be made small . . .

by vows I took centuries ago . . .

to an Order that would prefer me dead . . .

and my terror of a mindless animal . . .

that I can destroy with a thought.

He thought about the Nameless he had killed back in the clearing by the crashed shuttle. He had done it—

With a wave of my hand, Azlin thought.

Azlin Rell waved his hand, and every animal within five meters died in violent paroxysms, splitting and rupturing, their bodies spread across the leaves and soil in bright streaks of gore.

This is why I allowed Yoda to bring me back to the Jedi from my exile, he realized. *This is why I let them place me in that cell in the Temple, adhered to their rules, did what they asked. Not for them, but for me. Because on some level, I knew I needed them. I knew I had to find this place, and only the Jedi could help me do it.*

I needed to come to this world.

This is where I become.

"Azlin," said a familiar voice.

"Reath," Azlin said, turning to see the young scholar, a blaze of cool blue light.

Another figure emerged from the jungle some ten paces behind Reath. A woman, also ablaze, in yellow with hints of orange. A firelight person.

Ty Yorrick, Azlin thought. *The monster-hunter. The one who left the Order. Not like me. I never left. Never surrendered my place. I am still a Jedi, whether they like it or not.*

"Come with us," Reath said. "You don't need to be afraid. No one blames you for what happened—but we have to stick together. If we have any hope of salvaging this, we'll need every bit of knowledge we have. You know more than any of us about the Nameless."

"That's true," Azlin said.

"Enough, Reath," said Ty, moving closer. "You can't reason with him.

He's taken off his mask, his goggles. The planet's gotten into his head. He's gone mad."

"You think you're the first Jedi to hunt me?" Azlin said. "I've been alive for almost two hundred years. Jedi hunt darksiders on sight, especially those they consider apostate. But every hunter who ever came for me is dead, and I remain."

"We're not hunting you," Reath said, his voice calm. "We're asking you."

"I am fond of you, Reath," Azlin said, realizing it was true. "Walk with me. We will take the Rod of Ages and find the truth together."

Ty Yorrick snorted, and Azlin turned toward the insufferable woman. "You, however, I do not care about one way or the other."

He gestured, and the woman rose into the air, struggling against the grip of the Force. She reached for her belt, removed something from a pouch, and threw it at Azlin.

Her aim was good. Whatever she'd thrown burst into fire and shrapnel not far from his face. Azlin trapped the explosion, sealed it away, saved it for later. He smashed Ty Yorrick hard against the trunk of a nearby tree, and she slumped to the ground in silence.

Azlin turned to Reath, who had unleashed his lightsaber but was very obviously not going to use it.

"Take care of Ty or follow me, Reath. The choice is yours."

Reath didn't move. Strange colors flashed across his form—the colors of indecision, of inaction.

The colors of weakness, Azlin thought.

"Very well," Azlin said.

He turned and walked away, knowing Reath would not follow.

"Ty!" Reath said, falling to his knees next to the injured woman.

He reached to his belt, pulling out a flask of water, holding it toward her lips, not knowing what else to do. He wasn't a medic. He needed . . .

STAR WARS: TRIALS OF THE JEDI

Torban, he thought and felt his soul collapse.

Ty reached up and grabbed his wrist, pushing the flask away. "Help me up," she spat. "I'm going after him."

"What? You saw what Azlin's become—we need to stay away from him," Reath said. "We can't risk fighting him now, Ty. We have bigger problems to solve."

Is that the truth? he asked himself. *Or are you still, after all this time . . . curious? Do you want to know what Azlin learned out here? You've never seen him like that. He seemed strong, certain. Don't you want to know what you'd see if you followed him?*

Ty Yorrick seemed completely untroubled by anything like the questions swirling through Reath's mind. She pulled herself to her feet, holding on to the tree trunk for stability, her legs trembling—but her eyes were fierce.

"Azlin might have escaped all the Jedi who hunted him," she said, her voice gaining strength. She stood straight, no longer swaying. Her body had become a statue of pure focus and intent. "But I'm not a Jedi."

Chapter Twenty-One

THE NAMELESS HOMEWORLD

The four Jedi lifted Torban Buck's body from where it lay atop the crashed shuttle. They did this using the Force. It floated gently down, weightless, like a drifting leaf, past the corpses of the Nameless who had destroyed themselves at the terrible whim of Marchion Ro.

The body moved into the ship, where a length of cloth from the shuttle's stores became the Jedi's shroud.

The crude matter that was once a Knight of the Jedi Order spun gracefully in midair, the cloth wrapping around it, pulling tight, sealing away the indignity of the violence that had been done against Torban's body.

They moved him into the shuttle's engine compartment—a strong, spherical space at the ship's aft that remained intact after the crash. The Jedi set him down. They released the Force.

No one spoke. They had given Torban Buck the dignity he deserved upon his return to the Force. Nothing needed to be said.

Marchion Ro's getting away, Bell thought. *He's getting away and we just sit here.*

This was not entirely true. At that moment, Bell was helping Elzar Mann rig up a medical monitor for Terec. Before attending to Torban's body, they'd brought the unconscious Jedi to the crashed shuttle's engine compartment to ensure they were protected from any attacks by the local wildlife. With Torban's remains laid to rest as well as they could be, Elzar had asked Bell to help see what they could do for Terec.

The Kotabi was curled up in a position reminiscent of a fetus in the womb—knees to their chest, arms wrapped around their body. Neither Elzar nor Bell had been able to get Terec to relax the pose; the position seemed to be a defense or recovery mechanism. Terec's breaths came in long, slow whooshes, in and out, and their body was quite cool to the touch.

For all Bell and Elzar knew, the best course of action would be to leave Terec alone entirely. But leaving things alone was not in Elzar's character, so he had found the shuttle's emergency medical rig and hooked it up to Terec as best as he could while not disturbing the anti-Nameless armor. Terec's helmet was still mostly in place, although Elzar had lifted it to allow for an oxygen mask to be slipped over Terec's mouth and nose. Monitoring electrodes placed at Terec's neck and wrists provided wildly shifting readings—all but useless at conveying what was happening inside the Kotabi's body.

"Terec needs a medical droid," Elzar said. "I think they've put themselves into a healing coma—I've heard of species that do this—but I can't be sure. I'm not very well versed in Kotabi biology."

"Ceret's the only other Kotabi I've ever met," Bell said.

We need to go after Marchion, Bell thought again—but Elzar didn't seem to even be thinking about the Eye of the Nihil. Avar and Burryaga, too. They'd remained outside, examining the Nameless corpses, trying to . . . Bell wasn't sure. Maybe they were looking for some of the armor pieces they'd lost in the fight, from errant slashes from Nameless claws. Bell had lost a few himself, and he could feel the strange energies of the planet pulsing against his mind, clouding and shaking his composure.

Elzar made a small adjustment to Terec's medical monitor, outwardly calm. How was he so . . . passive? The others, too. Yes, they'd taken some hits. The loss of Torban Buck, Terec's injury, and of course the death of all those Nameless. But Marchion Ro was out there, alone, without his Nameless defenders or any Nihil troops. They could end him, right now, with a single slash of a lightsaber.

And beyond the opportunity itself, didn't the others understand the urgency? Marchion had made it clear that his intention was to accelerate the galaxy's destruction by killing every Nameless he could find on the planet. Every moment they let him do that was another moment the lives of everyone in existence were shoved closer to the edge of a cliff.

How can Elzar just stand there fiddling with that damn medical rig?

"Elzar . . ." Bell began.

The smell of smoke invaded the engine compartment—acrid, ammoniac.

Avar Kriss appeared at the chamber's hatch. Her face looked grim.

"What is it?" Elzar asked.

"With Terec's line of communication back to Coruscant cut off for the time being," Avar said, nodding at the unconscious Jedi, "I've been trying to use the Song to get a sense of what's happening in the galaxy after the death of so many Nameless at once."

"You can . . . do that?" Bell asked.

"She can do that," Elzar said. "Go on, Avar."

"The Blight feels like it's been supercharged, for lack of a better term. It's growing, spreading, appearing on more worlds. I think it might be moving faster, too."

"So we've lost," Bell said, his tone heavy. "It's over. Marchion won."

Elzar looked at him, raised an eyebrow.

"Are we alive, Bell Zettifar? Does the Force still roar and crash within us? Do we have our willpower and our training and our vows?"

"Of course, but—"

Elzar shook his head.

"Of course, Bell. I'm not going to pretend everything's fine. It's been one disaster after another. But we are here. It's only finished if we decide it's finished. Nothing is over."

"There's something you need to see out here," Avar said.

The three Jedi returned to the clearing together, leaving the unconscious Terec to hopefully recover and Torban's body to hopefully rest undisturbed.

Outside the shuttle, the smell of burning chemicals was much stronger. Avar and Burryaga had taken the Nameless corpses, moved them together with the Force, and lit them with their lightsabers, creating a funeral pyre for the beasts. Or possibly Ember had lit the fire for them—the charhound was pacing back and forth near the pyre, staying near Burry. The blaze burned weakly with an odd color, a greenish yellow that looked like it smelled. Bell's eyes began to water, and he blinked.

At least it's keeping the rest of the local wildlife away, he thought.

There had been no more attacks since the Nameless slaughtered each other, though shrieks and other odd sounds from the jungle suggested the planet's strange unrest continued.

Burryaga came to Bell, his eyes sad. Ember walked at the Wookiee's side, her head swinging back and forth, scanning the tree line, clearly uneasy after everything she'd experienced.

"I know, Burryaga," Bell said. "It's awful."

Avar and Elzar were standing near the jungle's edge, looking at something on the ground, speaking to each other in low voices.

Bell approached, Burryaga following. As he drew near to the other Jedi, he saw what Avar had wanted them both to see—a path of crushed vegetation, with splashes here and there of a pale liquid Bell recognized as Nameless blood. The path led into the jungle and vanished.

"One of them survived," Bell said.

"It makes sense," Avar replied. "Someone had to be the last one standing."

Burryaga hooted, squatting down and gesturing to a patch of blood.

"It's injured, yes," Elzar said. "Which also tracks, after that battle. The question is . . . where was it going?"

All four Jedi looked out into the jungle in the direction the Nameless had gone. There were no answers, just the thrashing, churning wilderness, full of screams and pain.

"This Nameless was free of Marchion Ro's control," Avar said. "I think it's going home, wherever it considers home."

"We need to follow it," Elzar said. "We have to learn more about them."

"I agree," said Avar. "That's why I brought the three of you out here."

"No!" Bell burst out, his patience finally gone. "We have to go after Marchion Ro! He caused all of this, and he's here with no backup. He even destroyed his own ship. He's trapped, with nowhere to go. We can find him, we can . . ."

Bell paused, thinking of what he would do when he found the Eye of the Nihil.

"Bring him to justice."

Avar and Elzar exchanged a glance.

"We can deal with Marchion later," Avar said. "The Blight has to be the focus. As you said, Bell, he's trapped, just like us. He has no way out. He doesn't have to be our immediate goal."

"Avar, I disagree," Bell said, realizing how much had changed for him in the past year or so.

There was a time he would have shown nothing but absolute deference to Avar Kriss. She was older, experienced, had shown her judgment and skill in countless situations. But at a certain point . . .

All Jedi walk their own path, Bell thought.

"Marchion is the threat," Bell said, jabbing two fingers into the palm of his hand to emphasize his words. "After everything we've seen him do . . . you really think he doesn't have a plan? You really think things can't get worse? We can't just let him run free out there. We need to get him while we can. That's what I'm going to do."

Elzar considered this, staring out at the tree line. "The group's already divided, Bell, and we've taken losses. I don't like the idea of splitting us up more than we already are. Avar's not saying we let Marchion go. We'll do

STAR WARS: TRIALS OF THE JEDI   259

it when we've gathered back together, when we understand more about what's happening on this planet. He's dangerous."

"So am I," Bell said.

The three Jedi looked at one another—two masters and a Knight. Avar and Elzar outranked him, and Avar was in command of the mission.

"What did you tell me back in the shuttle, Elzar?" Bell said. "That as long as we're alive, there's hope? That it's not over? If Marchion Ro kills us, *it will be.* You can do what you want. I'm going after him."

For Loden, Bell thought.

Avar nodded once.

"I'm not going to give you an order, Bell," Avar said, "and I don't think you'd follow it if I did. I have no doubt that you're dangerous—but believe me when I tell you that there is danger in this path for you as well. Go after Marchion, if that's what the Force is telling you to do. Be careful, walk in the light, and remember that you are a Jedi."

She turned, walking toward the edge of the jungle.

"We'll meet back here," Elzar said. "Comms don't work on this blasted world. We can all return here once we have information to share. Good luck. For what it's worth, I hope you—" He paused, seeming to realize what he had been about to say. "Bring him to justice."

Elzar loped away toward Avar, who waited for him at the edge of the forest.

Bell looked at Burryaga, who had stayed largely silent through the exchange.

"You ready, Burry? I'll need your help following Marchion."

He pointed at the top of the bluff.

"We'll start up there. He'll have left a trail. I might have trouble following it, but you're ten times the tracker I am. We'll get him. Once we find Marchion, we'll give him a chance to surrender. I don't think he'll take it, and he doesn't deserve it, but that's what we'll do."

And when he refuses, when he pulls out a blaster or one of those lightsabers he stole from the Jedi he's killed . . . well . . .

All Jedi walk their own path.

Burryaga didn't respond. He just stood there, his eyes slightly narrowed.

Bell loved the Wookiee like a brother—they were as close as any siblings he'd ever heard about—but Burry had a bad habit of keeping his thoughts to himself. Bell knew why. It was because almost no one outside the Wookiee homeworld of Kashyyyk understood Burry's native tongue, Shyriiwook. Even fewer spoke it. Bell had made a valiant effort and by now could understand about 70 percent of what Burryaga said if he spoke slowly. But as far as responding to Burry in his own tongue, making the whistles and groans and bassy trills that made up the Shyriiwook language, Bell was hopeless.

Burry knew that few people understood him, and so most of the time he didn't even bother speaking. That could be challenging, even frustrating. Bell had to remind himself not to make assumptions about what Burryaga was thinking or feeling, particularly not to assume Burry agreed with Bell just because he stayed silent. With Burryaga, you had to read his body language, his facial expressions.

And what Bell read on Burry's face at that moment was conflict.

"What's the matter, Burry?" Bell asked. "We don't have a lot of time."

Burryaga looked back toward the shuttle, his eyes sliding over the Nameless funeral pyre, now barely burning, mostly just putting out odd, oily smoke.

He said a single word, a name, a transliteration that was more the idea of the person than an attempt to reproduce it phonetically. *Terec* was the name Burry said, although what he actually said was closer to "the Half-One One."

"We've helped Terec as much as we can right now, Burry," Bell said. "They're locked away in the engine compartment. Nothing's getting in. Terec will be safe until we get back. They just need to rest."

Burryaga turned back to Bell, frowning. He spoke again, a longer series of sounds, keeping it precise and simple as if he were speaking to a child. Bell understood.

STAR WARS: TRIALS OF THE JEDI 261

Burry was not just concerned that Terec was hurt. It was that Terec was alone. If the Kotabi woke up, they'd be hurt, confused, sealed in a cold metal ball with no company other than the corpse of Torban Buck.

Bell could visualize that moment with perfect clarity, and he was ashamed that it had taken Burry to make him see it. That made sense, though, in a way. Burryaga understood all too well what it was like to be trapped, alone, and surrounded by death. For instance, in a cold, damp cave at the bottom of the Eiram sea with no hope of rescue. Terec's experience would be different, but it would also be the same, and Burryaga wanted to spare their fellow Jedi that terror if he could.

"I'm sorry, Burry," Bell said. "You're right. Stay with Terec. I'll go by myself. Or I'll take Ember. She can help track, too."

Burryaga reached out, putting his hand on Bell's shoulder in a gentle grip. Bell didn't often think about how physically strong Burry was, but in a moment like this there was no mistaking it. His claws could rip a good-sized tree in half. If a Wookiee didn't want you to move, you didn't move.

"I can't stay," Bell said. "Marchion Ro . . ." He took a deep breath. "Marchion Ro killed Loden Greatstorm. He killed many other Jedi, and lots of other people besides—people who matter—but Loden was my master. The best of us, Burry. I don't want revenge."

Burryaga just looked at him.

"I don't want revenge," Bell repeated. "But I can't let this chance go. I have to bring him in."

Burryaga nodded. He took his hand from Bell's shoulder and stepped back.

"Thank you, my friend," Bell said. "I'll see you soon."

Burry hooted in agreement.

"Come on, girl," Bell said, calling to Ember, who chuffed and came to his side.

Bell and Ember climbed the low hill where they had last seen Marchion Ro, looking for a trail. Bell found the spot where the Eye had stood, but the ground had been trampled by Marchion's Nameless. It was difficult to tell which way the man had gone.

"I knew we shouldn't have waited so long," Bell muttered to himself. "You smell anything, Ember?"

Bell didn't expect much from the charhound on that front. The horrible odor of the burning Nameless still lay heavy in the air.

Ember whuffed, the sound Bell associated with excitement.

"Mm?" he said, turning to look at her.

Ember was standing at the edge of the bluff, her hindquarters wiggling with excitement, white steam and little jets of flame shooting from her nostrils.

Bell looked down, back the way they'd climbed—and there was Burryaga, moving fast, headed straight for them. He had something on his back, white, shaped like a large backpack.

As the Wookiee drew near, Bell realized what Burryaga had done— Terec was lashed to his back, armor and medical gear and all, via a harness of wires and cloth. Burry must have woven it quickly out of materials he'd stripped from the shuttle.

Burryaga clambered up the side of the bluff four times as fast as Bell had managed. He reached the top, then gave Bell a self-satisfied look, turning to display Terec, snug and safe. The Kotabi was still unconscious, still curled up in that fetal position, but that made things simple—easier for Burryaga to carry.

"Aren't you clever?" Bell said, smiling, happy despite everything that was happening.

His friend had come.

Burryaga shook his head and coughed out a number of syllables in Shyriiwook.

Not clever. Stubborn. Unwilling to accept there wasn't a way to help you and Terec both.

Burryaga surveyed the ground, scanning across the bluff. He paused, then looked up in a direction that Bell would never have picked as the way Marchion had gone.

Without another word, Burryaga led the way.

Chapter Twenty-Two

THE *AUBERGE*

Porter Engle stepped through the hatchway and onto the bridge of General Viess's flagship. He paused, taking it in.

The room was dim, illuminated by purple accent lighting running in tracks along the walls and shining up from spotlights set into the floor between the control consoles. Most of the fixtures were chromed, shiny and reflective. The front wall was dotted with irregularly arrayed oval viewports of various sizes looking out to space—hyperspace, in this case. Porter realized the ship must have jumped away from Eriadu at some point after he boarded.

Honestly, the place reminded him of a nightclub. He suspected the vessel hadn't originally been a general's flagship. Maybe some rich person's toy, at least until the Nihil rolled up and decided they wanted it. Now it was just another thing they'd taken.

The thief herself stood silhouetted against one of the exterior viewports, perfectly positioned beneath one of the purple spotlights. General Abediah Viess, wearing that armor she liked. It was the same set she'd worn when Porter first met her back on Gansevor about a century and a half back. The only change: It had more beskar in it now, laced through it in filigree that had become increasingly detailed over the decades.

Viess's sword was beskar, too, pure-cast other than its hilt—not a bad weapon against a lightsaber. It was in its sheath, just as his lightsaber was in its holster. They were both creatures from an earlier era. There were formalities to be observed.

The center of the room was clear. The spot where the command chair had probably rested was now open, the seat removed to allow for the combatants to move freely throughout the dueling space.

Perhaps a dozen people stood in a circle against the far walls, their backs to the control consoles and instrument panels lining the bulkheads. Many wore black armbands slashed with purple, signifying them as Viess's longtime soldiers, her killers for hire. Others wore the masks of the Nihil, with the Eye's ugly, crude symbol on their clothing or skin. These had to be newer recruits, brought in after Viess took command of the Nihil military. They were all silent, watching. Spectators, not combatants.

Now that he had the measure of the space, Porter walked forward several paces. The hatchway slid smoothly closed behind him, locking with an audible click.

"General," Porter said.

"Jedi," Viess sneered.

A blaster bolt *cracked* out from behind Porter, the sound unmistakable. A flash of light, and the bolt returned to its place of origin. Another sound came, the sound of a body collapsing to the ground, some newly dead fool who'd thought perhaps he could end the fight before it began, thereby currying some kind of favor with the general. Sounds of awe and dismay rumbled from the crew.

Porter didn't turn to look. His palm tingled slightly from where he had sent the blaster bolt back.

"That didn't have to happen," he said to the crew, not taking his eyes from Viess. "I feel that I was *extremely clear,* but let me say it again. I don't want any of you to die. This is about your general, no one else. Don't bring yourselves into it."

STAR WARS: TRIALS OF THE JEDI 265

He kept his eyes on Viess, who stood waiting at the far end of the chamber.

"Apologies for that," the general said. "Zick was my second. With me a long time. Loyal."

"Maybe," Porter said. "Mostly just foolish. That's why he's dead."

A little rustle went through the watchers, a wave of disgruntlement at the disrespect shown to their noble leader and possibly to a now deceased colleague they might have liked. But no one did anything. Apparently, everyone else in the room was smarter than poor old Zick.

Viess drew her sword. It emerged silkily from the sheath, a tiny ringing note sounding as it came free. She held up the shining weapon and shifted her stance, moving her feet into a position that signaled a readiness to commence.

"This will be the last time we do this, Porter," she said.

"Sure will," he replied. "So it seems like we should chat first, even just for a minute."

The general nodded—but didn't sheath her weapon.

"I hope you approve of the space," Viess said. "The ship's former owner used to throw parties here. This was a dance floor. I thought it would be appropriate."

They watched each other for a few moments, taking the other's measure.

"So I've been asking myself something," Porter said. "We've had pretty serious fights, blade-to-blade, what . . . three times now?"

"Something like that," Viess replied, playing it casual, as if they didn't both remember every blow and block and riposte and cut from all the other times they'd clashed.

"Right. So this is the question: How is it possible you aren't dead?"

Viess seemed taken aback. She glanced at her crew. No commander liked to be mocked in front of their subordinates.

They were already dueling, whether the general knew it or not. Porter suspected she did, even if the subtleties might be lost on some of those watching.

"My skill speaks for itself, Jedi," Viess replied. "You aren't the first I've killed. I'll wager I have more lightsaber hilts in my cabin than your Temple's armory. I'm Mirialan. We're long-lived, just like you Ikkrukkians. I've had centuries to train, and I've used every day. Every *moment*. I've studied with the greatest swordmasters in the galaxy, honed myself into a perfect weapon. That's why I'm still alive, Porter Engle, and that is why you'll soon be—"

"Uh-huh," Porter said, cutting her off. "I'm sure that's all true. But come on." He spread his arms wide, letting a smile fall across his face. "I'm the Blade of Bardotta."

He placed his hand on his saber hilt, though he didn't draw. Just a warning. A point was coming in the conversation when Viess would have heard enough, and she'd lunge forward. Not that he'd have any trouble if she did, but he had a bit more to say first.

"If you're alive, it's because of me, not you," Porter said. "And Barash."

"Your sister," Viess said.

"My sister," Porter agreed, turning slightly to address the room. "About a hundred and fifty years back, your general here was the reason Barash Silvain left me forever. She was the best Jedi I ever knew, my guide to the higher simplicity of the Force. Barash made her own choices, made some serious mistakes, but it went as bad as it did because Viess is a monster, through and through. For the crimes your general committed on Gansevor alone, she should have spent her life in a cell."

Viess snorted in contempt.

"I did what I was hired to do," she said. "Don't blame me for making a living. I'm honest about who I am, just like everyone on this ship. People in my line are weapons, bought and paid for. We don't make the decisions any more than your lightsaber does."

Porter shook his head.

"The rationalization of the mercenary. Heard it plenty of times over the years. Doesn't work for me, Viess. Never has. Our choices are our own."

Porter took a single step closer. Viess tensed.

"So, General, let me tell you why I think you're still alive," he said. "It's

STAR WARS: TRIALS OF THE JEDI   267

because you're one of the only people left in the galaxy who actually knew Barash, even if only briefly. You were there the day she left. The day it all changed. She and I were as close as two people could be, and then it was gone."

He lifted a hand, pointed at Viess.

"If I kill you, it means I'd lose a kind of connection to Barash. One less person who knew what she looked like, how she spoke, how she lived, how it went down that day. So I haven't let myself do what needs to be done."

"No, Porter," Viess spat. "The reason I'm still alive is because *I'm better than you.*"

Porter could hear the tension ratcheting up in her voice. That was good. "Oh?" he said.

Porter flicked his left arm in a smooth motion, and a dark cylinder ornamented in gold slid into his palm from the hidden holster strapped to his forearm. He lit the lightsaber, the shorter secondary blade flaring to life. The atmosphere in the room changed, as it always did when a lightsaber came out. Anticipation, fear, awe, and even some level of desire to see the thing used, because anyone who wielded a lightsaber was by necessity one of the most skilled swordspeople in the galaxy.

"I held myself back in all our fights, Viess. I never went as hard as I could, never used my second blade. I didn't even realize I was doing it until the last time we met, when you said her name. When you told me that you know where Barash is now."

Viess shifted uneasily, her eyes locked on Porter's lit weapon.

Not long now, he thought.

He extinguished the blade and slowly, carefully, so as not to cause Viess to make any precipitous moves, returned it to his sleeve.

"I'm grateful to you, General," he said. "Hearing her name from your lips made me realize I've been letting you live for reasons that are, ultimately, selfish."

"You arrogant bastard," Viess said and swept forward.

Her beskar blade flashed, a high outside lunge designed to take out his throat. She was fast—Viess really *was* good. A fine sparring partner.

So few were. That was one reason Porter had chosen to retire from the daily work of the Order, before the Nihil conflict had called him back. He was the Blade. He was good at many things, but at the lightsaber, he was the best. No one could match him, and it had come to feel pointless, even depressing to unsheathe his weapons, to respond to duel requests from younger Jedi. The joy of the lightsaber was the idea that your dance partner might surprise you, might even best you. Only Barash had ever managed that, and she almost never used her lightsaber at all, and she was gone.

Porter sidestepped, and Viess surged past, correcting immediately and spinning into another attack.

So he seized her with the Force, lifted her off her feet, threw her across the bridge, and slammed her against the largest of the viewports looking out at the swirl of hyperspace. Viess's skull cracked against the hardened transparisteel, her armor clanging and rattling. Everyone flinched. The bridge viewport was reinforced, strong enough to repel hits from lasers and meteorite impacts. Porter would have needed to throw the general much harder to fracture it. But still—in space, the last thing you wanted was someone messing with the viewports.

"Hnnngh," Viess said, her voice thick.

It was clear that the general's bell had been pretty thoroughly rung, though to her credit she'd held on to her sword.

Keep it, Porter thought.

Now his lightsaber lifted from its holster, raised into the air via the Force. It whipped through the air, stopping suddenly very close to Viess's face, the emitter end a few centimeters from her eye.

"Do you see what I'm saying, General?" Porter said. "This was never a match. It's time for me to do my job."

He walked across the bridge, coming closer to her. Viess's eyes were locked on the lightsaber hilt hovering directly before her eye.

Porter rotated to face the killers scattered around the bridge.

"There are only about ten thousand Jedi," he said. "Even a single planet can have up to a trillion people. Relative to the galactic population, the Order is a whisper of a whisper. Our resources are best used to battle the dark in precise, targeted ways. If you need to field an army or blockade criminals across an entire sector, mostly we let the Republic handle it. But if the job is about stopping bad *individuals*..."

He gestured at Viess, still pressed hard against the window, still holding her sword. "We're incredible." He pointed at several of the Nihil in turn. "You know what I'm talking about. I know you do."

Uneasy murmurs.

"Even though we Jedi are very few in number, we can still be very effective at bringing light. Because when people consider being *really* bad, getting *truly dark,* there's always a little voice in the back of their head— *What if they send a Jedi after me?*"

Porter looked back at Viess, really looked at her, this sad woman who had devoted her entire life to death. Her long life.

Are you any different? Porter asked himself.

I try to be, came the answer.

"I am the Jedi they send, Abediah Viess, and I have come for you. Everywhere you go, people get hurt, people die. Your time is over. That's all there is to it. I'm certain."

"But your sister . . ." Viess gasped. "Don't you—"

"Barash is wherever she is," Porter said. "I'll find her if that's my path. I'm sick of you being part of my story with her."

Viess's face twisted, her lips thinning, her eyes clenching into dark little pits.

"I'll tell you where she is," Viess snarled. "She's dead. *She's in the dirt, Porter.*"

"If that's the case . . ." Porter Engle said.

The activation switch on his lightsaber triggered, just for a moment. A spear of bright-blue light flicked out and through the head of General Abediah Viess.

"Tell her I said hello."

Chapter Twenty-Three

THE *THIRD HORIZON*

Tactical displays projected across the command bridge told the story of the battle happening in the skies around the great ship and down on the surface of the planet below. Admiral Pevel Kronara scanned across the holos, looking for surprises, some unexpected twist in the tale. He saw nothing unusual, and had not expected to.

Kronara knew exactly how this story would go. He was writing its ending at that very moment.

Battles inevitably concluded in one of three ways: retreat, surrender, annihilation. The only real variation was the point at which the people involved in the fighting understood the battle was done, and then the choice made between the three options. One side often knew before the other, and that side often got to choose which ending it would be— though it wasn't always the side that won.

It looked like the Battle of Eriadu was one of those, although General Viess had not just made one decision. She had made two. She had chosen retreat for herself and annihilation for the Nihil forces remaining on the

STAR WARS: TRIALS OF THE JEDI

planet, the ones she had summarily abandoned once it was clear she was going to lose the fight.

Inspiring, Kronara thought, wondering how cowards like Viess could actually consider themselves warriors at all.

"This one's cooked, Admiral," said Lieutenant Commander Bekkitet, standing at his side. "Viess's battle fleet is almost entirely destroyed, although we've still got some stragglers to chase down. No ships larger than a corvette, though. Mostly fighters."

"And on the ground?" Kronara asked.

"Our reports are slightly less comprehensive," his XO said, "but our allies on the surface tell us the Nihil are either dead or preparing to surrender. The Eriaduans are . . . disinclined to accept that offer."

"Bloodthirsty bunch," Kronara replied.

"The Nihil only held this planet at all because they could call for backup from their offworld fleets," Bekkitet said. "Their garrisons here were lightly staffed, at least in comparison with the planet's local population."

"Not to mention that the local population is born with a knife between their teeth," Kronara said. "If it were me, I'd never have tried to occupy this planet at all. The Eriaduans already held a grudge after the Nihil slammed the planet with that Emergence a few years back."

"Perhaps you're smarter than the average Nihil, sir." His XO pointed at one of the displays. "These lone Nihil ships—the survivors. Do we hunt them down or let them try to escape?"

"I don't want to spend any additional resources here or put my people in unnecessary danger. Inform the Eriaduan security forces. I'm sure they'll take great interest in the location of Nihil survivors, and I suspect they won't remain survivors for long."

"Very well, sir," Bekkitet said. "Further orders?"

Kronara considered, running a hand through his beard. "The intelligence on the Stormwall is strong?"

Bekkitet nodded. "We've got it independently verified by multiple sources on the ground, Admiral. Nihil officers, comms relays we've been able to slice, intercepted messages. The Stormwall's control signal has vanished, as has any transponder information of any kind from the *Gaze Electric*."

"Like when we took out the Lightning Crash," Kronara said.

"Identical," Bekkitet replied. "It is possible that the Nihil turned off the Stormwall for reasons of their own, but our analysts have reviewed the data and are telling us the most likely conclusion is that the *Gaze* itself is gone."

Kronara thought about this. When the Nihil did things you didn't understand, it was often some sort of trap—but this didn't feel like that. Everything that had happened at Eriadu felt like an enemy making a gigantic strategic blunder. An overcommitment of forces, with huge losses suffered as a result.

This didn't feel like a trap. It felt like an opportunity.

"Issue a recall to all RDC personnel on the planet," Kronara said. "Send transports to bring them up to the fleet. Ask the Eriaduans if they need further assistance—they'll say no, and say they never needed us in the first place. That's fine."

He considered his displays.

"Bring me up a loss tally," he said.

Commander Bekkitet did as she was bid.

Kronara considered the numbers. They hurt—they always did. The RDC had suffered seven percent losses over the course of the battle. It was possible, with the tap of a button, to convert that seven percent into an actual casualty number, and with a few more to divide it among divisions, and then to pull up the individual names of the Coalition warriors who had lost their lives. You could go further, if you wanted—the system would deliver service records and personnel files for every person under Kronara's command, living or dead. You could understand everything that had been lost—if you wanted to.

But now was not the time. That level of consideration was for after the battle was done, and this particular fight was not over, no matter what General Abediah Viess might have concluded.

STAR WARS: TRIALS OF THE JEDI 273

Leaving the loss tally up, letting its significance guide his next set of decisions, Kronara selected another display. This depicted another front in the Battle of Eriadu, though this was far from the planet itself, farther out in the system.

When the Stormwall fell, a second RDC fleet, this one with a Jedi commander named Keeve Trennis, had headed for Naboo—an attempt to liberate that world just as Kronara's people had managed at Eriadu.

But once Trennis arrived, she found a system almost entirely empty of Nihil. General Veiss's call for reinforcements at Eriadu when the Stormwall went down had caused nearly every Nihil ship in the Occlusion Zone to head straight to Eriadu, including those at Naboo.

Keeve Trennis had understood what was happening and diverted her own forces to the Eriadu system. The Jedi-led fleet intercepted the Nihil reinforcements and commenced what sounded like a spectacular battle in its own right.

Kronara was grateful. If Trennis hadn't acted as quickly as she did, there was a good chance his fleet would have been caught in a pincer between two Nihil armadas. The day could have gone very differently.

"Once we have our people gathered up," Kronara said, "we'll head out to the *Gios* and see if Trennis needs any backup. Looks like they're doing just fine out there, but I'm sure our arrival will be welcome."

"And from there, sir? Do we try to find General Viess?"

"General Viess has made herself irrelevant, Major," Kronara said. "Her time will come, I'm sure. For now, we have a larger objective. The Nihil made an enormous mistake here at Eriadu. As I see it, the Nihil decided to send the vast majority of their fleet to this system because they expected the Stormwall to protect them. It went down, they lost, and now they're on the run. They won't be able to muster much strength for a while. I'm not inclined to give them that time."

The admiral left his command station and walked to one of the broad viewports built into the *Third Horizon*'s bridge. He looked down toward Eriadu. Columns of smoke rose from the surface—rings of fire where starships had crashed, wreckage floating against the curve of the planet. He saw his ships pulling themselves into formation, orderly and precise. He thought of the people aboard those vessels, all under his command, breathing sighs of relief that they had survived another fight.

"Fleet-wide comms," he said, and a junior officer appeared at his side holding a communications device, a long, thin cable running in tight curls back to his console.

Kronara lifted it and spoke.

"This is your commanding officer, Admiral Pevel Kronara. The Battle of Eriadu is over, and we have won," he began. "The Nihil fleet has been largely destroyed, and survivors are in disarray."

Aboard the bridge, cheers erupted, even though this information could not be news to anyone present. Survival was always a reason to celebrate.

"I am proud of every one of you. You have done honor to the precepts of our great Republic and liberated a world suffering under oppression. You have all earned the right to rest."

He paused.

"But I have more to ask of you. We have additional reinforcements within the system. My intention is for our fleet to link with theirs. I will take full command of the combined armada, and then we will drive through the Occlusion Zone to the place where this whole damn thing began, the world the Nihil stole and claimed as their flagworld.

"We will retake that planet for the Republic and destroy any Nihil resistance we find. We will never have a better opportunity to strike than now, this moment.

"We will reclaim everything the Nihil stole. We will show the lost worlds of the Occlusion Zone that we have not forgotten them. We are all the Republic, and we always will be."

Now the cheers were sincere, rattling the bridge.

"Major, inform Jedi Master Trennis that we are on our way. And then"—he permitted himself a grin—"set course for Hetzal."

The *Aurora III* eased its way into a landing berth in the *Third Horizon*'s hangar. Its fuselage was riddled with laser burns, ragged holes, and other evidence of near-misses and barely eluded destruction. As it landed, a strut partially collapsed under the ship's weight, causing the Longbeam to clang to the deck, listing to the side. Steam and smoke and sparks shot from its various vents and apertures.

To the eyes of the *Third Horizon*'s hangar crew, the Longbeam looked like it should not have been able to fly at all, much less execute a (relatively) safe landing.

With a wheezing grind, the *Aurie*'s primary hatch slid open and a landing ramp extended, sharply, almost unnavigably angled due to the vessel's cant.

A figure stood at the top of that ramp, a large humanoid shape, so wide that he almost entirely blocked the exit.

"I need a medical droid up here!" Joss Adren yelled, his voice booming through the hangar even amid the tumult and turmoil of multiple ships landing and taking off.

Hangar techs ran to the *Aurora III* as Joss stumbled down the ramp. A bloodstained strip of cloth was wrapped around his forehead, and he seemed barely able to keep his feet.

The techs reached for him.

"We'll get you to the medical bay, sir—don't worry, you're safe. You'll be all right."

Joss flexed, waving his arms with an intensity that would have sent the techs flying if they hadn't ducked and weaved out of the way.

"Get away! What are you doing? Not for *me*."

He turned and pointed up the ramp, where a second figure was silhouetted in the Longbeam's hatch. Short, petite but for a round belly, the meaning unmistakable.

"For our baby!"

The techs looked up, alarmed, realizing the situation might be more dire than they had first understood.

"I'm fine," Pikka said wearily. "The baby's fine, too. We just got shook around a little. Sure, I'll see a doc, but not until everyone who's actually injured gets their turn first."

She put a hand at the small of her back, stretched, groaned, and then began making her careful way down the landing ramp. Joss went to her, held her hand, helped her down.

"For instance," Pikka said, patting Joss's cheek, causing him to wince in pain, "my dear husband here."

The techs, not sure what they were actually supposed to do, looked at each other, then from Joss to Pikka, then back at each other.

Pikka sighed, taking Joss by the hand and leading him out of the hangar.

"Come on, big guy," she said. "To the medical bay we go. You'll be fine, I'll be fine, the baby's fine. We made it through."

"This time," Joss said. "We made it through *this* time."

His voice was husky, and Pikka looked a little closer . . . was he crying?

He'll blame it on the head injury if I ask him about it later, she thought, *and I'll let him.*

"We made it through this time," Pikka said, "which means we made it through."

<hr />

Eriadu City was a ruin. The Nihil bombardment had been relentless and total. The city was destroyed. But it was also a place of celebration, of victory, of liberation.

Emerick Caphtor sat in the open bed of a transport skimmer repurposed from its original job transporting goods from farm to market. Now it was in service as an ambulance, scanning for survivors in need of medical attention and bringing them to the nearest treatment center. Kantam Sy lay on a pad at his feet, an emergency medical droid monitoring the injured Jedi and several other patients they'd picked up. Kantam was

STAR WARS: TRIALS OF THE JEDI 277

stable, although the true extent of their injuries wouldn't be clear until the doctors had their turn.

Navaj Tarkin watched in silence as the devastation rolled by. Emerick could barely imagine what the young man must be thinking. The destruction disturbed Emerick on a soul-deep level, and this wasn't even his world.

"This is what you get," Navaj said, and the note in his voice was not sorrow but pride. "We are Eriadu. If you hurt us, it might take time, but we will burn ourselves to the ground rather than let the slight go unpunished."

"Imagine if everyone believed the same," Emerick said. "A galaxy of cinders."

The Jedi and the warrior stared at each other. Neither spoke. After a moment, they turned away, continuing to bear witness to what was left of Eriadu City.

Ghirra Starros's first inkling that something was wrong was when her personal flagship, the *Illustrious Reign,* dropped from hyperspace. This was not unusual—the ship needed to prepare for the unique processes required to transit the Stormwall and continue to Coruscant. What was unexpected, though, was that those processes no longer appeared to be necessary. Her captain had informed her that the Stormwall seemed to be . . . gone.

Ghirra had sent information requests to all corners of the Occlusion Zone, to all the relevant parties—Marchion Ro, her fellow ministers, the military leaders, anyone and everyone who could provide her with data about what was happening. All had responded, with the notable and expected exception of Marchion. The results had been collated into a report, and she had retired to her quarters to read it.

If the information was correct, it was over. The whole thing. The *Gaze*

Electric had vanished or been destroyed, and the mechanisms to operate the Stormwall along with it. The Nihil military had suffered a disastrous defeat at Eriadu, losing almost its entire fleet. The Occlusion Zone was wide open to the Republic, and RDC ships were already moving in.

Ghirra herself might even be in danger, even though the *Reign* was a designated diplomatic ship and supposedly could not be legally attacked by Republic-associated forces. The reality was this: The *Illustrious Reign* was a high-ranking ship of the Nihil Empire. In this new, rapidly evolving situation, that made it a target.

The Nihil Empire—there was a phrase. The Nihil had never quite become a fully functioning state, and now it was clear they never would. Ghirra had actually thought it might work. A few more years of solidifying, of holding Marchion Ro back from his worst impulses, of holding off the Republic . . . The Nihil would have become a true power, undeniable, not just a loose conglomerate of stolen worlds ruled by fear.

This could have been real, Ghirra thought with true sorrow.

She thought of her daughter, Avon, of everything she wanted to show her. To prove to her—about the Nihil and about her mother.

Ghirra reviewed the report a second time, then a third.

Disaster, she thought.

Part of her, even now, was unwilling to believe Marchion Ro had failed so utterly. After everything . . . it seemed impossible.

I believe in him, Ghirra thought. *I hate him, I love him, and I believe in him. He has a plan. I'm sure of it.*

Nevertheless, she had to act before the situation spiraled even further out of control. There were paths to a sort of victory here, still, even now. Not the one she had envisioned, not the galaxy she thought she and Marchion might build, but something.

Ghirra considered waiting for whatever Marchion was doing to reveal itself, but there was almost no time to make the move she was considering. Her window narrowed with every moment.

If Marchion has a plan, he'll have anticipated what I'm about to do, she thought. *And if not, well, maybe he should have let me in on it.*

STAR WARS: TRIALS OF THE JEDI

Ghirra tapped a communications console built into the desk in her quarters.

"Yes, Minister?" came the immediate reply.

Ghirra had trained her people properly. She seemed to be the only person associated with the Nihil who had.

Not that it mattered anymore.

"Send a communication to Supreme Chancellor Lina Soh of the Galactic Republic. Use my authorization codes. Tell the chancellor . . ." Ghirra swallowed, letting the dream fade away. "Tell her that I would like to negotiate the terms of the Nihil's surrender."

Chapter Twenty-Four

THE NAMELESS HOMEWORLD

"I didn't die on Starlight Beacon," Stellan Gios said. "I was badly hurt, but the Nihil took me off the station before it fell, and they've been holding me captive ever since."

Elzar froze on the trail he and Avar were following through the thrashing jungle of the Nameless homeworld. He stared at his old friend.

Stellan had stepped from behind an odd tree, its trunk bright orange with drops of bright-blue sap oozing from it.

His face showed evidence of terrible burns, his beard replaced with shiny scar tissue on the entire left side, but he'd clearly seen medical attention. Rough treatment, maybe, the kind offered to a prisoner. Stellan wore his mission robes—tattered, filthy, with the Jedi insignia torn or burned away. He stood in a clearing in the jungle, the odd, shifting light of the Nameless homeworld shining down on him. The rough, scarred skin of his cheek flexed oddly as he spoke.

"You knew I was still alive, Elzar," Stellan said. "You're no fool. You're one of the smartest Jedi in the Order. That's why the Council was always so afraid of you. Why they didn't want to make you a master."

Stellan shook his head—rueful, sorrowful, it was hard to tell. The semi-healed burns had changed the language of his emotions. Elzar couldn't read him the way he once had.

He took a single involuntary step backward, and Stellan's mouth twitched up in an awful, scar-mangled grimace. He took a step forward, pointing toward Avar, who was still walking along the trail farther ahead of them.

"You knew I was still alive," Stellan repeated. "It's why you were so upset when Avar came to the Occlusion Zone all by herself, why you tried so hard to get through the Stormwall. Because if Avar figured out I was alive, you knew she'd have saved me. Of course she would. Avar's astonishing. And once she did, well, it would just be the two of us, with a wall between us and you. No more pretending we all feel the same way about each other, no more pretending it's all friendly and nothing more. Avar could be what she always wanted to be with me."

Stellan smiled. Some of his teeth were cracked and broken.

"She's only with you because she can't have me. And you *knew* I was alive and you didn't tell her, because if you did, she'd have chosen me."

Elzar hated these words, hated them, hated how they made him feel, because they weren't just words Stellan was saying to him now but words he had said to himself in the dark, small hours. He knew they weren't true, he believed they were untrue, but that did not mean they were powerless.

Stellan took a step toward him. Elzar closed his eyes, knowing that whatever was to come, he deserved it, he did, because he had known his friend was alive and he'd just left him to rot—

A hand closed around Elzar's upper arm, and he leapt backward, scrabbling for his lightsaber.

"Elzar," Avar Kriss said. "Be easy. Breathe."

Elzar opened his eyes. Stellan Gios was gone, and Avar was with him, and he knew what was true.

"I think this planet is getting to me, even with the armor," he said. "Or maybe I'm just overwhelmed, exhausted."

"It's the same for me," Avar replied. "I'm seeing things that can't be there. People."

I wonder what she's seeing, Elzar thought. *I wonder who.*

"We'll just have to . . . focus," he said.

The solution to every problem a Jedi ever faced. Focus, find the Force. Push down whatever you were actually feeling in favor of control, control, control. There were times Elzar Mann found that maxim to be a bit stifling. Now, though, a bit of focus sounded very good indeed.

"You okay to keep going?" Avar said.

Elzar nodded.

"I'll have to be," he said. "We both will."

They were tracking the dying Nameless through the forest, following its glistening spoor, expecting to come across it at any moment. So far, the beast had stayed ahead of them, though many other creatures had attacked. Elzar wondered if the planet was always so . . . intense, or if its inhabitants were maddened by whatever imbalance was causing the Blight. Everything around them seemed to be killing or dying. If there was a place of greater horror for a Jedi, Elzar was having a hard time imagining it.

We came to this world with no plan, he thought. *It was reckless, foolhardy. I know the value of improvising, of finding ideas in the moment, but this was a terrible choice. We have no idea what we're doing, or what we're going to do. We—*

He stopped himself, realizing he was spiraling into yet another kind of fear. The world was insidious, full of tricks, always testing one's resolve one way or another. Elzar put his hand on his lightsaber hilt, looked for something to distract him from the negative thoughts hammering his mind.

Avar was a few meters ahead of him, her head swiveling back and forth—making sure they didn't lose the trail and weren't taken unawares by an attack from the planet's apparently endless supply of sharp-toothed, hinge-jawed creatures. Or maybe she was just looking for ghosts.

"What do you hear, Avar?" Elzar said. "What is the Song singing?"

"It's like . . . an orchestra where all the instruments have been hit with hammers," she said. "This is very wrong, Elzar."

STAR WARS: TRIALS OF THE JEDI 283

Elzar didn't experience the Force as directly and imminently as Avar did. For him, it was a sea, not a song, all around him at all times. He swam through it, moving up and down from light to the edge of darkness—more than once almost sinking into it, and if not for guidance from people like Orla Jareni—

"Elzar," Orla said, so pale, so pale, reaching out to him from the darkness, her voice like dust. Her face began to crumble, the dust like tears, her eyes collapsing, leaving sockets.

"Gah!" Elzar said, stumbling.

Avar turned back toward him.

"What is it?" she asked.

"You know," Elzar said. "Visions. Orla Jareni this time. But there have been others."

"I do," Avar said. She entwined her hand with his. "We know we're real, don't we?"

Elzar wished she wasn't wearing that mask, even though he knew she needed it. He needed his, too. But still, they should be looking into each other's eyes, especially if the end was as near as it felt.

If that happens, I'm ripping this thing off and hers, too. I'm not going back to the Force without seeing her again with my own two eyes.

"Yes, Avar," Elzar said. "We're real."

Behind her, Chancey Yarrow danced and skipped through the jungle, cut nearly in half by Elzar Mann's lightsaber almost a year before. Her pieces wobbled and slid, blood spattering the leaves.

The wound wasn't that bad, was it? I didn't do that *to her, did I? The lightsaber would have cauterized the—*

Elzar couldn't remember. That made it worse.

I'm a monster. I'm everything Stellan said I was. I did have those terrible thoughts. I did kill that poor woman. I did touch the dark side, and when I did, I wanted more. What am I doing here? I'm just going to fail again like I always do.

Avar tugged at his hand.

"Come," she said. "Focus on me. I'll focus on you. If we're feeling this, the other Jedi will be, too. This planet wants you to collapse, to fail, to become just another terrified beast flailing and killing. Don't let it. Swim against the tide.

"We're running out of time to find an answer, Elzar. That's why you're here. You see the things others don't. We need you."

In the forest, Chancey Yarrow capered and dripped.

The galaxy is full of Avars, and the people who love them, he told himself. *It has fallen to you to save them, Elzar Mann, even with all your flaws and failures. You can't change it, so just do it.*

"I'm all right, Avar," Elzar said. "I'm all right."

The two Jedi moved on through the forest, one hand on their lightsaber hilts, the second on the other—a shoulder, a hand, never letting the other be alone.

They followed the trail of the injured Nameless for another half kilometer. The landscape around them began to change. The essential wildness of the planet, a constant ever since their shuttle had crashed, lessened with every step. No longer did they hear the screams of beasts fighting and devouring. The winds stilled, and with them the eerie howls and screams. The trees thinned, then changed. Now strange dark shrubs sprouted from the ground, from which hung an odd, sticky red moss. No more did an endless variety of life slink and chitter all around them.

The Jedi emerged from the last bit of forest into a large circular clearing, a ring of slate-black stone. At its center was . . . something that was difficult to understand. Avar and Elzar paused at the edge of the clearing. The black stone gave way to a disk-shaped depression four meters across in which they could see the Veil, or at least a small portion of it. Churning, thrashing, vibrantly colored clouds moved in the disk, which somehow also appeared perfectly, preternaturally flat. At its edge lay the Nameless they had been tracking, its breath coming shallow and quick, one of its forelimbs torn away. The creature looked out of focus to Elzar, as if he were looking at the beast through eyes exhausted from twelve hours of poring over ancient Jedi texts.

The Nameless effect is getting through, he thought. *I'm trying. But the armor's still helping me, otherwise I wouldn't be able to see the creature with even this level of clarity.*

"The Nameless is almost gone," Avar said, her hand tightening on his. "Is there anything we can do to help it?"

"I'm not sure how," Elzar said. "I don't like watching any living creature suffer, but I also don't know how we can get near it. I would consider putting it out of its pain, but considering what that might do to—"

"We can't," Avar said. "No more can die. It might already be too late."

"I know," Elzar said, hearing the frustration in his tone. "Impossible choices. That's all we get."

"There is no impossible," Avar said, but it sounded rote, something a Jedi was supposed to say.

Ultimately, the choice was taken from them. The Nameless rotated its head to regard them, clearly aware of their presence. It gave them a look that seemed deeply mournful to Elzar, then turned back to the churning disk at the center of the clearing. It reached out a clawed hand toward the shapes. Just as it touched them, the creature collapsed, clearly dying or dead. Its body became a jumble of bones and skin, nothing more.

Elzar's senses immediately cleared.

"Ah," said Avar, and he knew she had experienced the same thing.

It's dead, he thought and was ashamed of the satisfaction he felt, even knowing what the creature's death could mean in the greater context of the ever-growing Blight.

"What is this place?" Avar said, taking a moment to look around. "It sounds strange. Open and closed at the same time."

Elzar took a moment to consider his own answer to that question, stretching out with every sense he had at his command.

"It's a place of transition," Elzar said. "It's where two very different states of being come into conjunction."

"I'll take your word for it," said Avar. "You have your own way of sensing things."

He released her hand and moved forward, toward the center of the stone clearing. The Nameless didn't stir as he approached—it had passed on, there was no doubt. It was one of the beasts Marchion Ro had brought to the planet—it had the Eye's symbol carved into its forehead, a raw, seeping wound. Elzar spared a thought for it, hoped it found more peace in death than it had in life. Then he refocused his attention on the strange, churning pool.

"What do you see?" Avar asked from behind him. "It looks like the Veil."

"It is the Veil," he said, and then he pointed up at the sky above. "Or at least its reflection."

Elzar crouched next to the strange substance, examining it. The Nameless's extended claw almost touched its surface—that's what it had been trying to do when it died. A breeze gusted across the clearing—strong enough to stir Elzar's robes—but the surface of the disk didn't move.

He had thought it might be some sort of hyper-reflective liquid, but up close, it no longer seemed like liquid at all. Whatever filled this depression was dense, something between a solid and a liquid, or neither. There was tension to it, in the way of a glass slightly overfilled. An energy. A barrier and a portal at once.

What would happen, he wondered, *if I touched it? The Nameless was going to. I wonder . . .*

Elzar Mann reached out a hand toward the surface of the strange mirror. Behind him, he thought he heard Avar gasping out a warning or a caution, but not in time, and he wasn't sure anything would have stopped him at that point, barring her cutting his hand off with her lightsaber.

The mirror pool had his attention, the strangeness of it, and Elzar couldn't resist a mystery. Not now, not ever.

Besides, he thought. *I'm wearing gloves.*

The gloves did nothing.

Elzar was in the light, the strange light of the Nameless homeworld, and then he was in the dark. He stood somewhere he did not understand, a great weight all around him, squeezing, compressing, though not killing—not yet.

STAR WARS: TRIALS OF THE JEDI

I'll have to fight to move, he thought. *I'll have to fight for every breath.*

Avar Kriss was there, suddenly, strangely. He could not see her, though he sensed her. Of course he did.

"Avar," Elzar said, his voice sounding strange, both echoed and not. "Where are we?"

"I don't know," she replied. "But, Elzar . . ."

A line of green light flared as Avar lit her lightsaber, pushing back the darkness only enough to reveal the look of abject horror on her face.

"I can't hear the Song."

Chapter Twenty-Five

THE NAMELESS HOMEWORLD

Have I ever felt this good before? Marchion Ro wondered.

He stood on the edge of a cliff, looking out across the Nameless homeworld. It spread before him all the way to the horizon, a riot of color and energy. Patches of bright-pink vegetation pushed up against turquoise lakes. Flocks of huge yellow creatures winged their way over rolling ocher hills. Every so often one of the fliers would swoop down and disappear beneath the surface of the hills—long grasses, he assumed—and come up with some wriggling creature clutched in its talons or beak, streams of glowing purple seeds scattering behind it as it rose.

Waves of energy pulsed through the sky, a daytime aurora twisting and winding around itself, light and dark bands spinning in an unending ballet.

And the sounds—the sounds! Crunching, swooshing, screaming, the trees shaking, the ground vibrating. This was nothing like his last trip to the planet, when he had first gathered the Nameless.

It's eating itself, he thought. *The world is chewing itself up, swallowing, opening its jaws to take another bite.*

A surge of pride filled his chest. Marchion exhaled, not sure how to process the sensation. He wasn't used to feeling such strong emotion. Was that something he had trained himself not to do, as a defense mechanism for the life he led? It seemed possible. Emotions were traps. Anger, fear, love—they all left you open to attack.

But he was feeling things now. He was feeling *everything,* and why not?

Marchion didn't need to protect himself, he didn't need to bide his time, he didn't need to save his feelings for some hypothetical moment in the future when he felt safe enough to allow himself to be a full person.

He was safe *now.* There was no more time to bide. There was nothing to protect himself from. He'd made sure of that.

This is the end, Marchion thought. *I am the end.*

The chaos happening here on the Nameless world was happening everywhere, just on a larger scale.

Marchion shook his head, just smiling, smiling as he thought about it. He tried to envision what was happening out there and realized it was beyond his capacity. Every image he called to mind—a building collapsing into a yawning pit of Blight beneath it, a sea turning gray as dead Blighted creatures floated to its surface, the expressions of people everywhere as they realized they had no time left—all too small. Nothing he imagined could possibly match the reality.

He looked up, considering the endless galaxy beyond the Veil. All those planets, those stars, everyone on them—*everyone,* everywhere, and not just the ones alive now but everyone who would ever live, who would have been born . . . all of them were gone. Dead.

Because of Marchion Ro.

No one is more than me. All those conquerors, warlords, emperors—they are all small compared to me. They had no ambition compared to me. No one will ever exert more control over more people than I have.

I am the only person who has ever mattered in all of existence.

He put a hand over his eyes, overwhelmed.

Is this what it feels like?

Joy?

I didn't know I ... could. I am like other people, he thought. *I can feel. I can be happy.*

"And the best part is," Marchion said aloud, looking out again over the view, watching the planet consume itself, "I won't have to be sad. There won't be any after. No comedown, no looking for the next way to feel like this, no anything. I'll just be dead like everyone else."

No, he thought. *Wrong. I won't die like everyone else. All they'll feel when they die is terror. I'll feel ... like* this.

A great white light bloomed in his chest, a feeling he could almost see. Marchion Ro's eyes welled up, and he closed them again.

A sound from behind—Marchion spun, his hand going to his belt, where any number of weapons rested. But it was not an enemy. It was a tool. A path. In a way ... a friend.

A Nameless.

The beast nosed its way out of the forest's edge, heading toward Marchion. This wasn't one of his—how could it be? He had killed them all. This was a native, not as emaciated or maddened as the beasts he'd taken from the world. Still deadly, though, still dangerous. The disturbed balance on the planet had affected this thing, too. It shook its head, bared its teeth, signaled an obvious intent to charge.

Marchion Ro raised the Rod of Power, showing it to the creature. It paused, uncertain. He exerted his will, took control of the beast as he had so many others. The Nameless reared back, fighting him, lifting its forelegs into the air.

"I don't think so, pretty," Marchion said and bore down.

The Nameless fell to its feet, shuddering.

"Better," Marchion said.

He gestured with the control rod. Without a sound, the Nameless walked, then ran, then galloped for the edge of the cliff. It passed Marchion and leapt forward into open space.

Marchion watched it fall, watched it explode against the rocks far below. The sound rolled up to him, pleasant and wet.

Did that change anything? he wondered. *Does the death of even a single Nameless increase the speed at which the Blight spreads? I hope so.*

Marchion found himself a little frustrated that he didn't know precisely what was happening in other parts of the galaxy. He wished he'd left himself a way to communicate with Ghirra. He wondered if she'd made it to Coruscant yet. Wondered when the Blight would get her, too. Wondered what was happening at Eriadu.

Marchion Ro wondered who was alive or dead, wondered how long it would be before people would realize the truth. It was irritating not to know these things.

He could already feel a shadow creeping in around the edge of his joy. He wanted more, wanted the end to be faster, bigger, deadlier, more agonizing.

He had an idea.

He lifted the control rod, holding it high above his head.

"Die," said Marchion Ro.

He put everything he had into the command. The gems on the control rod pulsed and flared, and Marchion knew it was working. He didn't need to be with the Nameless to kill them. The Rod of Power could amplify his will to let him touch all of the creatures, every one on the planet. He could send them all over the cliff at once. Every one that died would speed up the Blight, and with each death his happiness would grow.

The rod grew warm against his palm. This was new, but then he'd never tried anything like this before.

Marchion heard movement behind him, sound from the forest's edge.

They're coming, he thought, and his heart soared.

It occurred to him that he was standing at the edge of a precipice, with his back to any number of Nameless charging toward it to leap to their deaths. Not the best situation, perhaps, even with the control rod.

Marchion spun, his hand moving toward his weapons . . . and saw no Nameless at all.

Instead two Jedi stood at the edge of the forest—no, three. The Wookiee Burryaga carried one on his back like a mother with an infant. The bundled Jedi was Terec, apparently injured. A small black-and-orange creature stood hissing and steaming at Burryaga's feet, a charhound.

And then there was Bell Zettifar.

"You won't be able to kill any more of them," Bell said. "We won't let you."

Marchion watched, interested, as Burryaga carefully eased himself out of the harness holding Terec and set the injured Jedi down on the ground. The Wookiee didn't seem entirely steady. Neither did Bell, for that matter. Marchion's predator's eyes noticed that Bell's hands had the slightest tremor.

Pieces of the Jedi's armor were missing, his and Burryaga's both. It must have happened during their battles to reach this place. How sad for them.

"Are you feeling all right, young Bell?" Marchion said. "You seem . . . troubled."

"I've never been more calm," Bell said.

The Jedi reached to his waist and unsheathed his lightsaber, the green blade snapping to life. Beside him, Burryaga did the same, a gigantic blue saber blade hissing from the end of a huge, two-handed hilt. The charhound barked and growled at his side, little displays of meaningless aggression that Marchion ignored.

The two Jedi split up, moving to his left and right in coordination, attempting to flank him. Clearly they'd fought together before—although their movements were slow, overly precise, like they were both trying to maintain their footing in a great wind. Marchion watched them, unconcerned.

The Nameless effect, he thought. *Their armor must offer them some protection, but they've lost pieces, and now they can feel the terror creeping in. How wonderful.*

"This has been a long time coming," said Bell Zettifar, effecting a confidence he clearly did not feel.

"I suppose it has, Bell," Marchion replied.

He reached to his own waist, selected one of the lightsabers he had placed there. His trophies. He had several, and they were all special to him. But this moment called for one in particular.

He lifted the lightsaber from his belt, held it out to show Bell, made sure the Jedi knew exactly who its original owner had been, knew exactly where it had come from.

Loden Greatstorm's lightsaber flared to life, a yellow blade slicing the air. Marchion Ro grinned.

"Shall we?" he said.

PART THREE

THE RAZOR WINDS NEAR.
NOTHING CAN HOLD.

Interlude

ESTARVERA

Davet Colman and his eleven-year-old sister, Shanna, trudged down a street alongside hundreds of other slow-moving, stunned refugees. They were all headed toward Alowee Pond Park, where transports waited to whisk them away to safety, away from the Blight.

Davet was trying to inhabit the moment. More specifically, a moment in which he had not yet learned—for sure, irrevocably—that his parents were dead. It was a good moment. It kept him moving down the street as opposed to just collapsing to the ground.

He liked his parents very much. The idea that just because he was sixteen he was supposed to think they were embarrassing, seemed dumb. Was his dad a smooth operator? No, absolutely not. But Ryden Colman was smart. He got things done. He planned ahead, and the family always had enough credits for the things they needed even though the bakery they ran would never make them rich.

His mom was great, too—her recipes were the reason people came to the bakery in the first place, and she was infinitely better with the customers than his dad would ever be. Sure, there were challenges to be overcome because of her legs—they couldn't afford an operation to fix them—but Mom was a happy person. And with Sixbee to help out—

Sixbee's not going to be able to help anymore, Davet thought, remembering the sound the autocart made when it ran the droid down.

He put that aside.

The point was, when the Blight came, his dad had a plan for that, too. If things had worked out, all four of them could be on a starship right now, headed offworld to safety. No, six—Sixbee and Shanna's little scale-pig, Florg, would be with them, too. The whole family.

But things had not worked out.

How many of us are left? Davet thought. *Mom can't really move without her chair. What was Dad's plan when he sent us away? Was he going to carry her?*

Davet didn't think even his father could have made a plan to take into account a terrible corrosion plague methodically destroying the whole kriffing planet, or that the spaceport would be eaten just as they arrived, or that things would get so bad he'd have to send his kids away while he stayed back with his wife because she was paralyzed from the waist down and her hoverchair was lost.

Davet Colman was a lot like his dad. He liked to think ahead and use his brain to get around sticky situations. They shared that, and probably should have talked about it more while they had the chance.

But Davet was like his mom, too. She liked to say she "inhabited the moment." In the view of Calina Colman, it was important to experience your life as fully as you could while you were living it, because every moment lived was a moment lost. They never came back.

"Mom and Dad will be at the park," Shanna said, her voice a little muffled by her breathing mask.

Davet wore one, too, and was glad of it even though the thing was hot and he felt like his lungs were only getting about 80 percent full with each breath. The Blight might be floating through the air. When it ate things, big clouds of gray-white dust billowed up, and what would happen if you breathed it in? He didn't want to find out.

"They'll be there," Shanna said.

STAR WARS: TRIALS OF THE JEDI   299

"Uh-huh," Davet said, putting one foot in front of the other.

The first few times Shanna said these words, they'd been phrased as a question. Davet had answered by explaining all the ways their parents could have made it out of the *completely, obviously unsurvivable* situation back by the spaceport. She'd fall silent for a few minutes, then ask the same question again, to which he'd give a slight variation on the answer he'd just given her.

It got old fast, but Davet loved his sister and knew she was terrified. She was still asking, and he was still answering. It was just another way of inhabiting that good moment. That last good moment before they both had to face the truth.

I'm all she's got, he thought, *but she doesn't need to know that yet.*

He glanced at Shanna, who was clutching a little cloth bag close to her chest, from which a stubby, snuffling, green-fringed nose poked out.

I guess I'm not all she has, Davet thought. *She's still got Florg.*

Shanna whispered something to the little scalepig, and it broke Davet's heart. That was something she used to do when she was little. He hadn't seen her talk to the creature like it was a person in years.

Florg started to squirm in Shanna's hands, making that little yip sound it did when it was agitated in some way. It pushed against her from within the bag, suddenly consumed by what seemed like absolute terror.

"Ow! Quit it, Florg!" Shanna said.

She took the creature in both hands and held it away from her body, still in its bag.

"What's the matter with him?" Davet asked.

"I don't know! He's really upset. He scratched me, and he *never* scratches me."

Davet took his little sister's arm and pulled her toward the side of the street, finding a spot behind a parked speeder where they could get out of the flow of refugees. He looked at Florg. The little beast had its whole head out of the bag and was staring fixedly up the street in the direction they were headed. Its body language was clear—it leaned back, its little round plant-eating teeth bared, its nostrils flaring as it sniffed, taking big gulps of air, getting as far away as Shanna's grip would allow.

"Florg's afraid," Davet said. "But I can't see what frightened him. Maybe someone up ahead has some scary pet they're bringing along, and he smells it."

A low rumble reached both their ears, and both Davet's and Shanna's heads snapped up in unison. They knew this sound—they'd been hearing it all day. It meant part of the city was falling into another Blight pit. So far, they'd all been behind them, in the direction they'd come from.

Back where we left Mom and Dad, Davet thought.

This sound, though, was ahead of them. Screams started, and then the sound of running feet, and then the roaring, crunching sound of collapse, as if the entire world was cracking in half.

Davet reached for his sister—she was screaming, too. He held her close.

The ground shook, and panicked people rushed past. Davet felt lucky they'd moved out of the street before the collapse happened or they'd be at risk of being trampled. Clouds of white dust shot past them, and Davet felt lucky again. They had the masks.

Florg didn't, but Shanna tucked him back inside his bag and held it inside her tunic, and hopefully that would be enough.

The scalepig saved our lives, Davet thought, replaying the sequence of events in his mind. *It smelled the Blight. It must have.*

The rumbling slowed, then stopped. Davet gave it a good minute before he released his sister, looked into her tear-streaked eyes to make sure she was unhurt, and then stood up to get a look around.

At the end of the block, the street was . . . gone. Just a ragged edge of pavement and then a cloudy, swirling gray-white nothing.

The street was empty, too—everyone had fled. The exception was an old man, a long-faced Muun, staring into the horrible, blank cloud.

"I sent my husband on ahead," he said, and Davet wasn't sure who he was talking to. "I told him I needed a moment to catch my breath."

The old Muun walked forward, seemingly unaware that the road stopped and fell away into nothingness. Or maybe he just didn't care.

"Hey, wait!" Davet called out, but the man ignored him.

STAR WARS: TRIALS OF THE JEDI 301

Davet turned to make sure Shanna was still hidden behind the speeder—he didn't want her to see. She was, which was good. When he looked back toward the street, the Muun was gone. Only the billowing clouds of Blight.

"How are we going to get through?" Shanna said, joining him, staring up the street that had very literally become a dead end. "Mom and Dad are waiting."

Davet looked around, thinking. His comm still had no signal, but it had a subfunction that could display a map of the city on its little screen. He called it up, looking for another way to Alowee Pond.

"Here," he said, tracing a line on the screen, showing it to Shanna. "We can go this way. A little roundabout, but it'll get us there."

"But what if other streets are like that?" Shanna said, pointing at the Blight pit. "Or if they fall apart while we're walking on them?"

"Florg will help," Davet said. "He knew this street was bad—that's why he was afraid. We'll let him sniff out the right path."

Hope bloomed in Shanna's eyes, and Davet felt good, very good, even if he had no idea if his proposal would work.

"That's a good idea," she said.

"Of course it is," Davet replied, tweaking her ear. "We'll tell Mom and Dad about it. I bet they'll be impressed."

They set out, letting Florg lead. If they came across a street he didn't want to go down, they found another way. It took much longer than they wanted, and they saw many patches of Blight, but eventually the tall orange billyoak trees that surrounded Alowee Pond grew visible above the rooftops.

The streets grew more crowded as they approached, more and more people heading to the park for evacuation. It was all orderly, though. Safety officers made sure no one pushed or prodded or panicked, and every so often a transport took off, soaring into the air.

Davet found himself becoming somehow both more relaxed and more anxious the closer they got. The park meant safety. It meant a way off this death trap of a planet. It also meant he'd have to confront Shanna with the truth.

Our parents aren't waiting for us, he thought. *That goodbye they gave us back by the spaceport was the last goodbye.*

Davet's dad was a planner, which meant he'd known what was happening when he sent them away. Ryden had just made a new plan once things went bad, one that would get his kids to safety. He had lied to Davet and Shanna to get them to leave, but that was okay. Davet would have done the same thing, and he admired his parents for making such an impossible choice so quickly and well.

But part of him was angry, so angry, that they had left one of the hardest duties to him—he'd have to tell his little sister the truth.

But not yet. It could wait. She was smiling behind the mask as they got closer to where she thought their parents were waiting—he could tell. Better to let her feel good for as long as he could.

The idea of the park collapsing out from under them just like the spaceport did rose into his mind, and Davet shoved it away.

If that happens, it happens, he said. *Some things you can't plan for. If it does, just grab Shanna and make sure she knows she isn't alone.*

Then he was mad again, because who was going to make sure *he* wasn't alone.

"Davet!" he heard, and it was a voice he knew.

A voice he never expected to hear again, and his shock at hearing it now just underscored how certain he'd been that his parents were dead.

His father came up the street toward them, limping but moving fast. He was favoring a leg, Davet noted. Not too far behind was his mother, sitting on an emergency hoverchair. The thing was stripped down, didn't look very comfortable, but it kept her up and off the ground and that was good enough.

Davet found himself wrapped up in his dad's arms, the breath getting squeezed out of him, and that was fine, more than fine.

"Dad," he said, "Dad . . ." and that was about it because he could feel tears in his throat and couldn't say much more.

His dad pulled back, looked him over, looked back at Shanna, who was with their mother, doing something similar to what Davet and Ryden had just done.

STAR WARS: TRIALS OF THE JEDI 303

"You okay? You both okay? Where's Sixbee?"

Something was bothering Davet, but it was just a quiet sound in the back of his head, overwhelmed by the unexpected joy of finding his parents still alive.

"Sixbee didn't make it, but we're both all right, Dad. How did you and Mom get here?"

"Story for another time," Ryden said. "Once we're all on a transport."

Ryden let Davet go, then limped a few painful steps toward Shanna and Calina.

"Time to get going, ladies. We've already got a spot in line, but they'll give it away if we're late. Word from the security officers is that the Blight's really stepped up its pace. It's moving faster than they've ever seen it. Scans say things are still good under the park, so we've got time, but time's something you never want to waste!"

"Your leg, Dad," Davet said. "Are you okay?"

Ryden didn't answer, but as he got closer to Shanna, and more particularly Florg, the scalepig began yipping and squirming and scratching in the way he had on the way to this place, and that was answer enough.

Davet's mind snapped into focus, and he realized what had been bothering him since his parents' reappearance. There was a crucial difference between his mother and father, and it wasn't just that his mom was in that chair.

Calina was wearing a mask, very much like the ones he and his sister had on. Ryden was not.

"Dad . . ." Davet began.

Ryden held up a hand.

"I have a plan," he said, limping back toward Davet, his voice quiet. "I'll stay back while you go on with your mother and your sister. Someone has to make sure the bakery's okay."

"The bakery? Dad, what the hell are you talking about?"

"I didn't say it was a good plan, son," Ryden said and smiled.

It was a very sad smile.

Chapter Twenty-Six

THE NAMELESS HOMEWORLD

To a charhound born on the metal and stone and magnetic-field world of Elphrona, life was not complicated. Everything was good or bad or could be ignored.

Food was good. Friends who brought food and spoke in kind tones and rubbed Ember's back and scratched her ears and fought bad things were also good. Lying on a hot stone in the hot sun was good. Other charhounds were often good, though you couldn't always tell—it sometimes depended if food was around. Mating was good—although it had been a long time.

Being hungry was bad. Being hurt was bad. A friend being hurt was very bad.

Ember didn't call many beings her friends. Those who met the criteria were the most valuable beings in her world. They were the Goodest of the Good. She had known some friends almost all her life, since just after the Bad Hurt Time when she was a puppy and had crawled away from a fight with a spike-sparrow that had killed the other small charhounds and the two big charhounds who were all she had known up to that point in time.

It was good to have friends, even if spending time with them could

STAR WARS: TRIALS OF THE JEDI 305

make Ember's life frustratingly complicated. For instance, she spent much of her time with two beings—one she called Home Friend, and another she called Tall Friend. A long time ago, back on Elphrona, Home Friend had invited her to go with him into a metal cave. She did, and they waited there for a time. A while later, she followed him out, and everything outside was changed. Elphrona was gone. Since then, she had entered metal caves with Home Friend and Tall Friend many times and it was always the same. Coming out of the cave meant new sensations, new scents, new sights, new food. It was confusing at first—but as long as Home Friend or Tall Friend was around, it had stopped bothering her. Tall Friend and Home Friend were home. Simple enough.

Now, though, the metal cave had taken her to a place that was by far the worst she'd visited since leaving Elphrona. The *feel* of the place was just bad, a swirling mix of confusing energies she didn't understand. It felt like anything could happen at any time, good or bad. Danger could come from any side. Everything here wanted to eat her or hurt her friends.

Ember was not complicated, and this was a complicated place. She had decided that the best thing would be to stay close to Home Friend and Tall Friend and keep them safe. So she was with them when they found a new person, a person that was definitely not a friend.

Ember felt something like relief when she first assessed this new person. In a place defined by its ambiguity, it was nice to encounter someone she could quickly and definitively categorize as bad.

The being's scent was bad, like the feeling of something biting you. The sounds the being made were bad—negative, harsh sounding. The way Home Friend and Tall Friend felt about the being was bad—they thought he was a dire threat indeed.

In fact, her friends both had their hot bright sticks out—the things they used in their fights, the way Ember used her claws and teeth and burn. And lo, what was this? The bad being had a hot bright stick of his own! Home Friend's was green, Tall Friend's was blue, and the bad one's was yellow.

Ember had been a member of several packs during her life. Her first was composed entirely of charhounds, all of whom had died but her. Her second pack was also back on Elphrona, and she didn't see most of them anymore. Maybe they were dead, too.

Her pack now was Home Friend and Tall Friend, and the bad person wanted to hurt them—that was very clear. Home Friend and Tall Friend were moving slowly and carefully toward the bad one, getting ready to fight.

Packs came and went, but a very simple rule applied to them all. This rule held a place as high in Ember's decision-making hierarchy as Find Food and Love Well. The rule was this: Protect the Pack You Have.

Ember knew the bad person was paying attention to Home Friend and Tall Friend, not her. She could sense it. This was her moment. She moved, her strong, whip-thin legs shifting her to full speed in no time at all. The air ruffled her fur, and the ground vanished beneath her paws. She could feel the heat growing inside her. It felt good.

The bad one was bigger than she was, but that didn't matter. She could burn him. She could burn anything. This was a perfect burning time. In fact, Home Friend and Tall Friend clearly agreed—they had their hot bright sticks out.

But so did the bad person. Ember needed to remember that. He was dangerous, as dangerous as anything she'd ever encountered.

But not as dangerous as the burn. The bad one would burn, and then Home Friend and Tall Friend would be happy and safe.

There he was! He wasn't looking at Ember. His eyes—which made Ember think of mouths—were flicking between Home Friend and Tall Friend as they got closer to him.

Tall Friend made a loud sound, but Ember ignored it.

This was her chance.

She ran, as fast as she could, staying low to stay away from the bad person's sharp-toothed eyes. She pulled in a huge breath, letting the burn build, felt it filling her with the good heat.

Ember would burn this bad one. Her friends would be safe.

Her friends would be happy.

STAR WARS: TRIALS OF THE JEDI 307

Burryaga saw a flash of black-and-orange movement as he and Bell advanced toward Marchion Ro. Ember surged up from behind a little stand of rocks, barely two meters from where the Eye stood near the edge of the cliff overlooking the wild, thrashing planet. Burry had no idea how Ember had gotten so close. Charhounds were predators. Presumably she was born knowing how to stalk prey. Still, he should have seen her, should have sensed her.

Ember was too close to Marchion to warn her off. She was too close for Burryaga to do anything but shout her name—in Shyriiwook, it was a sharp snap like a log crackling in a fire.

But it was too late. Burryaga didn't think the charhound would stop even if she'd heard him. Ember was a good friend to him and Bell. She loved them. She was going to help no matter what.

Ember leapt into the air, wisps of steam pouring from her ears, flickers of flame around her snout. Burry heard Bell yell in alarm—also too late.

The charhound's body swelled as she sucked in a huge breath, stoking the forgefire in her lungs, clearly preparing to incinerate Marchion Ro where he stood.

She shot through the air, a creature of living flame. A rushing sound spilled from her, half snarl, half the sound of a roaring inferno.

Marchion Ro spun, a flicker of movement so fast Burryaga didn't know how he did it without the Force. He caught Ember around the throat as neatly as if she had thrown herself directly at his hand. The sound she'd been making stopped, strangled out of her, and her body whipped forward below her neck, the momentum of her leap carrying her onward.

She dangled from Marchion's slate-blue left hand, the dark claws at his fingertips digging into her throat. Her body was still swollen from the huge breath she had taken, the one she had intended to expel into Marchion Ro's face.

He held her so tight that the flames had nowhere to go.

Ember squirmed and struggled, her lithe body whipping back and forth, her eyes rolling crazily in her head. She whined, a sound of horrible pain.

She's cooking herself, Burryaga thought, horrified, realizing he could *smell* it. *She's cooking herself from the inside.*

Marchion Ro brought the whimpering charhound close to his face, inspecting her with cold, flat eyes.

Burryaga knew what he was going to do. It was the only option. Yes, Marchion could cut her in half with Loden Greatstorm's stolen lightsaber or snap her neck, but then the living fire inside her would spill out all over him.

Instead Marchion chose precisely the option Burryaga knew his calculating, evil mind would find.

He threw Ember over the cliff.

She disappeared, the flames already starting to spill from her mouth.

Burryaga howled and changed direction. He sprinted, faster than he'd been running before, no longer a tactical charge toward a lightsaber-armed opponent but a desperate dash. As he ran, he deactivated his lightsaber and slung it from his belt.

He was sorry to leave Bell alone, but part of him knew this was always going to be the other Jedi's fight.

Burryaga dived off the cliff.

Chapter Twenty-Seven

THE NAMELESS HOMEWORLD

Ty Yorrick knew how to track. Everything left a trail. Nothing moved without leaving some sign of its passage, even the stealthiest creature. Flying beasts disturbed the air, which disturbed the foliage, which left little curtainfalls of pollen. Burrowing beasts made sounds as they dug. Swimming creatures made currents.

The Force helped, too. Living things interacted with other living things in ways she could sense. Prey moved away from predators. Predators moved toward prey. To her, that's what the Force was—the great push and pull of all life. Birth, growth, life, death, decay, rebirth.

Ty could track beasts through any terrain, any weather. She just followed their path through the Force.

Her skill was such that she could have followed Azlin Rell if he were flying above a flat plain of solid stone.

But the ancient human was just moving through the forest, seemingly unconcerned that she and Reath Silas were following him. He was walking, his feet bare—she could tell by the shape of the prints she found in soft mud, and the infrequency of broken vegetation along his trail. Running feet made long, deep shapes in the ground, with the full foot rarely making an impression. Running creatures snapped branches and tore leaves. Walking creatures did none of those things.

They also didn't leave exploded carcasses of insects and small creatures in their wake, which littered the forest to either side of the trail.

Ty's head ached. Her side ached. Worse than both was the frustration she felt at being taken unaware by the ancient former Jedi's attack. It hadn't been a fair fight. For one thing, Ty was fighting with the equivalent of a hand tied behind her back. She'd been forced to leave behind so much of her standard gear load-out for this mission. If she had her full complement of weapons, perhaps her droid RO-VR . . . Azlin's cowardly sneak attack would have generated a very different outcome.

But Azlin wouldn't beat her again. Ty Yorrick had a plan.

She hadn't shared it with Reath yet. He was dutifully walking behind her, moving quietly. She appreciated that; no reason to advertise their presence either to Azlin or any of the maddened beasts that inhabited this strange, wild world. The young Jedi had activated that odd shield of his—she appreciated that, too. Reath had used it to save her life; maybe it would serve that purpose again. The young Knight seemed lost in thought, his standard mode of operation. Reath Silas was the thinking type.

Nothing wrong with that. Ty liked the kid. But there was such a thing as overthinking, too. Reath seemed conflicted, like he was having trouble understanding or accepting the truth about Azlin Rell. Ty didn't get it. To her, the situation with Azlin was crystal clear.

Was it fine that the old former Jedi had left the Order? Of course it was. Ty would be some kind of hypocrite if she judged Azlin for that. Was it even fine to conduct yourself within the Force however you wanted? Sure. Dark side, light side: For Ty, it all had its place.

But when you started hurting people because of your own fears, when you started killing indiscriminately . . . that was crossing the line from go-your-own-way iconoclast into monster territory.

And Ty Yorrick hunted monsters.

She felt sympathy for most of the beasts she hunted, and put them

STAR WARS: TRIALS OF THE JEDI   311

down as easily as she could. If there was a way to subdue a monster instead of killing it, she'd do it.

She'd even offer that courtesy to Azlin Rell. But she had her doubts that he'd give her the option. She thought Azlin was probably going to die.

She continued scanning the ground and the surrounding forest and the Force itself, making sure she was still on Azlin's trail. It only took part of her focus, though—the old darksider really wasn't making it difficult—and so Ty used the rest of her attention to run a mental inventory of her available tactical gear.

She had her lightsaber—useful but just one tool among many. A blaster. A second blaster. A hold-out blaster. Three daggers of varying composition and length—different beasts could be vulnerable to different metals or materials. A dart launcher, with a decent spread of options for poisons and tranquilizers. More grenades, although Azlin hadn't been particularly fazed by the last one she'd tossed at him. A sprayer that could produce insta-harden foam, enough to freeze a charging mudhorn in its tracks.

This was barely a quarter of what she usually carried, but there were some useful gadgets in there. The sprayer was the key. Bind Azlin up—he'd panic, dark side or not—and then she could knock him out, or if she had to, end it with her lightsaber. Either way, quick and easy.

Ty glanced back at Reath. She couldn't see his face under the white-and-gold helmet he wore—she wore one, too—but his body language said he wasn't happy. He was staring at his feet, his hands hanging limply at his sides.

Not good, she thought. *I need him focused.*

"Hey, kid," she said.

Reath's head snapped up. She knew he was frowning behind the mask.

"Hey," Ty amended.

"What is it, Ty?" he said.

"Tell me about this guy's weaknesses."

"The Nameless," Reath replied.

"Azlin didn't seem very weak to me," Ty said. "Maybe you missed it, but he wasn't wearing his armor. He acted like he was on vacation in the Core instead of a planet full of Nameless. You think we'd feel that calm if we took off our armor?"

"Probably not," Reath said.

The armor—that was another thing to take into account. Ty had lost a tasset and a pauldron during the fight with the Nameless back at the crash site, and she could feel the effects. Some of the carcasses Azlin was leaving in his wake seemed to be putting themselves back together. Seemed to be . . . dancing with each other.

She shook her head to clear it.

"You saw what Azlin did back there, when he fought us . . . I don't think we'd beat him in a direct assault, even two-on-one."

"Okay," Reath said.

"Hey, hold up here a second," Ty said, stopping, then turning and placing a hand flat against Reath's chestpiece.

The young Jedi watched her, waiting to see what she was going to say.

"I know this isn't easy, Reath. People have died, people are hurt. As far as we know, Marchion Ro just killed the entire galaxy when he had all those Nameless slaughter themselves. I also know you have some kind of connection to Azlin. I'm not saying you're friends, I'm not saying you'll go soft on him, but I can tell this is complicated for you."

Reath didn't respond.

"We need that blasted rod back," Ty said. "But he won't give it up without a fight. The only way I can see to do this is if he's distracted. I can only think of one thing that might get his attention." She moved her hand, changing it from a flat palm to a single pointing finger, right at Reath's heart.

"Me," Reath said.

"You," she agreed. "You're bait. Go to him, get his focus however you can. That's all you have to do. Just make sure he's paying attention to you and nothing else. I'll handle the rest."

"He's not evil," Reath said. "He's just afraid."

"Sure," Ty said.

⚜

Reath suspected Ty Yorrick planned to kill Azlin. And after what Rell had done, the power he'd shown, and his willingness to use it . . . there didn't seem to be a strong argument he could make against Ty's plan other than "Jedi don't kill unarmed old men."

But Ty wasn't a Jedi, and Azlin certainly wasn't unarmed.

He carried with him the dark side of the Force, and by all evidence, a powerful ally it was.

Reath thought of all the time he'd spent with Azlin down in that cell beneath the Jedi Temple on Coruscant. All their conversations about the nature of the Force, the truth of good and evil. Azlin had taught him many things, many important things.

He would never admit it, would never say it aloud, could barely think it, but Reath Silas had several masters—Jora Malli, who had been killed by the Nihil, then Cohmac Vitus, and finally, yes, Azlin Rell. He was the Jedi he was today because of *all* of their teachings.

Is this really my decision? he wondered. *Will I actually choose whether Azlin Rell lives or dies? How did this land on me?*

But Reath knew. Decisions didn't have some cosmic destiny. They landed on the people who had to make them. There was no reason to it. It was just how it was. Thinking about the situation, trying to analyze it, reflecting, studying . . . none of that would change the reality.

That reality was this: Azlin Rell had killed—directly killed— thousands upon thousands of people on Travyx Prime. He had done this by misleading and manipulating no less than Grand Master Yoda himself. Azlin had alluded to causing many other deaths in the century-plus he had wandered the galaxy after first encountering the Nameless and embracing the dark side.

Azlin was a murderer. If the Jedi Council had chosen to temporarily overlook that in light of the man's unique knowledge of the threat facing the galaxy, it did not change the facts.

And beyond all of *that,* something seemed to have happened to him out here.

Reath thought about the voice that had emerged from Azlin just before he attacked Ty. The old man's voice was extremely familiar to Reath by now; that sweet, soft, kind tone that could shift into a rasp of fury and terror when he became . . . agitated.

This had sounded different. Stronger, more confident.

Darker.

Reath made his decision.

"Yes, Ty," he said. "I'll help you deal with Azlin."

"Good," the hunter replied, turning and moving quickly ahead into the jungle. "Now let's move and stay quiet. We're catching up to him."

Ty turned out to be correct. Reath followed her as she moved stealthily through the jungle, making confident changes of direction, following a trail he couldn't see.

In not much time, Ty stopped, her body tense, her legs poised on the balls of her feet. She looked back at Reath. He couldn't see her face because of the mask she wore, but he imagined it—utterly focused, eyes gone cold. Ty did not speak, just pointed with two fingers farther along the path they had been following. Reath looked and saw that the vegetation seemed to clear in that direction, ten or so meters away.

Ty motioned again, tapping her own chest twice. She then moved her hand in a broad circle, and Reath understood.

She's going to circle around, get behind Azlin.

Then Ty tapped Reath twice on the chest and made that same pointing motion toward where Azlin waited. Reath nodded, and before he realized she was leaving, Ty was gone, vanished into the jungle.

That quickly, that simply, her hunt had begun.

Reath took a deep breath. He centered himself, found the Force within

STAR WARS: TRIALS OF THE JEDI   315

his spirit, an endless library that contained every story, every question, every answer.

He knew this was a moment that would define him forever—if not in the eyes of others, then in his own. The rest of the Jedi might never know what he was about to do, but he would carry it with him for the rest of his life.

Reath moved forward, using his shield to push the branches and vines out of the way. He was glad Ty had gotten them so close to the forest's edge. Without her skill, he could easily have become disoriented and lost.

But now the light awaited, and Reath moved toward it.

He pushed through a final stand of plants, long, thin stalks adorned by beautiful, delicate purple and red blossoms. The jungle opened up to a hilltop, where Reath could see Azlin Rell standing very still, facing away, toward whatever was on the other side of the slope.

"Azlin," Reath said.

The old man didn't turn, didn't respond. The Rod of Ages dangled loosely from his hand, the disk at its edge touching the ground.

Reath climbed the hill, very aware that somewhere nearby, Ty Yorrick stalked her prey.

"Azlin," he said again.

"Come to me, Reath," Azlin said, still not turning. "Tell me what you see down there. My sight is . . . different now. I don't trust what I see. I need you to be my eyes."

A sensation arose within Reath, the same that had driven so many of his decisions since he joined the Jedi Order, perhaps even his decision *to* join the Jedi Order, if a three-year-old child could be said to make any decisions at all. The same sensation that had caused him to delve deeper into the Jedi libraries than anyone he knew other than Elzar Mann—and he was sure he'd catch up with Elzar once he had a few more years under his robe.

The sensation was curiosity, and it was impossible for him to resist. Not when Azlin sounded like he was seeing the most fascinating, awe-inspiring sight in the galaxy. Reath knew his job was to distract Azlin so

Ty Yorrick could . . . well, could kill him. There was no point in pretending the situation was other than it was.

But that could wait. Until he saw.

Reath walked up the hill and joined Azlin. The lapsed Jedi put his hand on Reath's shoulder, and there was nothing uncomfortable about it, nothing threatening or strange. This was how it should be. Student and master.

"Tell me," Azlin said.

Reath looked.

"Is it real?" Azlin asked, a note of intensity creeping into his voice, fear dancing around its edges. "Tell me, boy. Do not keep me *waiting.*"

Reath felt Azlin's hand tighten on his shoulder, become almost painful.

Then a flash of movement he heard or felt or sensed—something fast, light, quick—and Reath spun, raising his shield.

The dart Ty Yorrick had fired spanged harmlessly off the shield.

Azlin started, coming back to himself.

"What?" the old man said.

Reath sensed another attack coming, lit his lightsaber, and lifted it just in time.

ZZSK!

The green blade hissed and crackled against Ty's purple lightsaber, the colors lighting her mask in a demonic glow. The hunter pushed hard against Reath's guard, her frustration obvious. The angle of her attack was clear. If Reath had been a fraction slower, Azlin Rell's head would have been cleaved in half.

"Reath," Ty spat. "What are you doing?"

"Thank you, my boy," Azlin said calmly, taking a step back, away from the clashing sabers. "I would have hated for it to end this way."

He lifted a hand, and Ty reared back, her free hand to her throat, gasping and choking.

"*NO!*" Reath shouted, and slammed the edge of his shield into Azlin's stomach.

STAR WARS: TRIALS OF THE JEDI 317

The ancient man cried out and doubled over. Ty sucked in a wheezing breath but never lowered her lightsaber.

Reath stood between them, his lightsaber and shield extended.

"Stop," he said. "Stop now. Both of you. This is more important than any of us."

"What are you talking about?" Ty said, her voice like broken glass.

"Look, Ty," Reath said, sweeping his lightsaber away from her, lowering his guard to use it to point down the hill. "*Look.*"

Ty climbed to the crest of the hill, looked, and saw what Azlin and Reath had seen.

Below them, a huge, bowl-like depression in the landscape, like a natural amphitheater. At its center, a large, perfectly circular, perfectly flat mirror-like surface reflected what hovered directly above it, a double spiral made of light and dark—huge, beautiful, terrible. It spun, the edges of each spiral ragged, crackling and hissing where they touched their opposite.

It was a thing of the Force, all of it, its power making the very air around it shimmer and vibrate. The light and the dark chased each other, spinning, battling, but also embracing. It was grand, so grand, but also horrible, because it was clear to see that the spiral was wrong. Damaged, out of balance, suffering, anharmonic. It vibrated with minute, ugly, irregular tremors, like an engine on the verge of tearing itself apart.

Whatever it was, it was hurt. It was dying.

All around this astonishing sight were Nameless. What seemed like hundreds, arrayed in a circle around the Force-sculpture spinning above them.

They were dying, too.

Chapter Twenty-Eight

THE NAMELESS HOMEWORLD

Burryaga was falling.

The air rushed past in a way that Burry knew well. He had fallen so many times. From trees on Kashyyyk in the years before the Jedi came for him. From tall platforms to padded floors in youngling and Padawan training exercises. From cliffs and ledges and balconies and rooftops. Leaps and falls were part of the life of a Jedi. He could handle them without fear.

Only once had that focus left him, one terrible fall that seemed like it would never end—but this was not that time. Now Burryaga's wits were with him, and so was the Force.

Ember was not handling it so well.

The charhound twisted in the air, emitting long gusts of flame that vanished in the wind, her way of screaming in terror. She had gone over the cliff's edge first, and so she was perhaps two seconds closer to the ground than Burryaga—but gravity could do a great deal in two seconds. She was already far away. If not for the long gouts of fire she kept shooting out, Burry could have lost track of her against the rapidly approaching, brightly colored landscape of the planet below.

STAR WARS: TRIALS OF THE JEDI 319

Burryaga threw out a hand, his fingers tensing with the effort. He called on the Force, choosing the easier path of pulling himself down toward the charhound rather than trying to draw her up against the pull of the planet.

He sensed Ember's terror and felt so sad for the creature. The charhound was closer to Bell, but Burry knew she loved him, too, in the pure, uncomplicated, bright-light way that beasts had for the companions that cared for them.

Her loyalty and care and good spirit deserved a better reward than being thrown to her death by a man who, even after he'd already murdered the galaxy, could not seem to stop killing.

A quick shot of despair washed through Burryaga's mind. He thought, for a moment, that it might be easier just to let Ember go. Everyone was going to die in any case. Marchion Ro had unleashed the Blight and killed the Jedi's chance to stop it. Maybe a quick end for Ember would be the merciful choice.

He shook the alien thought from his head, growling.

Ember deserved better.

Burry opened his heart and spirit and drew on his connection to the charhound, her life and his life together. He offered up his own uncomplicated bright-light love for this small, loyal beast, and through the Force he whipped through the air toward her, against gravity, against fate, against death, and he wrapped her in his arms.

Burryaga drew the terrified charhound to himself, knowing what this would mean. Even though he held her, she was no less afraid. Ember screamed, and Burryaga's fur was suddenly ablaze.

Now came pain, and it was not the first time he'd felt this particular kind. A vivid sense-memory returned to Burryaga of another fall, the bad fall. In an instant, he was back in it, back to that terrible time. His skin burned and blistering, the fur scorched away, Starlight Beacon collapsing around him, the station clearly in its final moments. An inferno raging all around him—an unsurvivable blaze. A rathtar—*a rathtar,* a monster of teeth and muscle and nothing else—snapping at his face. Burryaga was

CHARLES SOULE

holding it back, barely, but the strength in his arms and heart were failing. His lightsaber was lost, and a hundred different kinds of death spiraled closer to him with every moment.

It was a question of how he would die, not if.

Until a spear of wreckage fell, fast and merciless, almost like it had been thrown. The sharp end of the metal pierced the rathtar's skin, and it died. Burry remembered thinking that the Beacon was fighting for the light even as it fell.

Burryaga had avoided death by rathtar, but so many other endings still circled. He could not stop the Beacon's plummet from orbit above the world of Eiram. He could not put out the fires, he could not seal up the gash in the station's hull not ten meters away or still the rushing, churning wind from the atmosphere escaping through it, trying to pull him out into open space.

Burry did the only thing he could.

He shoved both hands deep into the rathtar's tooth-ringed maw, grasped whatever he found inside. His claws, made for climbing trees on Kashyyyk, now turned out to be equally adept at carving out the insides of rathtars. Double handfuls of long, stringy, acrid-stinking flesh emerged. Muscles, organs, tubes, and strings. Again he reached inside, and again, pulling out what he found. When it seemed like there might be enough space, Burryaga pushed himself inside, snatching his Jedi rebreather from his belt and shoving it into his mouth. The last piece of equipment he retained, and the only one he needed.

Such was the way of the Force.

From inside the rathtar's guts, Burryaga reached out with both hands, taking its jaws and muscling them closed. He sealed himself inside, into the dark.

He felt the carcass move, felt the rush of escaping oxygen pull it toward the rent in the hull, and then he heard nothing, just the quiet of outer space.

Rathtars could survive in vacuum, at least for a time. It was one of the things that made the beasts such potent subjects for scary stories told by

STAR WARS: TRIALS OF THE JEDI

Padawans to younglings before bedtime at the Temple. Rathtars' skin was so tough that it could even withstand the horrors of open space.

Now that skin would serve as the hull of Burryaga's makeshift escape pod. His horrifying, unlikely, uncontrolled escape pod.

From inside the rathtar's corpse, Burry briefly felt the float of low orbit, then increasing acceleration that he knew meant it had been captured by the gravity of Eiram, the ocean world that Starlight Beacon was above when it was attacked. He was falling—and then he was burning, the rathtar's skin heating up as it encountered the edge of the planet's atmosphere.

Burry's mind had left him for a time. When he woke, he was trapped in an undersea cave far below the surface of Eiram's ocean. There he had remained, down in the lonely dark, until his friend Bell Zettifar had come for him. Bell had suffered an ordeal of his own to effect that rescue, but he sought no gratitude, just as Burry wouldn't have expected thanks if the situation were reversed.

That was what you did for others.

When they were lost, you found them.

When they fell, you caught them.

Burryaga pulled himself back to the present. He ignored the pain of his fur crisping and burning away as Ember unleashed scream after scream. He murmured to the frightened creature, sounds that were not words but that she understood, and the charhound calmed.

Burry had seen the gleam of water below in the first moments of his fall, a shining pool at the base of the cliff. Now he steered toward it through the Force. His fur burned in the wind—he was a torch shooting through the air, but he pulled Ember closer to him, shielding her like the rathtar had done for him.

They crashed into the pond together, Burryaga calling upon the Force to slow them in the last few moments. The flames were extinguished, the water cool, soothing despite the pain of the impact.

Burryaga sank to the bottom, and through his agony and weariness, a single strong thought shot through his mind.

No more moments trapped in the dark. Not even one.

With all his remaining strength, Burry pushed hard off the bottom, breaking the surface and slowly pulling himself to shore.

Burryaga crawled from the pond, Ember next to him. He collapsed, rolling onto his back.

High above, at the edge of the cliff, he saw light—green and yellow flashes—the hiss and crackle of blades slashing against each other.

Burry hoped Bell won.

From the edge of the jungle, not far away, came the rustle of creatures slinking from the undergrowth, investigating the new arrivals, seeking easy, injured prey.

Burryaga was dimly aware of Ember chuffing out a warning, and then shortly after came the sounds of another fight, the signature sound of a charhound shooting out fire. Ember was protecting her friend.

I'll help, Burryaga thought, trying to lift himself up—but he had nothing left. He collapsed back into the mud.

He lay there, putting his faith in his friends.

Chapter Twenty-Nine

THE NAMELESS HOMEWORLD

Avar Kriss held her lightsaber high, trying to send its light as far into the dark void as she could.

"This is nothingness," she said, her voice sounding hollow and strange in her ears. "Are we anywhere at all?"

"I don't know, Avar," came Elzar's voice. "But there's ground beneath our feet. We have to be somewhere."

Elzar's own lightsaber flared to life, and in its bit of added light Avar could see something like oily spheres in the near distance, like a gigantic foam of sheened bubbles. They pulsed at different rates, some shivering, some slowly seeming to breathe. It was one of the most soul-inverting sights she had ever seen.

And inside each sphere, a reflection—her and Elzar, distorted, dark.

The sounds were no better. Skittering, crunching, something like laughter—but she couldn't see its source. No animals, just the implication of them, and her imagination developing them into horrific creatures out of nightmare.

But even worse than the sounds was the absence of sound. The Song of the Force did not exist here.

Avar wasn't entirely sure what that meant.

"Do you think we're dead?" she said.

"Not really," Elzar replied. "I don't think there's anything after death, and if there were, it's hard to imagine it would be like this." He reached over and placed his hand on her waist. "Besides, we're together. I can feel you, you can feel me. We're alive. We're just . . ."

"Lost," Avar finished, and Elzar murmured in soft agreement.

She stepped away from him and held her lightsaber out in front of her like a spear.

"Watch my back," she said. "I'm going to try something."

Avar let go of her hilt. She honestly wasn't sure what would happen. Either it would fall or it would respond to her attempt to use the Force and remain lit, hovering in midair.

"Okay," she said, watching the blade floating rock-steady in the gloom.

"What?" Elzar asked, his own lightsaber held in a guard stance as he kept a close watch on the darkness around them.

"I can't hear the Song, but I can still use the Force. That's what I was trying to figure out. The Force is here in this place, just . . . different."

"Maybe you're deaf to the Song," Elzar said, his tone thoughtful.

"Elzar, of all the things to—" Avar began.

"No, no, I'm sorry. I should have thought before I spoke. I apologize," Elzar said. "I didn't mean deaf in the traditional sense. Just because you can't hear the Song doesn't mean it's not there. There are many frequencies outside the range of human hearing. Some creatures speak in what seems to us to be silence, but to their ears their conversations are loud as a starship engine."

Avar considered this. "If I can't hear the Song, the information it usually conveys to me is gone."

"Welcome to the way the rest of us live, Avar," Elzar said. "Fortunately, we're still Jedi Masters. We're far from helpless."

He released his own lightsaber hilt. The blade floated into the air, casting its light, illuminating more of the space around them.

Avar plucked her hilt from the air and returned to a guard pose, not

STAR WARS: TRIALS OF THE JEDI

liking the idea of them both being unprotected in this strange place. She watched as Elzar lifted his hand and the lightsaber moved higher, soaring in ever-widening circles. The effect was hypnotic, reflecting off the odd dark foam structures around them in bizarre coruscations.

"Just trying to get a better sense of . . ." Elzar began.

The lightsaber stopped about five meters away, above an opening in the spheroid walls. A path, leading deeper into darkness. Deeper and downward.

"There," Elzar said. "A way through."

"A way through to where?"

"Let's find out," he said, and pulled the lightsaber back to his waiting hand. Elzar moved first, and Avar followed. She was still thinking about what he had said, about hidden frequencies.

The Song is here, she thought. *It's everywhere. It's just that here . . . it's not singing for me.*

But then . . . for who?

The two Jedi moved through the strange structures, now seeing occasional glimpses of the creatures that inhabited the void where they had found themselves. They had sharp teeth, claws—lean things that seemed evolved to hunt.

"This is bizarre," Elzar said as they passed a trio of savage-looking beasts about the size of tooka cats, each busily tearing each other to shreds even as they themselves were being torn to shreds—and all three of the same species. "Unnatural."

"What do you mean?" Avar said, her own eyes on a swarm of small orange buglike things devouring the carcass of a much larger beast, but also very clearly fighting among themselves.

"Every living thing we've seen down here is a predator," Elzar said. "I've never seen anything like it. Evolution suggests creatures find niches. Prey as well as predators. Plant eaters consume grass to keep it from growing out of control, and then a smaller number of predators eat the grass eaters to keep their numbers in balance, too. That's what we saw up on the surface, even if it was out of control. A standard ecosystem with the standard niches. But down here...everything just kills. Constant aggression. Taking instead of giving. Everything here must live in a perpetual state of . . ." He stopped, turning back to look at her.

"Fear," she finished.

And with that, she understood why she couldn't hear the Song. In the world she knew, there was a balance between light and dark, assonance and dissonance. Life and death. Here, there was only one of those two things.

"We're in the dark, Elzar," Avar said.

"I know," he replied, sounding mildly puzzled.

"The dark side," she clarified.

"Ah," he replied, the idea clearly opening up his perceptions as well.

This is the dark, Avar thought. *Whatever lives here must communicate using different senses than we use in the balanced world. The Song must be different here as well. Take a note and play it at the same time as its opposite frequency, its negative self, and the result is silence.*

The Song is here, I just can't hear it.

That understanding didn't make it any easier for Avar to operate in this bizarre place, but she could still consider it good news. It meant some of the more terrifying explanations for the Song's silence—her own death, or the death of the entire galaxy because of everything Marchion Ro had done—were less likely.

"I understand what's happening here, I think," she said to Elzar. "We can keep going, but we need to be careful. We might be the only light that exists in this place."

"Then this is exactly where we should be," Elzar said.

He was looking at her. She wanted to pull his mask off, see his eyes.

"Let's find the reason the Force brought us here," Avar said.

Down they went, following a curling path through the bizarre living, pulsing walls all around them. Avar was not afraid, and she knew Elzar was not, either. Whatever would come, would come, and they would deal with it like the Jedi they were.

They came to a bend in the strange path they were following, and when they turned, a sense of openness came to Avar, as if the darkness ahead was emptier than the darkness behind.

"Elzar . . . there's something," she said. "Do you see it? Far in the distance?"

"I'm not sure," he replied. "What is it?"

"A . . . light, I think. Faint. Far away."

"It might be easier to see without the lightsabers. Should we . . . ?"

Avar turned off her blade, and Elzar did the same. Darkness fell upon them like a wet, heavy cloak. Her eyes began to adjust, and she looked toward the light she thought she had seen.

From all around came a noise, a skittering, clattering sound, drawing closer. Something was coming for them.

"Avar . . ." Elzar said, his voice holding a tone of warning.

"Just another second," she said, her eyes straining.

There, she thought. *There.*

In the far distance, an impossibly faint pink glow.

"Now, Elzar!" she cried, and ignited her lightsaber.

All around her, creatures reared back, the light flickering off their dark shells, jagged, clawed arms flailing up to protect huge, sensitive, jellied eyes. The beasts were no more than half a meter away.

Without thinking, she stood back-to-back with Elzar. Their lightsabers cut, slashed, pushing the creatures back. They were huge, segmented things, and they quickly retreated—but not far. The beasts paused just outside the circle of light cast by the Jedi's blades, chittering in frustration and hunger.

"They're not going to run," Elzar said.

"No," Avar agreed.

They moved on, hearing the creatures as they moved with them, their rhythmic clacking occasionally roiling up into chaos as they attacked one another. She couldn't see the beasts but knew they were there, almost close enough to touch. That was worse.

The path was long, and the constant tension of being subject to attack at any moment was wearing, but in time they drew close to the glow Avar had seen. The light spilled from a kind of structure, the first sign of sentience they'd encountered beneath the planet. It was a building made of great slabs of chipped flint or obsidian, sharp edges glinting in the light. Anything brushing against it would be sliced to ribbons, which seemed to be the point. Pieces of the gigantic insectoid predators were scattered around its walls.

An arched opening was built into the structure where the path ended, and through it spilled the dim pink light that had called the Jedi down to this place. Energy shimmered at the entry, a nearly invisible barrier.

Elzar stepped close to it, examining it. "It's like the strange mirror above, the one that brought us here. There's surface tension. I think this is another transition point. Like a doorway."

"To where?" Avar asked.

"Well, Master Kriss, let's hope it's somewhere better than here." Elzar reached out, touched the surface of the barrier, and as had happened above, he seemed to be pulled through it.

He can't help himself, Avar thought as she followed him through.

When her perceptions resolved, she found herself in a circular chamber that reminded her of one of the larger classrooms or lecture halls at the Jedi Temple. It was suffused with the pink light they had seen from afar, similar to the sunlight of the world above, tinted by the Veil that surrounded this strange planet.

The floors sloped down from all sides to a flat, round area at the center, where three beings were gathered around the source of the light—a huge bowl filled with what seemed to be hundreds of soft, clear egglike objects.

The feel of the place was overwhelming, even though it was very simple. Avar felt small. She felt she was in the presence of something sacred. She had no other word for it.

Avar and Elzar both extinguished their lightsabers at the same moment, without speaking a word.

They walked down the sloped floor toward the beings and their strange treasure. A hum rose from them, each singing a different note, a long, slow harmony that sounded to Avar like nothing so much as the Song of the Force itself.

The Jedi drew near, and one of the beings noticed their approach. It turned, unveiling itself, its body stretching as it stood, using long, languid, deeply beautiful limbs. A familiar entity, though in this place not savage, not deadly, not ruined. Its true self.

The Nameless approached them.

Avar felt no fear at all.

It spoke, in a calm voice the Jedi heard with their minds, not their ears.

"Have you come to kill us, too?"

Chapter Thirty

THE NAMELESS HOMEWORLD

Reath stood alongside Ty Yorrick and Azlin Rell, their conflict set aside, the trio stunned into silence by what they saw below.

The Nameless, maybe all the Nameless left alive on this world, were twisted, agonized, their bodies contorted. These were not the ragged, shambling beasts Marchion Ro had used to hunt Jedi. These Nameless were strong, healthy. But all their eyes shone with the same deep-purple glow, and it was clear they were battling some powerful impulse toward self-destruction.

Reath watched a Nameless grasp its own head in its hands and twist it all the way around, collapsing a moment later to the ground. Another reached to its belly and tore itself open with its claws.

"They're . . ." he said.

"I know," Ty said. "Marchion Ro must have done this with that control rod he used back at the crash site. It's just like before. We have to help these creatures."

"Help them?" Azlin murmured, sounding fascinated. "Why would we do that? Let the monsters die."

"Because this is *wrong*," Ty said. "Don't you sense it?"

STAR WARS: TRIALS OF THE JEDI

"Your wrong is not mine," Azlin said.

Reath ignored them. He was thinking about the glow in the eyes of the Nameless, a purple color he'd seen before. He looked toward Azlin and saw it there again—the gem at the center of the Rod of Ages was glowing with the same shade.

"The control rod," Reath said. "That's the answer."

Azlin lifted it, looked at it, his face taking on an expression of mild curiosity.

"Yes, I see your reasoning, Reath," Azlin said. "The stories suggest the Echo Stone used to create the Rod of Ages has the ability to overpower other control rods. Marchion Ro has the Rod of Power—we could defeat his command for these Nameless to sacrifice themselves." He looked back at Reath, his eye sockets somehow seeming to glint. "But I ask you again . . . why would we ever do that?"

"Because they're living creatures!" Ty shouted. "You were a Jedi once. Have you forgotten?"

Azlin made a dismissive gesture toward Ty, and her lightsaber came up, her eyes narrowing. The corner of Azlin's mouth twitched up in a tiny signal of amusement.

"I have forgotten more than you've ever learned," he said.

Reath placed a hand on Azlin's arm.

"If you will not spare the Nameless for their own sake, then do it for yourself," he said.

He pointed at the spinning double spiral of the Force hovering in the air above the Nameless.

"That thing is the key to all of this. I'm sure of it. It's tearing itself apart, and with every Nameless that dies, it gets worse. Don't you sense it?"

"Of course," Azlin replied, gently patting Reath's hand. "Of course I do."

"Enough of this," Ty said, holding her lightsaber up by the side of her head, pointed directly at the fallen Jedi. "Give me the damn rod, Azlin, or I'll take it from you."

Azlin smiled and held up a finger. "You may try," he said. "Perhaps Reath would even help you, and perhaps you would succeed. But that is far from certain. The power of the dark side fills me, and my last act would be to destroy this silly trinket."

Azlin shook his arm free from Reath's grip, took a step back. He lifted the Rod of Ages, examining it.

"I spent a hundred and fifty years in thrall to my terror of the Nameless. It almost destroyed my life."

Azlin lifted a thin arm and extended a single bony, long-nailed finger to point toward the Nameless below.

"I have lived long enough. I will watch the Nameless die, and then I will die myself with the rest of the galaxy. But I will die free."

Sudden anger twisted in Reath's gut as screams rose from the Nameless below.

"No," he said, "you will die a pathetic old man."

A frown creased Azlin's thin lips. Ty's head turned slowly toward Reath, her eyes wide.

"Oh?" Azlin said.

"Do you think the dark side brought you here to watch someone else kill your enemies and then wait to die?" Reath said. "I don't. It's unworthy. And let me say it again. *Pathetic.*"

Azlin's lips pulled back from his teeth into an awful sneer. He raised his free hand. Reath didn't care. He believed every word he was saying.

"Imagine *living,* Azlin," Reath said. "Imagine inhabiting a galaxy where the Nameless still exist, and *then* feeling no fear. That is the path of a conqueror. If you were truly strong, you would find a way to make the Nameless *beneath your notice.* Any other decision and you'll remain in thrall to them until the moment your pathetic life finally ends."

Reath had never spoken to anyone like this, least of all Azlin Rell. It felt good.

"I am not a child, Reath Silas," Azlin said.

His voice was quiet, low, almost a hiss.

"Prove it," Reath said.

STAR WARS: TRIALS OF THE JEDI

Azlin lifted the Rod of Ages once again. He stared at the artifact. Reath wondered what he was seeing.

This was the moment.

Reath had no idea what Azlin was going to do, but he knew he couldn't beat him in a fight. Even if he fought alongside Ty, they might lose. She had to know that, too, but he heard her feet shift, sensed her getting ready to attack. If Azlin tried to destroy the control rod, she would do what she had to do, even if the effort was doomed. For that matter, so would Reath.

There would be no other choice. This was the moment.

Azlin turned toward the Nameless, and the strange spirals of energy spinning above them. He lifted the Rod of Ages, and the light from the Echo Stone at its center pulsed like a heartbeat.

"Live," he said.

Chapter Thirty-One

THE NAMELESS HOMEWORLD

"Do you feel special, Bell Zettifar?" Marchion Ro asked, weaving a slow, sinuous pattern in the air with the blade of Loden Greatstorm's lightsaber. "Here we are, just the two of us. I wonder how many Jedi believed they'd face me one-on-one? Dreamed of it ... fantasized about it ... desired that glory for themselves?"

Bell did not respond.

"Well, looks like you're the big winner," Marchion said. "This will be the last fight. There won't be time for any others. It's all done. Can't you feel it?"

Bell could. The planet had acquired a sense of accelerating doom ever since Marchion Ro forced the Nameless into their orgy of death. A chain reaction had been set in motion. Slow at first, but faster now, the way a single spot of flame could spread out into a roaring, racing conflagration.

"There's another wonderful thing, too," Marchion continued. "Let's say you win. You kill me. It won't matter. You are, like all Jedi, incapable of preventing me from doing anything I want to do. You can't stop anything, and you never could, not from the very first moment I set that Cloudship in the *Legacy Run*'s path.

STAR WARS: TRIALS OF THE JEDI 335

"The Jedi are the merest breeze. They can change nothing. While I, Marchion Ro, am a great, roaring hurricane of—"

"Enough, Marchion," Bell said. "Anyone ever tell you you're just . . . *tiresome?*"

He leapt forward, and the battle began.

Azlin Rell lifted the Rod of Ages. He poured the Force into the artifact, felt it fighting the will of the person who had commanded the Nameless to die. It was enormously challenging. Azlin had seen what Marchion Ro possessed, back when they had first encountered him on this cursed planet. Another control rod, designed to incorporate not one Echo Stone but two, the gems performing exactly as their name suggested. The willpower of anyone who used the Rod of Power was amplified, reflected back and forth between the two stones, becoming enormously strong.

The Rod of Ages had been designed specifically to overcome this— Azlin knew it to be true from his decades of research into the Nameless and the ways long-dead peoples had found ways to fight them. The power he needed rested within the artifact—he could sense it—but he was rapidly realizing he could not access it with the dark side alone.

Below, the Nameless moaned and howled, caught in the struggle between the commands from the two control rods.

"Reath," Azlin said. "I need you. I require the light side of the Force, but I am no longer able to reliably touch it. Join with me."

Ty Yorrick, that insufferable woman, decided to once again insert herself where she was unwelcome.

"Don't do it, Reath," she said. "It's a trick."

"What choice do I have?" Reath said.

His voice sounded sad.

Poor boy, Azlin thought.

Reath stood beside Azlin and laid his hand upon the Rod.

"Live," he said.

The glow from the Echo Stone intensified, and the disk itself began to glow. Strange energies crackled around its edge.

A whipcrack of power and light shot out from the Rod of Ages, striking both Azlin and Reath in their hearts.

Their bodies arched, their heads flew back. They screamed.

Bell called on every bit of his Jedi speed and agility. He lunged, thrusting his lightsaber forward. It was a powerful strike, designed to sever Marchion Ro's arm, ending the fight in one blow.

But Marchion was not there when Bell sliced down, and he had to spin and throw up his own blade to deflect a slash from a direction he was not anticipating.

How did he—

Bell did not finish the thought. Marchion delivered a flurry of blows, seeking a way past Bell's guard. Bell blocked them, but it was not easy. Any thoughts that his Jedi training with a lightsaber might let him make a quick end of Marchion Ro vanished.

He's trained, Bell thought, parrying, giving ground. *And not just with ordinary blades. He's worked with lightsabers.*

Marchion owned plenty, after all. One for each Jedi he'd murdered. Bell wondered if the Eye had found someone to teach him, some lapsed Jedi. Droids could be programmed to simulate a lightsaber-wielding opponent, too.

It didn't matter. However he'd acquired his skills, Marchion Ro was good. The Force made Bell fast, but Marchion was fast, too, a true killer. Bell knew Jedi reflexes alone would not save him.

"Do you know what I used this for?" Marchion said, taking a short leap back and holding up the glowing yellow lightsaber. "I cut off your master's head-tails with it."

STAR WARS: TRIALS OF THE JEDI 337

A surge of white-hot hatred rushed through Bell, so strong that it took everything he had not to let the emotion swallow him up. He was a Jedi, he was trained, but he was also a person, a young man who had loved his teacher.

Jedi were not emotionless automatons. They felt *deeply.* Want, need, anger and love and hate and fear—Jedi used those feelings to understand the needs of others, to find ways to help them.

Jedi gave, they did not take.

If Loden Greatstorm had taught Bell anything, he had taught him this. But staring at Marchion Ro . . . by the light, it was hard to remember the lesson.

"I just did one tail at first, but Loden didn't like it," Marchion said. His tone was light. He could have been discussing his breakfast. "He said he felt lopsided, uneven. He begged me to cut off the other." Marchion smiled, his sharp, dark teeth visible. "I'm not a cruel person. Of course I helped him."

Bell moved forward again to engage, letting out a sharp shout as he swung his blade. He told himself he was just releasing tension, using a technique he'd been taught by one of the Temple's blademasters—yells and screams and shouts could be a way to put the enemy off balance. Bell told himself that, but he knew the reason he cried out was not strategy, but rage.

Ty Yorrick did not know what to do. She knew how to hunt, to track. She worked with animals. She believed the greater mysteries of the Force would always be beyond her.

Azlin Rell and Reath Silas were surrounded by crackling shrouds of energy. Their bodies were bent backward, lifted up off the ground so their feet dangled. They screamed.

They both held the Rod of Ages.

Azlin had asked Reath to help him, to add the light side of the Force

338 CHARLES SOULE

to whatever he was doing with the dark. Was it working? Ty had no idea. It looked like they were dying.

Below them, the Nameless stood almost frozen in place, their bodies trembling.

This was the Force. She knew it. Nothing else was so powerful. Ty had left the Jedi because once, a long time ago, she'd tried to use that power to help someone—and had made a terrible mistake. Better to never try anything like that again. Better to live as a monster, alone.

"Ty . . . please . . ." Reath said, his voice cracked, agonized.

"Please what?" Ty said, gripping the hilt of her lightsaber as if that would do anything. "I don't know what to do!"

"Give us your strength," Azlin said. "The echo is too strong—needs another voice . . ."

"Can't do it . . . alone . . ." Reath said, his voice weakening.

Ty took a breath. She deactivated her lightsaber, stepped forward, and placed her hand on the Rod of Ages.

"Live," she said, and then it took her, too.

Bell's and Marchion's blades clashed again. This time, Marchion fell back, the cheerful mask of his face sliding into an expression of focused concentration.

That's right, Bell thought. *See how you like it.*

But Bell's own focus was clouded. He saw shapes moving out of the corner of his eyes, strange images. His body felt slow, his connection to the Force clouded.

It's the armor, he thought. *I've lost two pieces. The Nameless effect . . . it's getting through.*

Marchion, with his predator's instincts, must have realized Bell was struggling. He kicked out, hitting Bell on the thigh with his boot.

"Agh!" Bell cried, stumbling back.

Marchion pressed his advantage, sweeping his lightsaber in broad arcs, slashing aside Bell's attempts to parry, pushing him backward.

The cliff, Bell remembered, almost too late, and leapt, high and forward, somersaulting over Marchion Ro.

The Evereni reached up with Loden's lightsaber as Bell whipped through the air, a wild swing that didn't catch Bell's body—but nicked the strap securing the vambrace on his left arm. As he landed, the leather parted, and the armor fell away.

The fog invading Bell's senses surged. It was almost enough to bring him to his knees.

"Ah," Marchion Ro said, immediately realizing what had happened.

He walked slowly toward Bell, placing one boot methodically in front of the other like a stalking targon, Loden's lightsaber dangling from one hand.

"How are you feeling, Bell?" Marchion said. "How are you feeling?"

He laughed.

"How are you feeling?"

The Force swirled through Ty Yorrick, Reath Silas, and Azlin Rell, echoed and amplified, more powerful than any of them had felt before. The dark side from Azlin, unrestrained, and the light from Reath and Ty, echoing, building, growing through the Echo Stone at the rod's center.

The Jedi, the darksider, and one who was neither. Different people, with wildly different understandings of and beliefs about the Force, and yet slowly, with great effort and pain, their wills came into alignment.

All at once, at the precise moment an echo of an echo slashed through the gem within the Rod of Ages, they spoke as one.

"*Live,*" they said.

The Echo Stone exploded in a tiny supernova of pure-white energy, echoed by a much, much larger blast that shot out across the clearing, up into the air, its brilliance rivaling the Veil high above. Up and out it went, touching the Nameless who had been touched by Marchion Ro's evil command, freeing them.

The power released from the Rod of Ages moved across the world, searching, seeking.

Until finally, it came to the top of a cliff where the light and dark battled for the future of the galaxy. Marchion Ro had said a single word, and now that word echoed back to him.

Die.

A blast of light flashed across the clifftop, and with it two sharp cracks, one right after the other.

"Gah!" cried Marchion Ro, a sound of pain and shock.

Bell lifted his head, seeing Marchion stumble backward, all his deadly grace gone, a stunned look on his face. He reached behind his back and pulled free the long rod of metal he had used to control the Nameless. Its ends were blackened, the gems that had adorned it gone.

Marchion Ro's face twisted into a scowl. He tossed the rod to one side, discarding it to the dirt.

"It doesn't matter," he said, as if he was trying to convince himself. "I don't need it anymore."

He lifted Loden Greatstorm's yellow, crackling lightsaber and pointed it at Bell.

"There's really only one thing left to do," the Eye said.

Bell lifted his own blade, returning to a guard stance. He shook his head, trying to clear it. He wanted to rip that lightsaber from Marchion's hand with the Force, take his master's weapon from this evil man. But he didn't know if the Force would answer.

I want to kill him, Bell thought. *I want to take revenge for my master. I want it so badly. I've always wanted it, no matter what I've told myself. I've never looked it in the eye because I'm afraid of what it means. No true Jedi would want this.*

STAR WARS: TRIALS OF THE JEDI
341

Bell thought of Burryaga, gone over the cliff after Ember, and wondered if they were still alive. He thought about Terec, lying in the grass not far away. He wondered if the Kotabi had been dragged into the jungle to be eaten alive by one of the planet's monsters.

He thought of everyone who had come to this world to try to save the galaxy, and how utterly they had failed.

Marchion is right, he thought. *We haven't changed anything.*

"Bell, come on," said a voice he knew. "That's the most ridiculous thing I've ever heard."

Standing behind Marchion Ro was Loden Greatstorm, as he had been in life. Intact, strong, the bemused smile on his face so familiar.

Bell knew he wasn't actually there. Loden was dead. This was a vision. But not a vision of fear. This was not the Nameless. This was from the Force, or even just Bell himself.

"The how of it doesn't matter, Bell," Loden said. "I gave you enough of myself that I'm here when you need me. That's what a teacher does. Am I a vision? A memory? Who cares?"

"I know, Master," Bell said.

Marchion seized on this immediately. He showed his teeth. "Seeing things, little Bell?"

"This guy, huh?" Loden said, nodding disdainfully toward Marchion. "You weren't kidding. *Tiresome* is the word."

He gestured, and Marchion froze in place. Everything did. The wind, the thrashing jungle, time itself.

Loden Greatstorm walked forward, past Marchion Ro. He approached Bell, put a hand on his shoulder.

"Every living thing changes everything, Bell," he said. "You know that. It's all a web. It's all connection. No one and nothing is ever alone."

"But everything Marchion's done . . ." Bell said. "He's ended everything. Killed so many . . . and the Blight will take what's left. It's over."

"You can believe that if you want to, I guess," Loden said. "If that's a lesson you've learned, you certainly didn't learn it from me. If that's what you believe, then lie down and let Marchion kill you with my lightsaber.

Or jump off that cliff, but this time I won't be down there to catch you, and it sounds like you wouldn't be able to catch yourself."

Loden glanced at Marchion, whose face was frozen in an expression of amused hatred, the face of the man who was trying to murder every being in the galaxy and had probably already succeeded. Then Loden looked back at Bell, his face kind, sad.

"Nothing is over until it is over," he said. "And that decision is yours."

Bell realized he could see through his master. Whatever had brought Loden to him, whether memory or the Force, the effect was beginning to fade.

"Tell me why the Jedi matter," Loden said. "All my lessons were that one lesson. Tell me you learned it."

Bell closed his eyes, feeling his master's hand on his shoulder, the truth of his presence, the power of everything this person had taught him.

"When things are dark, and there is no one else, the Jedi are there," Bell said. "We don't have to know you, we don't want anything from you, we will not put ourselves above you because of the things we can do. We always help. We always save what we can, even if it costs us everything. We love all beings equally, without attachment or condition."

Bell felt lighter.

"You can believe in us."

"Good, Bell," came Loden's voice, growing faint. "By the light and the Force . . . this moment has fallen to you. Your path will end someday, just as mine did. The point is to use every moment you are given trying to make things better. That is the job."

Bell opened his eyes and saw the faintest echo of Loden Greatstorm's face fading away.

"I'm proud of you, my Padawan," were the last words he said.

Marchion Ro snapped his wrist, and Loden's yellow blade hissed out. Bell jerked his head backward, and the lightsaber barely missed. Then Bell rolled forward and *up,* and it was Marchion's turn to leap back—but too late. Bell's blade slashed him across the thigh, and Marchion cried out.

STAR WARS: TRIALS OF THE JEDI 343

"You little *whelp!*" he shouted.

Marchion's hand whipped down to his belt, and then he flung something small and dark out in an angle across the clearing. Bell followed it with his eyes, realizing, too late, that Marchion had thrown the thing at Terec, lying unconscious in the grass.

Without thinking, Bell flung out a hand, calling the object to him with the Force. It moved in midair, swinging toward him, and too late, far too late, Bell understood that this might not have been the best idea.

The mini grenade exploded three meters from Bell. His armor caught the brunt of the force, but the light and sound staggered him. He felt a piece of shrapnel pierce his outer shoulder, another cut through the meat of his calf. Pain shot through him, but he could manage it. The true problem was Bell's sight. The surge of light from the explosion had left him nearly blind. Behind the mask, he blinked, trying to focus through the Force, knowing Marchion would press his advantage.

And so he did. Bell parried a lightsaber slash, protected by instinct more than any training or skill. Then another, then a flurry of blows. Bell gave ground, and Marchion laughed, the sound coming from all sides. One of Bell's eyes cleared, the other didn't, the damage more severe, possibly even permanent.

Marchion seemed to know—how did he know? The monster always knew. He swept his lightsaber blade low, at Bell's legs. Bell leapt, avoiding the blow, but Marchion Ro danced in, seizing Bell's wrist and twisting. Bell's lightsaber fell, the hilt dropping into the grass, the blade going out.

Marchion punched forward, hitting Bell hard in the throat in the open space between his mask and his chestpiece. Bell felt something give way in his neck, and he collapsed backward, falling to the ground. Instantly, Marchion was on him, Loden's yellow lightsaber blade hissing and sizzling against his throat.

Bell could barely see. His ears felt blocked with wool. Everything was pain. Something was wrong inside him, deeply wrong. Things moved and ground against each other in Bell's body that should not.

"This has all been a little frustrating," Marchion Ro said. "I've killed everyone alive, but I couldn't look them in the eye when I did it. I couldn't tell them I was doing it. It feels good, don't get me wrong . . . but it's a little . . . *remote.*"

Marchion pulled back, put his boot on Bell's chest, pressed down. Bell felt a burning, crunching pain.

"We'll have to consider this a symbolic victory, Bell," Marchion said. "As you die, so dies every other life in the galaxy. I won't be able to feel the others, not the way I want to, but I'll feel yours. For me, your death will be everyone's. This death will be forever."

Bell was in agony. He had nothing left. He had lost, and his body knew it.

Even if I'd won . . . what would it have changed? he thought, despair seeping through him.

"Don't you want to find out?" came a voice. "Are you a Jedi or not? That's your decision, too."

Not Marchion. Loden? Was Bell talking to himself?

It didn't matter.

Am I a Jedi? Bell asked himself.

He decided he was.

His body was ruined. His strength was gone. But that was all right. He didn't need either. As long as he was alive, he was a conduit for something much stronger than his ravaged body.

The Force didn't want to die, didn't want the Blight to steal it from the galaxy. It loved being itself and wanted to continue—continue connecting everything in existence, binding them together and dancing through every insect, every mind, every stone and river and blade of grass.

The Force wanted to live, and what was Marchion Ro's ambition in comparison?

The Force had Bell Zettifar, and it would use him as its vessel.

STAR WARS: TRIALS OF THE JEDI 345

Bell is every living thing in the galaxy, all at once, all their energy and will to live—and whether that is literally true doesn't matter, because it's what his mind believes is happening. The strength comes, and Marchion Ro's boot lifts from Bell's chest, even though this is not what Marchion wants.

Bell gasps in a deep, rasping breath, begins to choke and cough. Meanwhile, Marchion is thrust back. Does Bell do this? Is it Loden, somehow? Is it the combined will of every being in the galaxy who wants to live?

Bell does not know.

He knows that he rolls over, pushing himself to his hands and knees, and looks at Marchion Ro, his gaze fierce through his one good eye.

Marchion Ro is shoved back, growls in anger and frustration.

Bell gets to one knee, rips the mask from his head. He does not need it.

Marchion feels his fingers loosening around Loden's lightsaber. He yowls, grasping the hilt with his other hand, but the fingers snap back, the bones breaking and cracking. Marchion Ro screams.

Bell stands, every part of him hurting. The Force burns through him, the dancing flames, pure light with a penumbra of darkness at its core. Like so many things—light and dark together, each unable to exist without the other.

Marchion Ro is lifted into the air, plucked up as if by a giant hand. Higher he goes, higher, and Bell is reminded of a time on Hetzal some years back, one of the last battles he fought with his master Loden Greatstorm at his side.

Bell looks up at Marchion, dangling in the air, his limbs spread, his face contorted in rage and agony. Bell speaks calmly, almost quietly, but Marchion hears every word.

"I'd like to show you something, Marchion Ro. I'd like to show you what the Force really is. Nothing's ever been able to stop life. Death doesn't stop life. Life always follows. That's why people like you will never win. There's never only dark. Light always comes."

Bell speaks with his own voice, and the voice of his master, and the voice of every Jedi.

"For life, and the light," he says.

Marchion Ro, in the traditional sense, did not know fear.

In another sense, fear was all he had ever known.

Now, suspended high above the ground, held there by a person he should have already killed, a small person, a nothing, a no-one person, who wielded a power he now realized was greater than he'd ever understood, Marchion felt a particular type of fear. It was the terror of someone who knew their death was at hand, and nothing they could do would stop it.

He wants to kill me, Marchion thought, and then the second thought, fast on its heels, *He has the power to kill me.*

The first thought, he had experienced many times. The second was new, and so he was afraid.

Marchion did not make peace with his end. He did not accept it as inevitable. He did not offer himself the rationalization that he and everything else in the galaxy would be dead soon enough anyway. He could not, because he was not in control. He was not choosing this death. It was being done to him.

He was being made small. What was worse—so much worse—was that he was beginning to realize he always had been.

The Jedi Bell Zettifar clenched a fist, and the power that held Marchion in the air vanished. He fell, so far, so fast. He found no peace in it, only terror.

He howled, panicking, and almost missed the slight reduction in speed just before he hit the stones at the cliff's edge. Bones in his body snapped. The agony was immense, all-consuming. He could not breathe from it.

Marchion Ro twisted his head, his eyes rolling in his skull, feeling vertebrae grate in his neck. He saw Bell Zettifar standing not far away, watching him with an expression he could not read.

Marchion ignored the pain in his broken fingers and wrist and flung

STAR WARS: TRIALS OF THE JEDI 347

his hand out in the Jedi's direction, releasing the row of razor-tipped stars he kept in a harness beneath his sleeve.

I will not die alone, he thought.

The stars flashed through the air, directly at Bell's bleeding, battered face. The Jedi held out a hand, and Loden Greatstorm's lightsaber hilt flew to him from where Marchion had dropped it.

Bell moved faster than Marchion could see, and the stars fell to the ground, each neatly bisected, a line of glowing heat marking the edges.

"At a certain point, Marchion," Bell said, "it becomes pathetic."

Marchion dropped into unconsciousness.

The last thing he saw—

Bell Zettifar, holding his master's lightsaber.

Chapter Thirty-Two

THE NAMELESS HOMEWORLD

"Have you come to kill us, too?" the Nameless said.

Had it spoken? Elzar considered. *Its mouth didn't move. A mind-speaker, then. A telepath.*

"We . . ." Avar said, clearly taken aback. "We aren't here to kill anyone."

The Nameless regarded them. It was regal, tall, sleek, glassine, its body shining with an inner light. So different from the creatures they had known.

Could they speak, too? Elzar wondered.

If the Nameless were all reasoning beings with the ability to communicate, the tragedy of what had happened to them, how they'd been used, was magnified a thousand times.

What Marchion Ro had made them do was horrifying. And, of course, the Jedi's response—unknowing, reactive.

Have you come to kill us, too? the being had asked.

The true answer was not no. It was *Not this time.*

The Nameless spoke again. "I believe that you mean us no harm. You are beings of light." It turned its head and set its beautiful, pale eyes on Elzar. "Though her more than you."

STAR WARS: TRIALS OF THE JEDI 349

Elzar did not know what that meant, either.

Yes, you do, he thought, and there was a time that would have terrified him, but now it was just something he had learned to accept about himself. *We all contain darkness. The danger comes when you pretend you don't.*

"I apologize for my companions," the Nameless said, gesturing back. "They would greet you as well, but all our focus must remain on maintaining stability."

Elzar looked over at the two other Nameless, crouched near what looked very much like a clutch of glowing pink eggs. The beings swayed and hummed, their long, elegant limbs occasionally reaching out to touch the other, offering support or reassurance, or just companionship.

There was energy here. Elzar could sense it. Great powers being shaped and moved with focus and intention.

"You are not here to kill us, but you are part of our end all the same," the Nameless said. Its tone was not confrontational. No aggression. But the way it was phrased . . . it had the hint of accusation about it, of certainty that some injury had been done.

"Can you explain what you mean?" Avar said. "If there is some wrong connected to us, we will accept blame and do our best to make it right."

The Nameless turned, extending its forelimb toward the clutch of eggs. "An egg appears whenever one of us dies. The planet gives them to us. Never before have we seen so many at once. Recently, they have begun to emerge with unusual frequency, and not long before you arrived, dozens appeared at once. This is a horror."

Avar and Elzar exchanged a glance, and although he could not see her face behind the mask, he sensed the same emotion he was feeling. Regret.

Not shame—they and the Jedi had done their best to preserve life— but the reality of what the Nameless actually were was very rapidly becoming clear. The Jedi had killed sentient beings, tormented to madness by their captivity. Not many, surely not as many as Marchion Ro, but some.

Elzar thought of Chancey Yarrow, a woman he had killed for the same reason the Jedi had killed Nameless. A lack of understanding. But now he knew the truth, and he knew something else, too—learning the truth didn't bring anyone back to life.

Will it ever end?

Avar reached up and lifted her crested helmet from her head.

"Avar," Elzar began, cautioning, but he stopped himself.

She was right. She was always right. They needed to face everything they had done. No more masks.

Elzar reached up and removed his own helmet, expecting a surge of disorientation and fear, hopefully mitigated by the other pieces of armor he wore. But there was nothing. He felt completely calm, in control of his own senses and perceptions. He realized he'd felt this way since the moment he and Avar arrived in this strange place. The shadows that had begun leaking into his vision back on the surface had ceased.

He wondered why. Perhaps because, unlike every Nameless he had ever seen, these beings were not . . . what? Angry? Hungry?

And if not, what were they?

Bereft was the word he settled on, sensing a profound sadness in all three of the beings.

Avar spoke.

"My name is Avar Kriss, and this is Elzar Mann. We are members of a spiritual order called the Jedi. We seek to bring light to the galaxy, and intentionally harming or killing any sentient being is anathema to us." Her voice was clear, and she did not attempt to dissemble or shy from the truth in any way. "We have encountered your people before, on other worlds. They seemed to be creatures without reason. Some of them attacked us, and a number of our fellows were killed. We defended ourselves, and some of your people did die. We offer you our gravest apologies."

The Nameless suddenly became agitated, rearing back, the fringe around its head trembling. So, too, did the others seated around the clutch of eggs. They seemed, to Elzar, to be absolutely aghast at what they had just heard.

"You . . . took us from this place?"

"Not us," Elzar said. "A man named Marchion Ro. But yes. Many were taken, and sent to other parts of the galaxy to be used to do great harm." He stepped forward, extending his hands to either side. "The galaxy is suffering. We believe it has something to do with this place. Can you explain this, perhaps help us stop it?"

The Nameless cocked its head, and Elzar realized how impossible that question probably was to answer for a being who had almost certainly never left this planet—was possibly only dimly aware that other planets existed at all.

"A blight has appeared on many worlds," Avar said. "Like a disease of reality. It begins small, in one spot on a world, and steals all light from everything there. Living things, even rocks and water. All that remains is empty dust, devoid of the energy that binds us all together. Do you know of this? We call this energy the Force."

The Nameless nodded but offered no further comment.

"We found a connection between your people being taken from this planet and this blight happening in the galaxy. The answer seemed to be to find your lost people and bring them here."

The Nameless waved an arm, seeming impatient. "Yes . . . of course. That is obvious. They were gone, and then some of them were returned . . . we felt it. But then . . . the returned *died.* The planet gave us more eggs than we had ever seen at one time. The balance tips."

"We are asking the wrong questions," Avar said, speaking quietly to Elzar.

"Let me try," he replied. "This is what I'm good at."

Elzar swept his arms in a broad circle. "I believe this world is not like most of the others I have visited. Can you tell me about its construction? How its pieces fit together?"

"It's not a machine, Elzar," Avar said quietly. "It's a world. It wasn't . . . built."

"Maybe not the way we understand, Avar, but I'm almost certain this planet is some kind of mechanism. At least I think so."

The Nameless pointed up with one claw, down with the other. "Light is above, dark is below," it said. "Within them both is this place, at the center. From here comes the hunger, kept in check by a balance of both the light and the dark. My people consume light or dark as needed to ensure neither grows too strong. We move back and forth between light and dark, consuming exactly what is needed to maintain balance. It is the dance of our lives, the rhythm.

"Here," the Nameless continued, gesturing around them, "it is both light and dark, and therefore also neither."

"That's why I can't hear the Song here," Avar said, a note of understanding and awe in her tone. "The Force is perfectly in balance here. Light and dark cancel each other out."

"If the hunger is released, terrible things happen," the Nameless said.

"They must have evolved around a Force vergence of some kind," Elzar said. "I've never heard of anything like it. Two spheres of oppositional Force energy working together to keep a hungry void at their center contained."

Elzar started to model the problem in his mind, his brain throwing up question after question, hypothesis after hypothesis. He wished he had access to the Temple Archives. This was almost more a question of philosophy than science. Odan-Urr's writings, perhaps—but he didn't have them and wasn't going to be able to get them.

Think, Mann, he told himself. *There's a solution here. You can feel it.*

"You said that the planet gives you these eggs?" Elzar said, pointing at the glowing ovoids.

"Yes," the Nameless replied. "It is a great honor to watch over them, a sacred duty."

Elzar turned to Avar, excitement surging in his voice. "Avar, this is the answer. We know the planet will bring itself into balance given time, as the eggs eventually hatch and the Nameless mature. We just need to find a way off the world. We can tell Chancellor Soh to blockade this planet— put everything the Republic's got into orbit here, and make sure the Nihil can't get anywhere near it. Then she can evacuate the Blighted worlds. The Blight moves slowly. Yes, it's been appearing on more planets, but if we just stay ahead of it . . . we can do this, Avar. We can do it!"

He turned back to the quiet, dignified being. "How long will it take for enough eggs to hatch so that the hunger is contained again?"

The Nameless did not answer. It moved back to the circle, to the place it had vacated when Avar and Elzar arrived. It settled itself, then turned back to the two Jedi.

"We are not here to help the eggs hatch and see balance return," it said. "We are holding vigil. Too many have been lost. Too many of us have died. The balance cannot be restored in time. It will take decades for even a single egg to hatch, and meanwhile the hunger is loose here, and in the galaxy from whence you came. It eats, and with everything it eats the Force grows less."

The Nameless made a little shudder of disgust or amusement.

"Do you Jedi think every problem can be solved?"

The Nameless returned to its vigil and began to sway in time with the others.

"Sometimes it is too late."

PART FOUR
THE TORMENT OF LOSS.

Interlude

ESTARVERA

From the spot where she had taken refuge with her family, Calina Colman could see the tops of the bright-orange billyoaks that ringed Alowee Pond. They were shaking. It was probably just one of the transports taking off . . . but was the ground rumbling, too?

Calina assessed the situation. She and her family had been reunited, which was astonishing and wonderful. She knew both she and her husband, Ryden, had never expected to see their kids again when they sent them away in those terrible first few moments of the spaceport collapse. But things didn't always go the way you expected, and that was true of good and bad.

They were all together again—her, Ryden, their son Davet and daughter Shanna, even Shanna's little scalepig, Florg. They were in a small courtyard off one of the main streets headed to Alowee Pond Park, where evacuation efforts had been relocated after the spaceport fell into a gigantic pit of chalk-white Blight. They weren't alone. Others were using the courtyard to shelter from the intense crush of people making their way along the narrow streets toward the park.

It wasn't violent out there yet, but the mood of the crowd grew darker with every transport that lifted off and zipped away into the sky. After all, what if there were no more transports, or there wasn't enough space, or the streets opened beneath them? To Calina, the streets leading to Alowee Pond felt like a storm on the verge of breaking.

So, despite her family's urgent need to get off the planet, she wasn't eager to put her kids in the middle of that. Or herself for that matter, considering she was in an emergency hoverchair and couldn't easily navigate a crowded street—much less a stampede, the light forbid.

And Ryden . . . he . . . Calina forced herself to look at the situation with clear eyes.

Ryden has the Blight. His left foot. Davet knows, because he saw the scalepig sniff it out. Shanna might not, but if that's true it's because she's deciding not to know.

There would be no hoverchair for her husband. Ryden was going to die. The medical reports they'd found on the holonet were very clear about that. The Blight consumed different people at different speeds. The only real consistency, and a particularly terrible one at that, was that supposedly the Blight moved faster in younger people. This was why Ryden was standing as far away from the kids as he could without making it obvious. They didn't want the other people in the courtyard putting two and two together. Who knew what they might do if they realized a Blighted person was among them?

Her husband would already have left—Calina had heard him mention the idea to Davet—but that was before the mood of the other refugees grew ugly. He'd decided to stay for the time being. Just in case he needed to protect them.

This has to be awful for him, she thought, looking at her husband.

Ryden looked pale. She hoped he wasn't in pain. They said the Blight didn't hurt. Calina wanted to hold him, to thank him, to love him, to be there for him the way he'd been for her, but she knew he wouldn't let her get that close.

How did it all fall apart so quickly? she thought. *Yesterday I was making a batch of goldcurrant scones.*

But Calina knew. It fell apart so quickly because that's how it always falls apart. The things you think are stable can collapse with no warning. The things that hold you up can fall away, and one day might be the last day you get to stand at all. One time you dance is the last time you dance. One time you run is the last time you run. One day you live is the last day you live. Appreciate whatever you have while you have it.

Because she knew all of this, she was, perhaps, better than some members of her family at ignoring questions like *How did this happen?* and focusing more on *What do we do now?*

"I don't like this," Ryden said, also looking at those shaking, trembling treetops in the distance.

The authorities had supposedly scanned below Alowee Pond and confirmed that the park was stable—no Blight cavities insidiously digging things out from beneath. But who knew what the Blight did, how fast it moved, where it even came from? The situation when those scans were run might not be how it was now.

The trees are shaking because a transport is taking off, Calina thought, trying to convince herself.

Screams in the distance, running feet. Blasterfire.

Blasterfire! Here, on this peaceful world! Somehow, hearing that sound was among the most shocking things Calina had experienced that day. She didn't know if she'd ever heard it before, outside a holodrama.

The arched entry to the courtyard offered a good view of the street beyond. Calina could see with perfect clarity as the densely packed crowd of refugees slowly marching toward the park stopped, began backing up, their faces uncertain, then filled with horror.

All at once, the people turned and ran, becoming a boiling wave of terrified, trampling beings. Some spilled into their little courtyard, and Calina tensed. Shanna drew closer to her, and both Ryden and Davet moved forward, ready to do whatever they needed to do.

And still, Calina had no idea what was happening out there. The Blight? A riot? An attack?

"If this is how it's going to be, then we're going to be together," she said. "Kids, Ryden, with me."

The moment they entered the courtyard, Calina had marked the ways they might get out. Beyond the archway leading back to the increasingly deadly streets, three buildings had entrances facing the little square. Calina chose the tallest one. She steered her hoverchair toward it, looking back to make sure her family was following.

Inside the building's lobby, she made another decision, potentially fatal if it turned out that the Blight was carving away the ground beneath the structure. But if that were the case, then she was out of options anyway.

Calina just acted, guided by nothing in particular, just making choices, giving her family the serenity that came from believing someone else knew what they were doing.

She steered her chair into the building's lift, and once her family gathered in with her, she tapped the control that would take the pod to the roof.

Calina reached out and took Davet's hand, and Shanna's, and offered a smile to Ryden, who had pressed himself deep into a corner, still trying to maintain distance. She loved him for it.

Up they went, and the lift doors opened, and the roof spread out before them.

"Ah," Calina said, once she could see.

From up here, you could see everything.

Turned out, it was the Blight after all.

Alowee Pond Park was gone, along with whatever relief efforts had been stationed there. From every direction came billowing clouds of Blight-white dust. Screams of horror and pain rolled up from below as people fled in any direction they thought was safe.

But from what Calina could see, there was no such direction.

"Ryden," she said, her voice tender. "Please get me out of this chair."

"But—" he began.

"It doesn't matter anymore, my darling."

He came to her, put his arms around her, and lifted her from the chair. His limp was much worse, but he didn't seem to be in any pain.

Ryden placed her on the roof, with her back to a decorative planter. It held a small tree that was producing beautiful turquoise-and-orange flowers. She'd never seen anything like it before and took a moment to look up and appreciate it.

After all, it wouldn't be there tomorrow.

"Come here, loves," she said and extended her arms.

Her children and her husband and even little Florg came and sat with her. She had an arm around Davet, cuddling him in a way she hadn't done in at least six or seven years. Her other stretched around Shanna. Ryden crouched nearby, looking at them, still trying to protect them by not getting too close.

"I love you all," she said. "You love each other. That's all we should be thinking about right now."

If this has to happen, Calina thought—and it surely seemed like it did, *then this is the best way it could.*

Chapter Thirty-Three

THE NAMELESS HOMEWORLD

Bell Zettifar was jealous of Marchion Ro. Many bones in the Evereni's body were probably broken, not to mention the various other wounds he'd sustained in their battle, plus the emotional hammer of reckoning with what might be the first time he'd ever lost a fight—to a Jedi, no less.

All that likely agony, and still Bell was jealous—because Marchion was unconscious, and Bell was awake.

Awake and feeling every cut, slash, and burn. Bell's leg was the worst, but his mind wasn't much better. He was missing four of the eight pieces of his armor, and the Nameless effect had turned his brain into a hive full of stinging insects, busily chewing tunnels through his mind and laying eggs in his sanity.

The Force had come to him at the end of his fight with Marchion in a way he'd never felt before. He didn't know how he'd managed to call up that much strength, such purity of focus. It had just happened. But it hadn't lasted, either. As soon as the immediate danger was over, once Marchion was no longer a threat, Bell's focus had dissolved and what had felt like the Force energy of half the galaxy along with it.

STAR WARS: TRIALS OF THE JEDI   363

He'd fallen to the ground, dropping Loden's lightsaber. He stayed there for a while on his hands and knees, just breathing, feeling like he'd been run over by a heavy lifter droid. But he couldn't stay there forever.

The armor, he thought. *Have to get my head back together.*

Bell cast his one good eye around the clifftop, looking for his helmet and vambrace, the two pieces he had lost during the fight with Marchion. They were each about ten meters away, in different directions.

He sighed and gathered his strength, contemplating what it might cost him to try to stand, knowing the Force was beyond his reach at that moment.

You know... maybe I'll just be happier crawling.

Bell went for the helmet first, because he thought, rightly or wrongly, that having the focusing metal around his brain might provide a more powerful antidote to the Nameless effect. He made his way through the grasses, looking at the tiny insects and crawling creatures moving through the soil. All this life. It was a whole other universe. There was probably another, tinier one below that, and below that. All those little universes were completely unaware of the battle that had just occurred, or that one man had tried to end their lives along with every other life in existence.

And succeeded, maybe, Bell reminded himself. *Just because I beat Marchion Ro doesn't mean I saved the galaxy. Marchion lost our fight, but that doesn't mean he lost.*

He hoped the others had more luck. Avar, Elzar... who knew, maybe even Azlin had come up with something.

Bell grasped the helmet and lifted it to his head. It was heavier than he remembered. But once it slid over his skull, his mind cleared. His body ached as much as it ever had, but at least he could think without pulling together every shred of focus he had to avoid collapsing into a puddle of fear.

Next, the vambrace, he thought, and laboriously turned himself to head in the opposite direction.

Several painful minutes later, he was reaffixing the piece of metal to his arm, knotting the severed bit of strap.

With that accomplished, and Bell feeling as strong as he thought he could barring some actual medical attention, he took a deep breath and shoved himself to his feet. He looked toward the spot where he'd left Marchion Ro, half expecting him to be gone. But no. The Evereni was still there, his eyes closed, still rasping out pained-sounding breaths. Bell was under no illusions that the Eye of the Nihil was no longer dangerous. For one thing, pretending to be unconscious in order to lure Bell close enough for a killing strike seemed to be exactly the sort of thing he'd do.

Bell moved toward Marchion, calling Loden's lightsaber to his right hand with the Force and igniting it. With his left, he pulled a pair of binder cuffs from an equipment pouch on his belt. They weren't part of the typical load-out for a Jedi Knight, but Bell had adjusted his equipment set during the months spent pursuing Nihil raiders near the Occlusion Zone frontier.

Bell pointed his blade at Marchion's head, then yanked the man's wrists together behind his back with the Force. He slapped the cuffs around them, one at a time, and activated them. A faint blue-white light appeared around the restraints. Bell stepped back, breathing a bit more easily.

All of this hadn't taken long, and Bell had proceeded in the correct order to ensure he wouldn't lose everything he'd gained if Marchion Ro unexpectedly woke up. But now that the Eye was secure, it was time to move on to the next task. Bell walked carefully, painfully to the cliff's edge.

Looking down took more courage than he'd needed to face Marchion Ro. Bell expected to see the bodies of two of his closest friends in all the world smashed against the rocks below. But no. He saw Ember and Burryaga, but they were not dead . . . yet. Far below, he saw the long, tall form of Burryaga lying on the shore of a small, bright-turquoise pond. Bell could tell he was alive—his body made slight movements every now and again—but that was about all.

Ember, on the other hand, was running back and forth, spewing blasts of fire at bright-yellow, long-armed forms that had surrounded her and

STAR WARS: TRIALS OF THE JEDI   365

Burry. They were lunging forward, trying to get past her guard, but Ember met them with gouts of flame at every attempt. Bell didn't know how long she could keep it up—didn't know if charhounds had an inexhaustible well of fire in their lungs—but he did know that her energy was not infinite. She'd presumably been fighting off the attackers through Bell's entire battle with Marchion. Ember was strong, but there were a lot of the creatures. It was just a matter of time before the inevitable calculus swung in the predators' direction.

"Burryaga!" Bell called.

The Wookiee lifted an arm, but it was unclear whether that was in response or just a weak attempt at trying to help Ember.

Bell didn't know what he'd actually have done if Burry had yelled back, asked for help. He didn't have a way to get down there other than a leap, and he wasn't sure he'd be able to land it properly in his current state, much less get back up. He couldn't leave Marchion Ro alone, either.

No choice, he thought, already weary beyond almost anything he'd ever felt. *I have to bring them up with the Force.*

Bell stood at the cliff's edge. He spread his feet and began to take deep breaths. He extended his hands, palms up, opening and closing his fingers in time with his breathing. The Force felt impossibly distant, and he felt impossibly weak. Calling Loden's lightsaber to him had been one thing. Bringing enough energy through him to bring a charhound and a Wookiee up from the bottom of a cliff might tear his poor battered body apart.

That is not reality, he thought. *That's fatigue talking, pain. You won't actually be lifting them. The Force will, and the strength of the Force is infinite.*

Bell summoned the fire, seeing it flicker deep within his mind. He imagined it roaring up into a blaze, reaching out and carrying his friends up to him, unquenchable, unending.

The Force did not seem to see things the same way. Not this time, at least. Bell was too tired, too hurt, and despite the armor, his focus was weak. He could barely even sense his friends, much less lift them.

Bell tried again, despair beginning to well up. He thought he could hear Ember far below, barking and fighting to save herself. Burryaga, too, roaring out a challenge, gathering what strength he had left.

The Force did not answer.

Bell tried again.

The Force did not answer.

Am I going to listen to them die? he thought. *No. If that's how it goes, I will leap down there. Marchion Ro be damned. I'll climb back up here and fight him again, if I have to.*

Bell tried again.

The Force did not answer.

"Come *on!*" he shouted.

Terec was alone. That was odd. They were never alone. Ceret was always present through the bond. But now Terec's eyes opened and they found themselves lying in a grassy meadow with no idea how they had gotten there.

Alone. Inside and out.

Terec sat up, quickly checking their gear. Lightsaber, armor, and an equipment pouch filled with a variety of medical supplies. Their head ached, and their throat was raw, and then the memories came back.

The death of Torban Buck. The slaughter of the Nameless. And then . . .

Azlin Rell tried to kill me. I must have fallen unconscious, and then someone brought me here. But who did that . . . and where is Ceret?

Terec looked again into their mind, seeking the place where their bond-twin usually resided. Nothing. That could mean any number of things. The bond could be disrupted by certain devices that generated the necessary interference, hyperspace travel . . . they could even turn it off themselves when they wanted to. Their injuries could be a factor. Or . . . Terec and Ceret hadn't been on the best of terms lately. Terec had been

STAR WARS: TRIALS OF THE JEDI 367

focused on greater independence, and perhaps Ceret had seen fit to give Terec what they wanted. Perhaps that was all it was.

Or perhaps Ceret is dead, Terec thought. *That would disrupt the bond, too. Forever.*

Deciding to ignore this idea, Terec gingerly rose. All around was a grassy meadow, with verdant forest on one side and the edge of a cliff on the other. The meadow bore signs of a battle, with trampled grass and singed vegetation that immediately suggested a lightsaber fight.

Terec's gaze moved toward the cliff's edge, first seeing Marchion Ro. The Eye of the Nihil was unmoving but probably wasn't dead, as his hands were bound. A short distance from him stood Bell Zettifar, right at the edge of the precipice, swaying unsteadily.

This was very alarming, and Terec moved toward the other Jedi quietly but with great haste.

"Come *on*!" Bell shouted.

"Be easy, Bell Zettifar," Terec said. "I am here."

Bell started. He turned quickly, surprised, his foot slipping, his Jedi poise leaving him. He began to fall.

So Terec reached out with the Force and pulled him back, holding Bell carefully and placing him down about a meter from the edge of the cliff.

"Are you all right?" Terec said.

"I'm fine, Terec," Bell said. "But Burryaga and Ember . . ." He pointed down, his meaning clear. "Beating Marchion left me pretty burned-out. I'm sure you aren't in great shape, either. But together, maybe we can . . ."

"Of course," Terec said, not needing any further explanation. "But first, very quickly—"

Terec opened the satchel slung across their body and removed two emergency painkiller injectors. They gave the first dose to Bell, sliding it under the edge of his helmet and depressing the injection button. Bell let out a long, slow sigh. Terec did the same at his own primary artery, which for a Kotabi was most easily accessible through the palm of the hand.

The pain at throat and head immediately lessened, and Terec stepped to the cliff's edge. Bell seemed better, too. They stood together, raised their hands, and brought their friends up. There was no discussion needed as to whether Ember should come first, or Burryaga. They brought them up together.

"We need to get Marchion Ro back to the crash site," Bell said as Terec gave Burryaga his own dose of anesthetic.

The Wookiee looked terrible. His fur had been singed off in broad patches across his body, and mud was matted into what was left. Raw, seeping burns were visible. Terec cleaned what could be cleaned, and gently placed juvan-infused medical patches across the ravaged flesh.

"I'm not sure if this will help much, Burryaga," Terec said, "but it can't hurt. We have no bacta. I wish I were better at this. I'm not really much of a medic."

At that, they all fell silent.

Burryaga slowly, painfully got to his feet. He looked around the cliff-top, then walked over to the still-unconscious Marchion Ro. He growled something Terec didn't understand, but Bell seemed to. It sounded like a question, from the Wookiee's inflection.

"No, Burry," Bell said. "This isn't over."

Burryaga crouched down over Marchion Ro, his big hands searching deftly through the Evereni's clothing. He found weapon after weapon, pulling them from hidden holsters and pockets. The blades, explosives, and blasters he snapped, disarmed, or tossed over the cliff. The lightsabers he kept, placing them inside his tunic and cinching it tight. He then lifted Marchion Ro easily with one hand and slung him over his shoulder, none too gently.

The Wookiee turned, and without another word, strode away through the meadow.

Chapter Thirty-Four

THE NAMELESS HOMEWORLD

Sometimes it is too late, Avar thought. *Do I believe that?*

"Yes," Elzar answered her, and Avar did not know if she had spoken aloud or Elzar just . . . knew. "Sometimes it is too late," he said, his eyes locked on hers but his spirit distant.

She wondered if he was remembering Chancey Yarrow, or Starlight Beacon, or something else entirely.

Then his eyes refocused, and he spoke again.

"But we don't know if we're in that situation, Avar. Think of all the things we might know that this being does not. Everyone has their own knowledge, their own perspective. To them, it's too late. But to us . . ."

"You know what?" Elzar said, interrupting his own chain of thoughts.

She looked at him. His face wore the expression of irrational optimism she'd seen many times since they were Padawans, Elzar Mann's *I don't care what everyone else thinks, I'm going to try it anyway* face, one of many reasons she felt about him the way she did. He failed as often as he succeeded . . .

But Elzar Mann always tried.

"It's not too late, because I don't want it to be too late," he said. "I don't accept that the galaxy is ending, that everyone out there will die. I don't accept that our time together is over. I haven't had enough. No one has had enough. And so I tell you, Jedi Master Avar Kriss . . ."

"It's not too late," she said.

Hope is a choice, Avar thought. *A choice no one else can make for you.*

She glanced around the chamber, softly lit by the glowing purple-pink eggs that could have saved the galaxy. "We have to get out of this place. Now that we have a sense of how the planet works, what it does, how the pieces fit together, I might have a better idea of what to look for. But I'll need the Song for that, and I can't hear it in here."

Elzar nodded. "Back to the surface?" he asked. "That will take some time, and I'm not even sure how we'll do it. I can ask the Nameless here. They might be able to tell us."

"No. Just outside this space. I think I understand what's happening. Below the surface, in the zone of the planet focused on the dark side, the Song isn't gone . . . it's just hidden. Different. I can find it."

"Then let's go," he said, not asking for further explanation.

Avar and Elzar retraced their steps until they reached the stone gateway that led back out into the dark, to the path they'd traveled to get to the world's core. Elzar pulled his lightsaber from his holster.

"I'll go first," he said. "If those creatures are still out there, I'll hold them off while you do what you need to do."

"We'll both go first," Avar said, lighting her own blade.

They stepped forward through the shimmering wall of energy projected across the gateway. Immediately, metallic snarls assaulted their ears, followed by flashes of movement they'd never have seen if not for the reflections from their lightsaber blades off the beasts' carapaces.

Two predators fell and died, their bodies bisected by glowing lines of seared heat. More were coming—many more, judging by the sound of clicking claws rushing toward them.

"Word must have spread down here," Elzar said. "Fresh meat."

"Do we go back?" Avar asked.

"No," Elzar said. "I'll keep them off you."

He looked at her and grinned, and it made her feel so sad.

If I can't do this, she thought, *he'll be gone.*

The first of the oncoming beasts leapt from the darkness, and Elzar's lightsaber began to flash and move. Avar heard strange shrieks of pain mixed with the sound of Elzar dancing and lunging around her. She felt something whick past her face and didn't know if it was Elzar, one of the creatures, or a piece of one or the other.

She was already sinking into deep concentration, searching within and without for the Song she knew had to be there. Calmly, Avar Kriss drew her legs up beneath her and rested within the Force, hovering a meter off the ground. She closed her eyes and listened.

This is a place where the darkness gathers. Only darkness. But darkness has its music. The opposite of the music of the light. It was always there, and I would experience it as dissonance or silence within the Song I was hearing. But that was wrong. There is a song of darkness just as there is a song of light. Of course there is.

The trick would be to find a way to hear it without opening herself to it. Avar did not want to use the dark side. She just wanted to try to understand it.

She considered what she knew. The dark side was not studied in depth by younglings or Padawans at the Temple. Its tenets, its seductiveness, its weapons and how to defend against them—yes. But the intricacies of its powers, the capabilities it might offer . . . those were reserved for study only by the most elevated of masters. And even then, it was considered a deeply treacherous path. Azlin Rell was proof of its dangers.

Avar listened but heard nothing. This did not surprise her. She was who she was—a person who had chosen the light again and again, in every moment of her life. She had to listen in a completely new way, attune herself to an aspect of the Force she had always rejected with her entire being. Not to mention that a person she loved with her whole heart was fighting for both of their lives just meters away, and—

Ah, Avar realized. *That's the answer. Elzar is the key.*

Elzar Mann understood the dark side better than she ever had. He had swum within it, dipped down into its depths before resurfacing into the light, had found a way to know it without being consumed by it.

CHARLES SOULE

Avar reached out to Elzar's spirit and established a link. With other Jedi, it took great effort, but with Elzar, it was easy. Once it was in place, she could listen through him as well as herself, all at once. She and Elzar listened together—even if he didn't know it was happening.

There. A note like a single plucked string on a zither, though reversed and inverted in some strange way. Twanging with an unsubtle buzz, an angry note that felt like it would hurt both instrument and musician to play.

Avar wondered how much of what she was hearing was real, and how much colored by what she thought the dark side should sound like—but it didn't matter. Everyone experienced things in their own way—saw, heard, tasted, felt. To Avar Kriss, the dark side sounded like bloodied fingers and screamed vocals and the insecurity of all artists everywhere wondering if their work would be loved or hated, of the ego, of aggression and crescendo without end and smashed instruments, the sound of which was its own kind of music, of feedback loops, of jealousy, of revenge, of rivalry, of power. The Song of the Dark was full of soloists, instruments wailing in their own worlds, alone, alone, alone.

But it told a story, too, and the more Avar listened, the more she came to understand that story, to see the world painted within it. The ravenous beasts surging toward her and Elzar had their own choir, as did all the life in the bizarre cavern. At the center of it all rested a strange blank spot of utter silence she knew to be the Nameless shrine holding the galaxy's only hope.

This isn't enough, she thought. *I still don't have the answer.*

Avar pushed her perceptions upward and outward. She knew the way the planet was constructed from the description the Nameless had provided. A central void surrounded by protective layers of the dark and light sides of the Force, which worked together in balance to contain the ravenous hunger at the center. Easy to describe, even relatively easy to visualize . . . impossible to understand. How did it actually *work*?

That was the question. Answering it was the task.

Avar Kriss listened to the Song of the Force, hearing it in full for the first time. It made her realize how limited her perspective had been. She had always heard both light and dark, but had only listened to the light. Was that bad? Some might say so. Call it limiting, even.

But everyone had their own part to play in the Song, their own melody strung through all the others. Avar Kriss's instrument was the light, and she found it limitless.

Avar took in the planet as a whole, a great mystery within the larger mystery of the Force. She saw how it had emerged in an eon long past, a Force vergence that seemed almost akin to the way a pearl might grow around a grain of sand within a mollusk. In this case, the sand was the Blight or whatever caused it, and the pearl was the world itself, and the creatures who kept the balance of the Force in good order upon it. Avar understood it all, and with that understanding came the realization of how she could save everyone.

No, she thought, rejecting what she had just learned.

Avar soared both deeper and farther out, falling into the Song, letting it swell and grow in her mind. She heard Burryaga, heard his pain and his strength as he carried Marchion Ro, who was awake now but was pretending not to be, and heard Marchion's rage—but eclipsing that his shame, his guilt. She heard Bell and Terec, and small, beautiful Ember, so happy to be with her friends. She heard Azlin Rell and Reath Silas and Ty Yorrick, as they all walked their own paths. Azlin falling joyfully away into the dark, and Reath sure of his current commitment to the light. Ty, deeply shaken, knowing her life had been forever changed by all that had happened to her in this strange place.

Farther yet. Indeera Stokes, Vernestra Rwoh, Ceret, consumed with a song of urgency. Porter Engle, a walking dirge. Yoda and the other members of the Jedi Council, taking great weight upon themselves, knowing they were looked to as paragons but were just beings like any other, with their own flaws and failings. Keeve Trennis, Sskeer, Ram Jomaram, Kantam Sy, Emerick Caphtor, Eve Byre, Amadeo Azzazzo, so many others—the younglings, the Padawans, the Knights, the masters, all across the galaxy.

And from there . . . Avar knew she shouldn't continue, but she couldn't help herself. She listened to the song of everyone. People all across the galaxy, all their beauty, their fear, their hope. Losses and loves, pain and joy. So many beings with so many ways to interpret the galaxy, all of them part of the same song, all of them linked.

She didn't have to stop there, either. The creatures, the plants. They had songs, too, and she could listen to them as well. If she wanted to, she could listen to everything that was.

Avar knew she could do it. All things were possible through the Force. She could hear it all. She would hear the Song of times past and future, the songs of Jedi from times long past or who had not yet been born. Stellan Gios, if she focused hard enough. The stones, the water, the worlds, the space between the worlds and all it contained, life and death and time itself.

And if she did that . . . what would separate her from the Force itself?

Avar could leave life behind, with its cares and struggle and effort, leave everyone else to their lives and their deaths and just be within the Song. She could be everywhere and everything and everyone.

She could be free.

Ah, she thought, understanding the source of this final impulse. *The dark side. There you are.*

Through all her listening, Avar Kriss had purposefully ignored one melody in the great chorus, almost as if she knew she might need it. She called it to herself now, anchored herself by it, pulled herself back from the enormity and infinity of the Force. It receded, replaced by the warm, regular music of waves crashing on a beach, of peace, of home.

"Avar," Elzar said, and she returned to herself, opening her eyes.

They were alone. His lightsaber was still illuminated, and in its blue glow she could see the evidence of the battle he had fought while she was off, away, listening. Corpses and pieces of corpses were scattered all around them. There was blood on his face and a larger stain on his side, running down from the gap between his chestpiece and his waist. It looked deep black in the blue light, darker even than the darkness all around them.

"Are you all right?" she asked, placing her hand on his cheek, trying to see his wound.

"Not really," he said. "The Blight truly will take everything. And soon."

"How do you know?"

"I saw what you saw, Avar."

Of course he had. She had borrowed from his perception of the Force to better understand the dark side—did she really think that would be a one-way channel?

"I couldn't have done any of this without you," Avar said. "Even if I'd somehow found my way in, I'd have gotten lost in the Song."

"I know," he said, placing his hand over hers. "I was there. I was there with you."

"Do you think that's why the Force brought us together?" she asked. "For this moment? So we could do this thing that neither of us could do alone?"

"I don't care," Elzar said. "I don't think the Force chose us. I think we did."

He kissed her palm and gently lowered her hand. He began to speak, his words coming quickly. There was very little time, and they both knew it.

"The planet produces exactly the right number of Nameless to preserve its balance between light and dark, and to keep the Blight contained," Elzar said. "The system can persist if some Nameless die, even many. But at a certain point, it can no longer compensate. Everything starts to collapse, faster and faster. In the engineering world, they call it a failure cascade."

"Which was the last one?" Avar asked. "Which Nameless put us over the edge?"

"The first, or the last, or one of the ones in between. It doesn't matter."

He turned to her, his face so sad. She knew hers must be the same.

"I know what we have to do," Avar said. "Do you?"

"Yes," Elzar answered. "I told you—I was there with you. I saw it all."

For a moment, Avar considered an idea. Elzar had been with her through her entire journey into the Song. She'd turned back at the last moment, but what if she hadn't? What if they'd gone together? The two of them could be out there now, lost in the Force. Together forever.

Avar set this aside. She was a Jedi.

"I can be the light," Avar said. "Azlin. Could he . . ."

Elzar gave her another sad smile.

"Come on. You want to leave the fate of the galaxy in the hands of *that* guy? It has to be us, Avar. You will be the light, and I will be the dark, and we will use our strength in the Force to maintain balance here on this world until the Nameless eggs can hatch."

"It will be decades," Avar said. "The rest of our lives. And once we begin, we will take the full weight of the vergence upon ourselves. We won't be able to stop, or it will all begin again."

"I know," Elzar said. "And you will be here, and I will be up above, and that's the only way it works. I know, Avar."

The corner of his mouth twitched upward, an acknowledgment of how little control anyone really had over their fate. Nothing was constant except that nothing was constant.

She stepped forward and kissed him, the way they both deserved, the way they had both earned, the way they both wanted. His hands moved up her back, and he pulled her close to him.

They stayed like that for a long moment, then broke apart. She saw tears on his face, and felt them on her own.

Avar saw all the things they might do together, the places they could go, the things they could see, all the memories they might make. She held them in her heart, and then she let them go.

All her moments with Elzar Mann and his with her, in trade for all the lives to be lived by every being in the galaxy, now and forever.

A bitter exchange. But more than fair. A bargain, really.

"Goodbye, Elzar," she said.

"Goodbye, Avar, my love."

They parted, knowing they would never touch each other again.

Chapter Thirty-Five

THE NAMELESS HOMEWORLD

Azlin Rell wandered along paths worn into the ground by generations of this strange world's creatures. Some of the beasts were curious, or hungry, or maddened, and Azlin dealt with them without sparing a thought. Beyond those, though, he left the world and its inhabitants alone.

He had even left Reath Silas and Ty Yorrick alive, even though it would have been easy to kill them after they lay stunned in the wake of their use of the Rod of Ages to save the Nameless. Azlin had recovered first and could have taken their lives with barely a thought. Instead he had tossed the now-useless control rod to the ground and slipped away into the jungle.

His mind was on other things.

I spared the Nameless, he thought. *What an astonishing decision.*

You are free. You have freed yourself, he thought.

Have I? he wondered.

He was no longer afraid, and this was so strange that he could almost barely understand it. It felt like some essential part of himself was missing. It felt like when he had first plucked out his eyes. But when he did that, nothing had truly changed. He had caused himself pain and lessened his ability to navigate the world in the way to which he was accustomed, but that was all. He had remained crippled by his fear of the Nameless.

Now, though, with the terror gone . . . Azlin found himself without a purpose, without a driving force for the first time in over a century. His feet took him where they would, wandering, thinking.

Turn here, he thought. *Just beyond the fallen tree.*

Azlin did.

Should I return to the Jedi? he thought. *I never truly left them, not in my heart, and they have allowed repentant apostates to return to the Order in the past.*

You know what is truly in your heart.

They would never take me back. I gave up everything to save them, but they would never let me return. What they say is not what they do.

Correct.

Azlin realized the path he was walking was not a wildlife trail. It was wider, older, deeper—more of a shallow gully carved into the jungle floor. He noticed an unusual stone at his foot and raised it into the air with the Force so he could see it clearly. It looked melted, or forged, as if it had been at one time subjected to great heat.

He let the stone fall to the ground and continued on.

If I do not return to the Jedi, then what will I do? My entire life has been defined by the Nameless. If I no longer care about them . . .

He tested this statement in his mind, and realized that yes, he no longer cared about the Nameless, or the Blight, or the Nihil, or any of the things that had so occupied his mind just a day before. The Blight was a problem, of course, but it felt like a *Jedi* problem, not so much an *Azlin Rell* problem. A curious distinction.

If the Jedi could solve the Blight and save the galaxy, they would. If they couldn't, then everyone would be dead. Either way, it was nothing for him to concern himself with. He had more important questions to answer.

Well, one question, really.

What will I do now? Who am I now?

You are free, he thought and also heard.

Let us see.

Azlin came to the end of the path, where the gully ended abruptly with what appeared to be a wall covered by the jungle's growth. He assessed it, moving to either side to get a better view, then climbing up the side of the gully to examine the structure more fully.

His new sight through the Force was strange—not well suited for perceiving items of technology in detail. Still, in time Azlin was able to realize he was looking at a small starship—some variety of transport.

Azlin swept the vines and dirt from the ship's hull with a wave of his hand, revealing an entry hatch. He approached the small set of steps leading to the sealed opening, sensing energy beyond. The ship's systems were not dead, despite it clearly having been on the planet for a very long time. He tapped the necessary control. The door slid open, and Azlin stepped inside.

Find the cockpit, he thought.

Azlin found his way forward. The ship's interior had been protected from the elements and so remained relatively pristine despite its obvious age. Indicator lights blinked here and there. Everything seemed to function.

Azlin reached the cockpit, where his gaze was immediately drawn to an object resting on the pilot's seat.

Through his new sight, it swirled and churned, a corona of bright green surrounding a cylinder of metal. A shape familiar to Azlin, though he had not owned one for a very long time.

A lightsaber.

Chapter Thirty-Six

THE NAMELESS HOMEWORLD

Reath Silas stepped from the jungle. He walked through the clearing, headed for the crashed shuttle that had brought him and the rest of the Nine to Planet X.

What was that thing? he asked himself, trying to remember every detail of the Force vortex he'd seen out there on the planet.

When he'd returned to himself after the Rod of Ages shorted out, Azlin was gone, the wrecked control rod discarded in the grass. The Nameless remained below, no longer under the control of anything at all, their eyes clear. They stood around the double spiral hovering in the air, their long arms extended toward it. It seemed more stable, although Reath could be imagining that.

Were they feeding on it? Manipulating it somehow? Worshipping it? Reath had no idea, and yet he knew the answer to that question was the key to everything here. The Nameless, the Blight . . . he knew it. He *knew* it.

But what did he actually know? Nothing. He'd seen, but he had not understood. It was like being on the wrong side of a deep, broad ravine, with the thing you needed visible on the other side but impossible to reach.

STAR WARS: TRIALS OF THE JEDI   381

He searched his memories for anything that could explain what he'd seen, what he'd sensed. He needed the Temple Archives. He needed Cohmac. He needed Azlin. He needed Yoda. Even Elzar Mann could help, although Reath had never considered him a true scholar, more of a serial experimenter with the Force who occasionally got lucky when one of his ideas actually worked.

But maybe that was what they needed. This situation was unprecedented. The double-spiral vortex contained both the light side and the dark. He, Ty, and Azlin had all sensed it. Reath had never encountered anything like it. It was out of balance, out of control. Why? Could it be fixed? If it could be fixed, would that stop the Blight?

Reath felt his mind spinning into a sort of logic-lock, where the ideas and hypotheses began to come faster and faster, one concept whipping to the next and each possible answer just opening up more questions.

Anxiety, he told himself. *It's not logic-lock. It's just anxiety. You're letting yourself fall into philosophical traps to avoid thinking about the bigger problems. The galaxy is still dying, and you don't know how to save it. That's why you're spinning out, trying to distract yourself. Pull yourself together.*

Reath took in a long, slow breath, held it, and released. He felt better, calmer. Amazing, the power in just a single breath.

Ty Yorrick emerged from the jungle. She'd been a few steps behind him on the return to the clearing, and now she walked to join Reath, her face twisted into a scowl. He thought about suggesting she take a breath herself—nothing about the Tholothian woman was calm. She was all agitation, frustration. Ty wanted to act, to hunt, to change their situation, but she didn't know how to do it any more than Reath did. The one path she'd been sure of—stopping Azlin Rell—he'd prevented her from pursuing.

Reath knew he'd done himself no favors there as far as any future friendship with the woman—she was prickly at the best of times. He also didn't care. He knew he'd made the right decision. He'd definitely saved either her life or Azlin's, possibly both—and it had taken all three of them to use the Rod of Ages. Without all of them, the Nameless in that bizarre place would have succumbed.

"Where is everyone?" Ty asked, taking in the clearing. "And what is that?"

A cloud of oily gray smoke rose slowly above a blackened, twisted pile on the far side of the clearing. The bodies—for that's what they were, dozens of partially burned Nameless corpses—seemed to be deliquescing in the strange light of the planet's sun.

"They should have used an accelerant," Ty said. "Something to get the flames hotter."

"This . . . doesn't feel right," Reath said. "Not anymore. Help me, Ty."

He raised his hand and used the Force to move one of the bodies to a spot in the center of the clearing. Then he did it again, and again, laying each Nameless next to the last. After a moment, Ty stepped up next to him and began to help, not saying a word.

In time, they brought the bodies together, laid out in tight rows, arranged with as much dignity as they could muster.

Ty pulled a trio of small devices from one of her pouches. She twisted a toggle switch on each, then placed them among the bodies. She stepped back, and they both watched as the incendiary devices lit up, bright flames consuming the bodies. Clouds of smoke rose up again, this time clean and white. While Reath would have expected it to be astringent, even acidic, the scent was gentle and strange. Like a breeze across a verdant meadow. Odors of flowers and rich soil and grasses.

They watched for a time, and then Ty turned and began to inspect the edges of the clearing.

"The others went off in two groups," she said, pointing. "Burryaga, Bell, and Ember went this way, and Elzar and Avar went off in this direction, following a blood trail. Before that, it looks like they gathered together near the shuttle. I'm guessing they were handling Torban's remains."

They were silent for a moment. They'd allowed themselves to focus on other things for a time, but the loss of the Chagrian healer was still waiting, ready to add its weight to the burden their spirits already carried.

"Burry and Bell must have gone after Marchion Ro," Reath said, recentering himself. "What about Terec?"

"Don't know," Ty said. "Don't see their tracks."

Reath wondered if Terec was inside the shuttle, too, dead and shrouded like Torban Buck.

"Should we split up? Each take a trail?" Ty asked.

"No. We should stick together. Too many dangers out here. We should follow Avar and Elzar. They need to know what we learned about the Nameless. What we saw out there. What we did with the Rod."

"You don't think we should go after Bell and Burry, see if we can help?" Ty said, her tone dubious. "I know those two are competent warriors, but who knows what surprises Marchion Ro might have stashed down here. He could have a whole army of Nihil with him. He's dangerous."

"Not as dangerous as he used to be," came a voice from behind them.

Reath and Ty spun to see Bell, Terec, and Burryaga emerging from the tree line, with Ember padding along beside them. Slung over Burryaga's shoulder . . . was Marchion Ro.

"You . . . you got him," Reath said, hating how stupefied he sounded, how young, but not being able to muster up much else.

The idea that the Eye of the Nihil was finally captured was just . . . after so long, after everything . . . Reath almost wouldn't let himself believe it.

"He dead?" Ty said, gesturing toward Marchion.

Burryaga growled in response, clearly answering in the negative.

"That's a mistake," Ty said. "I know you prefer not to kill. I follow that path myself. But there's a point when it's the only decision left."

At these words, she cast a glance at Reath. He ignored her.

"Are you all right?" Reath asked.

"No," Terec said. "We have all sustained injuries, some rather severe. We've administered basic first aid, but we should get into the shuttle to see if its medical equipment can be of more assistance."

"Need to secure Marchion, too," Bell said.

"You know he's awake, right?" Ty said.

Burryaga seemed startled, frowning and jostling the unconscious-to-all-indications Evereni. Marchion remained still.

"Trust me," she said. "I know when an animal's playing dead."

"This makes things easier," Reath said. "Ty, you and I can go after Elzar and Avar while the others stay here."

"Wait," Bell said. "Where's Azlin?"

Ty shot Reath a dark look.

"Could be anywhere," she said. "Reath had the bright idea to let him go."

Bell's eyes widened.

"What? After everything he's done? You were supposed to watch him. He was your responsibility!"

"Exactly," Reath said. "He was. I let him go because it was between that or possibly dying—him, me, Ty. We learned something out there, Bell—something more important than Azlin. I think I know what the Nameless are . . . their role on this planet. It explains the Blight, explains their hunger and why they were so desperate to get back here. It explains it all, and it changes everything."

"Yes, Reath, it does," came another voice, and again, everyone looked toward the forest.

Elzar Mann was walking toward them, his helmet off, one hand at his side, where a bloodstain marred his robes. That was shocking enough, but it was completely overshadowed by the fact that loping at Elzar's side was a Nameless, unlike any Reath had seen, even those he, Ty, and Azlin had found. This being was regal, elegant, beautiful, and much taller than the Jedi it walked beside.

Its eyes shone in the half-light of its homeworld, pearlescent and serene. The being's gaze slid over the remains of its fellows in the center of the clearing, now burned mostly down to ash. An expression of what Reath knew and sensed to be great anguish crossed its face.

"Avar?" Bell said, asking the question in all their minds upon seeing Elzar alone.

STAR WARS: TRIALS OF THE JEDI 385

"She's fine," Elzar said. "Alive, unharmed. But you won't be seeing her again. She needs to stay here, and so do I."

Burryaga growled in disbelief. He dumped Marchion to the ground, eliciting a grunt of pain from the Evereni. Burry placed his huge, heavy, clawed foot on the Eye of the Nihil's chest and pressed down a bit—an obvious warning. Then he turned back to Elzar, spread his arms, and hooted out a long, involved question.

"He wants to know what the hell's going on," Bell said.

"I got that," Elzar replied, smiling a little, although Reath thought it was the smile of a man under enormous strain, the smile of a man who didn't find much of anything funny at that particular moment.

"The beings we believed to be mindless animals are not," he went on, gesturing to the Nameless at his side. "They are sentient, although not in the way we typically understand it. This world is a Force nexus, a place where vast amounts of both the dark side and the light gather. The Nameless channel those energies and keep them in balance. That is all they have, and all they need. When Marchion Ro took them from this place, they became maddened and monstrous. They were starving and enslaved, their minds swallowed by hunger."

Reath had already come to understand much of this based on what he had seen in the forest, but the revelations hit harder for Bell, Burryaga, and Terec. Burry's gaze slid over to the smoldering remains of the dozens of Nameless who had died in this place, and his face became grim. He pressed down with his foot, and Marchion groaned.

"Take him to the shuttle, Burry," Elzar said. "Marchion's time is over. He has no part to play."

At this, Marchion's black eyes flashed open, and the look of hatred that shot from him seemed potent enough to split Elzar Mann in half.

"Sorry, Marchion," Elzar said. "You don't get to hear how we're going to fix this. All you'll know is that we did, and everything will go on without you. When all's said and done, you won't have mattered very much at all."

Burryaga lifted Marchion again, throwing him over his shoulder like a sack of grain. He jogged away across the clearing to the shuttle, his feet landing heavily. Reath thought the Eye of the Nihil had to feel every step in every broken bone in his body. He wondered if Burry was doing it on purpose and resolved never to make the Wookiee angry.

"The Blight," Bell said, as soon as Marchion was out of earshot. "Can we stop it?"

"In a way," Elzar said. "Truthfully, the Blight can never be stopped. Just . . . held. It is a symptom of the injuries done to this world, these people."

"All is broken," came a new voice, spoken directly into Reath's mind. "Only time can heal it."

That was the Nameless speaking, he thought. *It . . . no. No. We can't do this anymore.*

"What is your name?" Reath asked the being. "What you call yourselves?"

The tall, luminous entity drew itself up, its eyes studying Reath for a long moment. He felt no fear, and he understood why Elzar wasn't wearing his helmet. This being was no threat.

If anything, we're the threat, Reath thought.

The voice came again, chiming through Reath's mind.

"We are the—"

Here, the graceful being made a sound, an actual sound: a long, drawn-out sibilance. To Reath, it sounded like *Shrikarai.* The sound of water over stones.

"Shrikarai," Reath repeated. "Not Nameless."

The being bowed slightly in acknowledgment. Reath felt . . . not good, but better. He liked knowing the names of things, but this went beyond that. There were great wrongs to be repaired here, and this was a first step toward accomplishing that goal.

"How much time will it take?" Bell asked. "To heal whatever's holding back the Blight, I mean."

"Too much," Elzar said. "The planet can't do it on its own, and neither can the Shrikarai. They need help. That's why Avar and I have to stay here."

Elzar rubbed a hand across his forehead, leaving a smear of blood. The Jedi seemed impossibly weary. Burryaga had just returned from placing Marchion Ro in the shuttle, and he seemed to sense Elzar's fatigue as well. He hooted quietly and placed a hand on the other Jedi's shoulder.

"I'm all right, Burryaga," he said. "I just . . . need to get through this. There isn't a lot of time."

Elzar straightened, regaining his focus through what looked like willpower and little else.

"The Blight is within this world. The Shrikarai use the dark and light sides of the Force to ensure it remains sealed away. But now there are not enough of the Shrikarai left to do it. It falls to us. Avar will use the light, and I . . ."

Here, Elzar paused, steeling himself.

"I will use the dark."

Various reactions washed across the Jedi—disbelief, concern, apprehension. All Reath felt was pity. He knew what it meant to resist the call of the dark side and come out the other side stronger, forged into a purer instrument of the light. Elzar had done that, too. And now, to have to go back . . . it was awful.

Elzar gestured toward the enormous being at his side and said, "There are specific spots on the planet where the Force can be manipulated in the necessary fashion. Avar is already in her place, a single point of light in the dark. I must be the opposite. I will be shown the way."

"But how long, Elzar?" Bell asked. "How long will you and Avar have to do this?"

"I think . . ." Elzar began, and shook his head. "I think this is goodbye, Bell. Avar and I will be here for a very long time. There's another thing, too, and it's crucial that you understand."

The Nameless beside Elzar stepped forward, and looked at each of the

Jedi in turn, focusing its gaze on theirs. Burryaga, Ty, Bell, Terec, and finally Reath.

"This world must become lost to you and all your people," it said, speaking directly into their minds with a voice like all of time. "No one can know of the Shrikarai. The fate of all things rests upon it. This place must not be disturbed. Ever."

Elzar nodded. "You'll have to make the Council understand. The Shrikarai must be given the time they need to heal from the injuries done to them, and Avar and I must be left alone to do our work. I want you all to tell me that you understand and agree with what I'm saying. I need to hear you say it."

One by one, they agreed, and some of the weight seemed to lift from Elzar's shoulders.

Their heads all jerked upward as a sound split the sky—the telltale roar of a starship's engines. A small craft streaked across the sky, heading upward, clearly intending to leave the planet.

"Who . . ." began Bell.

"Azlin," Reath said, completely certain.

"Told you," Ty said. "You shouldn't have let him go."

The eyes of the Jedi turned to Reath. He felt pinned, caught—but he did not feel wrong.

"Azlin won't ever come back here again, or tell anyone, either," Reath said. "He wants to leave all of this behind. Believe me."

Is that true? Reath wondered. *Either way, it's my responsibility.*

"I hope you're right, Reath," Elzar said. "Everything depends on it."

"I'm glad you've found something to keep you busy, Elzar, but you do realize that the rest of us are stuck here, too, right?" Ty said, gesturing at the wrecked shuttle not far away. "I don't think you have to worry about us telling other folks about this place."

A sudden, sharp gagging noise, a strange intake of breath, and Reath looked to see its source—Terec. The Kotabi had stiffened, their whole body rigid, trembling slightly.

STAR WARS: TRIALS OF THE JEDI 389

Burryaga trilled in alarm, and Bell put a hand on Terec's arm, trying to see what was wrong.

"Terec! What is it?" he said.

The Kotabi fell to their knees, placing their hands on either side of their skull, like they were trying to hold it together.

"Nnnngh," Terec said. "I'm . . . we're . . ."

A calm settled over the Kotabi, their body relaxing. Terec's hands drifted down, and they looked up at the concerned faces of what remained of the Nine.

"I am sorry. I did not expect that to happen. Ceret's mind has been severed from mine for some time. It just returned, and my system took a moment to compensate for the shared sensations."

"Ceret? Why now? Did something happen?" Reath asked.

"Yes," Terec said. "Ceret left hyperspace, along with Indeera Stokes, Vernestra Rwoh, and the rest of the second team. They are about to thread the Veil, and will come down in a shuttle to retrieve us."

"But the Veil is why we crashed," Ty said.

"Vernestra is confident that she possesses the necessary information to see them through."

"She's not piloting, is she?" asked Bell.

"No. Indeera is flying the ship."

"Well, there's that, at least. Still, tell them to be careful."

"I will."

As one, they all looked up at the sky, watching for their rescuers to appear overhead. When Reath next thought to check, Elzar Mann and the Shrikarai were gone.

PART FIVE
THE QUIET DAWN.

Interlude

ESTARVERA

Ryden Colman's leg hurt.

This was a change. The Blight had been slowly creeping up from a patch on his foot, growing and spreading, but it had never hurt. The affected spots just felt . . . gone. That made it frightening, because it was unnatural. Damage should hurt. That's how you knew you were alive. Life hurt.

At the same time, Ryden had considered it good—because when the Blight came for his family, he could take consolation in the fact that it wouldn't cause any pain. And if it did . . . well, they were on a roof. He hated the thought, but he knew as well as his wife—maybe Davet, too—that there were worse ways to go than a quick end after a short fall.

With all of that rattling around in his head, Ryden wasn't sure how to think about the sudden pain that had sparked in his leg. A deep ache, spiking out from the parts of his ankle and heel the Blight had touched, now growing, surging—

"Agh!" he said, bending down, catching himself at the last moment before he touched his leg.

The Blight was contagious. Anything it touched, it took. He didn't want it on his hands.

"Ryden, what is it?" Calina asked.

"My . . . leg . . ." he said through gritted teeth.

Gingerly, he gathered the fabric of his pants at the thigh and tweaked them upward, pulling them away from his leg to get a better look.

The flesh where the Blight had appeared was still damaged. It was dark, mottled. *Necrotic* was the word that came to his mind, but he wasn't sure that was right. It did not, however, look Blighted. Before, his foot had been marred by a chalky gray deadness. Blighted flesh wasn't flesh at all, more like some kind of un-matter. An absence. But Ryden's leg felt fully present, even if the spots the Blight had touched were clearly in grave distress.

That's why it hurts, he thought.

"Oh, no," Calina said.

He looked at his wife, at the expression of terror on her face.

"No," Ryden said. "I think . . . don't be afraid, love."

He turned to his daughter. "Shanna, can you bring Florg over here? Let him get a good sniff of my leg?"

The little girl did as he asked, even though her face was pale. This was all too much for her.

You and me both, darling, Ryden thought.

Florg the scalepig sniffed the air near Ryden's leg. The little creature seemed to find nothing of interest, because it uttered a soft yip and then squirmed back around to hide its head inside Shanna's gently cupping hands.

"I'm okay," Ryden said. "I think the Blight stopped spreading. I mean, I'm not *great,* it hurts, but in this case that might be a good thing."

He limped over to his family. He reached out and took Calina's hand in his and held his free arm out to his son and daughter. They came together, and he drew them all close.

Life hurts, he thought. *But I'll take that over the alternative.*

The family looked out over their city. The sun was rising, and everything below had gone silent—but not the silence of death. This was the quiet of anticipation, of waiting to see what was to come.

The quiet of a new day they had not expected to see.

Chapter Thirty-Seven

THE JEDI TEMPLE

All at once, the Jedi holding vigil far below their Temple gasped as if a torrent of icy water fell over them. They started, shocked, emerging from the deep trances they had entered while using every drop of their focus to direct the Force against the patch of Blight that had emerged in the ancient Sith shrine.

The Jedi felt as if they had been using all their strength to move forward against a relentless, merciless wind—no, not move forward, simply stand still—but now, suddenly, without notice, the wind was gone. All of that energy had to go somewhere, and it did—with a loud reverberating bang, cracks spidered out through the walls of the shrine. Puffs of dust clouded the air, and chips of stone rained down to the floor.

"Calm," Yoda said. "Calm yourselves, you must. Focus, Jedi. Remember your training."

His voice was relaxed. No anxiety, no fear. Perhaps a touch of curiosity.

The shrine was completely filled with Jedi, wall-to-wall. Many more were gathered outside, extending up the stairs that led up to the main levels of the Temple. The Blight had pushed back against the Jedi's best efforts. The only way to keep it in check had been to bring more Jedi down to exert their will against its power—though all had known that at a certain point, there would be no more Jedi to deploy.

But something had changed. The Blight seemed to have stopped. Its relentless pressure to advance, to consume, was gone. The stone it had touched in the shrine still looked strange, dulled and dusty, but no longer felt so wrong, so malevolent.

For the first time since the Blight appeared below the Temple, the Jedi dared to hope.

Chapter Thirty-Eight

CORUSCANT
WEEKS LATER

When it came to predicting the way the political wind was about to blow, Ghirra Starros was a meteorologist, a sailor, a weather vane, a glider pilot, all rolled into one. Hell, she was basically an Evereni.

Still, she thought, sitting in the Senate building on Coruscant, watching the trial of Marchion Ro. *This was a tricky one. My masterpiece, I'd say.*

The Nihil were done. It had happened the moment the Stormwall fell. The technology to keep the wall running was aboard the *Gaze Electric,* and that venerable ship was now gone. It had been destroyed by its owner, her brutal, horrifying former lover, the narcissist Marchion Ro.

Why had Marchion destroyed his flagship and doomed the Nihil? Ghirra didn't know at the time, but had learned since that Marchion had wrecked the *Gaze* and brought down the Stormwall as part of an elaborate plan to murder every living being in the galaxy. This seemed laughable, impossible, the words themselves insane ... if applied to anyone except Marchion Ro, Eye of the Nihil.

Whatever the root cause, the Stormwall had fallen, and Republic attack fleets had defeated the Nihil forces gathered near Eriadu in a rather convincing fashion. General Viess was confirmed dead, and at that time Marchion was still missing. In their absence, leadership of the Nihil had fallen to none other than Ghirra Starros.

She'd worked so hard for Marchion, and even for the Nihil. They'd ignored her, and they'd lost, and now it was time for her to look out for herself. After all, none of this was her fault.

Her leverage to negotiate with the Republic had been cut down to almost nothing. But almost nothing was not nothing.

Ghirra began her work by calling Lina Soh and offering a conditional surrender. She would order the Nihil to cease all hostilities, and would return control of the entire Occlusion Zone to the Republic. In exchange, she requested that she be spared prosecution and be appointed liaison to the Senate in order to assist with the reintegration of the Nihil worlds into the Republic.

These demands were almost entirely predicated on Ghirra's hope that Lina's people did not know if she could turn the Stormwall back on, or if other weapons or war fleets were hidden within the Occlusion Zone. Ghirra did nothing to disabuse those concerns. She portrayed herself as a misled thrall of Marchion Ro who had realized the error of her ways, ready to return to the embrace of the Republic.

Lina Soh was not fooled. They understood each other. But Lina also knew the power of what Ghirra was offering, and accepted the surrender and Ghirra's terms—at least until the RDC had made its way far enough into the former Occlusion Zone to see whether there actually was any threat remaining from the Nihil. Ghirra knew they would find nothing. The Nihil had been once again reduced to a scattered rabble of raiders haunting the fringes of the Outer Rim. Still, the RDC's search would take time, which Ghirra would use to conduct the second phase of Operation Save Ghirra Starros's Skin.

Ghirra contacted the corporations. The San Tekkas, the Grafs, a group that had sprung up in the wake of the Great Disaster that was calling itself the Trade Federation, the venerable Banking Clan, the Techno Union. To them, she offered the true prize of the short-lived Nihil Empire . . . its science. The Nihil had never restrained their lines of research to conventional or approved zones. The Path Engines alone were incredibly valuable technology even if the Paths that had powered them were largely lost with the *Gaze Electric*'s destruction. Stormseeds, scav droids, the repellent but obviously profitable biotechnological advances created by Baron Boolan . . . even Baron Boolan himself.

Deals to quietly acquire these technologies and more were arranged, with Ghirra asking for comparatively little in return. To each of the power brokers, her request was the same: *Use your influence to ensure that I am allowed to return to the Republic in a position of power. If I am tried and executed, you will get nothing. Once I am safe, you will get what you desire.*

Now, weeks later, all that work had come to fruition, and Ghirra Starros found herself sitting in a prime seat in the Grand Convocation Chamber of the Galactic Senate building on Coruscant, watching the Republic's high and mighty try to figure out how to handle Marchion Ro.

Many Nihil war criminals had been brought before the Republic's justice. Ghirra had seen most of the trials. All were handled with scrupulous attention to applicable law, all given the full benefit of due process, legal advocates to argue on their behalf, and sentenced within existing parameters of the law. No one could accuse the Republic of being vindictive—only fair and correct. Which was, of course, the point. Drawing the contrast. Showing the many, many people watching across the galaxy that there was a better way. There was a path forward. Justice would be done.

But none of those poor fools mattered compared to Marchion Ro. He was, so to speak, the main event, which was why his trial was taking place in the Senate building as opposed to one of the many judicial halls on the planet. The magnitude of what he had done, and tried to do, was so great that he needed to face the entire galaxy he had tried to destroy, even if just symbolically.

Supposedly, the Evereni hadn't spoken a single word since his capture by the Jedi. They'd brought him in, shackled and broken—Ghirra did not know if the Jedi had done that to him. In the end, she supposed he had done it to himself.

The Republic's medical technicians had healed Marchion Ro's injuries. To Ghirra's eyes, he now looked much as he always had. He wore a red prisoner's uniform, just a loose tunic and trousers, but it did not diminish his power. Marchion's energy, his darkness, his desire, his rage and hunger and dismissiveness and disgust . . . all still radiated from him. His oil-dark eyes carried the weight of hammers. His teeth could rip out throats. His claws could slash the life from anyone who came too close.

Marchion Ro remained the beautiful predator he had always been.

And yet, here I am, and there he is, and only one of us is in chains, Ghirra thought. *You should have chosen us, Marchion. I could have saved you.*

Behind Marchion stood two Jedi—Bell Zettifar and Burryaga. It was Ghirra's understanding that they had brought Marchion in, and so had been afforded pride of place during his trial.

The Republic magistrate was nearly finished laying out the case against Marchion, supported by sworn testimony from the Jedi who had apprehended him plus other witnesses in a position to know his crimes with specificity. The little spy Nan seemed to have made her own deal—she'd had quite a bit to say during Marchion's trial. Ghirra herself had not testified—one of her conditions, to which Lina Soh had agreed under pressure from Ghirra's newly acquired corporate allies. Ghirra believed she had a future with the Republic. She didn't want people knowing too much about her role within the Nihil.

Ghirra had worked hard to create the perception of herself as an unwilling victim, coerced, co-opted, and converted to the cult of Marchion Ro. If she repeated it enough, and used her allies to ensure other people did the same, it would become the truth.

It would work. No one cared about what happened to Ghirra Starros, not really. Marchion Ro was the villain here. He had killed countless people, had tried to kill *all* people, everywhere, and had nearly succeeded. The onetime Eye of the Nihil hadn't denied any of his crimes, and the testimony and evidence against him were overwhelming. Jedi after Jedi had taken the stand, as had former associates of Marchion who had undoubtedly brokered their own deals. Some of the testimony was offered

STAR WARS: TRIALS OF THE JEDI 401

under seal—certain locations and other details were withheld—but the overall picture was very clear. Through it all, Marchion sat silent in his repulsorpod platform hovering in the middle of the Grand Convocation Chamber, with his two Jedi guards resplendent in their white-and-gold robes.

Now, at last, it was nearly over. The magistrate was gravely reciting all the many crimes with which Marchion had been accused, and finally ended with one called "Attempted genocide on a scale so vast it defies comprehension. The attempted murder of every being in existence."

Ghirra actually found that one a bit hard to swallow. The only evidence for that last claim was the sworn testimony of the Jedi who had captured Marchion on a planet they refused to name—but then again, they were Jedi. No one was willing to suggest they were lying, even to convict such a terrible enemy. Besides, whether Marchion Ro had almost murdered the galaxy didn't matter, from a legal perspective. The destruction of Starlight Beacon alone was enough to condemn the Eye of the Nihil to the harshest possible sentence.

"Who will speak for you, Marchion Ro?" the magistrate said.

Traditionally, this question would trigger the opening statement of the accused's advocate as they began to present their defense. But Marchion Ro had no advocate. The one assigned to him by the Republic had died during his first meeting with his client, which had occurred in a sealed, private chamber. Marchion was chained to a wall several meters away when it happened—no one knew how he could possibly have killed the man, but everyone assumed he had. The next two advocates the Republic had attempted to assign had both turned down the opportunity.

The truth was, no one spoke for Marchion Ro.

And it's no one's fault but his own, Ghirra thought.

Marchion Ro stood up. A gasp ran through the Senate chamber. Ghirra leaned forward with interest. This was the first acknowledgment by the Evereni that he was even aware he was on trial. Behind Marchion, the two Jedi remained calm. That made sense.

After all, they beat him once.

Marchion Ro shifted his all-consuming gaze across the Senate. Representatives from across the galaxy: worlds he had subjugated, worlds he had wrecked, worlds he had plundered, and—if the charges against him were to be believed—every last one a world he had tried to destroy. Marchion radiated nothing but contempt. It flowed out from him in waves.

Ghirra braced herself for the moment when Marchion would look into her eyes. He would understand immediately what she had done, the choices she had made, by virtue of the fact that she was free and he was not. Would he leap from his platform and fight his way to her? Try to seize a Jedi weapon and murder her? Or would he feel regret, knowing that if only he had followed her advice, had worked with her, had given her his loyalty, they might both be free?

Marchion's eyes slid over Ghirra without stopping. He looked right at her—it was impossible that he didn't see her—but he had no reaction at all. Not hatred, not jealousy or regret or love or lust. Just a complete lack of recognition.

She did not exist to him, and never had.

There was no sound in the chamber. Under the power of Marchion's gaze, everyone had fallen silent.

"You're all small," Marchion said. The corner of his mouth twisted. "Your Republic represents the combined power of too many beings to count. You could do anything. You do nothing." He gestured to himself. "I am alone."

Marchion Ro stood there unrepentant. He sought no clemency, offered no explanations. He was exactly what he was.

He leaned forward and exposed his teeth. "And I did everything."

The magistrate waited an appropriate amount of time, but once it was clear the defendant had nothing more to say, he raised the ornate staff, used only when a sentence was being handed down.

"Marchion Ro, Eye of the Nihil, it is the determination of this tribunal that you have forfeited your opportunity to live among other sentient beings. You are sentenced to a life of solitary imprisonment. You will be taken to a facility in deep space, staffed only by droids, with supplies

STAR WARS: TRIALS OF THE JEDI

403

sufficient for the rest of your life. The facility will be constructed by the droid stewards at a location randomly determined by them. Only the supreme chancellor and the Jedi High Council will know where you are. You will interact with no one. There will be no opportunity for parole."

The magistrate paused, then completed the proclamation: "As you said, Marchion Ro, you are alone. That is all you will ever be, until the day you die. This is the ruling of this tribunal. May the light bring you peace."

The staff struck the floor of the magistrate's platform with a boom that echoed through the chamber.

"These proceedings are concluded."

Babble broke out all around the chamber, voices erupting, debating the sentence. Clearly some thought the Republic was being too lenient, and would have preferred an execution. But Ghirra Starros knew Marchion Ro as well as anyone could. She thought the punishment was very well chosen indeed.

Alone, forever, with no one to listen to you, no one to acknowledge you, no one to corrupt or control. Just you, all alone, until the day you die.

Ghirra realized she was smiling.

I won, Marchion, she thought. *I got away with it.*

In the pocket of her gown, her comm chimed.

Ghirra removed the device and examined the message displayed on its screen. It was from a private investigator she had hired to locate her daughter and deliver a lengthy, heartfelt message. It was an apology, an acknowledgment of wrongdoing, an attempt at reconciliation. Ghirra understood that repairing her relationship with Avon would take time. But now she had all the time she'd need. This situation with Avon was just another form of politics. Ghirra had won back her place in the Republic. She would win back her daughter, too.

The message on her system was very simple: *Unable to deliver message. Subject deceased.*

Ghirra stared at these six words, so cold and precise.

Avon was a genius. She was capable of faking her own death in as convincing a manner as anyone could. That had to be what this was—an effort to get away from her mother once and for all. But if that was the truth, or if somehow . . . she actually was dead . . . the reality would be the same.

In the end, Ghirra Starros won nothing.

She was lost.

Chapter Thirty-Nine

MONUMENT PLAZA

Lina Soh knew that the Republic was, in essence, fiction. It was not "real" in the way that a stone was, or a piece of fruit, or gravity, or the Force. The Republic was just a story about a way people could live together successfully in large groups. Someone made up that story a long time ago, then convinced so many people of its truth that in time, everyone believed it.

But the main thing to remember, especially if you happened to be the supreme chancellor of that Republic, was that last part. For the Republic to continue to exist, people had to keep believing the story.

These were the key parts of that story:

The leaders of the Republic work toward a greater good for all people.

The many contrasting needs of those people will be acknowledged and balanced.

The institutions the leaders create can be relied upon to fulfill their various functions with efficiency and fairness.

The Republic will keep its people safe.

All people within the Republic are equal and have equal opportunity to improve their lives.

There is justice.

Lina Soh tried hard, very hard, to maintain those principles. The way to create faith in the Republic was to be a Republic that deserved that faith.

But a story was a story, and reality was reality. The pure, perfect Republic could never exist.

This was how the Republic truly operated, the actual story:

Elected leaders were just people. They could and did make mistakes. They could be selfish, venal, or afraid.

Some peoples within the Republic were more powerful than others, because of their wealth or their military or their technology.

Institutions were complex and could fail in any number of ways.

The Republic did its best to keep people safe but people still died constantly.

All people within the Republic had a voice, but some were listened to more closely than others.

There was justice—for most.

Now, the citizens of the Republic were not fools. They understood that the story they had chosen to believe was imperfect. In some ways, an outright lie. Lina Soh's job, and the job of all supreme chancellors, was to convince the people that the story of the Republic was better than any other they might choose to believe in its place.

It had worked. For centuries, it had worked. Until the Nihil.

Marchion Ro and his people had stripped the Republic bare, exposed and underscored the fictions upon which the whole thing was built. Doubt had crept in. Why be part of an institution that couldn't protect you? Why follow rules that didn't benefit you?

After everything the Nihil had done, people were starting to consider new stories, new ways of doing things. That was how Republics fell.

Lina Soh stood in Monument Plaza in Coruscant's Senate District, with her hand flat against the only natural surface left on the vast city-planet— the peak of the once proud mountain Umate.

The mountain was a great core of reality, vast, unchanging, its roots extending deep into the heart of the planet. Lina could see Umate. She could touch it. It was real.

STAR WARS: TRIALS OF THE JEDI 407

Lina's task now was to convince the galaxy that the Republic was the same. Despite the damage Marchion Ro had done, the story at the center of the Republic remained and stood strong, and everything that had been damaged or destroyed could be rebuilt.

Including faith.

And where do I place my own faith? Lina asked herself.

She knew, but it troubled her to admit.

Here was another story, one that was entirely true: The Jedi had saved the lives of everyone in the galaxy.

What is my responsibility to the Order? Lina thought. *They are so strong. We are so fortunate to have them, and fortunate that they actually seem to be what they claim: scholars of and warriors for the light side of the Force. If they ever sought control . . . how would I stop them?*

That was the central question. Lina knew she was not the first chancellor to ask it and would not be the last. She had studied the writings of those who held the office before her. The balance between chancellor and Order was never far from the minds of those who led the galaxy. But there was no answer, no ultimate solution, no way to solve the problem of a group of infinitely powerful, completely independent warrior-monks nestled deep within the heart and soul of the Republic.

When it came to the Jedi, you just had to have faith.

This time, it had been rewarded. But the Jedi were a story, too, and someday perhaps they too might break against some harsh, unyielding reality. Lina felt strongly that ever again relying on the Order to the degree she had during the Nihil crisis would be a mistake. The fortunes of the Republic could not be tied to ten thousand unusual individuals who did whatever they chose—no matter how trustworthy those people had proven to be. It was not a question of Lina's faith in the Jedi Order. It was a question of her responsibilities to the Republic.

Lina had already asked her aides to draft a measure to fund the construction of several additional *Emissary*-class cruisers, as well as the support ships and fighters to go with them. Nothing like a Galactic Navy, just a slightly increased force of peacekeepers empowered with the weight of the Galactic Senate. Not a replacement for the Republic Defense Coalition, but simply a way she might handle trouble spots across the Republic without involving the Jedi.

Trouble spots... Lina thought. *All I've got are trouble spots.*

The worlds of the Occlusion Zone had become a gigantic question mark. Most wished to return to the Republic, but some had become used to the quasi-independence of the Nihil regime. Others were still under the control of Nihil warlords. The risk of division was real, especially because a divided Republic could generate great profit for those poised to take advantage of it.

The Blighted worlds were another challenge. The immediate danger was gone, but people still needed help. The Senate was already beginning to rumble with conflict about which worlds would be helped first and how much the untouched worlds would be expected to pay to assist the damaged planets.

The Nihil were cowed, the Blight was gone, but the Republic was in as much danger as it had ever been.

The story of the great Galactic Republic felt less true than it had in living memory. It needed to be told again, in a new way, for this time, these challenges.

She was the supreme chancellor of the Republic. It was her job—no one else's.

This will be my greatest work, Lina thought.

She pulled her hand from Umate's implacable surface, that core that remained despite generations upon generations of attempts to lessen it, and turned to face the cameras.

Matari and Voru were at her side. She placed her hands on the two beautiful targons. The giant beasts purred, and she took comfort from them.

Lina Soh looked up. Hovering cam droids were set to record her words and send them to the holonet, where they would be relayed across the galaxy. Beyond them, she saw her aides, and ministers, and senators, and

STAR WARS: TRIALS OF THE JEDI 409

journalists, and behind them thousands of Coruscant's citizens, all come to hear the chancellor's words.

She began to speak. "What do you want from me? What do you want from the Republic? It's not a test. I think I know the answer. If I didn't, I shouldn't have this job."

Lina smiled. "That is not an invitation to have me replaced, by the way."

A small murmur of amusement from the assembled crowd.

Lina kept smiling, kept speaking.

"The point of this Republic is that we agree on more things than we don't, and the things about which we disagree are small in comparison with the things we all believe. Right? Let me tell you what I think those things are."

She held out her hands, extending a finger with every point she made.

"We choose peace over war. We believe there should be enough of everything for all to have their needs met. We believe there is value in people who are not like us. We choose to share, not to take. We choose to support, not to undermine. We do not dictate, we vote.

"We do not like selfishness. We do not like greed. We believe in success and advancement but don't like leaving people behind. We take care of the weakest among us because doing so does not make us less strong."

Lina paused to look directly into the cams. Both her hands were now fully open, extended before her.

"Am I saying anything you don't believe? I don't think I am. What I described is the Republic we've built. Look at your lives, look at your families, look at your friends and your communities. That *is* the Republic. In fact . . . and here it comes, you knew I was going to say this—

"We are all the Republic.

"I say that often. I mean it every time. Every single person in this Republic is as valuable as the entire thing. The Republic should offer the same truths, safety, and opportunity to every last one of its citizens.

"The Republic is not only for those who are strong. The Republic is for those who are weak, who are broken, who *need its help the most.*"

Lina paused here, giving herself a moment. This next bit was the challenge.

"We have been hurt so badly," she said. "The Nihil tried to destroy us and almost succeeded. But their time is over, their leader gone.

"We are all the Republic. That includes the worlds within the Occlusion Zone, now reunited with Republic space."

A ripple went through the crowd.

Lina kept speaking.

"I know some of you may have an instinct toward enmity, toward punishment, toward sanctions. You know that we have already brought many of the Nihil leaders to justice, including Marchion Ro. Others are yet to be found. I promise you, justice will be done. But do we treat those worlds as lesser, even those who took up with the Nihil freely? We cannot. If they wish to return, we will welcome them.

"We are all different in our individual lives. But in our hopes for what we want this galaxy to be, what we want to share with each other and hand down to our children, we are all the same.

"We are all the Republic. Our true strength lies not in what we do when things are easy, but when they are difficult."

Lina cast her eyes across the crowd, seeing shining eyes, clasped hands, people thinking not about the troubles of today but the promise of tomorrow.

"I believe that," she said. "I believe it with everything I have. I think you do, too."

She raised her hands into the air, fingers spread wide. All across Monument Plaza, thousands of arms shot into the air, echoing her gesture.

"Have faith, my friends," said Supreme Chancellor Lina Soh. "We'll do it together."

Chapter Forty

EVERYWHERE

Far from anywhere, floating in the vast, endless darkness, was a ship that once belonged to a Jedi named Barnabas Vim. Now it was owned by a man named Azlin Rell, who was once a Jedi but was now something else.

What he was and what he could be were yet to be determined. Azlin was allowing himself to enjoy being alive for the first time in over a century, and for now that was enough.

Azlin's hands moved, almost of their own accord. He had placed Barnabas Vim's lightsaber on the control console of the ship and opened the hilt. His fingers spidered over its components, fast and sure, disconnecting, opening, exposing. He sang a little song as he worked, one he'd known for well over a century. Once, it had terrified him, but now it just seemed like a lovely little melody with lyrics that he actually found rather inspiring.

"All you'll be," he sang, his voice quite pleasant, "is dust."

A small crystal caught the light, and Azlin carefully removed it from the lightsaber's hilt. He held it up, looking at it, seeing the strange sort of spirit it had. It was not alive, but it was certainly not dead. Its energies bent away from him, as if it knew what he was about to do.

As if it was afraid.

Do it, he thought.

Azlin recalled to his mind the moment the Nameless had first come to him, the fear washing through him, making him weak, a child, a captive, impotent and defenseless. He remembered how he hated himself for his inability to resist or fight back. The shame. The pain.

He remembered the feeling of his thumbs pressing into his eye sockets and *pushing,* of *gouging,* of the sharp, ragged edges of his nails *puncturing,* hoping for relief and then understanding that mutilating himself had achieved nothing, nothing at all. The long walk of years, existing, hating, pain, pain, *pain.*

In Azlin's sight, the little kyber crystal screamed. It screamed without sound, and in his strange newsight he saw its aura twist, compress, writhe . . . burn.

Azlin exhaled, a long, deep sigh of release and, astonishingly, relief.

His hands moved quickly again, reassembling the lightsaber, adjusting and modifying, already making the weapon into something that was his, no longer the weapon of a Jedi.

Azlin Rell ignited the lightsaber, and a smooth blade emerged from the hilt. He could not see its true color.

But he knew that it was red.

On the world of Eriadu, Joss and Pikka Adren stepped into a tavern, the sort that served all kinds. They walked up to the bar, sat. Pikka adjusted the child carrier strapped to her chest. Her baby stirred but did not wake.

Joss waved the bartender over.

"Got someone here we'd like you to meet," he said.

Slendo squinted at the child. He raised an eyebrow, then nodded. He pulled four shot glasses from behind the bar and filled them with something red and potent. He set three before the Adrens and lifted the fourth in a toast.

"Here's to you three," he said. "Looks like you've made a little world of your own."

⚜

Porter Engle traveled through hyperspace in a borrowed Nihil ship he had no intention of ever returning. The ship's navigation system was set for a trip to a world called Gansevor. He had only been there once, a long time ago. He had no idea what he would find there, but he knew that the person he was now was born in that place. It was time for a new version of Porter to be born, and Gansevor seemed as good a place as any to start.

That was also, of course, the last place he had ever seen his sister alive—Jedi Master Barash Silvain. Maybe she was gone, as General Abediah Viess had suggested. But maybe she wasn't. Either way, he needed to know the rest of her story. No matter how it ended, it began at Gansevor.

Porter was not thinking about Barash, though. He had spent enormous swaths of his life thinking about her, and he realized now that the end result of that choice was that he had not spent enough time thinking about himself.

The fierce and deadly Jedi who had infiltrated General Viess's flagship, terrifying everyone he encountered, was familiar to him. That Jedi was the reason he had retired from the Order to become a cook at that outpost on Elphrona where this latest chapter in his long life had begun. Every action that version of Porter Engle took seemed to lead to death, and no matter how well deserved or moral or necessary or earned that death might be, it was still death.

Perhaps the Jedi Order needed a destroyer among its ranks, even if it would not admit it to itself. Porter Engle had served in that role. He had tried to step away but had allowed himself to be pulled back. Or . . . had chosen to return, because part of him missed what he had left behind. The truth was unclear even to him.

He was certain, though, that the role of the destroyer was too much for him to carry alone. He was sick of it. Sick to death.

But he *was* alone. Porter had never allowed himself to get particularly close to anyone after Barash left. No Padawans, no true friendships beyond a jovial comrades-in-arms collegiality. Everyone in the Order liked Porter. No one knew him.

Solitude had been Porter's choice, his decision, stemming from a very obvious, basic calculation. If no one was close to him, it wouldn't hurt him if they left, and he couldn't hurt anyone, either.

He could be the death dealer, the killer, so no one else had to be.

Despite what he tried to tell himself, despite the Force his constant companion, that razor-sharp blade of light and dark . . .

"I am alone," Porter Engle said.

But not for long. Not forever. Of that, he was certain.

The Jedi Temple chimed with the sounds of celebration. A memorial service was under way—a grand ceremony honoring all who had passed since the Nihil crisis began. The event was joyful, full of food and laughter and music, exactly the sort of gathering Torban Buck, that good man, would have enjoyed while he was alive.

The Jedi came together in an acknowledgment of everything they had endured, everything they had survived, all they had accomplished. They honored their dead, lauded their heroes, told stories, ate and drank more than they should have, danced, were silly and were somber.

Kantam Sy was there, head bandaged but swirling around the Temple terrace that had been repurposed into a dance floor. Emerick Caphtor danced, too, with a guest from outside the Order, a woman named Sian Holt. Arkoff complained loudly about the way his leg itched where it was attached to his new prosthetic. Terec and Ceret provided a performance— they recited poetry in unison and then in harmony and then in syncopation, demonstrating to themselves as much as anyone else present that they could be united and also apart, and neither meant they were any less.

Ram Jomaram and Burryaga and Reath Silas and Cohmac Vitus and

STAR WARS: TRIALS OF THE JEDI   415

Indeera Stokes and Yaddle and Vernestra Rwoh and so many more. The Council took a moment to declare the Guardian Protocols rescinded, which earned a resounding cheer from all assembled.

Younglings ran around, getting underfoot. Padawans tried to get away with things and mostly succeeded.

Hundreds of Jedi had come together here . . . thousands, perhaps, gathered in a celebration of light and life.

A drift of Vectors shot through the sky above the Temple, one of the largest seen in many years—assembled not for combat, but for the joy of it. The ships swooped and dived, their pilots linked by the Force, their wingtips mere meters from one another, like a flock of songbirds chiming through the air, shining in the sun.

Yoda, that grand and venerable Jedi, stood alone at the edge of the revels, pondering what the Order would become after enduring such deep, existential threats. Whatever it had been, it was no longer. The trials they had survived would echo through the Jedi's choices for generations to come.

A pang of loss washed across the old Jedi, momentarily drowning out the sounds of celebration. Many had become one with the Force, so many more than the Jedi were directly memorializing that day.

Yoda thought of them, held them in his heart.

All that pain had stemmed from the choices of just a single lost person, a being consumed with greed and possessiveness. A woman named Elecia Zeveron, who had called herself the Mother, though her only true child was tragedy. No stranger to the Force, though Elecia's path took her through its shadow much more than its light. The Mother's decisions had reverberated down through the centuries, all the way to Marchion Ro, and had almost ended all things.

Yoda considered what might be learned from the tragedies the Order had faced, and thereby the lessons that might be taught to future generations. What was it about the Jedi that had allowed them to survive such a focused assault by such powerful enemies and overcome fear beyond anything most in the Order had ever known? Yoda believed the answer did not rest with the Jedi's power over the Force or any specific knowledge its members held. He thought it came from the Order itself, in the connections between its members. From the earliest days, younglings formed bonds with one another, with their teachers. These strengthened as they became Padawans and then Knights and masters in their own right. The Jedi who came before and the Jedi to come, all linked in an intricate web of trust, learning, and understanding. This was the great strength of the Order, why the Jedi were able to triumph over even a threat as terrible as Marchion Ro and his sad corruption of the Shrikarai.

No Jedi ever stood alone. Within the Force, all was connected, and so too within the Order, all the way back to the very first Jedi knight. The Order mirrored the Force itself, and what was greater than the Force? Nothing. Nothing at all. And so . . . there was nothing to fear.

Yoda wondered if he could have done more to ensure that this truth rang within the spirit of every Jedi. Perhaps the tragedies suffered by the galaxy could have been lessened if the Order, or if he, had been more perceptive, if he had seen what the Force was trying to show him earlier, if—

He stopped himself.

He could only move forward. He could remember the lessons he had learned, pass them on, hope they took root, all while keeping the secrets that must be kept. This last gave Yoda pause. Nothing should be hidden within the light. But the risk connected to the Shrikarai was so great, and the injuries visited upon them so severe, that the Jedi would keep them hidden as part of the Order's commitment to the safety of the galaxy entire. A burden. A compromise. And yet, as Yoda and the Council had decided, a necessity.

The Jedi Order was safe. In time, new challenges would appear, new threats would arise—that was inevitable. But the Jedi were stronger for what they had survived. Whatever came, they would face it as they always did—together, within the great light of the Force. Unafraid.

STAR WARS: TRIALS OF THE JEDI 417

Yoda sighed deeply, then realized he might not be using his time very well. This was, after all, a party. For once, he decided, perhaps even the wise and wonderful Grand Master Yoda could save the pondering for another day. He smiled, chose to trust in the Force, and headed toward the feast tables to see what delights might await.

Ty Yorrick had returned with the Jedi to Coruscant. She told herself it was because she had left her things there, and there were many irreplaceable weapons and pieces of gear she did not want to leave behind.

She also wanted to pay her respects to Torban Buck, who had saved her life.

Ty watched the Vectors shoot by overhead, all those Jedi working together, becoming more than they could ever be alone.

She was not a Jedi and was still unsure that she should ever be one—although her views on that front were evolving.

Some time after the memorial, Reath Silas, with the approval of the Jedi Council, left Coruscant in a Vector.

Reath had decided to search for Azlin Rell. He had brought both his shield and his lightsaber, because he did not yet know the choice he would make once he found his quarry. Azlin was lost, in more than one way. It was Reath's job to find him. Beyond that . . . he would trust in the Force.

Bell did not see Loden Greatstorm again. He did not need to.

CHARLES SOULE

Burryaga took time for himself after the defeat of the Blight. He returned to the Temple, meditated, taught the younglings' art class, healed.

But one day, he walked to a spot in the Temple's central hall that he had determined to be the exact center of the entire gigantic building. Burry closed his eyes, breathed, and listened to the Force. His senses expanded, and he felt all the emotions of his great Order churning around him. Joy, purpose, curiosity, peace—but not only these good things. The Jedi were people, after all, and they felt as deeply as any other being. Confusion, frustration, longing, regret, even fear—Burryaga sensed these things, too.

After a few moments, the Wookiee came to believe he had located the most troubled person in the Temple—a Padawan who had convinced themselves they were not strong enough to be in the Order. They had not yet found their path and were ashamed of their failures. Confusion and pain churned through them.

Burryaga opened his eyes and began heading in the Padawan's direction.

He thought he might be able to help.

Chapter Forty-One

WITHIN THE VEIL

Avar Kriss is deep inside the enormous cavern that comprises the interior of the planet that protects the galaxy from the Blight. The beings native to that world call their home Sophros, which translates to "the Balance"—though the word has never been spoken aloud.

Great beasts prowl around Avar, but she is not afraid. She is deep within the Force, a single spot of light within a great penumbra of dark.

Avar is in dialogue with Elzar Mann, singing a song without words. He is up on the surface, seated atop the sun-drenched peak of the planet's highest mountain—the best spot for him to serve as a single spot of dark within a great corona of light. Near him, a strange construct made of the Force rotates slowly in the air, one of a number on the planet, now more stable than they have been in a very long time.

If you were to pull back and observe this world with eyes attuned to the Force, you would see both light and dark, two endless curved half circles each of which contained the whole universe. Within each, a tiny spot of the opposite—this is Avar and Elzar.

They are together in spirit but separated in body, and now that they have begun the process of ensuring the balance of light and dark on the planet of the Shrikarai is maintained, they cannot shift or change. They can, with great effort and focus, come to the places where the two great energy fields touch—any of the shining mirrors of the type that originally led them to the planet's core. They can see each other, even speak— but never for long lest their focus waver. They cannot touch, or all would collapse.

This is a loss, but they both accept it. They are connected more deeply than they have ever been before. They are grateful for what they have, and are untroubled by what they do not. They fear nothing.

Avar and Elzar love each other truly and deeply, but do not need each other. They are content knowing both of their lives will be spent ensuring the persistence of life, and the light.

They are Jedi.

Epilogue

NOWHERE

The Republic was not cruel.

Marchion Ro's prison had many amenities. It was built into a small, hollowed-out asteroid and contained a number of facilities beyond just his cell. An exercise room, a space with table and chair where he might take his meals if he wanted a change of scenery. A fairly well-stocked hololibrary—though it was never updated, because no communications ever came to or left his prison.

The facility included a droid attendant and a number of droid maintenance workers. None of them had vocal circuits.

The droids had brought him to this place in a ship. As promised during his sentencing, the vessel was stocked with a lifetime's worth of supplies and then some. Nothing fresh, of course, but sufficient food and water to keep Marchion alive forever.

Or, for that matter, for as long as he chose to live. The prison featured an air lock, which Marchion could access at any time.

The Republic, after all, was not cruel.

The droids chose an asteroid traveling through the void on a path that would not intersect with any known world or shipping lane. They set to work building Marchion's new home using assemblers and other construction technology. The work progressed quickly and incorporated materials from the ship itself, although the engines and navigational technology were destroyed. There would be no opportunity given for Marchion Ro—a notoriously resourceful improviser—to build a new ship from scraps.

Over the years, he tried various routes of escape, all of which failed. He attempted to slice into his droid attendants to find communications circuits or any resources he might use, and succeeded only in nearly destroying the closest things to companions he had. In desperation, he effected clumsy repairs, praying the droids would reactivate once he turned them back on. Most did, one did not, and Marchion mourned the loss of his friend.

Marchion Ro began to lose confidence, lose faith that even his ability to turn any situation to his advantage would see him through.

He was alone, alone, alone.

Marchion considered the air lock but could not abide that being the conclusion to his story. It seemed such a pathetic end—Bell Zettifar's final words to him were never far from his mind.

Marchion grew older. He did not use the exercise room. He ate sporadically. He slept.

He was surprised that he was not visited by his ancestors. Surely Marda Ro might appear to tempt or taunt him? Or his father, Asgar, glowering with rage and paternal disappointment. Even Shalla, his grandmother, and who knew what she would say. She had never thought of Marchion as a person, just an instrument.

Eventually, Marchion Ro grew ill, feeble. Pain and weakness came for each part of his body in turn—all but his mind, and that was its own source of pain.

So it went, until the day he drew his last, lonely, agonized breath, his lungs full of blood, his body a withered shell.

In all that time, no one came for Marchion Ro.

Not even ghosts.

Acknowledgments

This is a big one. The novel you're holding (or listening to or reading on your gadget of choice) can't really be looked at as a singular piece of work. I couldn't have written it without the work of dozens of other people, in a way that goes beyond the typical small army that gathers to bring any novel into the world—first readers, copy editors, everyone in editorial, marketing, design, and so on. *Trials of the Jedi* is unique because of the way it's built atop so many other stories that came before, each of which had their own small army making that story happen, too. I'll do my best to acknowledge everyone who contributed to this book and the High Republic as a whole. In advance, to anyone I foolishly fail to include, I apologize! You're amazing.

First and foremost, my family, who have been a part of the High Republic since the very start in all kinds of ways. Amy and Rosemary, I am deeply grateful for the patience, the listening, the insightful notes, the encouragement, the support and good counsel in low moments, the pride, and all the shared excitement and joy.

Next, Michael Siglain, to whom this book is dedicated—I'd like to specifically acknowledge his vision and constant focused effort to pull the High Republic into existence from nothing. Few people reading this will ever really understand how much Mike did along the way for the authors, for the initiative, and for all of it. A project with the scope of the High Republic is a massive garden requiring constant tending if it's going to succeed. That's what Mike did—nonstop adjustments here and there to deal with whatever might be needed on a given day. And because of all that work, the High Republic went way beyond mere success. In just four

ACKNOWLEDGMENTS

years, it ushered in an entirely new era of Star Wars with all-new characters, villains, conflicts, ships, style, and more. We saw dozens of interconnected stories told across various publishing mediums, many of which were bestsellers in their formats. The High Republic has appeared in AAA video games and television shows, and is in every way a firmly established part of the timeline. In just four years! It's beyond difficult to pull off something like this, especially within a pop culture force as strong and well-defined as *Star Wars*. It took more people to make it happen than just Mike Siglain—but I can confidently say that none of it would have happened without him. Well done, sir. Your authors are grateful.

Speaking of those authors . . . there are eleven High Republic authors now, but we started with just five. In the beginning, it was Cavan Scott, Claudia Gray, Daniel José Older, Justina Ireland, and me. I met them all in a hotel lobby in northern California in 2019, and a conversation began that's ongoing to this day. We built the High Republic together, and then we poured our ideas and care into it for years. We spoke to one another constantly in the beginning, probably every day as things were really ramping up. The High Republic was special from the start, in a way that's difficult to convey if you weren't there. I hope my life is filled with creativity until the day I shuffle off to become one with the Force, but no matter where my work might take me moving forward, it's hard to imagine much will outshine the light of the High Republic or the relationships I built within it. Again, I am grateful.

That gratitude is also offered, of course, to the second tranche of authors who came in to tell their own stories after we first five almost broke ourselves against the relentless, wonderful cascade of projects that constituted Phase I of the High Republic Initiative. Tessa Gratton, George Mann, Lydia Kang, Zoraida Córdova, Alyssa Wong, and of course Rosemary Soule—they all came into a project that already had an established dynamic and relationships. It couldn't have been easy to make sure their own voices and perspectives rang out as strongly as they did, but they all managed it, and the High Republic became bigger, better, and stronger for it.

ACKNOWLEDGMENTS

425

Every story each of those people wrote is part of the one you just read. *Trials of the Jedi* would not be what it is without every tale that preceded it in the initiative.

It also would not be what it is without the dedicated work of the people at Lucasfilm who kept me from tripping over my own words and ideas more times than I can remember. Mike Siglain (yep, him again) had a big editorial role in this book, as he did with all the High Republic projects. Jennifer Heddle's close reads were instructive and insightful in ways I hugely appreciated, as was the editorial acumen of Rob Simpson and Brett Rector. Pablo Hidalgo, Matt Martin, Leland Chee, Kelsey Sharpe, Emily Shkoukani, and everyone else in the vaunted Story Group—their job is both infinitely more interesting and challenging than you'd think, but they all rise to the occasion every time. Kathleen Kennedy at Lucasfilm championed this story from the start. James Waugh worked so hard to open new doors for the High Republic and its creators. Troy Alders and Phil Szostak were the steady hands on the tiller for the High Republic's many designs and visual elements. Max Taylor, Michael Garcia, Josh Rimes, and Shaun Sutton thought about new places the High Republic might go. Kristin Baver, Krystina Arielle, Sammy Holland, Lyssa Hurvitz, Kelly Forsythe, Joe Sullivan, and Crystal McCoy have done so much to promote the initiative and put its stories front and center for the fans. Leslye Headland, Rayne Roberts, and others worked on *The Acolyte* to realize the High Republic in live action, and other teams created *Young Jedi Adventures, Jedi: Survivor,* and the other projects that took the era to new audiences. The work of people like Dave Filoni, Rian Johnson, Tony Gilroy, and so many others served as constant sources of inspiration. And finally, thanks to the person who began it all, George Lucas.

Heartfelt thanks to Elizabeth Schaefer at Del Rey (I know it's Random House Worlds now, but it'll always be Del Rey to me), as well as the talented team of designers, copy editors, and everyone else at that vaunted publishing house for doing the work to bring this book (and *Light of the Jedi,* and so many other wonderful books) to the world, and bearing with me through draft after draft . . . after draft after draft.

426 ACKNOWLEDGMENTS

I can't ignore Marc Thompson's work on the High Republic audiobooks—if you haven't listened to his work, do yourself a favor and listen to the way he brings the era and its zillions of characters to perfectly realized and distinct life—which is also true for all the High Repulic audio narrators. Such a talented crew. Similarly, Grant Griffin, Phil Noto, Jama Jurabaev, Iain McCaig, and many other powerfully skilled artists helped us see the High Republic and its characters as if they'd always been part of the galaxy far, far away.

Are you starting to see? So many people worked on all of this. *Trials of the Jedi* would not be what it is without all of them.

More personally, I want to acknowledge the work here of my spectacular literary agent, Seth Fishman, who never stops looking for opportunities for me, even the out-of-the-box stuff, and has been working with me for most of a decade to help make some of my longest-held dreams come true.

This book had a number of first readers, as all my stories do. I want to specifically call out Shawn DePasquale, Tommy Stella (who is not just a great person to read through your draft, but also toils away at what I am certain is the worst gig in any creative field: being my assistant), Daniel José Older, Amy Soule, and Rosemary Soule. They all went through this book in its early versions, before I knew what the hell I was doing with it, and helped me figure out what the hell I was doing with it.

And now, it's your turn. If you're reading this, whether this is your first High Republic story or the culmination of years of following this saga through all its twists and turns in every comic, novel, handbook, and more, thank you. The fans have been here for this project every step of the way, from the earliest days when all we'd shown was a single slide at a convention panel teasing something called Project Luminous, up to this very story you just enjoyed. You responded to the High Republic by bringing it to life through incredibly creative, beautiful, and intricate cosplay, fan art, rampant speculation about upcoming stories, online communities, memes, and an outpouring of support like nothing I've ever seen. We couldn't have told this story—and by that I mean the big story, the whole

ACKNOWLEDGMENTS

High Republic thing—without you. I hope, now that you've seen how it all ends, you think we achieved our goal: to tell a gigantic, interconnected, powerful, and beautiful story set in this world we all love . . . to bring something new to *Star Wars* that was in conversation with and honored all that had come before . . . to entertain but also do something the galaxy far, far away has always been wonderful at doing—offer moments of inspiration.

To everyone I mentioned here, to everyone I wish I'd remembered to, to everyone I've met on this incredible journey, and the people I haven't met yet who will encounter our work in years to come . . .

Thank you.

We are all the Republic.

Charles Soule
February 2025
New York City

About the Author

CHARLES SOULE is a #1 *New York Times* bestselling novelist and comic book author. He has spent over a decade creating stories for some of the most enduring characters in popular culture, from Superman to Darth Vader, with much of his work adapted for film, television, and video games. He is the writer of numerous bestselling, critically acclaimed original comic series such as *Eight Billion Genies* and *Undiscovered Country*, as well as three original novels for HarperCollins, the latest of which is *The Endless Vessel*. Charles is a creative consultant for Lucasfilm, Ltd., and is one of the founding architects of *Star Wars: The High Republic*, a multiplatform *Star Wars* saga kicked off by his bestselling novel *Light of the Jedi*. He lives in New York City.

About the Type

This book was set in Hermann, a typeface created in 2019 by Chilean designers Diego Aravena and Salvador Rodriguez for W Type Foundry. Hermann was developed as a modern tribute to classic novels, taking its name from the author Hermann Hesse. It combines key legibility features from the typefaces Sabon and Garamond with more dynamic and bolder visual components.

A long time ago in a galaxy far, far away. . . .

STAR WARS

Join up! Subscribe to our newsletter at ReadStarWars.com or find us on social.

𝕏 @StarWarsByRHW

◙ @StarWarsByRHW

f StarWarsByRHW

....

Disney · LUCASFILM |

© 2025 Lucasfilm Ltd. & ® or ™ where indicated. All rights reserved.